喚醒你的英文語感！

Get a Feel for English !

喚醒你的英文語感！

Get a Feel for English !

愈忙愈要學
100個商業動詞

風行**500**大企業的*Leximodel*字串學習法

BIZ ENGLISH
for
BUSY PEOPLE

由龐大的商務語料庫中
彙整出最關鍵的 100 個動詞，
並提供數百個相關衍生字串！
搭配最常見的商務情境例句，
一次補足商務口説和寫作的競爭能量！

附1片實戰
MP3

貝塔語言出版
Beta Multimedia Publishing

作者◎商英教父 Quentin Brand

Contents

Part 1　第一組 **25** 個動詞

Unit 4 詞彙

Part 2 第二組 25 個動詞

Unit 5 寫作

Unit 6 口說

Unit 7 詞彙

Part 3 第三組 25 個動詞

Unit 8 寫作

Unit 9 口說

Unit 10 詞彙

Part 4 第四組 25 個動詞

Unit 11 寫作

Unit 12 口說

Unit 13 詞彙

附　　錄

前言

引言與學習目標

　　英語成為全球通用的商業語言，已經是既定的事實了。近幾年來，無論總公司和市場位於何處，已有愈來愈多的公司採用英文當作正式的商業語言；區域性的公司也會使用英文開發海外市場，和客戶建立和維持良好的關係；跨國公司用英文與子公司做跨國界的溝通；懷有雄心大志或想在當地市場中獲取更優渥工作機會的人，也需要具備良好的英文技能。

　　然而許多人發現在學校學到的英文，在商業環境中卻不是那麼的好用。或者對英文的記憶已太久遠，有些基本文法和詞彙已經忘得一乾二淨。甚至不大清楚商業英文和其他種類的英文到底有何分別。

　　本書旨在教你商業英文中必備的能力。現在已有人研究分析實際商業環境中使用的英文語法，並以電腦分析語文模式和詞頻，本書便是以這些研究為依據，並以商業英文說和寫雙方面使用頻率最高的一百個動詞為基礎。雖然這些核心詞彙中大部分的動詞你都很熟悉，或許你會希望知道在使用這些動詞時，自己犯了哪些錯誤，以及應該如何避免這些錯誤。你可能希望更加了解商業英文的口說和寫作當中，如何精準地使用這些動詞，也可能希望以這些動詞為基礎，建立新的詞彙。你甚至可能只是很單純地希望加強商業英文能力。本書的用意便在於幫助你達成這些目的。在接下來的章節當中，我會更詳細地介紹這些動詞。為了讓你發揮最大的學習效果，現在請你先做一個Task。

前言 TASK1

請思考以下問題，寫下答案。

1. 你購買本書的原因為何？
2. 你希望從本書中學到什麼？
3. 你在用英文交談和寫作時遇到哪些問題？

答案🅠

請閱讀可能的答案，勾選出最貼近自己想法的項目。

1. 你購買本書的原因為何？
   - ☐ 我買這本書是想找到一個學習英文的方法，來滿足我專業上的需求。
   - ☐ 我看過《愈忙愈要學英文系列》中其他的書，但覺得以我的英文程度而言太難了。我想找一本比較簡單的書。
   - ☐ 我已經看過《愈忙愈要學英文系列》中其他幾本書，現在想找一本比較一般性的書，而不是專攻某個特定的商業技巧。我想學商業英文中必備的英文能力。
   - ☐ 我知道我英文動詞的用法問題很大，尤其是搞不清楚時態或分不清楚及物動詞和不及物動詞。我希望這本書可以幫我解決這些問題。
   - ☐ 我想要一本可以放在電腦旁邊隨時查閱的書，有一點像商業英文的聖經。

2. 你希望從本書中學到什麼？
   - ☐ 我想知道商業英文中有哪些必備要領，包括自己最常犯的錯誤有哪些以及避免的方法。
   - ☐ 我想學會如何使用英文，但對英文為什麼要這樣用沒什麼興趣，我沒時間，更何況我沒有語言學的背景，所以有時候看到一大堆文法解釋感覺就像在看天書。我覺得這就是我以前都學不好英文的原因。
   - ☐ 我想學會在客戶關係管理（customer relationship management，CRM）方面最實用的英文，因為我知道這在商業英文中很重要。.
   - ☐ 我想學會如何自修加強英文能力。我在英文環境中工作，但知道自己沒有充分利用這個優勢加強專業的英文能力。我希望這本書可以教我怎麼做。

3. 你在用英文交談和寫作時遇到哪些問題？
   - ☐ 有時我怎麼都找不到適當的詞彙或慣用語表達想法。可能我懂的詞彙太少了。
   - ☐ 我不知道自己犯了哪些錯誤，所以不知道我說的或寫的英文正不正確。
   - ☐ 我很害羞，不敢和外國人說英文，因為我不知道自己有沒有說錯話。我不想說錯話，冒犯別人。
   - ☐ 我知道我的發音不清楚，但是我不知道該怎麼改善。
   - ☐ 聽力是我的罩門。外國人講話好快，有時候二個詞聽起來像一個詞，有些詞我應該知道卻聽不懂。有的口音我也聽不懂。

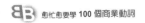

你可能同意以上這幾點的部分或全部，你也可能有其他我沒有想到的答案。不過請先容我自我介紹。

我是 Quentin Brand，我教了超過十五年的英文，對象包括來自世界各地的商界專業人士，就像各位這樣，而且有好幾年的時間都待在台灣。我的客戶包括企業各個階層的人，從大型跨國企業的國外分公司經理，到擁有海外市場的小型本地公司所雇用的基層實習生不等。我教過初學者，也教過英文程度非常高的人，他們都曾經表達過上述的心聲。他們所想的和各位一樣，那就是要找一種簡單又實用的方法來學英文。

各位，你們已經找到了！這些年來，我開發了一套教導和學習英文的方法，專門幫像各位這樣忙碌的生意人解決疑慮。這套辦法的核心概念稱作 Leximodel，是以一嶄新角度看語文的英文教學法。目前 Leximodel 已經獲得全世界一些最大與最成功的公司採用，以協助其主管充分發揮他們的英語潛能，而本書就是以 Leximodel 為基礎。

本章的目的在介紹 Leximodel，並告訴各位要怎麼運用。我也會解釋要怎麼使用本書，以及要如何讓它發揮最大的效用。看完本章後，各位應該就能：

❑ 清楚了解 Leximodel，以及它對各位有什麼好處。
❑ 了解 chunks、set-phrases 和 word partnerships 的差別。
❑ 在任何文章中能自行找出 chunks、set-phrases 和 word partnerships。
❑ 清楚了解學習 set-phrases 的困難之處，以及要如何克服。
❑ 清楚了解本書中的不同要素，以及要如何運用。

但在往下看之前，我還是要先談談 Task 在本書中的重要性。各位在前面可以看到，我會請各位停下來先做個 Task，也就是針對一些練習寫下一些答案。我希望各位都能按照我的指示，先做完 Task 再往下看。

每一章都有許多 Task，它們都經過嚴謹的設計，可以協助各位在不知不覺中吸收新的語言。做 Task 的思維過程比答對與否重要得多，所以各位務必要按照既定的順序去練習，而且在完成練習前先不要看答案。

當然，為了節省時間，你大可不停下來做 Task 而一鼓作氣地把整本書看完。不過，這樣反而是在浪費時間，因為你要是沒有做好必要的思維工作，本書就無法發揮最大的效果。請相信我的話，按部就班做 Task 準沒錯。

The Leximodel

在本節中，我要向各位介紹 Leximodel。Leximodel 是看待語言的新方法，它是以一個很簡單的概念為基礎：

Language consists of words which appear with other words.
語言是由字串構成。

這種說法簡單易懂。Leximodel 的基礎概念就是從字串的層面來看語言，而非以文法和單字。為了讓各位明白我的意思，我們來做一個 Task 吧，做完練習前先不要往下看。

前言 TASK 2

想一想，平常下列單字後面都會搭配什麼字？請寫在空格中。

listen	_____
depend	_____
English	_____
financial	_____

你很可能在第一個字旁邊填上 to，在第二個字旁邊填上 on。我猜得沒錯吧？因為只要用一套叫做 corpus linguistics 的軟體程式和運算技術，就可以在統計上發現 listen 後面接 to 的機率非常高（大約是 98.9%），而 depend 後面接 on 的機率也差不多。這表示 listen 和 depend 後面接的字幾乎是千篇一律，不會改變（listen 接 to；depend 接 on）。由於機率非常高，所以我們可以把這兩個片語（listen to、depend on）視為固定（fixed）字串。由於它們是固定的，所以假如你不是寫 to 和 on，就可以說是寫錯了。

不過，接下來兩個字（English、financial）後面會接什麼字就難預測得多，所以我猜不出來你在這兩個字的後面寫了什麼。但我可以在某個範圍內猜測，你在

English 後面寫的可能是 class、book、teacher、email、grammar 等，而在 financial 後面寫的是 department、news、planning、product、problems 或 stability 等。但我猜對的把握就比前面兩個字低了許多。為什麼會這樣？因為能正確預測 English 和 financial 後面接什麼單字的統計機率低了許多，很多字都有可能，而且每個字的機率相當。因此，我們可以說 English 和 financial 的字串是不固定的，而是流動的（fluid）。所以，與其把語言想成文法和字彙，各位不妨把它想成是一個龐大的字串語料庫；裡面有些字串是固定的，有些字串則是流動的。

總而言之，根據可預測度，我們可以看出字串的固定性和流動性，如圖示：

The Spectrum of Predictability 可預測度

```
         ◄─────  ┌──────────────┐        ┌──────────────┐  ─────►
                 │  listen to   │        │English grammar│
                 │  depend on   │        │financial news │
fixed            └──────────────┘        └──────────────┘       fluid
固定                                                            流動
```

字串的可預測度是 Leximodel 的基礎，因此 Leximodel 的定義可以追加一句：

Language consists of words which appear with other words. These combinations of words can be placed along a spectrum of predictability, with fixed combinations at one end, and fluid combinations at the other.

語言由字串構成。每個字串可根據可預測度的程度區分，可預測度愈高的一端是固定字串，可測預度愈低的一端是流動字串。

你可能在心裡兀自納悶：我曉得 Leximodel 是什麼了，可是這對學英文有什麼幫助？我怎麼知道哪些字串是固定的、哪些是流動的，就算知道了，學英文會比較簡單嗎？別急，輕鬆點，從現在起英文會愈學愈上手。

我們可以把所有的字串（稱之為 MWIs = multi-word items）分為三類：chunks、set-phrases 和 word partnerships。這些字沒有對等的中譯，所以請各位把

這幾個英文字記起來。我們仔細來看這三類字串，各位很快就會發現它們眞的很容易了解與使用。

我們先來看第一類 MWIs：chunks。Chunks 字串有固定也有流動元素。listen to 就是個好例子：listen 的後面總是跟著 to（這是固定的），但有時候 listen可以是 are listening、listened 或 have not been listening carefully enough（這是流動的）。另一個好例子是 give sth. to sb.。其中的 give 總是先接某物（sth.），然後再接 to，最後再接某人（sb.）。就這點來說，它是固定的。不過在這個 chunk 中，sth. 和sb. 這兩個部分可以選擇的字很多，像是 give a raise to your staff「給員工加薪」和 give a presentation to your boss「向老闆做簡報」。看看下面的圖你就會懂了。

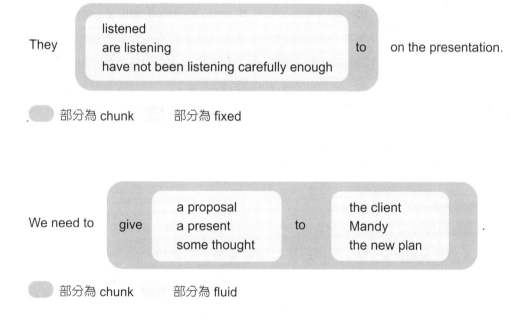

相信你能夠舉一反三，想出更多例子。當然，我們還可以把它寫成 give sb. sth.，但這是另外一個 chunk。它同樣兼具固定和流動的元素，希望各位能看出這點。

Chunks 通常很短，由 meaning words（意義字，如 listen、depend）加上 function words（功能字，如 to、on）所組成。相信你已經知道的 chunks 很多，只

是自己還不自知呢！我們來做另一個 Task，看看各位是不是懂了。務必先作完 Task 再看答案，千萬不能作弊喔！

前言 TASK 3

閱讀下列短文，找出所有的 chunks 並畫底線。

Everyone is familiar with the experience of knowing what a word means, but not knowing how to use it accurately in a sentence. This is because words are nearly always used as part of an MWI. There are three kinds of MWIs. The first is called a chunk. A chunk is a combination of words which is more or less fixed. Every time a word in the chunk is used, it must be used with its partner(s). Chunks combine fixed and fluid elements of language. When you learn a new word, you should learn the chunk. There are thousands of chunks in English. One way you can help yourself to improve your English is by noticing and keeping a database of the chunks you find as you read. You should also try to memorize as many chunks as possible.

【中譯】

　　每個人都有這樣的經驗：知道一個字的意思，卻不知道如何正確地用在句子中。這是因為每個字都必須當作 MWI 的一部分。MWI 有三類，第一類叫做 chunk。Chunk 幾乎是固定的字串，每當用到 chunk 的其中一字，該字的詞夥也得一併用上。Chunks 包含了語言中的固定元素和流動元素。在學習新字時，應該連帶學會它的 chunk。英文中有成千上萬的 chunks。閱讀時留意並記下所有的 chunks，將之彙整成語庫，最好還要盡量背起來，不失為加強英文的好法子 。

答案

現在把你的答案與下列語庫比較。假如你沒有找到那麼多 chunks，那就再看一次短文，看看是否能在文中找到語庫裡所有的 chunks。

商用英文必備語庫 前言1

· … be familiar with n.p. …	· … every time + n. clause …
· … experience of Ving …	· … be used with n.p.…
· … how to V …	· … combine sth. and sth. …
· … be used as n.p. …	· … elements of n.p. …
· … part of n.p. …	· … thousands of n.p. …
· … there are …	· … in English …
· … kinds of n.p. …	· … help yourself to V …
· … the first …	· … keep a database of n.p. …
· … be called n.p. …	· … try to V …
· … a combination of n.p. …	· … as many as …
· … more or less …	· … as many as possible …

✎　語庫小叮嚀

◆ 注意，上面語庫中的 chunks，be 動詞以原形 be 表示，而非 is、was、are 或 were。

◆ 記下 chunks 時，前後都會加上 …（刪節號）。

◆ 注意，有些 chunks 後面接的是 V（go、write 等原形動詞）或 Ving（going、writing 等），有的則接 n.p.（noun phrase，名詞片語）或 n. clause（名詞子句）。我於「本書使用說明」中會對此有詳細的說明。

　　好，接下來我們來看第二類 MWI：set-phrases。Set-phrases 比 chunks 固定，通常字串比較長，其中可能有好幾個 chunks。Set-phrases 通常有個開頭或結尾，或是兩者都有，這表示完整的句子有時候也可以是 set-phrase。Chunks 通常是沒頭沒尾的片斷文字組合。Set-phrases 則在電子郵件中非常常見，現在請研讀下列的語庫並做 Task。

 **TASK 4**

請看以下常見的商業英文 set-phrases，把認識的打勾。

商用英文必備語庫 前言 2

❑ Apologies for the delay in getting back to you, but …

❑ Thanks for your reply.

❑ Going on to n.p. …

❑ I look forward to hearing from you.

❑ I'd like to draw your attention to the fact that + n. clause

❑ I'd now like you to look at n.p. …

❑ If you have any questions about this, please do not hesitate to contact me.

❑ If you look at this (chart/graph/table), you can see that + n. clause

❑ If you look here, you can see that + n. clause

❑ Just to confirm that + n. clause

❑ Just to let you know that + n. clause

❑ My recommendation here is to V …

❑ My suggestion here is for n.p. …

✎ 語庫小叮嚀

◆ 由於 set-phrases 是三類字串中最固定的，所以各位在學習時，要很仔細地留意每個 set-phrases 的細節。稍後對此會有更詳細的說明。

◆ 注意，有些 set-phrases 是以 n.p. 結尾，有些則是以 n. clause 結尾。稍後會有更詳細的說明。

學會 set-phrases 的好處在於，使用的時候不必考慮到文法。你只要把它們當作固定的語言單位背起來，原原本本地照用即可。本書的 Task 大部分和 set-phrases 有關，我會在下一節對此有更詳細的說明。但現在我們先來看第三類 MWIs：word partnerships。

這三類字串中，word partnerships 的流動性最高，其中包含了二個以上的意義字（不同於 chunks 包含了意義字與功能字），並且通常是「動詞＋形容詞＋名詞」

或是「名詞 + 名詞」的組合。Word partnerships 會隨著行業或談論的話題而改變，但所有產業用的 chunks 和 set-phrases 都一樣。舉個例子，假如你是在製藥業服務，那你用到的 word partnerships 就會跟在資訊業服務的人不同。現在來做下面的 Task，你就會更了解我的意思。

前言 TASK 5

看看下列的各組 word partnerships，然後將會使用這些 word partnerships 的產業寫下來，請見範例。

1.

- government regulations
- drug trial
- patient response　hospital budget
- key opinion leader
- patent law

產業名稱：*製藥業*

2.

- risk assessment
- non-performing loan
- credit rating
- share price index
- low inflation
- bond portfolio

產業名稱：＿＿＿＿＿＿＿＿＿

3.

- bill of lading
- shipment details
- customs delay
- shipping date

· letter of credit
· customer service

產業名稱：＿＿＿＿＿＿＿＿＿＿

4.

· latest technology
· user interface
· system problem
· repetitive strain injury
· input data
· installation wizard

產業名稱：＿＿＿＿＿＿＿＿＿＿

答案

請看以下提供的答案。

2. 銀行與金融業
3. 外銷／進出口業
4. 資訊科技業

假如你在上述產業服務，你一定認得其中一些 word partnerships。

現在我們對 Leximodel 的定義應要修正了：

Language consists of words which appear with other words. These combinations can be categorized as chunks, set-phrases and word partnerships and placed along a spectrum of predictability, with fixed combinations at one end, and fluid combinations at the other.

語言由字串構成，這些字串可以分成三大類——chunks、set-phrases 和 word partnerships，並且可依其可預測的程度區分，可預測度愈高的一端是固定字串，可預測度愈低的一 端是流動字串。

新的 Leximodel 圖示如下：

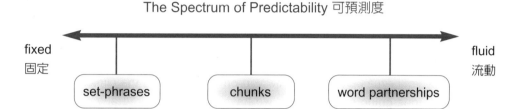

學英文致力學好 chunks，文法就會進步，因為大部分的文法錯誤其實都是源自於 chunks 寫錯。學英文時專攻 set-phrases，英語功能就會進步，因為 set-phrases 都是功能性字串。學英文時在 word partnerships 下功夫，字彙量就會增加。因此，最後的 Leximodel 圖示如下：

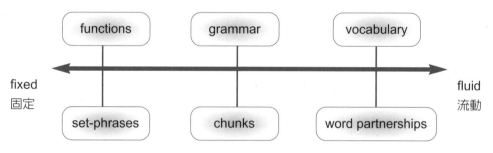

Leximodel 的優點以及其對於學習英文的妙用，就在於說、寫英文時，均無須再為文法規則傷透腦筋。學習英文時，首要之務是建立 chunks、set-phrases 和 word partnerships 的語料庫，多學多益。而不是學習文法規則，並苦苦思索如何在文法中套用單字。這三類 MWIs 用來輕而易舉，而且更符合人腦記憶和使用語言的習慣。本節結束前，我們來做最後一個 Task，確定各位對於 Leximodel 已經完全了解。如此一來，各位就會看出這個方法有多簡單好用。在完成 Task 前，先不要看語庫。

 **前言 TASK 6**

請看這分報告和翻譯，然後用三種不同顏色的筆分別將所有的 chunks、set-phrases 和 word partnerships 畫底線。最後請完成下表。請見範例。

Dear Mary,

Thanks for your email. Just to update you on the situation, the clinical trial of the new drug is going smoothly and we have not encountered any problems. We expect the trial to be completed by the end of this quarter. If all goes well, we can get approval for the drug by the end of the year. Our team has already started working on the marketing strategy for the drug. We intend to have a public awareness campaign using TV, print ads, and bus posters. We are also assembling a team of doctors to help introduce the product to hospitals throughout the north.

I hope this helps with your plans. Once we get the go-ahead from headquarters, I'll be in touch to finalize the plans for the advertising campaign.

Best regards,

Albert

【中譯】

瑪莉您好：

　　謝謝您的來信。向您報告一下目前情況，新藥的臨床試驗進行順利，我們尚未遇到任何問題。我們預期試驗將在本季末以前完成。如一切順利，藥在年底以前便可獲得核准。我們的工作小組已經開始為此藥研擬行銷策略。我們計劃透過電視、平面廣告和公車海報等來做公共宣傳活動。我們也正在延攬一組醫生，幫助我們在北部各地的醫院引薦產品。

　　希望以上報告對您的計劃有所幫助。一收到總部的許可，我便會和您聯絡，確定公共宣傳活動的計劃。

祝　安好

亞伯特

set-phrases	chunks	word partnerships
Thanks for your email	*... the end of sth.*	*marketing strategy*

答案 🎧

請利用下面的必備語庫檢查答案，並閱讀語庫小叮嚀。

商用英文必備語庫 前言 **3**

set-phrases	chunks	word partnerships
· Thanks for your email.	· ... update sb. on sth. ...	· clinical trial
· Just to update you on ...	· ... any problems ...	· new drug
· If all goes well, ...	· ... be completed by ...	· go smoothly
· I hope this helps...	· ... expect sth. to V ...	· encounter problems
· I'll be in touch...	· ... the end of sth. ...	· get approval
	· ... this quarter ...	· marketing strategy
	· ... approval for sth. ...	· public awareness campaign
	· ... work on sth. ...	· print ads
	· ... intend to ...	· bus posters
	· ... a team of ...	· get the go-ahead from
	· ... ntroduce sth. to sb. ...	· advertising campaign
	· ... plans for sth. ...	
	· ... help with sth. ...	

✎ 語庫小叮嚀

◆ 注意，set-phrases 通常是以大寫字母開頭。

◆ 刪節號 ...，表示句子流動的部分。

◆ 注意，chunks的開頭和結尾都有刪節號，表示 chunks 大部分為句子的中間部分。

◆ 注意，word partnerships 均由意義字組成。

　　假如你的答案沒有這麼完整，不必擔心。只要多練習，就能找出文中所有的固定元素。不過你可以確定一件事：等到你能找出這麼多的 MWIs，那就表示你的英文已經達到登峰造極的境界了！很快你便能擁有這樣的能力。於本書末尾，我會請各位再做一次這個 Task，以判斷自己的學習成果。現在有時間的話，各位不妨找一篇英文文章，像是以英語為母語的人所寫的電子郵件，或者雜誌或網路上的文章，然後用它來做同樣的練習。熟能生巧哦！

本書使用說明

　　到目前為止，我猜各位大概會覺得 Leximodel 似乎是個不錯的概念，但八成還是有些疑問。對於各位可能會有的問題，我來看看能否幫各位解答。

我該如何實際運用 Leximodel 學英文？為什麼 Leximodel 和我以前碰到的英文教學法截然不同？

　　簡而言之，我的答案是：

　　只要知道字詞的組合和這些組合的固定程度，就能簡化英語學習的過程，同時大幅減少犯錯的機率。

　　以前的教學法教你學好文法，然後套用句子，邊寫邊造句。用這方法寫作不僅有如牛步，而且稍不小心便錯誤百出，想必你早就有切身的體驗。現在只要用 Leximodel 建立 chunks、set-phrases 和 word partnerships 語庫，接著只需背起來就能學會英文寫作了。

本書如何使用Leximodel 教學？

　　本書以 chunks、set-phrases 和 word partnerships 介紹商業英文口說和寫作中 100 個最常出現的動詞，並說明 MWIs 的學習與運用方法。本書也會教各位要怎麼留意每天都可以看到和聽到的語言，以及記下這些語言的方法。

為什麼要留意字串中所有的字，很重要嗎？

　　不知道何故，大多數人對眼前的英文視而不見，分明擺在面前仍然視若無睹。他們緊盯著字詞的意思，卻忽略了傳達字詞意思的方法。每天瀏覽的固定 MWIs 多不勝數，只不過你沒有發覺這些 MWIs 是固定、反覆出現的字串罷了。任何語言都有這種現象。這樣吧，我們來做個實驗，你就知道我說的是真是假。請做下面的 Task。

前言 TASK 7

看看下面表格中的 set-phrases 和 chunks，並把正確的選出來。

☐ Regarding the report you sent me, …	☐ … contact sb. …
☐ Regarding to the report you sent me, …	☐ … get in contact sb. …
☐ Regards to the report you sent me, …	☐ … contact with sb. …
☐ With regards the report you sent, …	☐ … get contact with sb. …

不管你選的是哪個，我敢說你一定覺得這題很難。你可能每天都看到這個 set-phrase 和 chunk，但卻從來沒有仔細留意過其中的語言細節。（其實第二欄的第一項才是對的，其他的都是錯的！）

如果多留意每天接觸到的固定字串，久而久之一定會記起來，轉化成自己英文基礎的一部分，這可是諸多文獻可考的事實。刻意注意閱讀時遇到的 MWIs，亦可增加學習效率。Leximodel 正能幫你達到這一點。

需要小心哪些問題？

本書中許多 Task 的目的，即在於幫你克服這些問題。學固定 MWIs 的要領在於：務必留意 MWIs 中所有的字。

從前言 Task 7 中，你已發現自己其實不如想像中那麼細心注意 set-phrases 和 chunks 中所有的字。接下來我要更確切地告訴你學 set-phrases 和 chunks 時的注意事項，這對學習非常重要。

學習和使用 set-phrases 時，需要注意的細節有三大類：

1. **短字**（如 a、the、to、in、at、on 和 but）。這些字很難記，但是了解了這點，即可以說是跨出一大步了。Set-phrases 極為固定，用錯一個短字，整個 set-phrase 都會改變，等於是寫錯了。

2. **字尾**（有些字的字尾是 -ed，有些是 -ing，有些是 -ment，有些是 -s，或者沒有 -s）。字尾改變了，字的意思也會隨之改變。Set-phrases 極為固定，寫錯其中一字的字尾，整個 set-phrase 都會改變，等於是寫錯了。發音也非常重要，發音不正確，聽者便無法 set-phrases 掌握的意義。

3. **Set-phrase 的結尾**（有的 set-phrases 以 n. clause 結尾，有的以 n.p. 結尾，有的以 V 結尾，有的以 Ving 結尾），我們稱之為 code。許多人犯錯，問題即出在句子中 set-phrase 與其他部分的銜接之處。學習 set-phrases 時，必須將 code 當作 set-phrase 的一部分一併背起來。Set-phrases 極為固定，code 寫錯，整個 set-phrase 都會改變，等於是寫錯了

4. **完整的 set-phrase**。Set-phrase 是固定的單位，所以你必須完整地使用，不能只用前面一半或其中的幾個字而已。

　　Set-phrases 是 Leximodel 中最固定的 MWIs，因此以上大部分的注意事項都圍繞著 set-phrases，但這些注意事項在使用 chunks 時往往也都能派上用場。學習和使用 chunks 和 set-phrases 時，重點在於留心檢查小地方。最常出錯的正都是那些小地方，英文就有一種說法：The devil is in the details！

　　教學到此，請再做一個 Task，確定你能夠掌握 code 的用法。現在請做前言 Task 8。

前言 TASK 8

請看以下 code 的定義，然後將詞組分門別類填入表格中。請看範例。

　　n. clause = noun clause（名詞子句），n. clause 一定包含主詞和動詞。例如：I need your help.、She is on leave.、We are closing the department.、What is your estimate? 等。

　　n.p. = noun phrase（名詞片語），這其實就是 word partnerships，只是不含動詞或主詞。例如：financial news、cost reduction、media review data、joint stock company 等。

　　V = verb（動詞）。

　　Ving = verb ending in -ing（以 -ing 結尾的動詞）。以前你的老師可能稱之為動名詞。Ving 是看起來像名詞的動詞。

1. arrange	9. having	17. require
2. Can you help?	10. he is not	18. return
3. doing	11. helping	19. sending
4. general meeting	12. It's not right	20. talking
5. get approval	13. knowing	21. telephone call
6. get on with	14. I made make progress	22. we are going to
7. give instructions	15. Mary is on leave	23. we don't know
8. go ahead with	16. prepare to	

n. clause	n.p.	V	Ving
		annual report	

商用英文必備語庫 前言 4

n. clause	n.p.	V	Ving
· he is not	· get approval	· arrange	· helping
· we are going to	· give instructions	· return	· knowing
· Mary is on leave	· telephone call	· require	· doing
· we don't know	· annual report	· prepare to	· having
· It's not right	· general meeting	· go ahead with	· sending
· Can you help?		· get on with	· talking
· I made progress			

✎ 語庫小叮嚀

◆ 注意 n. clause 的 verb 前面一定要有主詞。

◆ 注意 n. p. 基本上即為 word partneships。

所以總而言之，在學習 set-phrases時，主要會碰到的問題有：

1. 短字
2. 字尾
3. Set-phrases 的結尾

不會太困難，對吧？

如果沒有文法規則可循，我怎麼知道自己的 set-phrases 或 chunks 用法正確無誤？

很簡單，參考一下你面前的這本書吧。為了助你一臂之力學好英文，本書提供了 language banks（語庫）。你只需檢查自己用到的 set-phrases 和本書語庫的一模一樣即可。張大雙眼，用心看我上面講述的所有細節準沒錯。別擔心為何你用的 set-phrases 不對，或者運用或違反了哪些文法規則，依本書的語庫完整照用就沒問題。熟能生巧！現在請再做下面的 Task，記住，做完後再往下看答案。

前言 TASK 9

請看下面句子中的錯誤，並與前言語庫 2 中的 set-phrases 作比較。請研究這些錯誤，並寫出正確的句子和錯誤原因的編號 (1. 短字；2. 字尾；3. Set-phrases 的結尾；4. 完整的 Set-phrases)。請看範例 A。

A	If you have any question about this, please do not hesitate to contact me.	2
B	Apologize for the delay in getting back to you, but I've been very busy.	
C	I look forward to hear from you.	
D	Just to confirm that the party.	
E	My recommendation here is to moving to a bigger office.	
F	I'd like to draw your attention to the sales figures last year were better.	
G	Just let you know that I have received it.	

前言 TASK 10

好了，在你檢查前言 Task 9 的答案之前，請修正以下句子。

A	If you have any question about this, please do not hesitate to contact me.	*If you have any questions about this, please do not hesitate to contact me.*
B	Apologize for the delay in getting back to you, but I've been very busy.	

C	I look forward to hear from you.	
D	Just to confirm that the party.	
E	My recommendation here is to moving to a bigger office.	
F	I'd like to draw your attention to the sales figures last year were better.	
G	Just let you know that I have received it.	

現在請檢查前面兩個 Task 的答案。

答案

前言 Task 9 的範例答案。

B 2　　C 2　　D 3　　E 3　　F 4　　G 1

前言 Task 10 的範例答案。

A	If you have any questions about this, please do not hesitate to contact me.
B	Apologies for the delay in getting back to you, but I've been very busy./ I apologize for the delay in getting back to you, but I've been very busy.
C	I look forward to hearing from you.
D	Just to confirm that the party is going ahead.
E	My recommendation here is to move to a bigger office.
F	I'd like to draw your attention to the fact that the sales figures last year were better.
G	Just to let you know that I have received it.

　　如果你的答案與上述的範例答案截然不同，請回頭再把本章節詳讀一遍，並且特別注意前言 Task 8 和對於 set-phrases 細節四個問題的解說。

本書有許多 Task 會幫你將注意力集中在 set-phrases 的這些細節上，你只須作答和核對答案，無須擔心背後原因。

本書的架構爲何？

這本書分成四篇。每篇分別教 100 個動詞中的 25 個動詞，並會從最容易使用的教起，然後一路進階到挑戰性最高的，也就是說第四篇會比第一篇的難度高。此外，每篇都有一個單元教寫作和文法，一個單元教聽力和口說，還有一個單元幫你擴充詞彙。

寫作單元教的是寫電子郵件管理客戶關係（customer relationship management，CRM），也會提供 chunks 幫你更準確的用商業英文寫作。

口說單元的主題會著重在商業英文和社交英文。這些單元也會教你不同的情況中應該使用的時態。第一篇的教學重點在於不受限的時間，第二篇的教學重點在於現在時間，第三篇的教學重點在於過去時間，而第四篇的教學重點在於未來時間。除此之外，口說單元也會幫助你改善聽力和發音。

詞彙單元會教你一些關鍵動詞的主要 word partnerships、片語動詞和慣用語，擴充你的詞彙庫。

本書更附有「常見錯誤欄」，告訴你大家在使用動詞時一些最常見的錯誤。

本書的利用方法有四種：

1. 如果想從初階學到高階，加強商業英文各方面的能力，你可以跟著本書從第一篇一直學到第四篇，按照順序學習裡面的各單元。
2. 如果你只想加強寫作和文法，可以僅僅學習本書各篇的第一個單元，也就是第二、五、八、十一單元。如果希望加強客戶關係管理技巧，只要學習每個寫作單元的第一節即可。
3. 如果只希望加強口說和聽力，只需要學習本書每篇的第二單元，也就是第三、六、九、十二單元。如果只想學動詞時態，可以只看每個口說單元的第一節。

4. 如果只想增加詞彙，可以只看本書每篇的最後一個單元，也就是第四、七、
十、十三單元。

不論你選擇用什麼方式使用本書，我強烈建議你先從第一單元學起，如此一來，
不論選擇哪一個途徑研讀本書，你都會學到英文動詞的關鍵正確用法。

我如何充分利用本書？

在此有些自習的建議，協助你獲致最大的學習效果。

1. 本書的 Tasks 很重要，有助於你記憶所學的語文項目，並加強你對這些語文項
目的理解力。
2. 建議用鉛筆做本書的 Tasks。寫錯時還可以擦掉。
3. 做分類 Tasks（請見第二單元 Task 2.1）的時候，只要在每個 MWI 旁做記號
或寫下英文字母即可。不過建議你在有空時，還是回來把 MWIs 抄寫在正確的
一欄中。還記得當初是怎麼學中文的嗎？抄寫能夠加深印象！
4. 做聽力 Tasks 的時候，請先將 MP3 聽至少三遍，然後再翻閱其下的答案。
5. 做口說 Tasks 的時候，請用錄音機錄音，聽過自己的答案之後再做一次
Task。你可以比較自己在同一個 Task 中的答案，看有沒有進步。請把音檔儲
存在電腦中，並花一點時間整理。
6. 利用書末附錄的「學習目標記錄表」追蹤自己的學習狀況，如此有助於你挑出
想學的語文項目。選擇的時候，不妨記住以下重點：
❏ 選擇困難、奇怪或新的用語。
❏ 如果可以的話，避免使用你已經知道或覺得運用自如的用語。
❏ 特意運用這些新的用語。
7. 如果你下定決心要進步，建議你和同事組成 K 書會，一同閱讀本書和做
Task。

在我開始之前有沒有什麼需要知道的事情？

Yes. You can do it!

開始閱讀第一單元前，請回到前言的「學習目標」，勾出自認為達成的項目。希
望你全部都能夠打勾。

祝學習有成！

Unit 1 英文動詞概論

引言與學習目標

本書將教你商業英文中最常見的100個動詞，這些動詞可以運用在口說和寫作上。按照字母排列，這些動詞如下：

A	contact	hope	**N**	see
accept	continue	**I**	need	send
agree	**D**	implement	note	serve
allow	decide	improve	**O**	set
apologize	discuss	include	offer	show
appreciate	do	increase	**P**	suggest
arrange	**E**	inform	pay	**T**
arrive	enjoy	interest	plan	take
ask	ensure	involve	prepare	talk
attach	expect	**J**	propose	tell
attend	**F**	join	provide	thank
B	feel	**K**	put	think
base	find	keep	**R**	try
be	follow	know	read	**U**
become	**G**	**L**	receive	understand
begin	get	learn	recommend	use
believe	give	leave	regret	**V**
bring	go	let	remember	visit
C	**H**	like	request	**W**
call	handle	look	require	want
cause	have	**M**	return	wish
come	hear	make	review	work
complete	help	meet	**S**	write
confirm	hesitate	mention	say	
consider	hold		schedule	

Word List
- implement [ˋɪmpləmənt] v. 履行；實施（契約、計劃等）
- interest [ˋɪntərɪst] v. 使（人）感興趣；使……參與

本書將這 100 個動詞分成四組，每組 25 個動詞。我會按照各組動詞容易學習和理解的程度，逐一為你解說，而不是按照其出現頻率。

為什麼要選擇教動詞呢？

首先，如果把一個句子想像成一輛汽車，汽車有輪子、窗戶、座椅、汽車音響和駕駛操控裝置等，而句子則有主詞、受詞，可能還有幾個介系詞片語、幾個分詞子句，當然也有一些詞彙。汽車裡面最重要的配備就是引擎，少了引擎，即使具備其他配備，汽車也無法發動。而句子中最重要的部分就是動詞，動詞就像句子的引擎一般，有了動詞，句子才會活起來。這就是為什麼加強英文能力最有效的辦法，便是學會英文動詞。

第二，從中文人士使用英文的錯誤分析中顯示，中文人士最常犯的錯誤就在於動詞。這些關於動詞的錯誤可分為兩種，一種是時態上的錯誤；另一種則發生在我們稱為動詞補語（verb complements）或其他搭配動詞使用的詞彙上，例如受詞、介系詞等等。我會在本單元中介紹一些概念，幫你解決這兩種問題。

本單元結束時，各位應達成的「學習目標」如下：

❏ 更加了解中文動詞和英文動詞的差別。
❏ 更加了解英文動詞的時態系統。
❏ 更加了解動詞 chunks 和片語動詞的差別，以及為什麼要了解這兩者間的差別。
❏ 更加了解不同種類的動詞 chunks 模式。
❏ 更加了解慣用片語動詞和非慣用片語動詞的差別。
❏ 更加了解雙受詞動詞。

好，我們這就開始探討大家使用動詞時會犯的第一類錯誤：動詞時態。

動詞時態

　　中英文動詞最主要的差別在於：從中文動詞只能看出動作的資訊，而從英文動詞中除了能得到動作的資訊，同時也能知道動作發生的時間。在中文裡，如果想在句子中提供動作發生的時間，必須加上時間 chunks，例如昨天、明天、之後、之前等。然而在英文中，透過動詞時態便可傳達動作發生的時間，不見得非得在句中放進時間 chunks 以說明時間。請做下面的 Task，你就會明白我的意思了。

TASK 1.1

請將適當的時間 chunks 放入下面的句子中。

at the moment	now	two years ago
next week	tomorrow	yesterday

　　　　　　　　　 1. We attend the trade fair in Hong Kong.
　　　　　　　　　 2. I fly to Tokyo for a meeting.
　　　　　　　　　 3. I meet the customer.
　　　　　　　　　 4. I join the company.
　　　　　　　　　 5. I work in the finance department.
　　　　　　　　　 6. We develop a new product.

答案

希望你沒辦法做這個 Task！事實上這個 Task 是有陷阱的。問題就出在所有的動詞都是原形動詞，完全看不出發生的時間。少了時間的資訊，這些時間 chunks 根本沒辦法放進句子中。我們再試一次，請做下頁的練習。

TASK 1.2

請將適當的時間 chunks 放入下面的句子中。

at the moment	now	two years ago
next week	tomorrow	yesterday

_____ 1. **We're going to attend the trade fair in Hong Kong.**

_____ 2. **I'm going to fly to Tokyo for a meeting.**

_____ 3. **I met the customer.**

_____ 4. **I joined the company.**

_____ 5. **I'm working in the finance department.**

_____ 6. **We're developing a new product.**

答案

現在這個練習應該比較容易做了吧？這些動詞透露出動作的發生時間，時間 chunks 便比較容易放入句子中了。以下是我的建議答案：

1. Tomorrow/Next week/At the moment/Now we're going to attend the trade fair in Hong Kong.

2. Tomorrow/Next week/At the moment/Now I'm going to fly to Tokyo for a meeting.

3. Two years ago/Yesterday I met the customer.

4. Two years ago/Yesterday I joined the company.

5. At the moment/Now/Next week/Tomorrow I'm working in the finance department.

6. At the moment/Now/Next week/Tomorrow we're developing a new product.

　　這些動詞時態透露了動作發生的時間，看得出來嗎？掌握這點非常重要。在句子中放進適當的時間 chunks，只是更具體地指出動作發生的時間，例如指出動作是發生在昨天還是二年前，如此而已。倘若把句子中的時間 chunks 拿掉，我們還是能夠透過時態，大概知道動作發生的時間。反觀中文句子，如果把時間 chunks 拿出來，就不知道動作是何時發生的了。

好，既然現在你已經知道動詞時態的重要性，接下來要學的就是不同的時間要使用哪一種動詞時態。

在英文中有四個時間範圍：現在時間、過去時間、未來時間和不受限的時間。現在時間也可視為未完成的時間，例如今天便是尚未完成的時間。過去時間可視為是已完成的時間，例如昨天。前三個時間範圍很容易理解，但是最後一個──不受限的時間──可能難度就比較高一點。但是花一點時間思考，就會發現其實許多我們說和寫的東西都和時間無關。請看下面的範例：

1. Taiwan is an island.

2. I am a man.

3. I don't know.

4. He is pretty stupid.

5. She is amazing.

6. This is a difficult market to do business in.

7. The company has 200 employees.

這些句子和時間並沒有很大的關係。舉一個例子，在說台灣是一座島的時候，不表示明天或昨天台灣就不是一座島。或者說我是男人時，不表示明天我起床的時候就會發現自己變成女人！這些句子要表達的是概念或看法，無關乎時間。

了解我的意思後，接下來的部分就很簡單了。你只需要學會使用動詞時態，來傳達這四個不同的時間範圍即可。

TASK 1.3

請仔細研讀下面的表格。

	時間範圍	時態	一般／商業英文中的適用情境
1	不受限	簡單現在式	◆慣例和程序 ◆永恆不變的事實 ◆看法 ◆與時間無關的一般性描述

時間範圍		時態	一般 / 商業英文中的適用情境
2	現在	現在進行式	◆當下正在進行的事情 ◆目前的市場情況 ◆發生中的商業趨勢和活動
		現在完成式	◆生活經驗 ◆某些當下的情況 ◆銷售或預測的結果
		簡單現在式	◆非只有現在為真的事實 ◆非只有現在為真的看法 ◆非只有現在為真的一般性描述
3	過去	簡單過去式	◆過去發生的事件 ◆公司過去的重要事件
4	未來	各種不同的時間 chunks	◆個人安排 ◆預定好的事件 ◆與個人無關的預測

　　表達不受限時間的事情時，必須使用簡單現在式（present simple）。你可能以前學過，表達現在時間時要用簡單現在式，但我的教法不同，我在接下來的章節裡很快就會教你不受限時間的說法和寫法。

　　表達現在時間的事情時，可以使用的時態有三種，端視你所要表達是哪一種現在時間而定。如果想表達的是正在進行的事情，或在講的當時還沒完成的事情，可以用現在進行式（present continuous）。如果想表達結果和生活經驗，請用現在完成式（present perfect）。如果你想表達的事實或看法不是只有現在才是真實的，那麼可使用簡單現在式（present simple），並搭配一個現在時間 chunks。例如：Currently, this market is very difficult to do business in. 或者 The company has 200 employees at the moment.。如果沒有在句中放進時間 chunks，你的讀者或聽者會假設你的看法永遠不變。我會在第六單元中更加詳細地說明現在時間的說法和寫法。

　　表達過去的事件時，一般來說用簡單過去式（past simple）即可。你可能在高中時便學會過去進行式（past continuous）和過去完成式（past perfect），但無需太擔

心這兩種時態，因為這兩種時態在文學作品裡比較常用，在商業英文甚至一般的日常生活會話很少用到。我在第九單元中會更詳細說明過去時間的說法和寫法。

表達未來的事件時，你可能以前學過是用 will。然而描述未來事件沒那麼簡單，事實上未來時間的時間 chunks 有很多，端視你想表達的是哪一種而定。我會在第十二單元中更詳細地教你未來時間的說法和寫法。

TASK 1.4

請根據 Task 1.3 的表格，將適當的時間範圍編號寫在以下例句旁。見範例。

A	2	I am not happy with my job these days.
B		I go to the gym every Wednesday evening.
C		I have never been to Japan.
D		I really hated learning English at school.
E		I saw that movie last week.
F		I think my boss is very cool.
G		I went to Japan in 1999.
H		I work in the accounting department.
I		I'm doing an EMBA.
J		I'm going to go to the movies with my boyfriend tonight.
K		I'm working on a new design.
L		I've completed my MBA.
M		It's really cold today.
N		My company is a global market leader.
O		My flight leaves at 9:00.
P		Sales have gone up this month.
Q		Sales will probably fall in the first quarter.
R		The company was founded in 1966.
S		The economy grew by 0.02% last year.
T		The market is expanding.
U		The meeting starts at 8:30.
V		We are getting married next month.

答案

A	2
B	1
C	2
D	3
E	3

F	1
G	3
H	1
I	2
J	4

K	2
L	2
M	2
N	1
O	4

P	2
Q	4
R	3
S	3
T	2

U	4
V	4

　　我猜你 C、L、O 和 U 的答案寫錯了，你是不是以為 C 和 L 是指過去的事件？別忘了我前面說過的，現在完成式不代表過去時間。我會在第六單元裡更詳細地解說現在完成式。另外，或許你以為 O 和 U 是指不受限的時間，因為這兩者用的都是簡單現在式，但其實這是特殊的未來式，我在第十二單元中會詳加說明。

　　請注意 E、G、R 和 S 都有過去時間 chunks。然而如果把時間 chunks 拿掉，我們還是知道這些句子談的是過去時間，因為裡面用到了簡單過去式。

　　請注意 J 和 V 也都有未來時間 chunks。然而因為句子中使用的時態，就算我們把這些時間 chunks 拿掉，我們仍然可以理解句子談的是未來時間。另外還有特殊未來式，我會在第十二單元中更詳細地為你解說。

　　在現階段請不要擔心是否答錯。答錯有可能是因為你還沒掌握這些動詞時態的確切意義。我在接下來的相關章節中會更加詳細地教你。

　　在英文中，動詞時態非常重要，希望你從本節中已經了解這一點。如果時態用錯，你的讀者和聽者會一頭霧水，不知道事情究竟發生在哪一個時間範圍。

　　好，現在我們繼續往下學習，看一看動詞運用上常見的第二類錯誤：動詞補語。

動詞補語

你可能還記得以前學英文時，老師說有些動詞是及物動詞（vt），有些是不及物動詞（vi）。你可能不清楚兩者到底有何分別。分辨及物和不及物還有一種方法，那就是先學會動詞的 chunks。我們現在要學的正是這種方法。接下來請務必仔細閱讀，找出所看到的模式。

所有的動詞補語均可分成兩種：搭配介系詞的動詞，即片語動詞（phrasal verbs）；另外就是未搭配介系詞的動詞，簡單地說即是動詞 chunks。

TASK 1.5

請仔細研讀以下 chunks，並將它們分類歸入下表中。

1. arrange n.p.	18. inform sb. about sth.
2. ask sb. to V	19. involve Ving
3. begin to V	20. keep after sb.
4. believe that + n. clause	21. keep on at sb.
5. continue to V	22. look at sth.
6. continue Ving	23. look into n.p.
7. decide that + n. clause	24. offer sb. sth.
8. discuss sth. with sb.	25. prepare to V
9. do away with n.p.	26. recommend that + n. clause
10. do sth. for sb.	27. remember n.p.
11. enjoy Ving	28. require sb. to V
12. feel that + n. clause	29. try Ving
13. find n.p.	30. understand n.p.
14. get sth. from sb.	31. use sth. to V
15. go into sth.	32. want to V
16. go to n.p.	33. send sb. sth.
17. help sb. to V	34. tell sb. sth.

未搭配介系詞的動詞 （動詞 chunks）	搭配介系詞的動詞 （phrasal verbs）

答案

請看我在下面提供的答案並研讀語庫小叮嚀。

商用英文必備語庫 1.1

未搭配介系詞的動詞 （動詞 chunks）		搭配介系詞的動詞 （phrasal verbs）
· arrange n.p.	· offer sb. sth.	· want to V
· ask sb. to V	· prepare to V	· discuss sth. with sb.
· begin to V	· recommend that ＋ n. clause	· do away with n.p.
· believe that ＋ n. clause	· remember n.p.	· do sth. for sb.
· continue to V	· require sb. to V	· get sth. from sb.
· continue Ving	· send sb. sth.	· go into sth.
· decide that ＋ n. clause	· tell sb. sth.	· go to n.p.
· enjoy Ving	· try Ving	· inform sb. about sth.
· feel that ＋ n. clause	· understand n.p.	· keep after sb.
· find n.p.	· use sth. to V	· keep on at n.p.
· help sb. to V		· look at sth.
· involve Ving		· look into n.p.

🖊 語庫小叮嚀

◆ Sb. 和 sth. 與 n.p. 的意義一樣。但有時有必要分辨是指人還是指事。如果只是接 n.p.，就不需要分了。

◆ 未搭配介系詞的動詞 chunks 還有其他幾個種類，但是我要在相關的寫作單元中才會一一向你介紹。

目前學的都挺簡單吧？

現在我們來深入學習動詞 chunks。動詞 chunks 可根據模式粗略的分成五、六組。請做下面的 Task，你就會明白我的意思了。

TASK 1.6

請仔細研讀以下動詞 chunks，並將它們分類歸入下表中。

1. arrange n.p.
2. ask sb. to V
3. begin to V
4. believe that + n. clause
5. continue to V
6. continue Ving
7. decide that + n. clause

8. enjoy Ving
9. feel that + n. clause
10. find n.p.
11. help sb. to V
12. involve Ving
13. prepare to V
14. recommend that + n. clause

15. remember n.p.
16. require sb. to V
17. try Ving
18. understand n.p.
19. use sth. to V
20. want to V

V + n.p.	V that + n. clause	V to V	V + Ving	V sb./sth. to V

答案

請以下列語庫核對答案。

商用英文必備語庫 **1.2**　　動詞 chunks　　　　　　　　MP3 03

V + n.p.	V that + n. clause	V to V	V + Ving	V sb./sth. to V
· find n.p. · understand n.p. · arrange n.p. · remember n.p.	· feel that + n. clause · believe that + n. clause · decide that + n. clause · recommend that + n. clause	· want to V · continue to V · prepare to V · begin to V	· continue Ving · enjoy Ving · involve Ving · try Ving	· help sb. to V · ask sb. to V · require sb. to V · use sth. to V

動詞 chunks 很重要，非知道不可，因為學會動詞 chunks 之後才能正確地運用在句子中。許多人句子結構會出錯，其實都是錯在動詞 chunks。因此學會動詞 chunks 有助於避免此類錯誤，並提高英文文法的準確性，進而表達更清楚。

現在我們繼續往下學習片語動詞吧。片語動詞比動詞 chunks 難一點，但基本上片語動詞有兩種：慣用（idiomatic）和非慣用（non-idiomatic）片語動詞。

非慣用片語動詞很簡單，因為意思顯而易見。當介系詞接上動詞的時候，動詞的意思不會改變。例如 listen to（例：Listen to the presentation.）或 look at（例：Let's look at the figures again.）或 go to（例：Are you going to the meeting?）。

慣用片語動詞比較複雜，因為動詞在搭配了介系詞之後，意義就會改變，例如：look sth. up（例：I need to look this up in my dictionary.）。

有的片語動詞有時是慣用語，有時是非慣用語，端視用法而定。例如：I took off my wet rain coat. 是非慣用語，但 The flight took off on time. 卻是慣用語。

TASK 1.7

請填寫表格的最後一欄。如果你認為該片語動詞是慣用語，請寫 i；如果認為是非慣用語，請寫 ni。見範例。

1	look at sth.	Look at that! That's amazing!	*ni*
2	look into n.p.	We need to look into the situation carefully.	
3	keep after sb.	My boss is keeping after me for the report.	
4	keep on	He kept on working.	
5	go to	I'm going to Singapore for a meeting.	
6	go into sth.	The report goes into great detail.	
7	do sth. for sb.	Can I do something for you?	
8	do away with	We've done away with the old office procedures.	

答案

請看我在下面提供的答案。

1	look at sth.	Look at that! That's amazing!	*ni*
2	look into sth.	We need to look into the situation carefully. look into sth. 意為「仔細地檢視某事」	*i*
3	keep after sb.	My boss is keeping after me for the report. keep after sb. for sth.意為「一直提醒某人要做某事；嘮叨某人」	*i*
4	keep on	He kept on working.	*ni*
5	go to	I'm going to Singapore for a meeting.	*ni*
6	go into sth.	The report goes into great detail. go into sth. 意為「仔細地描述某事」	*i*
7	do sth. for sb.	Can I do something for you?	*ni*
8	do away with sth.	We've done away with the old office procedures. do away with sth. 意為「擺脫；去除某事」	*i*

1、4、5 和 7 是非慣用語，因為可以從句子中隱約猜出這些動詞 chunks 的意義。

2、3、6 和 8 的意思則比較難從字面上判斷，必須已經認識這些慣用語才行。

片語動詞很重要，因為很多情況和意義都必須靠片語動詞描述，使用正式英文時更是如此。有時片語動詞可用一個同義詞取代，但有時卻不行，也就是說該情況非得用片語動詞描述不可。我稍後會教你更多好用的片語動詞。

最後在本單元中，我們必須再學一種動詞補語，這種動詞補語有一個以上的受詞，稱作雙受詞動詞（two-object verbs）。以下是一些範例：

EX

discuss sth. with sb.	offer sb. sth.
get sth. from sb.	send sb. sth.
inform sb. about sth.	tell sb. sth.

從這些範例中，你可以看出通常一個受詞是指事物（sth.）；而另一個受詞通常是指人（sb.）。

雙受詞動詞有兩種，一種受詞順序可以調換，我們稱為可倒置雙受詞動詞（invertible two-object verbs），另一種受詞順序不可以調換，又稱不可倒置雙受詞動詞，（non-invertible two-object verbs）。上面左欄的是不可倒置雙受詞動詞，例如 discuss sth. with sb. 不能說或寫成 discuss sb. with sth.。上面右欄的是可倒置雙受詞動詞。

就不可倒置雙受詞動詞而言，可以只有一個受詞，不過如果想要再加一個受詞來釐清語意，則需要多加一個介系詞。這些動詞的困難之處，就在於要記得加哪一個介系詞。

EX

| discuss sth. (with sb.) |
| get sth. (from sb.) |
| inform sb. (about sth.) |

以可倒置雙受詞動詞來說，請看調換受詞位置後的結果：

offer sb. sth. ▸ offer sth. to sb.

send sb. sth. ▸ send sth. to sb.

tell sb. sth. ▸ tell sth. to sb.

希望你能看出，在調換受詞順序之後，第二個受詞前面便得多加一個介系詞 。我會在本書每一篇的寫作單元中更深入地教你這類雙受詞動詞。

雙受詞動詞很重要，因為一百個最常見和最好用的動詞當中很多都是雙受詞動詞，而且由於這類動詞很難使用，大家經常栽在這類動詞上。

好了，本單元要教的動詞到此結束。在本單元結束前，請看下頁的圖，以複習和整理所學到的動詞補語。

TASK 1.8

請看此圖，以了解動詞補語。

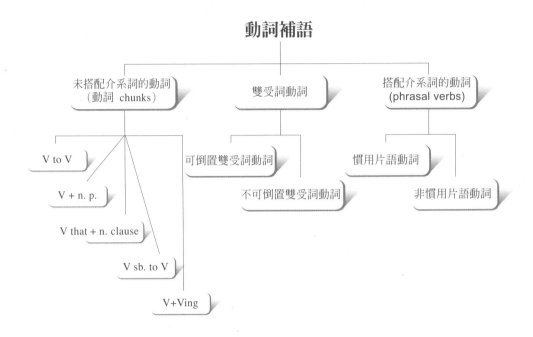

　　我會在相關章節中更詳細地教你每一個動詞補語，但現在你只需要清楚知道動詞的一些基本概念。在往下學習第二單元之前，請回到本單元前面的學習清單，確定你已確切掌握了每一項概念。

PART 1

Biz
Verbs

導讀

　　在第一篇中我們要學的是下面的 25 個動詞。在開始學習之前，我想先請你做兩個 Task，之後在第一篇結束前我會請你再做一次這兩個 Task。透過比較這第二次的答案，你就會了解自己在使用這 25 個動詞時犯了哪些錯誤，並知道自己的學習成果。

第一篇 開頭 Task 1

請研讀以下動詞，並利用每一個動詞來各造一個句子。

第一組 25 個動詞

· thank	· let	· give	· find	· accept
· know	· hope	· take	· help	· meet
· like	· appreciate	· call	· need	· want
· make	· send	· receive	· wish	· think
· look	· see	· get	· feel	· come

第一篇 開頭 Task 2

請勾選覺得使用上有困難的動詞和難造的句子。

Unit 2 寫作

引言與學習目標

　　本單元的學習重點在於將這 25 個動詞運用在寫作上，我們也會學習這些動詞在 set-phrases 和 chunks 中的用法。Set-phrases 可用來寫電子郵件，維繫你和收件人的關係並執行業務；chunks 則可增加用語的準確性。你在本單元學到的 set-phrases 很適合用來寫電子郵件，chunks 則適用於所有的寫作類型，商業或一般寫作皆然。

　　本單元結束時，各位應達成的「學習目標」如下：

　　　　　❑ 學會許多可用於客戶關係管理的 set-phrases。
　　　　　❑ 練習如何使用這些 set-phrases。
　　　　　❑ 學會許多動詞 chunks。
　　　　　❑ 學會許多雙受詞動詞 chunks。
　　　　　❑ 練習運用學到的新字串。
　　　　　❑ 寫作時可以更精準和有自信地使用動詞。
　　　　　❑ 了解寫作上一些常見的錯誤並知道該如何避免。

Set-Phrases

客戶關係管理（customer relationship management，簡稱 CRM）即建立和維持與消費者或客戶間關係的過程。你和公司的客戶多半是用電子郵件溝通，可見電子郵件是建立和維持這層關係最重要的環節。本節中我們要探討的是電子郵件中可以使用的 set-phrases，重點會擺在電子郵件中開頭和結尾的 set-phrases。

◀ 用於電子郵件開頭與結尾的 Set-Phrases ▶

我們就從電子郵件中用於開頭與結尾的 set-phrases 開始著手吧。首先要學的動詞是 thank，因為 thank 是商業溝通中最常用到的動詞。

TASK 2.1

請將下列 set-phrases 分門別類，填入下表中。

1. Thank you for your email about n.p./Ving …
2. Thank you for your email.
3. Thank you for sending n.p. …
4. Thank you for sending me n.p. …
5. Thank you very much for your help.
6. Thanks and sorry for any misunderstanding.
7. Many thanks for your understanding on this.
8. Thank you very much.
9. Thanks in advance.
10. Thank you in advance for your time.
11. Thanks in advance for your help.
12. Thank you again for choosing n.p. …
13. Many thanks.
14. Thanks for your help.
15. Thanks for your reply.
16. Thank you for purchasing n.p. …
17. Thank you for your message.
18. Thank you for your message about n.p./Ving …

Opening	Closing

答案

請以下列語庫來核對答案,並閱讀語庫小叮嚀。

商用英文必備語庫 **2.1** 包含 thank 的開頭與結尾的 set-phrases ⚪MP3 04

Opening（開頭）	**Closing（結尾）**
· Thank you for your email about n.p./Ving … · Thank you for your email. · Thank you for sending n.p. … · Thank you for sending me n.p. … · Thanks for your reply. · Thank you for your message. · Thank you for your message about n.p./Ving …	· Thank you very much for your help. · Thanks and sorry for any misunderstanding. · Many thanks for your understanding on this. · Thank you very much. · Thanks in advance. · Thank you in advance for your time. · Thanks in advance for your help. · Many thanks. · Thanks for your help. · Thank you again for choosing n.p. … · Thank you for purchasing n.p. …

✎ 語庫小叮嚀

開 頭

◆ 這些 set-phrases 中,thanks 和 thank you 可以互換。但不能寫成 Thanks you … 。
◆ 請注意,send 後面不一定非得接 me 不可,除非是希望使用比較個人的口吻。

結 尾

◆ Thanks and sorry for any misunderstanding.
   如果你和收件人間因溝通不良而造成某些誤解,此時便可使用這個 set-phrase。
◆ Many thanks for your understanding on this.
   如果有商業問題必須解決,這時可使用這個 set-phrase。
◆ Thanks in advance.、Thank you in advance for your time.、Thanks in advance for your help.
   如果想對收件人施加壓力,請對方幫你一個忙,這些 set-phrases 便能派上用場。既然已經預先感謝對方做某事,對方便比較有義務幫你忙了。好用吧?

◆ Thank you again for choosing n.p. ...、Thank you for purchasing n.p. ...
初次寫電子郵件連絡客戶，謝謝對方選擇你的產品、服務或公司時，可以使用這些 set-phrases。這樣的表達方式有助於建立良好的消費者關係。

現在我們就來學這些 set-phrases 吧。請一面學習，一面仔細留意我在前言提到的 set-phrases 細節。

TASK 2.2

請改正下列句子中 set-phrases 的錯誤，見範例。

1. Many thank for your understanding of this.
   Many thanks for your understanding on this.

2. Thank you for send me the form.

3. Thank you in advanced for your time.

4. Thanks you and sorry for any misunderstanding.

5. Thanks for getting back me so quickly.

6. Thanks for your email about finishing the project soonly.

7. Thank you for your helping.

8. Thanks in advance about your help.

答案

請比較自己的答案和下面提供的答案。

2. Thank you for sending me the form.

3. Thank you in advance for your time.

4. Thanks and sorry for any misunderstanding.

5. Thanks for getting back to me so quickly.

6. Thanks for your email about finishing the project soon.

7. Thank you for your help.

8. Thanks in advance for your help.

常 見 錯 誤 ＞ ＞ **make** 和 **let**	
錯 誤	正 確
Thank you for your inviting me.	Thank you for inviting me.
Thank you for your coming.	Thank you for coming.
Thank you for your replying.	Thank you for replying.
	Thank you for your reply.
· 千萬不要寫： Thank you for your + Ving， 除非 Ving 是動名詞當形容詞 用。如：Thank you for your entertaining presentation.	

　　現在我們繼續往下學習如何使用 hope 和 wish 的 set-phrases，這兩個動詞在 CRM 裡非常好用。許多人分不清楚這兩個動詞在意義上有何分別。建議你先把用到 這兩個動詞的 set-phrases 背起來，而不要鑽研每個詞的意義。做過下面的 Task 之 後，你自然就會發現兩者的差別。我們就先從 hope 學起吧。寫電子郵件時，hope 可用於開頭也可用於結尾。

TASK 2.3

請將以下用到 hope 的 set-phrases 分門別類，填入下頁的表格中。

1. I hope this email finds you well.

2. I hope this helps.

3. I hope this is clear.

4. I hope this is OK.

5. I hope this is the beginning of a long and prosperous relationship.

6. I hope to hear from you soon.

7. I hope to see you there.

8. I hope we can move this along quickly.

9. I hope you are feeling better now.

10. I hope you are well.

Word List　▪ prosperous [ˋprɑspərəs] adj. 興盛的；成功的

11. I hope you had a good trip.
12. I hope you had a nice weekend.
13. I hope you have a good trip.

14. I hope you understand our position on this.
15. I hope your meeting was successful.
16. We hope to be hearing from you soon.

Opening	Closing

答案

請利用下面的必備語庫來核對答案，並閱讀語庫小叮嚀。

商用英文必備語庫 2.2 包含 hope 的開頭與結尾 set-phrases　

Opening（開頭）	Closing（結尾）
· I hope you had a nice weekend.	· I hope this is clear.
· I hope you had a good trip.	· I hope we can move this along quickly.
· I hope your meeting was successful.	· I hope this is OK.
· I hope you are feeling better now.	· I hope to hear from you soon.
· I hope this email finds you well.	· I hope this helps.
· I hope you are well.	· I hope this is the beginning of a long and prosperous relationship.
	· We hope to be hearing from you soon.
	· I hope to see you there.
	· I hope you have a good trip.
	· I hope you understand our position on this.

✎　語庫小叮嚀

◆ 語庫中的 set-phrases 大多在信件的其他部分也可以使用，只是左欄傾向於在開頭使用，右欄則傾向於在結尾使用。

◆ 看得出來嗎？這些 set-phrases 中，hope 的後面大部分都會接一個名詞子句。在本書後面的單元裡，我會教你 hope 的其他意義和用法。

◆ 另外也請注意，如想要正式一點的表達方式，主詞務必每次都要寫出來，如：I hope ... 而不是 Hope ...。

◆ I hope this is clear. 的使用時機為收件人不是很明白你的信件內容，而你想要更進一步解釋時，這個 set-phrase 便可派上用場。

◆ I hope we can move this along quickly.
　如收件人拖延回信或者你欲加快進度時，便可使用這個 set-phrase。基本上這個 set-phrase 就是「請加快進行」的意思。

◆ I hope this is the beginning of a long and prosperous relationship.
　初次寫電子郵件與客戶聯繫，或者初次締結一項商業合作時，可以使用這個 set-phrase。

◆ I hope you understand our position on this.
　如需婉拒客戶的要求，可使用這個 set-phrase。

現在我們來學 wish 的用法吧。

TASK 2.4

請研讀下面的必備語庫和語庫小叮嚀。

商用英文必備語庫 2.3 包含 wish 的 set-phrases　

> · We wish you all a Happy New Year.
> · I wish you great success in your new job.
> · I wish you all the best.
> · We wish everyone there a pleasant holiday.
> · We wish you a Merry Christmas and a Happy New Year.
> · We wish you every success.
> · We wish you good luck.
> · We wish you the best of luck.
> · We wish you success in n.p. ...

　　語庫小叮嚀

◆ 從這些 set-phrases 可以看出，寫電子郵件或信件時如以 wish 結尾，wish 後面大部分要接一個 n.p.

◆ 我會在下一單元中教你 wish 的不同意義和用法，讓你在交談時表達個人願望和夢想。

◆ 同樣地，正式一點的表達方式為：I wish ... 而不要只有寫 Wish ... 。如欲在特別的時刻裡表達祝福之意，這些 set-phrases 都可以派上用場。

　　現在我們來看一看 appreciate 這個動詞，這個動詞在 CRM 裡也非常好用。想正式請求協助、感謝對方幫忙或在有人請你幫忙，你卻愛莫能助的時候，appreciate 都可派上用場。

TASK 2.5

請將下面的 set-phrases 分門別類，填入下頁的表格中。

1. I appreciate all that you have done.

2. I appreciate you taking the time to help me with this.

3. I would appreciate your attention to this matter.

4. I appreciate your concerns, but I'm afraid I am not able to help you.

5. I would appreciate a prompt reply.

6. I would appreciate a response.

7. I would appreciate any assistance you can give.

8. I would appreciate your help with this.

9. We hope you can appreciate our position.

10. We appreciate having you as a customer.

11. We appreciate it.

12. We appreciate your business.

13. We appreciate your efforts.

14. We appreciate your help.

15. We appreciate your interest in our company/products/services.

16. We appreciate your support.

17. We very much appreciate your help with this.

18. We would appreciate it greatly if you could V …

19. We would appreciate it if you would V …

20. We would appreciate prompt action.

21. We would appreciate prompt payment.

22. We would very much appreciate it if you could help us.

23. Your help with this would be much appreciated.

Word List　▪ prompt [prɑmpt] adj. 迅速的；立刻的

Requesting Help	Thanking sb. for Their Help	Refusing a Request for Help

答案

請看下面必備語庫和語庫小叮嚀。

商用英文必備語庫 2.4 感謝、請求和婉拒幫忙的 set-phrases

Requesting Help （請求幫忙）	Thanking sb. for Their Help （感謝某人）
· I would appreciate your attention to this matter. · I would appreciate a prompt reply. · I would appreciate a response. · I would appreciate any assistance you can give. · I would appreciate your help with this. · We would appreciate it greatly if you could V … · We would appreciate it if you would V … · We would appreciate prompt action. · We would appreciate prompt payment. · We would very much appreciate it if you could help us. · Your help with this would be much appreciated.	· I appreciate all that you have done. · I appreciate you taking the time to help me with this. · We appreciate having you as a customer. · We appreciate it. · We appreciate your business. · We appreciate your efforts. · We appreciate your help. · We appreciate your interest in our company/products/services. · We appreciate your support. · We very much appreciate your help with this.
Refusing a Request for Help （婉拒幫忙某人）	

· I appreciate your concerns, but I'm afraid I am not able to help you.
· We hope you can appreciate our position.

✎ 語庫小叮嚀

◆ 無論是電子郵件或是一般信件，這些 set-phrases 都常被拿來當作結尾使用。

◆ 請注意，在請求幫忙的時候，appreciate 必須搭配 would 使用。

TASK 2.6

從 wish、hope 或 appreciate 中選出適當的動詞填入下表，完成句子，見範例。

1	I _____ all that you have done.	*appreciate*
2	I _____ to hear from you soon.	
3	We _____ you all a Happy New Year.	
4	I would _____ your help with this.	
5	I _____ you understand our position on this.	
6	I _____ you all the best.	
7	We _____ having you as a customer.	
8	I _____ you great success in your new job.	
9	I would _____ a prompt reply.	
10	I _____ this is OK.	
11	I would _____ a response.	
12	We _____ you can _____ our position.	
13	We _____ your help.	
14	I _____ your meeting was successful.	
15	We _____ your support.	
16	We _____ to be hearing from you soon.	
17	We very much _____ your help with this.	
18	We _____ everyone there a pleasant holiday.	
19	I _____ you have a good trip.	
20	We _____ you every success.	

答案

1	appreciate	6	wish	11	appreciate	16	hope
2	hope	7	appreciate	12	hope/appreciate	17	appreciate
3	wish	8	wish	13	appreciate	18	wish
4	appreciate	9	appreciate	14	hope	19	hope
5	hope	10	hope	15	appreciate	20	wish

在第二題裡，wish 也是可能的答案，比較不可能發生的原因是聽起來比較傲慢無禮。

現在請練習用這些 set-phrases 寫電子郵件。

TASK 2.7

請使用適當的開頭 set-phrases 和結尾 set-phrases，完成下列電子郵件。有些空格有多個答案。

Dear Jonathan,

(1)_____. I will be attending the meeting in KL on the 19th.
(2)_____.

Dear Lucy,

(3)_____ me the report. I'll read it later and get back to you on Monday. (4)_____.

Dear William,

Could you tell me when you can let me have the report on the Dubai project?

I need to pass it on to the regional office. (5)_____.

Dear Joyce,

(6)_____. Regarding our meeting last week, I

apologize for the delay in getting back to you, but we have been very busy here. The price for the new product has indeed changed. When you quote the price, please add 10% to the old price. (7)_____.

Dear Jack,

Please find the attached report for your information. (8)_____.

答案 🔊

(1) Thank you for your email.

　　Thank you for your message.

(2) I hope to see you there.

(3) Thank you for sending

(4) I hope this is OK.

(5) I hope to hear from you soon.

　　We very much appreciate your help with this.

(6) Thank you for your message.

(7) I hope this is clear.

　　Thanks and sorry for any misunderstanding.

(8) I hope we can move this along quickly.

動詞 Chunks

　　在本單元接下來的第二節當中，我們要學的是這 25 個動詞的動詞 chunks。在往下學習前，建議你複習第一單元中學到的動詞 chunks，因為這和接下來要學的東西有關。還記得嗎？你在第一單元中學過的動詞 chunks 有五、六個不同的模式。

TASK 2.8

請將下面的動詞 chunks 分門別類，填入下表中。見範例。

1. 'd like sb. to V
2. feel that + n. clause
3. find n.p.
4. 'd like to V
5. find that + n. clause
6. feel adj.
7. know n.p.
8. accept n.p.
9. help sb. to V
10. want to V
11. meet n.p.
12. help sb. V
13. know that + n. clause
14. let sb. V
15. like n.p.
16. need n.p.
17. accept that + n. clause
18. think that + n. clause
19. need to V
20. want sb. to V
21. need sb. to V
22. know wh-clause
23. want n.p.
24. see n.p.
25. make sb. V

V + n.p.	V that + n. clause	V to V	V sb. to V	V sb. V	Other
feel n.p.	*feel that + n. clause*	*'d like to V*	*'d like sb. to V*	*help sb. V*	*feel adj.*

答案 🔊

請利用下面的語庫核對答案。

商用英文必備語庫 **2.5** 動詞 chunks　　　　MP3 08

V + n.p.			V that + n. clause		
· accept n.p.	· like n.p.	· see n.p.	· accept that + n. clause	· find that + n. clause	· think that + n. clause
· find n.p.	· meet n.p.	· want n.p.	· feel that + n. clause	· know that + n. clause	
· know n.p.	· need n.p.				

V to V	V sb. to V	V sb. V	Other
· 'd like to V · need to V · want to V	· 'd like sb. to V · help sb. to V · need sb. to V · want sb. to V	· help sb. V · let sb. V · make sb. V	· feel adj. · know wh-clause

🖋 語庫小叮嚀

◆ 請注意，有的動詞會有一個以上的 chunks。例如 accept n.p. 和 accept that + n. clause 以及 help sb. to V 和 help sb. V。

◆ 請注意，feel adj. 和 know wh-clause 這兩個無法歸類的 chunks，我將在下一單元中更詳細地說明這兩者。

◆ 用 'd 開頭的動詞 chunks 可能看起來有一點奇怪。'd 就是 would 的意思，例如：I'd like to、she'd like to。寫作用到這種動詞 chunks 的時候，你可以自由決定是要用縮寫還是完整拼出 would like to。然而交談的時候，比較常用 I'd like to，比較少用 I would like to。

好，現在來看電子郵件中這些動詞 chunks 的用法。

TASK 2.9

請閱讀以下電子郵件，找出必備語庫 2.5 中的動詞 chunks 並畫底線。留意這些動詞 chunks 的用法。見範例。

EX

Dear Jojo,

Thank you for your proposal, which we have studied carefully. We <u>like the proposal</u>, but we <u>need you to provide</u> more information about the market before we <u>know what</u> financial resources we need to make available for the project. In particular, we <u>need more information</u> about the intended market segment. We already know the product, but we still <u>would like you to think</u> about the marketing strategy more carefully.

Word List
• intended [ɪn`tɛndɪd] adj. 擬議的；有企圖的
• segment [`sɛgmənt] n. 部分

67

Please <u>let me have</u> this information as soon as possible so that we can look at it again.

Dear Lucy,

Please find the attached project outline. I know that this is urgent, as the supervisor wants everyone to read it. Please confirm when you will be able to come to our office to discuss it in more detail.

If you have any questions, please call me.

Dear Kevin,

Thanks for your email explaining your poor performance over the last few months. I'm sorry you feel that your contribution to the team is not being recognized, and I do accept that your salary is rather low compared to others in the group. I am looking into this and would like to meet you to discuss it further. I'll be in touch.

Dear Tom,

I'm sorry I don't know any other service providers in our area, but let me try to come up with some alternatives. I think that an old colleague of mine may be able to help us locate one.

Dear Calvin,

I know about your problems with your family, and I feel sorry that you are in such a difficult position. I want to help. Please accept my good wishes, and don't hesitate to contact me if there's anything I can do.

Word List	▪ contribution [ˌkɑntrəˋbjuʃən] n. 貢獻
	▪ alternative [ɔlˋtɝnətɪv] n. 選擇；替換方案
	▪ colleague [ˋkɑlig] n. 同僚；同事

Dear George,

I find that it's best to have at least three people edit the reports before they're sent out. There are some spelling mistakes in the section written by Brad. Please see my changes in Section 10. If you have enough time, I'll make Brad proofread the entire document. Please confirm.

答案

Dear Lucy,

Please find the attached project outline. I know that this is urgent, as the supervisor wants everyone to read it. Please confirm when you will be able to come to our office to discuss it in more detail.

If you have any questions, please call me.

Dear Kevin,

Thanks for your email explaining your poor performance over the last few months. I'm sorry you feel that your contribution to the team is not being recognized, and I do accept that your salary is rather low compared to others in the group. I am looking into this and would like to meet you to discuss it further. I'll be in touch.

Dear Tom,

I'm sorry I don't know any other service providers in our area, but let me try to come up with some alternatives. I think that an old colleague of mine may be able to help us locate one.

Word List　▪ proofread [pruf, rid] v. 校對

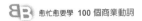

Dear Calvin,

I <u>know about</u> your problems with your family, and I <u>feel sorry</u> that you are in such a difficult position. I want to help. Please <u>accept my good wishes</u>, and don't hesitate to contact me if there's anything I can do.

Dear George,

I <u>find that</u> it's best to have at least three people edit the reports before they're sent out. There are some spelling mistakes in the section written by Brad. Please <u>see my changes</u> in Section 10. If you have enough time, I'll <u>make Brad proofread</u> the entire document. Please confirm.

常 見 錯 誤 > > make 和 let	
錯 誤	正 確
It makes me to feel tired.	It makes me feel tired.
My boss lets me to go home early.	I am allowed to go home early. / My boss lets me go home early.
My supervisor makes me to do overtime.	I am made to do overtime. / My supervisor makes me do overtime.

· 不要寫成 make sb. to V 或 let sb. to V，因為 make 和 let 是使役動詞，後面直接接原型動詞即可。
· 將 make 改成被動語態時，可以寫成 be made to V；同理，let 的被動語態可以改用 be allowed to V。

Word List　　▪ overtime [`ovə,taɪm] n. 加班

雙受詞動詞 Chunks

　　你應該還記得，在第一單元中有些動詞有兩個受詞，這些雙受詞動詞中有的受詞是可以倒置，有的則是不可倒置。如果需要溫習一下，請在繼續往下學習之前回顧第一單元。在接下來的章節裡，我們要探討的即是這兩種雙受詞動詞，首先來看一看不可倒置的雙受詞動詞。

TASK 2.10

請看下面的必備語庫。

 **2.6** 不可倒置的雙受詞動詞 chunks　　MP3 09

- get sth. from sb.
- call sb. about sth.
- receive sth. from sb.
- take sth. from sb.
- take sth. to sb.

TASK 2.11

請將下列句子與括弧內的受詞組合成完整的句子，請看範例。

1. Can you get the report as soon as possible, please? (from the consultant)

   Can you get the report from the consultant as soon as possible, please?

2. I need to call the SVP to close the department. (about her decision)

   _____

3. I receive about 25 emails every day. (from foreign customers)

   _____

4. I don't want to take any money. (from them)

   _____

5. I don't want to take the projector. (to the meeting)

   _____

答案 🔊

請看下列我所提供的參考答案。

2. I need to call the SVP about her decision to close the department.

3. I receive about 25 emails from foreign customers every day.

4. I don't want to take any money from them .

5. I don't want to take the projector to the meeting.

　　請注意，括弧內的資訊不是必要的。如果想在句中包含這些資訊，記得要在第二個受詞的前面放入適當的介系詞。

　　請務必準確地背下這些 chunks。背這些 chunks 的難處就在於記住第二個受詞前面用的是哪一個系詞。

　　好，現在我們來學習可倒置的雙受詞動詞 chunks。

TASK 2.12

請研讀下列語庫與電子郵件，找出必備語庫中的動詞 chunks 並畫底線。注意這些動詞 chunks 的用法。

商用英文必備語庫 2.7　可倒置的雙受詞動詞 chunks　　　MP3 10

· give sb. sth.	· send sb. sth.
· give sth. to sb.	· send sth. to sb.

Dear Mary,

I apologize for the delay in replying to you. Further to your questions about filing procedure, please see the description below.

1. When you send someone a report, please also give the filing clerk a copy.

2. If someone gives a document to you, send a copy of it to the filing clerk.

Hopefully this will all be much easier when we get the system computerized, but till then, please follow the above procedure.

If you have any questions, call me.

Regards,
Henry

答案

Dear Mary,

I apologize for the delay in replying to you. Further to your questions about filing procedure, please see the description below.

　1. When you send someone a report, please also give the filing clerk a copy.
　2. If someone gives a document to you, send a copy of it to the filing clerk.

Hopefully this will all be much easier when we get the system computerized, but till then, please follow the above procedure.

If you have any questions, call me.

Regards,
Henry

TASK 2.13

請利用語庫 2.7 來改正以下句子，見範例。

1. I'll give to you the report later.
   I'll give you the report later.
2. Please send the details of the project me as soon as you can.

3. She usually sends to her boss the figures every Friday.

4. We need to give more space the new people.

_____

5. Can you give Mary to a hand?

_____

6. They have to send everything us by courier, as their server is down.

_____

7. We usually give to our workers a bonus on their birthday.

_____

8. Please do not send to us any junk mail.

_____

答案

請看下面提供的參考答案，每個句子依受詞擺放的位子不同有兩種不同的寫法。

2. Please send the details of the project to me as soon as you can.
   Please send me the details of the project as soon as you can.
3. She usually sends the figures to her boss every Friday.
   She usually sends her boss the figures every Friday.
4. We need to give the new people more space.
   We need to give more space to the new people.
5. Can you give Mary a hand?
   Can you give a hand to Mary?
6. They have to send us everything by courier, as their server is down.
   They have to send everything to us by courier, as their server is down.
7. We usually give a bonus to our workers on their birthday.
   We usually give our workers a bonus on their birthday.
8. Please do not send us any junk mail.
   Please do not send any junk mail to us.

　　每個錯誤的句子有兩個正確答案，端視你想先用哪一種受詞而定。你認為最重要的受詞必須放在後面。

Word List　▪ by courier 用快遞

現在來加強練習你已學會的雙受詞動詞。

TASK 2.14

請閱讀下面的電子郵件，在雙受詞動詞 chunks 下面畫線。

Dear Jojo,

Please contact Lawrence about the press launch next Monday. When I try to call him about it, I get no response from his answering service. Ask him what we need to bring, and to give us directions to the location. Ask him also if we need to take the report file to the meeting, or if we should send it to him by courier beforehand. We need to receive this information from him by close of business today.

Thanks for your help.
Lawrence

答案

Dear Jojo,

Please contact Lawrence about the press launch next Monday. When I try to call him about it, I get no response from his answering service. Ask him what we need to bring, and to give us directions to the location. Ask him also if we need to take the report file to the meeting, or if we should send it to him by courier beforehand. We need to receive this information from him by close of business today.

Thanks for your help.
Lawrence

Word List　• press launch 新聞發表會

TASK 2.15

現在請幫 Jojo 回信給 Lawrence，寫作的時候，請留意動詞 chunks 的正確性。

答案

以下是我建議的範例答案。

Hi Lawrence,

Regarding the press launch next Monday, please let me know what we need to bring to the launch. Could you also give us directions to the location and let us know if we need to take the report file to the meeting or if we should send it to you by courier beforehand. I need to receive this information from you by COB today.

Thanks in advance for your help.
Jojo

　　好了，本單元的學習到此結束。請回到單元前面的學習目標，確定每一項都確實學會了。

Word List ▪ COB (=Close of Business) 停止受理業務時間

Unit 3 口說

引言與學習目標

　　本單元的學習重點是學會在交談時運用這 25 個動詞，時態也是我們的學習重點。如同我在第一單元中提到的，英文有四個時間範圍，每一個時間範圍都得以不同的時態表達。如果你已經忘記這四個時態的意義，建議你回到第一單元將 Task 1.3 的表格再複習一下。本單元中我們的重點將會放在簡單現在式。我之所以選擇從簡單現在式學起，是因為這個時態最容易理解也最容易應用，而不是因為本單元中所有的動詞都只能用這個時態。我們就從簡單的時態開始著手，然後循序漸進地慢慢建立你的英文能力。

　　本單元結束時，各位應達成的學習目標如下：

❑ 對商業英文中簡單現在式的意義有清楚的了解，並學會正確的用法。
❑ 有能力使用本單元的一些重要動詞，表達自己的想法和願望。
❑ 有能力以簡單現在式使用本單元的一些重要動詞，口頭說明工作慣例和程序。
❑ 有能力聽出弱讀時的疑問助動詞，並且確認自己的發音正確。
❑ 知道一些常見的口說錯誤並避免犯錯。
❑ 做完一些口說、聽力和發音練習。

時態：不受限時間

在商業英文中，下列項目要用口說和寫作的方式表達時，應該使用簡單現在式：

Opinions	Routines	Facts or General Statements	Desires	Procedures
看法	慣例	事實或一般性陳述	願望	程序

TASK 3.1

請看以下句子，把代表句子種類的字母寫在表格右欄中，有些句子可填入的種類不只一個，見範例。

Opinions	Routines	Facts or General Statements	Desires	Procedures
O	R	F-GS	D	P

1	I think we can increase our market share by 3%.	O
2	I don't know about this case.	
3	I feel excited about the new project.	
4	I hope you can do this.	
5	I usually meet my clients in their offices.	
6	I want this project to be completed as quickly as possible.	
7	I call my client about his account every Monday.	
8	I wish you a Happy New Year.	
9	The office looks untidy.	
10	We give a one-month bonus at Chinese New Year.	
11	You need to send a copy of every document you receive to your boss.	
12	You need to keep a record of all expenses.	

Word List　• untidy [ʌn`taɪdɪ] adj. 凌亂的；雜亂的

答案 🔊

請利用下面的表格檢查答案。

1	I think we can increase our market share by 3%.	O/F-GS
2	I don't know about this case.	F-GS
3	I feel excited about the new project.	F-GS
4	I hope you can do this.	D/F-GS
5	I usually meet my clients in their offices.	R/F-GS
6	I want this project to be completed as quickly as possible.	D/F-GS
7	I call my client about his account every Monday.	R/F-GS
8	I wish you a Happy New Year.	D/F-GS
9	The office looks untidy.	O/R/P/F-GS
10	We give a one-month bonus at Chinese New Year.	R/F-GS
11	You need to send a copy of every document you receive to your boss.	R/P/F-GS
12	You need to keep a record of all expenses.	R/P/F-GS

　　有沒有注意到，有些句子的確切意義比較不明顯，也有些句子可能有兩或三個答案。這是因為若對句子的背景沒有提供足夠的資訊，有時很難分辨出句子表達的是看法還是願望。

　　很多人經常搞不清楚什麼叫現在時間，之所以會不懂實在是因為被這種時態的名稱弄糊塗了，以為簡單現在式便一定是指「現在時間」。但事實上這個時態常被用來描述事情。前面 Task 中的句子，除了是在描述發生在當下的行為或狀況外，也都是在說明事實、表達要求或陳述看法。等我們進入第六單元學習用現在時間說寫某個行為時，你就會更加明白我的意思了。

　　在往下做口說和聽力練習之前，請做下面的 Task，以複習目前已學到的簡單現在式。

TASK 3.2

請重新閱讀第二單元中的所有電子郵件，留意其中簡單現在式的用法。

表達看法的 Set-Phrases

TASK 3.3

請聽 MP3 中的對話，對話中的主角 Joe 和 Kelly 正站在咖啡機旁聊天。那一天是星期幾？他們對本身的工作有何看法？

答案

那天是星期一。他們很喜歡自己的工作，但對工作時間不盡滿意。

如果因聽不懂對話而無法回答，沒關係，等一下在 Task 3.6 會附上完整的對話內容。

　　現在我們來看一看 Joe 和 Kelly 表達看法的方式。請看下面的 set-phrases 並做 Task。

TASK 3.4

請將下列 set-phrases 分成四類填入下表中。

1. Do you know what I mean?
2. I know exactly what you mean.
3. I don't know what you mean.
4. I think + n. clause
5. I don't think so.
6. I feel the same.
7. I don't really like n.p./Ving …

8. What do you think?
9. I feel that + n. clause
10. How do you feel about that?
11. I find that + n. clause
12. Do you find that + n. clause?
13. I really like n.p./Ving …

Giving Opinions	Asking for Opinions	Agreeing	Disagreeing

答案

請利用下面的必備語庫來核對答案，並注意其後的語庫小叮嚀。

商用英文必備語庫 3.1 　表達看法的 set-phrases 　　　　MP3 11

Giving Opinions （給予意見）	Asking for Opinions （請教意見）	Agreeing （表達同意）	Disagreeing （表達不同意）
· Do you know what I mean? · I think + n. clause · I feel that + n. clause · I find that + n. clause · I really like n.p./Ving … · I don't really like n.p./Ving …	· What do you think? · How do you feel about that? · Do you find that + n. clause?	· I know exactly what you mean. · I feel the same.	· I don't know what you mean. · I don't think so.

✎　語庫小叮嚀

◆ 你有沒有發現？Do you know what I mean? 乍聽之下好像是在請教他人看法，但實際上卻是在表達自己的看法。表達自己的看法時，你可以在句子最後加上這個 set-phrase。請再聽一次對話，同時注意這個 set-phrase 的用法。

◆ 請注意，這些 set-phrases 中，find 和 feel 後面都會接 that，然後才接 n. clause，但是 think 卻不會，使用時要特別銘記在心。

◆ 我們在前言中學過、也練習過使用 set-phrases 和 chunks，還記得嗎？當時我強調 MWIs 中所有的小細節務必都得確實學會，這一點不論在口說或寫作時都很重要。

TASK 3.5 　　　　　　　　　　　　　　　　　　　MP3 11

請練習必備語庫 3.1 中 set-phrases 的發音。

TASK 3.6

請再聽一次 Joe 和 Kelly 的對話，並利用必備語庫 3.1 把聽到的 set-phrases 勾出來。

答案

請利用下面完整的對話內容來核對答案。

Joe ： So how's your day going?

Kelly: It's not too bad, although I always feel tired on Mondays.

Joe ： Yeah right! I think they should give us Monday off because we work on Saturday, do you know what I mean?

Kelly: I agree. Everybody else has a two day weekend, why can't we?

Joe ： Right. And I find that working late in the evening means I have no social life.

Kelly: I wish I had a social life! I really want to have some fun. I feel that this job doesn't give me any personal time.

Joe ： I feel the same.

Kelly: I mean, I really like the job, but the hours are ridiculous.

Joe ： I know exactly what you mean.

Kelly: You know, it's really hard to meet new people when you have to work while other people are enjoying themselves.

Joe ： Maybe we just need a change.

常 見 錯 誤 ＞ ＞ **like**	
錯　誤	正　確
I very like my new coworkers.	I really like my new coworkers.
．要表達非常喜歡……時，千萬不要說成 I very like ...，這是中式英文！	

　　現在繼續往下看，學習 Joe 和 Kelly 表達願望的方法。

表達願望或要求的 Set-Phrases

TASK 3.7

請將下面的 set-phrases 分門別類,要分成幾組和幾個類別都由你決定。

商用英文必備語庫 3.2 表達願望或要求的 set-phrases

MP3 13

· I wish I could V …	· I wish it would V …
· I really want to V …	· I wish it was Ving/n.p. …
· I wish I had n.p. …	· I really need n.p. …
· I wish I didn't have to V …	· I wish it wasn't Ving n.p. …
· I really need to V …	· I really want n.p. …

答案

無論你的分類方式為何,一個辦法就是根據動詞是 want、wish 或 need 來分類。

✎ **語庫小叮嚀**

◆ 請注意,這些用到 wish 的 set-phrases 與前一單元中所學的截然不同。前一單元中用到 wish 的 set-phrases 是用來管理消費者關係的,尤其是用於電子郵件的結尾。當時學到的 set-phrases 大多是用 I wish you n.p. 的句構,但用口說表達願望和要求時,這些 set-phrases 的用法卻迥然而異。現在學到的 set-phrases 是用 I wish + n. clause 的句構,主詞是 I 或 it。請比較必備語庫 3.2 和 2.3 中的 set-phrases,確定你全部都理解了。

◆ 請注意,I wish I … 和 I wish it … 後面永遠都是接簡單過去式。這並不是表示過去時間,而是表示與現在事實相反的假設。你可以用這些 set-phrases 表達很強烈但不大可能實現的願望,如:I wish it would stop raining.

TASK 3.8

MP3 12

請再聽一遍對話,並利用必備語庫 3.2 把聽到的 set-phrases 勾出來。留意對話中 set-phrases 的使用方法。

描述工作程序的 Set-Phrases

TASK 3.9

（MP3 14）

請聽 Kelly 對新進員工 Sam 解釋工作程序的內容。Sam 的職務內容為何？

答案

Sam 負責處理小額的現金報帳。

對話中的用語可能會有點艱澀，如果聽不懂別擔心，請邊聽邊參閱下方的對話。

Kelly: OK, Sam, this is the petty cash register. Let me show you how it works——it's quite easy. Any staff member who wants petty cash reimbursement completes this form, form QT7. Here's an example. See how it works?

Sam : Yes, OK, so they fill in these boxes here——what they spent the money on, amount ——yes, it's quite clear.

Kelly: OK. They attach a receipt, and a copy of the receipt to the form, like this.

Sam : Both, the copy and the receipt?

Kelly: Yes, that's right.

Sam : Why do we need both?

Kelly: Well, that's just procedure. It's designed to make life easier for the accounting department, who check everything at the end of the quarter.

Sam : OK. Then what happens?

Kelly: When they're completed the form, their manager signs the QT7, in this box here. If it's not signed, they don't get their reimbursement.

Sam: Wow, tough, huh?

Kelly: Yes. At the end of the month, you send an email to all staff members telling them you are going to do petty cash. They give you their completed and signed forms, with the attachments.

Sam : OK.

Word List
- petty cash 小額的現金收支；零用金
- reimbursement [ˌriɪm`bɝsmənt] n. 退款償還
- receipt [rɪ`sit] n. 收據

Kelly: The receipts have to have a tax number on it, so look carefully at each receipt to make sure it's there. See? When you're satisfied that everything is correct, you give them the cash from the cash box, and file the QT7. Got it?

Sam : Got it.

Kelly: If you have any problems or you're not sure about anything, just call me.

Sam : Thanks, Kelly!

TASK 3.10

現在請閱讀下列 Sam 做的筆記。這些筆記的順序是錯的。請按照正確順序將他的筆記填入下表中，見範例。如有困難請再聽一次 MP3。

· The accounting department checks everything at the end of the quarter.
· I file the QT7.
· I give the staff their reimbursement from the cash box.
· I look carefully at the receipts to check the tax number.
· I send an email to all staff members at the end of the month.
· Staff members fill out the QT7 form.
· Staff members give me the completed form.
· Their manager signs the QT7.
· They attach a receipt, and a copy of the receipt, to the form.

1	*Staff members fill in the QT7 form.*
2	
3	
4	
5	
6	
7	
8	
9	

答案 🔊

請利用下面的表格檢查答案。

1	Staff members fill in the QT7 form.
2	They attach a receipt, and a copy of the receipt to the form.
3	Their manager signs the QT7.
4	I send an email to all staff members at the end of the month.
5	Staff members give me the completed form.
6	I look carefully at the receipts to check the tax number.
7	I give the staff their reimbursement from the cash box.
8	I file the QT7.
9	The accounting department checks everything at the end of the quarter.

建議你邊看答案邊聽 MP3，重複聽幾次，直到有信心聽清楚全部的對話為止。

請留意，Kelly 在解說時及 Sam 在筆記中用到的動詞全部都是簡單現在式，因為他們談的工作程序不限於特定的時間範圍。

常　見　錯　誤　>　>　call	
錯　誤	正　確
I give a phone call to her if I need help.	I call her if I need help.
I call to her if I need help.	I call her if I need help.
・請不要說 give a phone call to sb. 記住，這是中式英文！ ・Call to sb. 並不是打電話給某人的意思，而是「呼叫／叫喊某人」的意思。	

TASK 3.11

請練習口述自己工作上的一項職責，別忘了用簡單現在式。建議你用錄音機錄下你的答案，方便檢視你的口說表現。

答案 🔊

雖然現在你會用的動詞很有限，不過我希望你在描述自己的工作內容時，先把焦點放在時態的正確性。
請按照我在前言中的說明，用錄音機來檢視動詞的用法及發音，並練習加快說話速度。

發音

在本節中我們要學的是疑問助動詞的發音。有時和外國人說話時，疑問助動詞不容易聽清楚，這是因為以一般速度說話時，有時助動詞會和後面的詞連在一起，形成語音 chunks，因此聽起來含糊不清。如果你能學會疑問助動詞的正確發音，不僅說話的語調聽起來會更自然，聽力也會更上層樓。

注意，這些只是可能或常見的發音方式，有時發音方式會因說話的語氣而有不同，如：興奮、困惑、生氣等。

我們接著來練習簡單現在式的 be 動詞和助動詞 do 的發音。

TASK 3.12

請看下面的表格並同時聽 MP3。

MP3 15

寫作	發音 MP3
Do you …?	[dʊˋju]
Does he …?	[dəˋzhi]
Does she …?	[dəˋzʃi]
Does it …?	[dəˋzɪt]
What do you …?	[ˊhwɑdəju]
What does he …?	[ˊhwɑdəzhi]
What does she …?	[ˊhwɑdəzʃi]
What does it …?	[ˊhwɑdəzɪt]
Are you …?	[ərˋju]
Is he …?	[ɪˋzhi]
Is she …?	[ɪˋzʃi]
Is it …?	[ɪˋzɪt]
What are you …?	[ˊhwɑdərˏju]

你會注意到明明寫出來是兩個或三個字，聽起來卻像一個詞。

當在助動詞的前面加一個 wh- 詞，助動詞和主詞仍舊聽起來像一個詞。遇到 What do you ...? 和 What are you ...? 時請小心，因為這兩者最常聽錯。

請先做完下面的練習，確定所有的語音 chunks 都聽清楚了。

TASK 3.13

現在請聽 MP3 中的問題與回答，一邊聽，一邊留意說話者語音 chunks 的用法。

1. <u>Do you</u> enjoy your job?
   Yes, I do.

2. <u>What do you</u> enjoy about it?
   I like the challenge.

3. The boss is really upset. <u>Does he</u> often get angry?
   Yes, he does, unfortunately.

4. She looks great. <u>Does she</u> always look so good?
   Yes, she does!

5. The printer is broken again. <u>Does it</u> often break down?
   Yes, it does, unfortunately.

6. <u>Are you</u> hungry?
   Yes.

7. <u>What are you</u> doing?
   Nothing.

8. David seems really stressed. <u>Is he</u> often like this?
   Yes, he is.

9. Donna is really nice. <u>Is she</u> married?
   Yes, she is.

10. It's cold today. <u>Is it</u> always this cold here?
    At this time of year, yes, it is.

TASK 3.14

現在請用以上學到的語音 chunks 來練習提問，並錄音以檢視發音。

好了，本單元的學習到此結束。請回到單元前面的學習目標，確定每一個項目都學會了，然後再繼續往下研讀。

Unit 4 詞彙

引言與學習目標

　　在本單元中我要教你一些最有用和使用頻率最高的詞彙，讓你能夠搭配本篇的一些動詞使用。我們先從 word partnerships 學起，然後再學片語動詞。請在往下學習之前，回頭再複習一遍前言第一節的 word partnerships。也建議你閱讀第一單元的相關章節，複習片語動詞。

　　本單元結束時，各位應達成的學習目標如下：

　　　　❑ 學到商業英文口說和寫作中許多使用頻率高而且也非常實用的
　　　　　 word partnerships。
　　　　❑ 學到商業英文口說和寫作中許多有用的片語動詞。
　　　　❑ 學到一些有用的商業慣用語。
　　　　❑ 已練習過如何運用新詞彙。
　　　　❑ 知道常見的英文錯誤有哪些並知道該如何避免。

Word Partnerships

　　在本節當中我們要學一些含有 make、get 或 take 的 word partnerships，下面的語庫表納入了一些最常見的商業名詞，可分別和這三個動詞搭配使用。也就是說學會了這些「動詞＋名詞」組合，你就學到了商業英文中最常出現、也最有用的 word partnerships。本節的 word partnerships 都不是慣用語，意即只要了解語庫表中的生字，就能輕鬆理解這些 word partnerships 的意思。閱讀本節的同時，建議一本你用字典輔助學習。

TASK 4.1

請研讀下面的 word partnerships 語庫表以及例句。

商用英文必備語庫 4.1 含 make 的 word partnerships 　　MP3 17

make	· a change · a choice · a comment · a comparison · a contribution to · a copy · a deal · a decision · a difference to · a discovery	· a mistake with · a note about · a phone call · a point of · a presentation on · a profit · a request · a reservation for · a suggestion about · a trip	· an application for · an appointment · an effort to · an impact on · an impression on · an offer · arrangements · inquiries about · money · payment · progress

 EX

1. I need to make a decision on this quickly.

2. Please make a point of returning all files to their correct place.

3. Most new companies don't make a profit until they've been in business for several years.

4. Please let me know how I can make payment.

Word List　· inquiry [ɪnˋkwaɪrɪ] n. 查問；詢問

 商用英文必備語庫 4.2 含 get 的 word partnerships　(MP3 18)

get	· a chance to V	· approval for sth. (from sb.)
	· a feel for n.p.	· involved (in sth.)
	· a good price for n.p.	· lucky
	· a great deal on n.p.	· ready for n.p.
	· acquainted with n.p.	· sth. done
	· an/some insight into n.p.	· started
	· an understanding of n.p.	· together

 1. Bob always manages to get a great deal.

2. It takes new staff some time to get acquainted with the systems here.

3. Can you get this done as soon as possible, please?

4. It's a great idea but we couldn't get approval for it from the board.

商用英文必備語庫 4.3 含 take 的 word partnerships　(MP3 19)

take	· some time to V	· an active role in n.p.
	· a taxi	· an interest in n.p.
	· a rest	· care of n.p.
	· a chance on n.p.	· control of n.p.
	· a course in n.p.	· sb. to court for n.p./Ving
	· a day off	· effect
	· a long time to V	· legal action against sb.
	· a look at n.p.	· note of n.p.
	· a message to sb.	· part in n.p.
	· a picture of n.p.	· responsibility for n.p./Ving
	· advantage of	

1. I think we should take a chance on this new computer system.

2. She's taking a course in finance in her free time.

3. My boss takes an interest in his staff's professional development.

4. The new rules take effect on Monday.

Word List	▪ acquainted [əˋkwentɪd] adj. 熟識的
	▪ insight [ˋɪn͵saɪt] n. 洞察；眼光
	▪ involved [ɪnˋvɑlvd] adj. 捲入的；涉及的

TASK 4.2

下面的句子都被分成兩半，請將其連成一個完整句。見範例。

A

A bigger budget usually makes	• a copy of the report for me.
Business is not so good. We need to get	• a point of being polite to his staff.
Can you make	• an impression on his audience.
It's always a busy time of year. Get	• lucky.
My boss always makes	• ready for the rush!
His presentations always make	• a difference in the quality of the ad.

B

I don't want to get	• a feel for the market so we can lift sales.
I really like making	• an insight into the China market.
If you live there for two months, you can get	• involved in this problem.
We need to get	• money!
Because it's so complex, it takes	• time to get acquainted with new staff.
There are so many of them so it takes	• some time to understand the new system.

C

Let's make	• a message to him for me.
Please call the hotel and make	• a picture of it and put it on the website.
You are always late. Please make	• a reservation for the 23rd.
I can't get in touch with Tom. Please take	• an effort to arrive on time for work.
The new office looks great! Take	• an offer they can't refuse.
They are quite tricky, so make sure you take	• note of the terms in the contract.

Word List　　▪ terms [tɜmz] n.（合約的）條款

D	I don't like dealing with them. They always take ◆	◆ a good price for the car when you sell it.
	Try to get ◆	◆ advantage of us.
	We don't usually take ◆	◆ approval from head office for this.
	We don't want them to take ◆	◆ part in this kind of deal.
	We need to get ◆	◆ us to court if they discover our mistake.

答案

有些句子或許有多個可能的答案，不過請參考下列我的建議答案。

A	A bigger budget usually makes	◆ a difference to the quality of the ad.
	Business is not so good. We need to get	◆ lucky.
	Can you make	◆ a copy of the report for me.
	It's always a busy time of year. Get	◆ ready for the rush!
	My boss always makes	◆ a point of being polite to his staff.
	His presentations always make	◆ an impression on his audience.

B	I don't want to get	◆ involved in this problem.
	I really like making	◆ money!
	If you live there for two months, you can get	◆ an insight into the China market.
	We need to get	◆ a feel for the market so we can lift sales.
	Because it's so complex, it takes	◆ some time to understand the new system.
	There are so many of them so it takes	◆ time to get acquainted with new staff.

C	Let's make	◆ an offer they can't refuse.
	Please call the hotel and make	◆ a reservation for the 23rd.
	You are always late. Please make	◆ an effort to arrive on time for work.
	I can't get in touch with Tom. Please take ◆	◆ a message to him for me.
	The new office looks great! Take	◆ a picture of it and put it on the website.
	They are quite tricky, so make sure you take	◆ note of the terms in the contract.

D I don't like dealing with them. They always take
- advantage of us.

Try to get
- a good price for the car when you sell it.

We don't usually take
- part in this kind of deal.

We don't want them to take
- us to court if they discover our mistake.

We need to get
- approval from head office for this.

TASK 4.3

現在請利用 make、get 和 take 這三個動詞的語庫表，為每一個動詞造三個句子。

答案

相信你在研讀完這麼多例句之後，必能利用學過的 word partnerships 及合宜的情境造出合宜的句子。

片語動詞

　　在下一節中我們要學的是片語動詞，這些片語動詞可以用在英文口說和寫作上，處理某些層面的工作。

◤ 處理訊息的 **15** 個片語動詞 ◢

TASK 4.4

請研讀下列片語動詞的意義及例句。

商用英文必備語庫 **4.4**　處理訊息的片語動詞　　　　　MP3 **20**

know about sth./sb. 知道很多特定的或專門的資訊	▶ He knows a lot about the bond market. Ask him.
know of sth./sb. 知道某事，但不是很了解	▶ I know of him, but I don't think I know much about his ideas.
let on 洩密	▶ I never let on what I know.
let sb. into sth. (英式) let sb. in on (美式) 告訴某人一個秘密	▶ You never let me into what's going on. You never let me in on what's going out.
look for sth. 尋找某物	▶ We are always looking for opportunities to do business.
look sth. over 快速瀏覽某物	▶ Please look your reports over one last time before you hand them in.

Word List　▪ bond [bɑnd] n. 債券

look through sth. 快速瀏覽某物	▶	I usually look through important memos over the weekend when I have more time.
look sth. up 查詢資訊	▶	Can you look her number up for me please?
make sth. up 捏造或編造某事	▶	I usually just make the figures up if I don't have the correct ones.
make of sth. 解讀某事（用於否定句或疑問句）	▶	What do you make of their report? I don't know what to make of it.
send sth. back 因有瑕疵而退還某物	▶	If it's not correct, send it back and ask for another one.
send sth. off 當完成某物時寄給某人	▶	When the report is ready, you can send it off to the client.
send sth. on 將收到的東西轉給別人閱讀	▶	If you find anything interesting, please send it on to the other people on the team.
send sth. out 將某物同時寄給很多人	▶	We send a company newsletter out to all our customers every month.
think of sth. 對某事有何看法 （用於否定句或疑問句）	▶	What do you think of my suggestion? Actually I don't think much of it.

TASK 4.5

請在空格中填入介系詞，完成下列句子，見範例。

1. When you finish looking _through_ the article, please remember to send it (1)_____ to the other members of the team.

2. Please look (2)_____ the copy one last time before you send it (3)_____ .

3. Let me know what you think (4)_____ the newsletter before you send it (5)_____ .

4. We need to think (6)_____ new ways of looking (7)_____ new customers.

Word List   • newsletter [ˈnjuzˌlɛtə] n.（公司、機關的）簡訊；業務通訊

答案 🎧

請核對你的答案。

(1) on　(2) over/through　(3) off/on/out　(4) of　(5) out/off/on　(6) of　(7) for

TASK 4.6

MP3 21

請填入適當的介系詞，完成下面的對話。接著再聽 MP3 來檢查答案。

Conversation 1

A: What do you make (1)＿＿＿＿＿ the latest official figures?

B: I think they made them (2)＿＿＿＿＿ .

Conversation 2

A: What do you know (3)＿＿＿＿＿ our main competitor's new CEO?

B: Well, I know (4)＿＿＿＿＿ him, of course, he's well-known. But I don't know much (5)＿＿＿＿＿ his ideas or ways of doing business.

A: Can you look (6)＿＿＿＿＿ his biography for me?

Conversation 3

A: Can I let you (7)＿＿＿＿＿ a secret?

B: Sure. I won't let (8)＿＿＿＿＿ . What is it?

A: My boss and his secretary are having an affair.

B: Wow. People are going to ask me for details.

答案 🎧

如果覺得聽得有點吃力，可以參閱下方的解答。如果你在上面所寫的答案和解答有一點出入，請回頭閱讀必備語庫 4.4，確定你對語庫裡的片語動詞都確實理解了。

(1) of　(2) up　(3) about　(4) of　(5) about　(6) up　(7) into　(8) on

Word List　▪have an affair 偷情

處理問題的 6 個片語動詞

TASK 4.7

請閱讀下面的必備語庫。

商用英文必備語庫 4.5　處理問題的片語動詞

call for sth. 需要某物	▶	The situation calls for an immediate response.
come down to sth. 回歸到最簡單的因素	▶	It all comes down to the fact that we don't have the resources for this project.
come up against sth. 遇到麻煩或問題	▶	We frequently come up against problems of this kind.
let up 變得較和緩	▶	Business usually lets up over the Chinese New Year period.
look into sth. 調查某事	▶	We need to find someone to look into this and find out what the problem is.
make sth. up 彌補某事	▶	If we work overtime we can make up the delay.

TASK 4.8

請在空格中填入介系詞，完成以下的電子郵件。

1. We've come up (1)＿＿＿＿＿ a number of serious problems with the project that are delaying it. We are looking (2)＿＿＿＿＿ ways of solving the problem, and we hope to be able to make (3)＿＿＿＿＿ the time lost. However, the problem seems to come (4)＿＿＿＿＿ (5)＿＿＿＿＿ the fact that we do not have enough team members to complete the project on time.

2. The situation in the southern branch calls (6)＿＿＿＿＿ a long-term solution, not just a quick fix. Without a long-term solution, I think the bad situation there will not let (7)＿＿＿＿＿ soon.

答案

(1) against　(2) into　(3) up　(4) down　(5) to　(6) for　(7) up

處理人際關係的 5 個片語動詞

TASK 4.9

請閱讀下面的必備語庫。

商用英文必備語庫 4.6　處理人際關係的片語動詞 　　　　　MP3 23

get after sb. 要求某人盡快將某事完成	Can you get after them? We need the designs quickly.
get on with sb. (英式)	I really get on with my supervisor. She's so nice!
get along with sb. (美式) 與某人相處愉快	I really get along with my supervisor. She's so nice!
let sb. down 讓某人失望	He always lets me down when I ask him to help me.
see sth. through 完成某事	He finds it difficult to see projects through.
take sb. off sth. 使某人退出某專案或任務	We should take him off the project. He doesn't have enough time to help us anyway.

TASK 4.10

MP3 24

請在空格中填入適當的介系詞，完成以下對話，接著聽 MP3 檢查答案。

A: I don't know what to do about William. He's so slow. I keep getting (1)＿＿＿＿＿ him to finish stuff on time. He doesn't really get on (2)＿＿＿＿＿ the other team members either, so he's difficult to work with. And he can't see things (3)＿＿＿＿＿.

B: Hmm. We might have to take him (4)＿＿＿＿＿ the project. It's important that we don't delay it. That would really let the customer (5)＿＿＿＿＿.

答案

如果你覺得很難聽懂，可以參閱下方的解答。

(1) after　　(2) with　　(3) through　　(4) off　　(5) down

處理工作的 7 個片語動詞

TASK 4.11

請閱讀下面的必備語庫。

商用英文必備語庫 4.7　處理工作的片語動詞

 MP3 25

get around to doing sth. 抽時間做某事	▶ I haven't gotten around to sorting out my inbox yet.
get down to sth. 講到重點	▶ Let's get down to what our customers really want: low prices.
get on with sth. 繼續進行某項工作	▶ I must get on with this. It's already late.
get through sth. 完成某項工作	▶ I can't get through all the work I have.

see about sth. 安排完成某事	▶	Let me see about getting you a new computer. Yours is too slow.
see to sth. 照料某事	▶	Can you see to it that everything is shipped out by tomorrow?
take sth. on 接下更多工作	▶	We always take more work on at this time of year.

TASK 4.12

MP3 26

請在空格中填入適當的動詞或介系詞，完成以下對話，接著聽 MP3 來檢查答案。

A: This time of year is always very busy for me, because the company (1)＿＿＿＿＿ on more Christmas orders in our overseas markets. I've got to (2)＿＿＿＿＿ to five new customers. I don't know how I'm going to get (3)＿＿＿＿＿ it all before the weekend. I think I need to (4)＿＿＿＿＿ about getting a temp to help me. Oh well, I suppose I'd better just (5)＿＿＿＿＿ on with it.

B: Did you get (6)＿＿＿＿＿ to getting your haircut?

A: Huh! Are you kidding? Look, let's talk later. I need to get (7)＿＿＿＿＿ to some work.

B: OK. Bye.

答案 🔊

如果你覺得很難聽懂，可參閱下方的解答。

(1) takes   (2) see   (3) through   (4) see   (5) get   (6) around   (7) down

連繫用的 3 個片語動詞

TASK 4.13

請閱讀下面的必備語庫。

商用英文必備語庫 **4.8** 連繫用的片語動詞　　MP3 27

call sb. back 回電給某人	▶ He never calls me back.
get back to sb. 稍後再聯絡某人	▶ You need to get back to me quickly on this.
get through to sb. 聯絡上某人	▶ I always find it hard to get through to him. He never answers his phone.

TASK 4.14

MP3 28

請在空格中填入動詞或介系詞，完成以下留言，接著聽 MP3 來檢查答案。

A: Hello. This is Sam. Can you please ask Joyce to (1)＿＿＿＿＿＿ me back? It's about the report she sent me. I've tried to (2)＿＿＿＿＿＿ back to her several times, but I can't get (3)＿＿＿＿＿＿ to her. If you see Joyce, please tell her to get on to Michael about the report. It's urgent. Thank you.

答案

(1) call　　(2) get　　(3) through

常 見 錯 誤 ＞ ＞ **back**	
錯　誤	正　確
I back home now.	I'm going back home now.
I returned back the letter.	I returned the letter.
‧記住，back 不是動詞。 ‧使用 return 時，無須再多加 back 一字，因為 return 就帶有 back 的意思了！	

商業慣用語

在第一節中你學到了包含 make、get 和 take 的非慣用 word partnerships。在本節中我們要學的是比較接近慣用語的 word partnerships，也就是說這些 word partnerships 的意思較難單從個別的字義上辨別，必須將其視為是一個整體來學習。

在本節中我會教你一些可在交談時用上的慣用 set-phrases。

TASK 4.15

請研讀下面的必備語庫以及例句。

商用英文必備語庫4.9 含 take 的慣用語 MP3 29

take	a bit of getting used to	不習慣某事
	a dim view of sth.	不贊同某事
	the long view (of sth.)	以長遠的角度來看待某事
	a firm stand against sth./on sth.	不同意某事並預防該事發生
	charge of sth.	掌管某事
	place	發生

EX
1. This new job takes a bit of getting used to.
2. My boss took a dim view of my request for a three-week holiday.
3. Training is expensive, but we take the long view.
4. He takes a firm stand against staff members accepting gifts from customers.
5. After I resign, Mr. Braddock will take charge of HR.
6. The board meeting takes place every Monday morning.

商用英文必備語庫 4.10 含 make 的慣用語 MP3 30

make	the best of sth.	用正面的態度來看待某事
	a quick buck	輕鬆賺到錢，但有時手段不正當
	ends meet	努力讓收支平衡

	a go of sth.	努力讓某事成功
make	a killing	快速地賺到很多錢
	do	將就著用

 1. Business is very bad at the moment, but we have to try to make the best of it.

2. He's always trying to make a quick buck.

3. I find it hard to make ends meet on my salary.

4. We don't have much funding, but let's try to make a go of it anyway.

5. We always make a killing on this kind of deal.

6. We don't have enough resources, so we'll just have to make do with what we've got.

商用英文必備語庫 4.11 含 get 的慣用語

	to the bottom of sth.	找出錯誤或問題發生的原因
	sth. off the ground	一開始做某事就很成功
get	the hang of sth.	慢慢地知道要如何做某事
	the picture	了解
	fired	因做錯事而被炒魷魚

 1. We must get to the bottom of this before the client finds out.

2. It's always difficult to get a new product off the ground.

3. I get the hang of new systems quite easily.

4. I get the picture. You want me to resign, right?

5. She got fired after only two weeks.

在學習和使用慣用語的時候，很重要的一點就是要把慣用語視為一個整體來學習，因此要特別注意其中的每一個字，因為當慣用語中有一個字弄錯了，便會失去原本的意義，變成又怪又沒意義的片語。

慣用語中唯一能夠更動的是動詞。使用時請務必確定時態符合上下文情境並且是正確的。此外，若是第三人稱的簡單現在式，動詞後面一定要加 s 或 es。

TASK 4.16

請更正下面句子中的錯誤。有些是慣用語本身的錯誤；有些則是時態上的錯誤。

1. We must getting to the bottom of the problem.
2. It's usually quite easy to get this kind of project off the earth.
3. He can never get the hang from new vocabulary.
4. I get a picture. You want to quit your job, right?
5. Even though the situation is not good, we must try to make the better of it.
6. I'm more interested in the long-term view than in making a quick cent.
7. I have a second job to make the ends meet.
8. She always make a go of anything she does.
9. We always kill someone when we launch a new product.
10. I'm very good at making a do.
11. My new boss used to take a bit of get. He's really strange.
12. She take a dim view of my work.
13. Planning involves looking at the long view.
14. We stand firm against lateness in this company. Please arrive on time.
15. I in charge marketing strategy.
16. Month closing take place at the end of every month.

答案🔊

請看下面提供的答案。檢查答案的時候，建議你將完整的慣用語圈起來，以增加你對慣用語的印象。

1. We must get to the bottom of the problem.
2. It's usually quite easy to get this kind of project off the ground.
3. He can never get the hang of new vocabulary.
4. I get the picture. You want to quit your job, right?
5. Even though the situation is not good, we must try to make the best of it.
6. I'm more interested in the long-term view than in making a quick buck.
7. I have a second job to make ends meet.
8. She always makes a go of anything she does.
9. We always make a killing when we launch a new product.
10. I'm very good at making do.
11. My new boss takes a bit of getting used to. He's really strange.
12. She takes a dim view of my work.

13. Planning involves taking the long view.
14. We take a firm stand against lateness in this company. Please arrive on time.
15. I'm in charge of marketing strategy.
16. Month closing takes place at the end of every month.

現在我們來學交談時會用到的一些 set-phrases。在下一個 Task 中,許多 set-phrases 的確都非常口語,也可能會有一點沒禮貌,所以請務必注意使用的對象。

TASK 4.17

請研讀以下 set-phrases。

商用英文必備語庫 4.12 慣用語 set-phrases

· Take it or leave it.	要不要隨你。
· Take it from me.	相信我。
· Take it easy!	放輕鬆!
· Don't make me laugh!	你的話很可笑!
· Make up your mind!	快一點做決定!
· Make it snappy!	快一點!
· Get your act together.	請有條理和有效率一點!
· Get cracking!	快開始進行!
· Don't get me wrong.	不要誤會我的意思。

TASK 4.18

MP3 33

請閱讀以下對話,並從必備語庫 4.12 挑選適當的慣用語填入下列空格,接著聽 MP3 來核對答案。

Conversation 1

A: I can give you a 20% discount and no more. (1)＿＿＿＿＿.

B: OK, let me think about it some more.

A: Well, do you want to buy it or not? (2)＿＿＿＿＿. We want to close the shop.

B: OK, I'll take it. (3)＿＿＿＿＿.

A: OK, I'll (4)＿＿＿＿＿.

Word List　· snappy [ˋsnæpɪ] adj. 敏捷的;迅速的

109

Conversation 2

A: It's really easy to learn Chinese. (5)_____.

B: Don't make me laugh! You have to learn thousands of characters! How can that be easy?

A: (6)_____ ! I'm just talking about speaking and listening. Sure, reading and writing are hard.

Conversation 3

A: I'm so angry I could kill someone!

B: Wow, (7)_____ ! What happened?

A: I can't find my wallet and my car keys and I'm late for an important meeting.

B: Gee, (8)_____ !

答案 🔊

請聽 MP3 檢查答案，如有困難請參閱下方的解答。

1. Take it or leave it!
2. Make up your mind.
3. Make it snappy.
4. get cracking.

5. Take it from me.
6. Don't get me wrong.
7. take it easy
8. get your act together

常 見 錯 誤 >　> **against**	
錯 誤	正 確
I against this. I never against my boss.	I am against this. I never go against my boss.
· 請記住，against 不是動詞。 · 請用 go against 或 be against。	

好，本詞彙單元到此結束。在繼續往下學習之前，請回到本單元最前面的學習目標，確定每一項都學到了。

在本篇一開始我曾請你用本篇中所有的 25 個動詞造句，然後請你勾選出覺得不容易造的句子，現在我們來看一看你到本篇末的學習成果。

學習評量

第一篇 結尾 Task 1

請再次研讀下面的動詞,並運用你在本篇中學到的字串,為每個動詞造一個句子。

thank	let	give	find	accept
know	hope	take	help	meet
like	appreciate	call	need	want
make	send	receive	wish	think
look	see	get	feel	come

第一篇 結尾 Task 2

請比較你在本篇中為開頭 Task 1 與結尾 Task 1所造的句子,並思考以下問題:

◆ 你學到了什麼?

◆ 比起開頭 Task 1,你寫結尾 Task 1 時感覺輕鬆了多少?

◆ 你覺得在運用哪幾個動詞時還有問題?為什麼?

◆ 你進步了多少?

PART 2

Biz Verbs

導讀

在第二篇中我們要學的是下面這 25 個動詞。在開始學習前，我想請你再做一次跟第一篇中一樣的兩道 Task。如此一來，等學習結束時，你就會知道自己下了多少功夫，並進步了多少。

第二篇 開頭 Task 1
請研讀以下動詞，並利用每一個動詞來各造一個句子。

第二組25個動詞

· learn	· offer	· discuss	· continue	· request
· regret	· interest	· work	· say	· become
· provide	· understand	· keep	· put	· confirm
· use	· hear	· believe	· include	· suggest
· write	· ask	· attach	· pay	· follow

第二篇 開頭 Task 1
請勾出覺得困難的動詞，以及難造的句子。

Unit 5 寫作

引言與學習目標

　　本單元的學習重點是學會這 25 個動詞的 set-phrases 和 chunks，並利用他們來寫作。如同我在第二單元中提到的，set-phrases 可用來清楚表達電子郵件的內容，並維持你和收件者的關係。Chunks 則可讓你的文字更加準確。無論正式或非正式的電子郵件，本單元學到的 set-phrases 絕對可以派上用場，甚至某些種類的正式商業信件也都適用，儘管這類正式商業信件已非常少見。此外，本單元所教的 chunks 則無論一般或商業寫作，任何種類的文章都適用。

　　本單元結束時，各位應達成的學習目標如下：

- ❏ 學到許多用於客戶關係管理 的 set-phrases。
- ❏ 練習過如何使用這些新的 set-phrases。
- ❏ 學到很多動詞 chunks。
- ❏ 學到很多雙受詞動詞 chunks。
- ❏ 練習過如何使用新字串。
- ❏ 在寫作時能夠更準確、更有自信地運用動詞。
- ❏ 知道寫作中常見的錯誤並知道該如何避免。

Set-Phrases

　　在本節中，我們要來學習清楚表達郵件內容的方法。寫電子郵件時務必將內容表達清楚，收件者才能一目了然，知道你整封信的主旨為何。從客戶關係管理的角度來看，有的電子郵件比較難寫。舉例而言，回應壞消息很難，告知別人壞消息更難。現在來看一看該如何下筆吧。

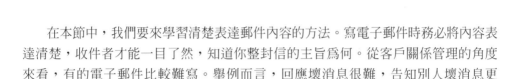

說明來信目的的 Set-Phrases

　　我們首先要學的是開頭 set-phrases，可以讓你用來說明來信目的。第一組是用於正式電子郵件的 set-phrases，例如介紹公司或產品、應徵工作、初次寫電子郵件聯絡客戶，或者和客戶建立關係後但在初期仍較生疏時。

TASK 5.1

請研讀下面的必備語庫以及例句，然後試著自己造句。

商用英文必備語庫 5.1　說明來信目的的 set-phrases MP3 34

I am writing	· in response to n.p. · in regard to n.p.	· in connection with n.p. · on behalf of n.p.
I am writing to	· ask about n.p. · confirm n.p. · confirm that + n. clause · cancel n.p. · request n.p. · clear up n.p. · enquire about n.p.	· inform you of n.p. · inform you that + n. clause · let you know that + n. clause · let you know about n.p. · tell you that + n. clause · thank you for n.p./Ving

1. I am writing to cancel our appointment next Thursday.

2. I am writing to let you know about our new product line.

3. I am writing to inform you that your policy is due for renewal.

4. I am writing to clear up the misunderstanding caused by one of our employees.

5. I am writing in response to your inquiry about prices.

6. I am writing in connection with the job ad in the *Taipei Times*.

7. I am writing on behalf of my employer, OMD Chemicals.

8. I am writing in regard to your email complaining about our service.

接著，我們就來學習該如何用 set-phrases 來確認或要求確認某事，這跟上一組 set-phrases 一樣都屬於常見的電子郵件語句。

TASK 5.2

請將下列 set-phrases 分門別類，填入下表中。

1. I am pleased to confirm that + n. clause

2. Just a short note to confirm that + n. clause

3. Please confirm our n.p.

4. Would you please confirm that + n. clause

5. Please confirm receipt of n.p.

6. Please confirm whether + n. clause

7. We wish to confirm that + n. clause

8. Please confirm that + n. clause

9. Please give me a call to confirm that + n. clause

10. I can confirm that + n. clause

11. This is to confirm that I will be attending n.p.

12. This is to confirm that + n. clause

13. Please confirm if + n. clause

14. We hereby confirm that + n. clause

15. We wish to confirm the following: …

Making Confirmation	Requesting Confirmation

Word List
- policy [ˈpɑləsɪ] n. 保單
- due [du] adj. 到期的；應付的
- renewal [rɪˈnuəl] n. (契約等) 展期；續約

答案 🔘

請利用必備語庫檢查答案，並閱讀語庫小叮嚀。

商用英文必備語庫 5.2 向對方確認或要求確認的 set-phrases　　🎵MP3 35

Making Confirmation（確認）	**Requesting Confirmation**（要求確認）
· Just a short note to confirm that + n. clause	· We hereby confirm that + n. clause
· This is to confirm that + n. clause	· Please confirm our n.p.
· This is to confirm that I will be attending n.p.	· Please confirm if + n. clause
· I can confirm that + n. clause	· Please confirm whether + n. clause
· I am pleased to confirm that + n. clause	· Please confirm that + n. clause
· We wish to confirm that + n. clause	· Please confirm receipt of n.p.
· We wish to confirm the following: …	· Please give me a call to confirm that + n. clause
	· Would you please confirm that + n. clause

✎　語庫小叮嚀

◆ 必備語庫中的 set-phrases 是根據正式程度由低至高排列，愈下面的愈正式。

◆ 你可自由決定不同的情境中該用哪一個 set-phrase。請先考量你和收件者的關係再決定。

TASK 5.3

請改正下列句子中的錯誤，見範例。

1. I am pleased confirm that we can go ahead with the deal.

   I am pleased to confirm that we can go ahead with the deal.

2. Just short note to confirm that the project is on schedule.

   _____

3. Please confirm a receipt of the attached document.

   _____

4. Please confirm weather you would like someone to pick you up.

_____

5. We wish confirm that payment has been received.

_____

6. Please confirm that payment received.

_____

7. Please give me a phone to confirm that you have received my email.

_____

8. This to confirm that I will be attending the meeting on the 29th.

_____

9. This is confirm that the meeting is cancelled.

_____

10. Please confirm you need more information.

_____

11. We here confirm that the project has been completed according to our agreement.

_____

12. We wish to confirm following: the Z9 is actually an earlier version of the Z7.

_____

答案

請比較你改正過的句子與下面的參考答案。這個練習並不難，你只需仔細檢查眼前的句子，比較裡面的 set-phrases 與必備語庫中的 set-phrases，即可挑出錯誤的地方。

2. Just a short note to confirm that the project is on schedule.
3. Please confirm receipt of the attached document.
4. Please confirm whether you would like someone to pick you up.
5. We wish to confirm that payment has been received.
6. Please confirm that payment has been received.
7. Please give me a call to confirm that you have received my email.
8. This is to confirm that I will be attending the meeting on the 29th.
9. This is to confirm that the meeting is cancelled.

10. Please confirm whether you need more information.

11. We hereby confirm that the project has been completed according to our agreement.

12. We wish to confirm the following: the Z9 is actually an earlier version of the Z7.

　　現在繼續往下研讀，學習客戶關係管理中的另一項重要技巧：處理壞消息。處理壞消息很棘手，因為在告訴收件人壞消息時，必須同時顧及你和對方的關係，避免造成傷害。在下面的 Task 中你會學到一些得體的 set-phrases，適合用來處理壞消息。

處理壞消息的 Set-Phrases

TASK 5.4

請將下列 set-phrases 分門別類，填入下表中。

1. We're sorry to learn of n.p.
2. We regret having to V
3. I'm sorry to learn about n.p.
4. We regret that + n. clause
5. We regret that we have to V
6. We regret to advise you that + n. clause
7. We are sorry to learn from sb. about/of sth.
8. We regret to announce that + n. clause
9. We regret to inform you that + n. clause
10. We regret to say that + n. clause
11. We regret to tell you that + n. clause
12. I am very sorry to learn that + n. clause
13. We regret we cannot V
14. I regret to report that + n. clause

Giving Bad News	Responding to Bad News

答案 🎧

請利用必備語庫檢查答案，並閱讀語庫小叮嚀。

商用英文必備語庫 **5.3** 處理壞消息的 set-phrases

MP3 36

Giving Bad News （發布壞消息）		Responding to Bad News （回應壞消息）
· We regret to announce that + n. clause · We regret to inform you that + n. clause · We regret we cannot V · I regret to report that + n. clause	· We regret having to V · We regret that + n. clause · We regret that we have to V · We regret to say that + n. clause · We regret to tell you that + n. clause · We regret to advise you that + n. clause	· I'm sorry to learn about n.p. · We're sorry to learn of n.p. · We are sorry to learn from sb. about/of sth. · I am very sorry to learn that + n. clause

✎ 語庫小叮嚀

◆ 注意，所有告知壞消息的 set-phrases 都用到 regret 一字，而所有回應壞消息的 set-phrases 都用到 learn 一字。

◆ 當然，每一個 set-phrase 的主詞都可以替換，與收件者關係較親近時可用 I，關係較遠時可用 we。

TASK 5.5

請將下列句子組合成完整句。見範例。

We regret to	◆	◆ your resignation.
We regret to	◆	◆ Jason of your difficulties.
I regret to	◆	◆ your business is closing down.
We regret any inconvenience	◆	◆ we cannot supply this item at present.
We regret that	◆	◆ to tell you that I am leaving the company.
I regret	◆	◆ this problem may have caused.
I'm sorry to learn about	◆	◆ the problems you are having with the product.
We are sorry to learn that	◆	◆ report that the figures are down this week.
We are sorry to learn from	◆	◆ inform you that the post is filled.
We're sorry to learn of	◆	◆ announce the department is closing.

Word List	· resignation [ˌrɛzɪgˋneʃən] n. 辭呈 · post [post] n. 工作；職位

答案 🔊

請利用下面的表格來核對答案。

We regret to	announce the department is closing.
We regret to	inform you that the post is filled.
I regret to	report that the figures are down this week.
We regret any inconvenience	this problem may have caused.
We regret that	we cannot supply this item at present.
I regret	to tell you that I am leaving the company.
I'm sorry to learn about	your resignation.
We are sorry to learn that	your business is closing down.
We are sorry to learn from	Jason of your difficulties.
We're sorry to learn of	the problems you are having with the product.

告知有附件的 Set-Phrases

　　寫電子郵件時，常常會同時附上其他重要資訊。附上其他資訊的方法有兩種，第一個是把資訊另外存檔，當作附件寄送；還有一個方法是將資訊直接貼在電子郵件中。不論是用哪一種方法，你都得特別告知收件者，電子郵件中有重要的附件，所以現在我們就來學習告知收件者有其他相關附件的表達方式。

TASK 5.6

請將下面的字串分門別類，填入下表中。

1. I am attaching n.p. for your consideration.

2. ... the following: ...

3. I am attaching n.p. for your interest.

4. I have attached n.p ....

5. I'm attaching n.p. for your interest.

6. ... n.p. is attached.

7. Please find the attached n.p.

8. ... as follows: ...

9. Please find the attached.

10. Please find the n.p. attached.

11. Please refer to the attached n.p.

12. The following is n.p.

13. Please see the attached n.p.

14. Please see the attached.

15. ... the following n.p.

16. Please see the attachment.

17. Please see the n.p. attached.

18. The n.p. is attached for your consideration.

Attaching Information	Inserting Information

答案 🔊

請參照下面的必備語庫並閱讀語庫小叮嚀。

商用英文必備語庫 **5.4** 告知有附件的 set-phrases

MP3 37

Attaching Information （附加附件）	· n.p. is attached. · I am attaching n.p. for your consideration. · I am attaching n.p. for your interest. · I have attached n.p. · I'm attaching n.p. for your interest. · Please find the attached n.p. · Please find the attached.

Attaching Information （附加附件）	· Please find the n.p. attached. · Please refer to the attached n.p. · Please see the attached n.p. · Please see the attached.	· Please see the attachment. · Please see the n.p. attached. · The n.p. is attached for your consideration.
Inserting Information （插入附件）	· ... as follows: ... · ... the following: ...	· ... the following n.p. · The following is n.p.

✎　語庫小叮嚀

◆ 在此類字串中，常用到的字不外乎下列幾項： the attached、the following 和 as follows。

◆ 特別注意 set-phrases 中的標點符號，有時會用到冒號，千萬別搞混了。

◆ 注意，附加附件中的 I'm attaching n.p. for your interest. 是英式用法。

　　好，現在就來練習運用以上學到的字串，然後再繼續往下學習。

TASK 5.7

請在空格中填入適當的 set-phrases，完成下列電子郵件，有些空格可填入多個答案。

Dear Mary,

(1)_____ due to the SARS outbreak in Taiwan, we are closing down our Taipei office for three weeks. This will affect our business, but we hope to keep operating efficiently.

Thanks for your understanding.

Dear Sue,

(2)_____ the shipment has still not arrived. This order is very urgent, and we are very disappointed. Please try to make sure shipments arrive on time in future.

Thanks.

Word List　▪ outbreak [ˋaut͵brek] n. 爆發

Dear Eric,

(3)_____ we are scheduled to meet in the lobby an hour before the start of our presentation. Let me know if there's a more convenient time.

Dear Mr. Lee,

(4)_____ your inquiry about our new product lines. (5)_____ catalogue. If you have any questions about prices, or would like to place an order, please do not hesitate to contact me at the following number:(02) 2234-5678.

Dear Mr. Marks,

(6)_____ Unlimited Liability Insurance Company Ltd to introduce you to our new range of insurance products. We are moving into your area at this time, and can send a salesperson to your office when it is convenient for you.

Dear Howard,

(7)_____ your resignation. We wish you all the best in your new job and will certainly miss your lively sense of fun here!

Good luck.

Dear Lulu,

(8)_____ you are still using the customer database on a regular basis. Thanks.

Dear Ms. Lin,

Thanks for your inquiry regarding model number XYZ123. (9)_____ the product you are interested in has recently been discontinued. If you would like more information about other products, please do not hesitate to contact me at (10)_____ number: 0953-124-678.

Dear Ms. Chu,

(11)＿＿＿＿＿＿ we have received your payment. Thank you very much.

Dear Tom,

(12)＿＿＿＿＿＿ your email account is now working.

答案

請看下面的建議答案。有些空格有多個答案，請記得依你與收件者的關係及訊息的性質來調整。

1	· I am writing to inform you that · I am writing to let you know that · I am writing to tell you that · We regret to tell you that	· We regret to advise you that · We regret to announce that · We regret to inform you that
2	· We regret to tell you that · We regret to advise you that	· We regret to inform you that
3	· Just a short note to confirm that	· This is to confirm that
4	· I am writing in response to · I am writing in regard to	· I am writing in connection with
5	· Please find the attached	· Please refer to the attached
6	· I am writing on behalf of	
7	· We're sorry to learn of	
8	· Please confirm whether	
9	· We regret to say that · We regret to tell you that	· We regret to advise you that · We regret to inform you that
10	· the following	
11	· Just a short note to confirm that	· This is to confirm that
12	· Just a short note to confirm that · This is to confirm that	· I can confirm that · Please confirm whether

動詞 Chunks

在本節中，我們要學的是動詞 chunks，本單元的動詞 chunks 有五種模式，這些模式與第二單元的略為不同。

TASK 5.8

請將下列動詞 chunks 分門別類，填入下表中。見範例。

1. use n.p. to V
2. understand that + n. clause
3. understand n.p.
4. suggest Ving
5. suggest that + n. clause
6. say that + n. clause
7. request that + n. clause
8. request n.p.
9. provide n.p.
10. offer to V
11. keep Ving
12. keep n.p.
13. hear that + n. clause
14. hear n.p.
15. follow n.p.
16. continue Ving
17. continue to V
18. believe that + n. clause
19. believe n.p.
20. attend n.p.
21. ask sb. to V

V + n.p.	V that + n. clause	V to V	V n.p./sb. to V	V + Ving
provide n.p.	*understand that + n. clause*	*offer to V*	*use n.p. to V*	*continue Ving*

答案

請利用下頁的必備語庫來檢查答案。

商用英文必備語庫 5.5　動詞 chunks

 MP3 38

V + n.p.	V that + n. clause	V to V	V n.p./sb. to V	V + Ving
· provide n.p. · understand n.p. · keep n.p. · request n.p. · hear n.p. · follow n.p. · believe n.p. · attend n.p.	· understand that + n. clause · suggest that + n. clause · say that + n. clause · request that + n. clause · hear that + n. clause · believe that + n. clause	· offer to V · continue to V	· use n.p. to V · ask sb. to V	· continue Ving · suggest Ving · keep Ving

語庫小叮嚀

◆ 注意，有的動詞有二個以上的 chunks。例如 hear n.p. 和 hear that + n. clause。

◆ Continue to V 和 continue Ving 的意思一樣。

◆ 若提出的建議與自己相關，可用 suggest Ving 的句構，如：I suggest raising the price.。若想表明是為他人提出建議，與自己無關，可用 suggest that + n. clause，如：I suggest that you raise the price.。在使用 suggest that + n. clause 時，若要把自己也包含進去，子句裡的主詞可以改為 we。在這種時候，I suggest raising the price. 跟 I suggest that we raise the price. 的意思是一樣的。

◆ Ask sb. to V 是要求（request）或需要（require）某人做某事的意思。Ask 單獨使用時則是詢問（enquire）的意思，我會在下一節中教你更多包含 ask 的動詞 chunks。

常 見 錯 誤 ＞ ＞ suggest	
錯　誤	正　確
I suggest to start again.	I suggest starting again./ I suggest that we start again.
I suggest we should start now. I suggest we can start now. I suggest we must start now.	I suggest that we start now.

> ・Suggest 後面要接 Ving，不可接 to V。
> ・不要用 suggest 搭配 must、can 或 should。只要在其後所接的子句中用簡單現在式就好，如：I suggest that we start now.。

好，現在來學這些動詞 chunks 在電子郵件中的用法吧。

TASK 5.9

請閱讀下面在 SARS 危機發生時所寫的電子郵件。找出必備語庫 5.5 中的動詞 chunks 並畫底線。注意這些動詞 chunks 的用法，見範例。

Dear Mary,

Just a quick note to confirm that we are interested in your proposal. We <u>believe that</u> there is a good opportunity for this kind of project, but we would like to hear more.

Dear Winston,

Thank you for your application. I regret to tell you that because of the current situation here, we are not looking for new staff members. I have kept your application on file for future reference.

Dear Customer,

I have recently received a call from our customer service department saying that you are not happy with our service. Despite the current emergency, we are continuing to do our best to provide high quality service. We are currently working out how to deliver the products on time without putting our delivery-men in danger of infection from SARS. We appreciate your patience.

Word List   ・infection [ɪnˋfɛkʃən] n. 感染

Dear All,

During the current crisis, we need to take care with personal hygiene. The government has provided guidelines for entering and leaving buildings, and it is important that we all understand and follow them. Can I also request that all visitors to the office wear a mask, and that you all use soap to wash your hands. I also need someone to offer to help screen visitors entering the building. I appreciate everyone's efforts to keep SARS out of our office!

Dear Mandy,

Regarding your question about sick leave, we need to work out a new procedure. Due to the situation, many people have not had leave since last year. I suggest that we extend the amount of sick leave time we offer to three weeks.

答案 🔊
請核對你的答案。

Dear Winston,

Thank you for your application. I regret to tell you that because of the current situation here, we are not looking for new staff members. I have kept your application on file for future reference.

Dear Customer,

I have recently received a call from our customer service department saying that you are not happy with our service. Despite the current emergency, we are continuing to do our best to provide high quality service. We are currently working out how to deliver the products on time without putting our deliverymen in danger of infection from SARS. We appreciate your patience.

Word List	• hygiene [ˈhaɪdʒin] n. 衛生
	• sick leave 病假

Dear All,

During the current crisis, we need to take care with personal hygiene. The government has provided guidelines for entering and leaving buildings, and it is important that we all understand and follow them. Can I also request that all visitors to the office wear a mask, and that you all use soap to wash your hands. I also need someone to offer to help screen visitors entering the building. I appreciate everyone's efforts to keep SARS out of our office!

Dear Mandy,

Regarding your question about sick leave, we need to work out a new procedure. Due to the situation, many people have not had leave since last year. I suggest that we the extend the amount of sick leave time we offer to three weeks.

常 見 錯 誤 > > request	
錯 誤	正 確
I requested for a pay raise.	I requested a pay raise./ I put in a request for a pay raise.
I requested to transfer to another department.	I request a transfer to another department.
I request you to stop smoking.	I request that you stop smoking.

- 請留意，request 可以當名詞也可以當動詞。
- Request 的動詞 chunk 是 request n.p. 或 request that + n. clause；名詞 chunk 則是 a request for sth.。
- 注意，pay raise 是美式用法；pay rise 是英式用法。

雙受詞動詞 Chunks

　　在第二單元中我們學過可倒置與不可倒置的雙受詞動詞，再幫你複習一次，不可倒置的動詞 chunks 受詞位置不可調換，且第二個受詞可寫可不寫；而可倒置動詞 chunks 的受詞位置可調換，不過調換受詞位置後需加上適當的介系詞。在本節中你會學到更多這類的動詞 chunks。請做下面的 Task，看看你對這類動詞的用法是否還熟悉。

TASK 5.10

請將下面的雙受詞動詞 chunks 分門別類，填入下表中。

1. ask sb. (about n.p.)
2. attach sth. (to sth.)
3. include sth. (in sth.)
4. pay sb. (sth.)
5. offer sb. sth.
6. provide sth. to sb.

7. offer sth. to sb.
8. pay sth. (to sb.)
9. discuss sth. (with sb.)
10. provide sb. with sth.
11. ask sb. (about wh-clause)
12. say sth. (to sb.)

Non-Invertible	Invertible

答案

請利用下面的必備語庫檢查答案。

商用英文必備語庫 5.6 雙受詞動詞 chunks

Non-Invertible（不可倒置）	Invertible（可倒置）
· ask sb. (about wh-clause)	· offer sb. sth.
· ask sb. (about n.p.)	· offer sth. to sb.

· attach sth. (to sth.)	· pay sb. (sth.)
· discuss sth. (with sb.)	· pay sth. (to sb.)
· include sth. (in sth.)	· provide sb. with sth.
· say sth. (to sb.)	· provide sth. to sb.

✎ 語庫小叮嚀

◆ 使用不可倒置的雙受詞動詞時，第二個受詞可寫可不寫，不會影響句子的正確性，只是意思較不清楚而已。

◆ 注意，provide sth. to sb. 在英文中比較少用。我會建議你用 provide sb. with sth. 或改用 give sth. to sb.。

◆ 注意，ask sb. (about wh-clause) 和 ask sb. about n.p. 是「詢問某人關於某事」的意思。而 ask sb. to V 則是「要求某人做某事」的意思。

現在我們來做一些不可倒置雙受詞動詞的練習。

TASK 5.11

請將下列片語放入句子裡適當的位置，然後將完整的動詞 chunks 畫線。

1. Please ask John. I need it as soon as possible.

   (about why he is taking so long to turn in his expense claim)

   _____

2. You should always attach the receipt. This makes it easier to confirm the details of the claim. (to your expense claim)

   _____

3. Please don't say anything to the others, but keep me posted. (about this)

   _____

4. I think we need to discuss this issue. They always want us to keep them abreast of new developments. (with the client)

   _____

Word List · keep sb. abreast of 告知某人……的最新消息

5. Should we include last month's figures? They may help to confirm our current position. (in the report)

_____

6. I have asked my department head. However, she thinks it will put too much of a strain on our resources. (about your request for a bigger budget)

_____

答案 🎧

請比較你的答案與我在下面提供的答案。

1. Please <u>ask John about why</u> he is taking so long to turn in his expense claim. I need it as soon as possible.

2. You should always <u>attach the receipt to your expense claim</u>. This makes it easier to confirm the details of the claim.

3. Please don't <u>say anything about this to the others</u>, but keep me posted.

4. I think we need to <u>discuss this issue with the client</u>. They always want us to keep them abreast of new developments.

5. Should we <u>include last month's figures in the report</u>? They may help to confirm our current position.

6. I have <u>asked my department head about your request</u> for a bigger budget. However, she thinks it will put too much of a strain on our resources.

常 見 錯 誤 > > **discuss**	
錯　誤	正　確
We need to discuss about the project.	We need to discuss the project.
I need to discuss with my boss.	I need to discuss this with my boss.
· 你應該沒那麼快忘記吧！Discuss 是不可倒置的雙受詞動詞，因此要與他人討論某事時，discuss 的後面要先接一個受詞才能再接 with sb.。	

TASK 5.12

請閱讀下面的電子郵件，並找出必備語庫 5.6 中的雙受詞動詞 chunks，並畫底線。
注意這類動詞 chunks 的用法。

Dear John,

Thank you so much for offering the new overseas post to me. I feel very honored, although I do think you should have offered Mike the job since he has been with the company for a lot longer than I have.

I have already asked Lucy to provide me with a full report on the situation in the new branch, but I would be grateful if you could also provide any useful information to me. The more I know about it, the better.

Many thanks again.

Mario

Dear Oliver,

Regarding our conversation on the phone a few days ago, the client has not paid their bill for three months. This is really affecting our cash-flow siluation, as we need to pay our own supplier.

Please, could you ask XYZ to hurry up?

Thanks.

Tracy

答案 🔊
請核對你的答案。

Dear John,

Thank you so much for <u>offering the new overseas post to me</u>. I feel very honored, although I do think you should have <u>offered Mike the job</u> since he has been with the company for a lot longer than I have.

I have already <u>asked Lucy</u> to <u>provide me with a full report</u> on the situation in the new branch, but I would be grateful if you could also <u>provide any useful information to me</u>. The more I know about it, the better.

Many thanks again.

Mario

Dear Oliver,

Regarding our conversation on the phone a few days ago, the client has not <u>paid their bill</u> for three months. This is really affecting our cash-flow situation, as we need to <u>pay our own supplier</u>.

Please, could you <u>ask XYZ</u> to hurry up?

Thanks.

Tracy

TASK 5.13

請調換下列句子中受詞的位置，改寫每一個句子。

1. Please provide me with directions to your office.

_____

2. Do you offer your clients a discount for early payment?

_____

3. I think we should offer a 20% discount to our most important customers.

_____

4. They usually provide very good service to their customers.

_____

5. We are providing you with an invoice. Please see the attachment.

_____

6. Please pay your bill to the finance department.

_____

Word List   • invoice [ˈɪnvɔɪs] n. 發票

7. We need to pay the supplier 20% in advance.

答案 🔊

請比較你的答案與我在下面提供的答案。

1. Please provide directions to your office to me.

2. Do you offer a discount for early payment to your clients?

3. I think we should offer our most important customers a 20% discount.

4. They usually provide their customers with very good service.

5. We are providing an invoice to you. Please see the attachment.

6. Please pay the finance department your bill.

7. We need to pay 20% in advance to the supplier.

還記得我稍早教過的 provide sth. to sb. 嗎？上面答案中含 provide 的句子文法均正確，不過比較常用的還是改寫前的那個句子。

常 見 錯 誤 ＞ ＞ **offer**	
錯 誤	正 確
He is offering me to do it.	He is offering to do it for me.
·切勿使用 offer sb. to do sth.，請使用 offer to do sth. for sb.	

Unit 6 口說

引言與學習目標

在本單元中，我們要學的是將本篇 25 個動詞中的部分動詞運用在口說中。我們也會學習現在時間的時態。在開始學習前，建議你回到第一單元閱讀 Task 1.3 的時態概要表，溫習一下。

本單元結束時，各位應達成的學習目標如下：

❑ 對現在時間中的三種時態，也就是現在完成式、現在進行式和現在完成進行式有清楚的了解，並知道如何正確地運用。

❑ 有能力以現在進行式和現在完成進行式運用本篇的一些重要動詞，談論目前的工作計劃、目前的市場趨勢和暫時的現況。

❑ 有能力運用本篇的動詞及正確的時態，談論個人做過的事、計劃結果和生意結果。

❑ 知道哪些時間 chunks 該和哪些現在時間的時態搭配使用。

❑ 有能力聽出口說中常會有的連音，並學會發音的技巧。

❑ 知道一些常見的口說錯誤並知道該如何避免。

❑ 做過一些口說、聽力和發音練習。

時態：現在時間

　　英文中現在時間的用法有兩種。一個是強調動作本身，如：I am writing my report.「我正在寫報告。」（報告還沒寫完）；另一個是強調動作目前完成的結果，如：I have written my report.「我已經寫完報告。」（報告已經完成，我們現在就看得到結果，即已完成的報告）。

　　如果你希望把重點擺在動作本身，便應該使用現在進行式（be + Ving），或者現在完成進行式（have been + Ving）。現在進行式強調的是某事現在正在進行；而現在完成進行式強調的則是某事持續在進行。如果你希望把重點擺在現在已經完成的結果，便應該使用現在完成式（have + p.p.）。

　　現在來進一步學習這些時態的用法，我們就從談論動作本身的用法學起。談話中把動作當作重點的情況有三種：談目前正在處理的工作計劃、談目前的市場或業界趨勢、談目前暫時的現況。現在請做下列 Task 以了解這三類事情所指為何。

TASK 6.1

請將這些句子分門別類，填入下頁的表格中。

1. At present I'm living with my sister until my new apartment is finished.

2. At present I'm working on the marketing strategy for next year.

3. Lately our share of the US market has been declining.

4. At the moment I'm designing a new CRM software program for my company.

5. I haven't been feeling well recently.

6. I'm still organizing an event for our new product launch.

7. I'm still studying for my MBA.

| Word List | ▪ decline [dɪˋklaɪn] v. 下降；下跌 |
| | ▪ launch [lɔntʃ] n. 新產品推出 |

8. I've recently been dealing with some of the outstanding payments.

9. Nowadays I'm working for a bigger company.

10. Our brand profile is increasing nowadays.

11. These days the market in China is growing very quickly.

12. We are presently expanding our market share in Europe.

Talking About Current Projects
Talking About Current Market Trends
Talking About Present Situations That Are Temporary

答案

請利用下面的表格來和你的答案做比較。

Talking About Current Projects （談論目前的計劃）
· At present I'm working on the marketing strategy for next year.
· At the moment I'm designing a new CRM software program for my company.
· I'm still organizing an event for our new product launch.
· I've recently been dealing with some of the outstanding payments.

Word List · outstanding [ˈaʊtˈstændɪŋ] adj. （負債等）未付的

Talking About Current Market Trends （談論目前的市場趨勢）

- These days the market in China is growing very quickly.

- We are presently expanding our market share in Europe.

- Lately our share of the US market has been declining.

- Our brand profile is increasing nowadays.

Talking About Present Situations That Are Temporary （談論目前暫時的現況）

- Nowadays I'm working for a bigger company.

- I'm still studying for my MBA.

- At present I'm living with my sister until my new apartment is finished.

- I haven't been feeling well recently.

TASK 6.2

現在請為以下三類事項各造兩個句子，描述：(1) 目前正在處理的計劃；(2) 目前你所從事的行業或市場上的趨勢；(3) 你目前生活中一個暫時的情況。

答案

我能夠為這個 Task 提供的答案有限，在此提醒你要記得使用現在進行式或現在完成進行式來談論這三類事項。

　　現在我們繼續往下看，學習現在時間的另一種用途，也就是強調動作的結果。

TASK 6.3

請將下列句子分門別類，填入下頁的表格中。

1. Costs have also risen since June.
2. I haven't been to Japan yet.
3. I've already been to New York three times in the last two years.
4. I've finished three presentations so far.
5. I've had five meetings about this problem since yesterday.
6. I've just received my EMBA.

7. I've just written a report.

8. I've known John for ages.

9. I've recently talked to Malcolm about the problem with the specs.

10. Our targets have just increased.

11. Sales have risen for the last three months.

12. This means that profits have so far remained the same.

Talking About Things sb. Has Done	Talking About Project Results	Talking About Business Results

答案

請利用下面的表格比較答案。

Talking About Things sb. Has Done （談論某人做過的事）
· I've already been to New York three times in the last two years.
· I've just received my EMBA.
· I've known John for ages.
· I haven't been to Japan yet.
Talking About Project Results （談論計劃結果）
· I've recently talked to Malcolm about the problems with the specs.
· I've had five meetings about this problem since yesterday.
· I've just written a report.
· I've finished three presentations so far.
Talking About Business Results （談論生意結果）
· Sales have risen for the last three months.
· Costs have also risen since June.
· This means that profits have so far remained the same.
· Our targets have just increased.

TASK 6.4

現在請為下列三類事項造兩個句子，描述：(1) 個人做過的事；(2) 計劃結果；(3) 生意結果。

答案

同樣的，我無法預測你會寫出什麼樣的句子，不過請務必記得，這三類事項要使用現在完成式來描述。

現在來學習不同時態下可以使用的時間 chunks。

TASK 6.5

請把下列的時間 chunks 分門別類，填入其後的表格中。

1. already
2. at present
3. at the moment
4. currently
5. ever

6. for
7. for ages
8. just
9. lately
10. now

11. nowadays
12. presently
13. recently
14. since
15. so far

16. still
17. these days
18. yet
19. never

Present Perfect	Present Perfect Continuous	Present Continuous

答案

請利用下面的必備語庫比較答案。

商用英文必備語庫 6.1　現在時間 chunks

Present Perfect（現在完成式）		
· so far · yet · now · just	· for · already · since · recently	· lately · never · ever · for ages

Present Perfect Continuous（現在完成進行式）		
· lately · these days · since	· for ages · nowadays · still · recently	· just · for · currently · these days
Present Continuous（現在進行式）		
· at present · nowadays · now	· at the moment · these days · still	· currently · presently

✎ 語庫小叮嚀

◆ 有些時間 chunks 可用於多個時態，請務必特別注意。

◆ 在美式用法中，presently 的意思等同於 currently（現在；目前），因此屬於現在時間 chunks；在英式用法中，presently 則是 soon（即將）的意思，因此是未來時間 chunks。

◆ Ever 和 yet 多用於疑問句或否定句中，如：Have you ever seen it?、I haven't seen it yet.。Never 要搭配肯定動詞使用，但必須用於帶有否定意思的句子中，如：I have never seen you before.。

◆ Since 必須搭配某個特定的時間點使用，如：I have been here since noon.、I've been studying English since I was 9 years old.；for 則必須搭配某段特定的時期使用，如：I've been here for 20 minutes.、I've been studying English for about 15 years.。

◆ 如果你想描述的事實和狀態只有在談話當時為真，或者可能是短暫的，則所有的現在時間 chunks 都必須搭配簡單現在式來使用，如：We currently have 20 sales people.、At the moment we are quite busy.。

TASK 6.6

請再閱讀一遍 Task 6.1 和 6.3 中的句子，這次注意句子中的時態和時間 chunks 的用法。

答案 🎧

針對其中時間 chunks 的用法，有下列幾點需注意：

1. Just 要直接接在 have 的後面。

2. Still 要直接接在 be 動詞的後面。

3. 其他大部分的時間 chunks 可以接在第一個動詞，也就是 be 動詞或 have 的後面，或者也可直接放在句首或句尾。

現在就來練習將時間 chunks 運用在正確的時態上。

TASK 6.7

請用不同時態改寫下列的句子，並改正任何你找到的錯誤，見範例。

1. I am already asking Lucy to provide me with a full report.
   I have already asked Lucy to provide me with a full report.

2. The client is not paying their bill for three months.

3. So far we are not having any problems.

4. Macey just calls me about the budget.

5. Our business has had difficulties these days.

6. We don't see each other for ages.

7. I don't finish yet.

8. I recently receive a call from our complaints department.

9. We currently work out how to deliver the products.

10. I have not ever hear of anyone getting fired from this company.

11. Many staff do not have leave since last year.

12. The product you are interested in is lately discontinued.

13. Have you still used the computer system?

答案 🔊

請比較你的答案和下面提供的答案。

2. The client hasn't paid their bill for three months.

3. So far we haven't had any problems.

4. Macey just called me about the budget.

5. Our business has been having difficulties these days.
   Our business is having difficulties these days.

6. We haven't seen each other for ages.

7. I haven't finished yet.

8. I recently received a call from our complaints department.

9. We are currently working out how to deliver the products.

10. I have never heard of anyone getting fired from this company.

11. Many staff have not had leave since last year.

12. The product you are interested in has lately been discontinued.

13. Are you still using the computer system?

常 見 錯 誤 > > **ever**	
錯 誤	正 確
I ever go to Japan. I haven't ever seen it.	I went to Japan once./I've been to Japan. I have never seen it.
·注意，ever 大多用在否定句及疑問句中，如：Have you ever + p.p.? ·請用 I have never p.p.，而不要用 I haven't ever p.p.	

在進入下一節之前，請先做下面的閱讀練習，複習已學過的三種現在時間時態。

TASK 6.8

請重新閱讀第五單元中所有的電子郵件，這次留意其中現在完成式、現在完成進行式和現在進行式的用法。

表達或接受慰問時的 Set-Phrases

TASK 6.9

MP3 41

請聽 MP3 中的對話。Nadia 和 Oliver 正在飲水機旁邊聊天。Nadia 的老闆 Bob 對她做了什麼事？為什麼？Oliver 的反應是什麼？

答案

1. Bob 威脅了 Nadia 後又請她走路。
2. Nadia 負責的計劃發生了一些問題，她老闆對事情有不同的認知，結果因為受到 Nadia 挑戰，便打了 Nadia。
3. Oliver 非常擔心。
   這整件事情非常戲劇化，對不對？

　　如果沒有聽懂對話中所有內容，別擔心，多聽幾次，直到比較能夠理解為止。如果還是覺得有困難，可以參閱下方完整的對話內容。

Oliver: Are you OK? You look terrible.

Nadia: Not really. Actually, I've just been fired.

Oliver: What? I don't believe it.

Nadia: Yup. I've just had a meeting with Bob, and he got really angry with me and fired me. Just like that. Can you believe it?

Oliver: Gee. Tell me what happened. What reason did he give?

Nadia: Well, you know the ICM project?

Oliver: The ICM project? Oh, yes.

Nadia: Well, we've been having problems with the client. The client is really, really difficult to work with, you understand, and blames all his mistakes on us. As I'm the team leader, naturally it gets blamed on me.

Oliver: I'm sorry to hear that.

Nadia: I feel terrible about it, of course,

Oliver: I can understand that.

Nadia: You know, it's OK when people make mistakes. What I don't understand is when they try to blame them on other people. It's so dishonest and unprofessional. Do you understand what I mean?

Oliver: I hear you!

Nadia: Anyway, so, at the moment we're working on the launch for the new product, and according to him, we've gone over budget by several million dollars.

Oliver: Several million dollars? I find that hard to believe.

Nadia: Right. I don't believe a word of it. So I told him.

Oliver: So what did he say?

Nadia: He threatened me.

Oliver: What? I can't believe my ears! Bob threatened you?

Nadia: Yeah, it was scary. And then he apologized, and asked me to forget about it. Then he offered me some money not to say anything! When I refused, he fired me! He's totally unprofessional.

Oliver: I can understand how you feel. Here sit down. Golly. I can't believe it. So what are you going to do?

Nadia: Well, I'm going to contact my lawyers and see if I can sue Bob. I'm too angry to simply forget about it.

Oliver: Wow, I can believe it. Maybe he'll apologize again and offer you your job back.

Nadia: Yeah right! I'll believe it when I see it.

 **TASK 6.10**

MP3 41

請研讀下列 set-phrases，並重聽一遍對話，將聽到的 set-phrases 打勾，接著思考對話中這些 set-phrases 的使用方法及意思。

1. … you understand …

2. Can you believe it?

3. Do you understand what I mean?

5. I can believe it.

6. I can understand how you feel.

7. I can understand that.

8. I can't believe it.

9. I can't believe my ears!

10. I can't understand it!

11. I don't believe a word of it.

12. I don't believe it.

13. I find that hard to believe.

14. I hear you!

15. I'll believe it when I see it.

16. I'm sorry to hear that.

17. What I don't understand is wh-clause

| Word List | • golly [ˈgɑlɪ] interj. 哎呀！ |
| | • sue [su] v. 控告；對……提起訴訟 |

答案

如果覺得很難聽懂，建議你借助上一個 Task 的對話內容。不必每一個字都聽懂，只要專心聽 set-phrases，學會 set-phrases 的意思和用法即可。

TASK 6.11

現在將上述 set-phrases 分門別類，填入下表中。

Asking for Sympathy	Showing Sympathy

答案 🔊

請利用下面的必備語庫檢查答案。

商用英文必備語庫 6.2 慰問的 set-phrases　　　　　（MP3 42）

Asking for Sympathy （尋求慰問）	Showing Sympathy （表達慰問）
· I can't understand it! · Do you understand what I mean? · What I don't understand is wh-clause · … you understand … · Can you believe it?	· I'm sorry to hear that. · I hear you! · I can understand how you feel. · I can understand that. · I find that hard to believe. · I can believe it. · I don't believe it. · I can't believe it. · I can't believe my ears!

✎ 語庫小叮嚀

◆ 如果想確定對方是否注意聽你講話，可以在句子中說 … you understand …。

◆ 如果想表示非常同意對方，可以說 I hear you!。請閱讀下列對話：

　A: I really hate this hot weather.　B: I hear you!

◆ 請再聽一次對話並閱讀對話內容，確定你已確實掌握這些 set-phrases 的用法了。

TASK 6.12

  43

請聽 MP3 中的句子，並運用剛剛學到的慰問 set-phrases 回答。做這個 Task 的時候，別忘了錄下你的答案以便評量。

答案

MP3 44

請聽 MP3 中的參考答案。你的回答可能不同，但沒有關係，因為可以使用的 set-phrases 本來就有很多 。

◀ 描述改變的 Word Partnerships ▶

　　動詞 become 通常會搭配現在進行式或現在完成式來使用，幾乎很少會用簡單現在式，可用來表示從一個狀態改變到另一個狀態，因此非常適合用來說明變化帶來的結果或者進行中的改變。我們就來進一步學習這個動詞吧。

TASK 6.13

請研讀這個 word partnerships 語庫表以及下面的例句。

商用英文必備語庫 6.3　描述改變的 word partnerships

MP3 45

become	· available (to sb.)	可用的；可取得的
	· aware of n.p.	知道某事
	· aware that + n. clause	知道某事
	· clear (to sb.) that + n. clause	某事對（某人而言）是清楚的
	· dependent (on n.p.)	依靠某事物的
	· dissatisfied (with n.p.)	對……不滿的
	· eligible (for n.p.)	對……有資格的
	· familiar (with n.p.)	對……熟悉的
	· more + adj.	更……
	· necessary to V	必需的

Word List　· eligible [ˈɛlɪdʒəbl] adj. 合格的；適任的

1. It has become necessary to lay off 200 factory workers.
2. We have become too dependent on the Japanese market, and are now suffering for it.
3. I'm becoming dissatisfied with your performance.
4. It's gradually becoming clear to me that we need to withdraw from the market.
5. I'm happy to inform you that you have become eligible for promotion.
6. It's becoming more difficult to do business here.

✎　語庫小叮嚀

◆ 如果重點在於改變帶來的結果，則 become 要用現在完成式；如果重點在於改變的過程，則 become 必須使用現在進行式。
◆ 請注意，become 後面通常會接一個形容詞 chunk。
◆ 如果描述的重點在於狀態或事實，而非改變，那麼 word partnerships 中的 become 可以用 be 動詞取代，如：I am dissatisfied with your performance.、It's difficult to do business here.、It's necessary to lay off 200 factory workers.。

請使用在語庫 6.3 中學到的 word partnerships 改寫以下句子，別忘了先思考句子的意義，判斷句子的重點是在結果還是改變過程，見範例。

1. You are eligible for a 10% reduction.

   You have become eligible for a 10% reduction.

2. Are you familiar with the China market?

3. We are more efficient now.

4. It is necessary to update our records more frequently.

5. The raw materials are now more readily available to us.

Word List	▪ lay off　（暫時的）解雇
	▪ withdraw [wɪðˋdrɔ] v. 退出
	▪ raw [rɔ] adj. 未加工的

6. We are aware that your company is experiencing financial difficulties.

_____

7. We are too dependent on credit.

_____

8. I'm dissatisfied with their service, so I'm looking for another provider.

_____

9. It is clear to me that the new product is not selling.

_____

答案

請比較你寫的句子和我在下面提供的建議答案。

2. Are you becoming familiar with the China market?
3. We have become more efficient now.
4. It has become necessary to update our records more frequently.
5. The raw materials are now becoming more readily available to us.
6. We have become aware that your company is experiencing financial difficulties.
7. We are becoming too dependent on credit.
8. I have become dissatisfied with their service, so I am looking for another provider.
9. It's becoming clear to me that the new product is not selling.

　　你可能是選擇用現在完成式，而不是現在進行式，或者恰好相反，兩者都沒錯，因爲這個練習的重點在於先仔細思考你所想表達的意思，然後以適當時態來運用動詞。

常　見　錯　誤　>　>　**change**	
錯　誤	正　確
The changement of the system is good.	The change to the system is good.
· Change 也是名詞。因此它的名詞 chunk 就是 the change to n.p.，請留意。	

發音

　　在本節中，我們要學的是 be 動詞當助動詞用時的發音。英文人士在說話速度很快的時候常常會把它的音弱化，因此很難聽出來，這類連音在疑問句中尤其明顯。現在我們先做一些練習。

TASK 6.15

請研讀下面的表格，並同時聽 MP3。

寫作	發音
Are you (Ving) …?	[ərˋju]
Is he (Ving) …?	[ɪˋzhi]
Is she (Ving) …?	[ɪˋzʃi]
Is it (Ving) …?	[ɪˋzɪt]
What are you (Ving) …?	[ˋhwɑdər͵ju]
When is he (Ving) …?	[ˋhwənɪ͵zhi]
Why is she (Ving) …?	[ˋhwaɪzʃi]
Who is (Ving) …?	[huz]
Where are you (Ving) …?	[ˋhwɛrər͵ju]
How are you (Ving) …?	[ˋhaʊrju]
Who are you (Ving) …?	[ˋhurju]

答案 🎧

這些詞組寫下來時都有三個字，不過口說時聽起來卻像一個字。

請注意，如果 when 是搭配現在進行式，句子則含有未來意義。我會在第十二單元中更詳細地為你說明。

TASK 6.16

現在請聽一些問句與答句。一邊聽，一邊注意說話唸語音 chunks 的發音。 (MP3 47)

1. <u>Are you</u> enjoying your vacation?
   Yes, <u>I'm</u> having a great time.

2. <u>What are you</u> enjoying the most?
   <u>I'm</u> enjoying the beach.

3. The boss is coming. <u>Is he</u> coming?
   Yes. <u>He's</u> walking down the hall. Quick, look busy.

4. <u>Is she</u> working on the project, too?
   Yes, <u>she's</u> doing the planning.

5. <u>Is it</u> raining outside?
   Yes, <u>it's</u> pouring.

6. When <u>is he</u> leaving?
   <u>He's</u> leaving tonight.

7. <u>Why is she</u> crying?
   <u>She's</u> crying because her boyfriend dumped her.

8. <u>Who is</u> using the printer.
   It's broken. <u>They're</u> fixing it.

9. <u>Where are you</u> going?
   <u>I'm</u> going to get some lunch. Want some?

10. <u>How are you</u> doing with the new project.
    OK. <u>We're</u> getting on fine with it.

11. <u>Who are you</u> talking to?
    <u>I'm</u> talking to the client.

TASK 6.17

現在請利用剛學過的語音 chunks，練習使用這些 chunks 發問。記得用錄下你的聲音以便評量。

現在來看 be 動詞用於肯定句時的發音。在口語中，be 動詞和主詞幾乎都會用省略法連結。請研讀下面的表格。

TASK 6.18

MP3 48

請研讀下面的表格，並同時聽 MP3。

寫作		發音
I am Ving …	I'm Ving …	[aɪm]
You are Ving …	You're Ving …	[jur]
He is Ving …	He's Ving …	[hɪz]
She is Ving …	She's Ving …	[ʃɪz]
It is Ving …	It's Ving …	[ɪts]
We are Ving …	We're Ving …	[wir]
They are Ving …	They're Ving …	[ðer]

寫作時，非正式的句子可以用省略法，但比較正式的句子則不要用。

TASK 6.19

MP3 47

現在請再聽一次 Task 6.16 中的問句與答句，這次留意回答的部分。注意說話者是如何唸這些語音 chunks 的。

常 見 錯 誤 > > **happen**	
錯 誤	正 確
Lots has been happened. What happen? Something happen.	Lots has happened. What happened? / What's happened? Something happened. / Something's happened.
· Happen 不能用被動語態，即使是以物當主詞都不行！ · Happen 比較常用現在完成式和過去簡單式表示。	

好了，本單元的學習到此結束。請回到本單元前面的學習目標，確定全部都學會了之後再往下學習下一個單元。

Unit 7 詞彙

引言與學習目標

在本單元中我們將學習一些常見的詞彙，以搭配本章 25 個動詞中的部分動詞。如同我們在第四單元中做過的練習，我們會從 word partnerships 著手，然後學習片語動詞，最後再學習一些慣用語。

本單元結束時，各位應達成的學習目標如下：

❑ 學到很多使用頻率高的 word partnerships，可用於商業英文的口說和寫作。
❑ 學到很多片語動詞，可用於商業英文的口說和寫作。
❑ 學到一些很有用的商業慣用語。
❑ 練習過如何使用新學到的詞彙。
❑ 知道一些常見錯誤並知道該如何避免。

Word Partnerships

我們就先從一些以 keep、pay 和 put 三個動詞為主的 word partnerships 開始學起。動詞 keep 經常用於處理資訊。在下面的 Task 中你會發現，含 keep 的 word partnerships 通常是用來傳遞或保留資訊。

TASK 7.1

請研讀含 keep 的 word partnerships，並將其分門別類填入下表中，見範例。

keep	· a promise	· sb. informed of/about sth.
	· a record of n.p.	· sb. posted as to sth.
	· in contact	· sb. posted as to wh-clause
	· in mind that + n. clause	· sb. up to date as to wh-clause
	· in touch	· sb. up to date on n.p.
	· it in mind	· sb. updated on n.p/wh-clause
	· sb. abreast of n.p.	· sth. on file
	· sb. advised of n.p.	· the books
	· sb. in mind for sth.	· track of n.p.
	· sb. in the loop (on n.p.)	

Communicate Information	Store Information
keep sb. informed of/about sth.	*keep a record of n.p.*

答案🎧

請利用下面的必備語庫來核對答案。

商用英文必備語庫 7.1 含 keep 的 word partnerships　　　MP3 49

Communicate Information (傳達訊息)	**Store Information** (保留訊息)
· keep sb. informed of/about sth.	· keep sth. on file
· keep sb. posted as to sth.	· keep the books
· keep sb. posted as to wh-clause	· keep a record of n.p.
· keep sb. up to date on n.p.	· keep track of n.p.
· keep sb. up to date as to wh-clause	· keep sb. in mind for sth.
· keep sb. updated on n.p/wh-clause	· keep in mind that + n. clause
· keep sb. advised of n.p.	· keep a promise
· keep sb. abreast of n.p.	· keep it in mind
· keep in touch	
· keep in contact	
· keep sb. in the loop (on n.p.)	

✎　語庫小叮嚀

◆ 語庫中含有 posted 的 word partnerships 的意思等同於 keep sb. updated，也就是「使某人得知最新消息」的意思。Keep sb. abreast of n.p. 和 keep sb. advised of n.p. 同義，都是「告知某人某事的最新消息」。

◆ Keep sth. in mind 和其他含有 mind 的 word partnerships 一樣，都有「記住某事」的意思。

◆ Keep the books 意為「記帳」。

TASK 7.2

請先判別下頁句子是要傳達訊息還是要保留訊息，接著再利用語庫 7.1 中適當的 word partnerships 改寫以下句子。每個句子會用到的 word partnerships 可能不只一個，見範例。

1. Please let me know about the situation.

   Please keep me posted as to the situation.

2. Please remember that the figures must be checked by your supervisor.

3. I'm telling the client everything that they need to know about the situation.

4. Please store all your email correspondence with clients for six months.

5. Please inform Joy about the new ideas for the campaign.

6. I hope you will remember me for future projects.

7. Please let me know how the situation develops while I'm away.

8. His job is to write down the details of all financial transactions.

9. We are trying to record all transactions as they happen.

10. It was so nice to see you! Let's make sure we stay in contact.

答案🔊

請比較你的答案和下面提供的範例答案。

2. Please keep in mind that the figures must be checked by your supervisor.

3. I'm keeping the client up to date on everything that they need to know about the situation.

   I'm keeping the client abreast of everything that they need to know about the situation.

4. Please keep a record of all your email correspondence with clients for six months.

   Please keep all your email correspondence with clients on file for six months.

Word List

- correspondence [ˌkɔrəˋspɑndəns] n. 通信；（信函的）往返
- campaign [kæmˋpen] n. 宣傳活動
- transaction [trænsˋækʃən] n. 交易；買賣

---

5. Please keep Joy in the loop about the new ideas for the campaign.
   Please keep Joy updated about the new ideas for the campaign.

6. I hope you will keep me in mind for future projects.

7. Please keep me posted as to how the situation develops while I'm away.
   Please keep me abreast of the situation while I'm away.
   Please keep me updated on how the situation develops while I'm away.

8. His job is to keep a record of the details of all financial transactions.
   His job is to keep the books.

9. We are trying to keep track of all transactions as they happen.

10. It was so nice to see you! Let's make sure we keep in touch.

TASK 7.3

現在請用 keep 的 word partnerships 練習造句。

答案

請在造句的同時回想已學過的動詞時態,確定 keep 的時態適用於句子中。

　　現在往下學習另一個動詞的 word partnerships。Pay 通常是用在處理金錢和付帳方式。

TASK 7.4

請將含 pay 的 word partnerships 分門別類,填入下表中,見範例。井字號(#)代表數字。

pay	· sb. to V · a bill (of #) (for sth.) · a fee (of #) (for sth.) · a fine (of #) (for sth.) · a high price (for sth.) · a penalty	· by electronic transfer · compensation (for sth.) · for sth. · good money for sth. · in cash

Word List	▪ penalty [ˋpɛnltɪ] n. 不利 ▪ compensation [͵kɑmpənˋseʃən] n. 補償金;賠償金

pay	· a premium	· in full
	· a reasonable price (for sth.)	· in installments
	· a total of	· income tax
	· a visit (to sb.)	· interest (on n.p.)
	· attention to n.p.	· off a debt
	· back the amount owed (to sb.)	· off a loan
	· bribes	· off a mortgage
	· by check	· operating costs
	· by credit card	· overhead (on sth.)
	· by direct debit	· rent
		· sales tax
		· capital gains tax
		· taxes
		· wages

Business Costs	Payment Method
pay a bill (of sth.)	*pay by check*

- premium [ˈprimɪəm] n. 額外的費用；保險費
- installment [ɪnˈstɔlmənt] n. 分期付款
- bribe [braɪb] n. 賄賂
- mortgage [ˈmɔrgɪdʒ] n. 抵押貸款
- overhead [ˈovəˌhɛd] n. 經常開支
- capital gains tax 資本收益稅

答案

請以下列語庫來核對答案。

商用英文必備語庫 7.2 含 pay 的 word partnerships

Business Costs（企業成本）		Payment Method（付款方式）
· pay a high price (for sth.)	· pay bribes	· pay by check
· pay a realistic price (for sth.)	· pay capital gains tax	· pay by credit card
· pay a total of	· pay income tax	· pay in cash
· pay a visit (to sb.)	· pay interest (on n.p.)	· pay in full
· pay compensation (for sth.)	· pay operating costs	· pay in installments
· pay good money for sth.	· pay overhead (on sth.)	· pay by direct debit
· pay a bill (of #) (for sth.)	· pay rent	· pay by electronic transfer
· pay a fee (of #) (for sth.)	· pay sales tax	
· pay a fine (of #) (for sth.)	· pay wages	
· pay a penalty	· pay taxes	
· pay a premium	· pay off a debt	
· pay back the amount owed (to sb.)	· pay off a loan	
	· pay off a mortgage	

> 🖊 語庫小叮嚀
>
> ◆ Pay good money for sth. 是指付了錢買了某物，但某物卻不如人意的意思，如：
> A: Your computer is kind of slow.　B: Yeah, and I paid good money for it, too.

　　現在來學習動詞 put。在商業英文中，put 的用法相當多，chunks、word partnerships、片語動詞或慣用語裡都會用到，但卻不易掌握。然而這個動詞值得學，因為 put 的使用頻率很高，也非常有用。我們就從最常見的 word partnerships 學起吧。

　　大致上含 put 的 word partnerships 可依其意思大略地分成六組：

　　第一組是寫或記錄的意思，如：Let me put you on our mailing list.。
　　第二組是開始運作的意思，如：We need to put this into effect by next week.。

第三組有表明優先考量的意思，如：We need to put the client first at all times.。
第四組則含有負面意義，如：My boss is really putting pressure on me to resign.。
第五組可處理人際關係，如：I'm putting you in charge of the team.。
第六組則是搭配名詞，以表達比較抽象的意義，如：Let's try to put this problem into perspective here.。

TASK 7.5

請將下面含 put 的 word partnerships 分門別類，寫在下面的表格中，見範例。

| put | · a stop to sth.
· a strain on resources/capacity/cashflow
· oneself out for sb.
· pressure on sb.
· sb. in a difficult /embarrassing/awkward position
· sb. in charge of n.p.
· sb. in the picture
· sb. in touch with n.p.
· sb. on a mailing list/waiting list | · sth. into effect
· sth. into perspective
· sth. into service
· sth. on file
· sth. onto the market
· sth. to good use
· sth. to one side
· sth. to use
· sth. to work
· the matter right |

Record	Abstract Meaning
put sb. on a mailing list/waiting list	*put the matter right*

Negative Meaning	Begin Functioning
put pressure on sb.	*put sth. to work*

Relationships	Prioritize
put sb. in touch with n.p.	*put sth. to one side*

Word List
- strain [stren] n. 拉緊；繃緊
- awkward [ˋɔkwəd] adj. 難爲情的；不自在的

答案

請比較你的答案和下面的必備語庫。

商用英文必備語庫 7.3 含 put 的 word partnerships　MP3 51

Record（做記錄）	Abstract Meaning（抽象意義）
· put sth. on file · put sb. on a mailing list/waiting list	· put sb. in the picture · put sth. into perspective · put the matter right
Negative Meaning（負面意義）	**Begin Functioning**（開始運作）
· put a stop to sth. · put a strain on resources/capacity/ cashflow · put sb. in a(n) difficult/embarrassing/ awkward position · put pressure on sb.	· put sth. into service · put sth. into effect · put sth. onto the market · put sth. to work · put sth. to use
Relationships（人際關係）	**Prioritize**（表明優先考量）
· put oneself out for sb. · put sb. in charge of n.p. · put sb. in touch with n.p.	· put sth. first · put sth. to good use · put sth. to one side

◆ Put sb. in the picture 是英式用法，意為「將目前發生的事解釋給某人知道」。

　　好，現在來鞏固我們在本節中學到的 word partnerships 吧。

TASK 7.6

連連看，請將下面未完成的句子組合成完整句。有些句子的答案不只一個，見範例。

A

Can you put	my promises. That's why people trust me.
Did we pay	by direct debit, as the amount is the same.
How much rent	me in the picture and tell me what's going on?
I always keep	in an embarrassing position when he kissed me.
I usually pay my supplier	do you pay on your office?
I was put	capital gains tax last year?

B

I won't forget your help. I'll keep	a visit to the factory next week.
I'd like to pay	on file.
I'll put you	myself out for them. They never appreciate me.
I'll put your request	it in mind.
I'm going to put this report	in touch with our supplier. They are very good.
I'm not going to put	to one side and concentrate on the budget.

C

Keep the customer	me to work on the new project. I'm very excited.
My boss has put	a strain on our capacity. It's too big.
Please keep me	to good use. Don't waste it.
Please pay attention	to all matters related to this important client.
Please put the extra budget	informed on the situation while I am away.
This big order is putting	advised about the progress of the order.

Word List   • direct debit 直接扣款

D	We are going to have to pay ◆	◆ a stop to card fraud. It's costing us millions.
We are now in a position to pay ◆		◆ the loan for the new plant.
We finally managed to pay off ◆		◆ taxes this year.
We need to keep ◆		◆ to clean the windows. They're filthy.
We need to pay someone ◆		◆ the books better. The inspector is not happy.
We need to put ◆		◆ back the amount owed.

E	We paid ◆	◆ You put the matter right.
We usually pay ◆		◆ in full, or in installments?
We're working on putting ◆		◆ you updated on the location of the hipment.
Our new tracking system keeps ◆		◆ the new design onto the market by June.
Would you like to pay ◆		◆ a premium price for early delivery.
You caused the problem. ◆		◆ a penalty becausewe entered the market too soon.

答案 🎧

由於有些句子有多個可能的答案，請參考以下的建議答案。

A	Can you put	◆ me in the picture and tell me what's going on?
Did we pay		◆ capital gains tax last year?
How much rent		◆ do you pay on your office?
I always keep		◆ my promises. That's why people trust me.
I usually pay my supplier		◆ by direct debit, as the amount is the same.
I was put		◆ in an embarrassing position when he kissed me.

Word List
• fraud [frɔd] n. 詐欺
• filthy [ˈfɪlθɪ] adj. 髒的

B I won't forget your help. I'll keep ◆ it in mind.

I'd like to pay ◆ a visit to the factory next week.

I'll put you ◆ in touch with our supplier. They are very good.

I'll put your request ◆ on file.

I'm going to put this report ◆ to one side and concentrate on the budget.

I'm not going to put ◆ myself out for them. They never appreciate me.

C Keep the customer ◆ advised about the progress of the order.

My boss has put ◆ me to work on the new project. I'm very excited.

Please keep me ◆ informed on the situation while I am away.

Please pay attention ◆ to all matters related to this important client.

Please put the extra budget ◆ to good use. Don't waste it.

This big order is putting ◆ a strain on our capacity. It's too big.

D We are going to have to pay ◆ taxes this year.

We are now in a position to pay ◆ back the amount owed.

We finally managed to pay off ◆ the loan for the new plant.

We need to keep ◆ the books better. The inspector is not happy.

We need to pay someone ◆ to clean the windows. They're filthy.

We need to put ◆ a stop to card fraud. It's costing us millions.

E We paid ◆ a penalty because we entered the market too soon.

We usually pay ◆ a premium price for early delivery.

We're working on putting ◆ the new design onto the market by June.

Our new tracking system keeps ◆ you updated on the location of the shipment.

Would you like to pay ◆ in full, or in installments?

You caused the problem. ◆ You put the matter right.

片語動詞

在接下來的一節中，我們要再學一些英文寫作和口說中會用到的片語動詞來處理工作上某些層面的事務。本節的模式有些和前面第四單元一樣，因此建議你在往下學習的同時，溫習一下那些片語動詞。

◤ 處理採購和銷售的 6 個片語動詞 ◥

TASK 7.7

請研讀下面的必備語庫。

商用英文必備語庫 7.4 處理採購和銷售的片語動詞　　　MP3 52

work sth. out 計算成本或價錢	▶ I'm working my budget out for next year.
work out to sth. 總計	▶ Your final bill works out to $1,570.
interest sb. in sth. 想推薦某物給某人，希望他人能購買	▶ Can I interest you in our new product?
be interested in sth. 對某事有興趣	▶ We're interested in forming an alliance with your company.
put sth. at (#) 猜測或粗略計算價錢	▶ I put the final cost at $150,000. What have you got?
put in an order 下訂單	▶ If you put in your order before the end of the month, we'll give you a discount.

TASK 7.8

請用上面學到的片語動詞，完成下面的對話，接著聽 MP3 來檢查答案。 MP3 53

A: While we're here, we also are interested (1)＿＿＿＿ the XYZ1. Can we (2)＿＿＿＿ an order for 1,000 units for that as well?

B: Of course you can. However, can I (3)＿＿＿＿ you in the XYZ2, which is a more up-to-date model of the XYZ1 and has more functionality? Here, take a look.

A: Hm, yes, that is good. OK, we'll take a thousand units of the XYZ2 then, instead of the XYZ1. What does that (4)＿＿＿＿?

B: OK, let me just (5)＿＿＿＿ it ＿＿＿＿. Mmm. Er. OK. I (6)＿＿＿＿ that ＿＿＿＿ $125,000. Is that OK?

A: Wow, that's a lot. Can you give me a discount?

答案

特別注意 it 和 that 在句子中的位置，這些受詞有時會分開動詞與介系詞。

如果你在上面練習中寫的答案與我的答案不同，請回頭看必備語庫 7.4，確定所有的片語動詞都完全懂了，也知道如何運用了。

(1) in　　(2) put in　　(3) interest　　(4) work out to　　(5) work/out　　(6) put/at

---

處理問題的 7 個片語動詞

TASK 7.9

請看下面的必備語庫。

商用英文必備語庫 7.5 處理問題的片語動詞 MP3 54

| work around sth.
儘管出現問題阻礙了你，
你仍想辦法處理 | We haven't got the resources we need?
Well, we'll just have to work around it. |

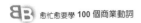

use up sth. 耗光某物	▶	We need to get some more paper for the copier. Somebody just used up the last box.
ask around 四處詢問	▶	Let's try to find a cheaper supplier. Let me ask around.
put up with sth. 容忍某事	▶	We'll just have to put up with his rudeness since he's such an important client.
put sth. aside 暫時擱置某事	▶	Let's put this aside for now and talk about it after the meeting.
put sth.back 拖延某事	▶	This mechanical failure is going to put the project back about two months.
put sth.off 延後某事	▶	Let's put off this project until we can find a buyer for it.

TASK 7.10

MP3 55

請利用上述片語動詞完成下面的對話，然後聽 MP3 來檢查答案。

John: OK, let's move on to the next item on the agenda now. Mary, do you have anything to report on your project? I understand that you've been having problems with it.

Mary: Yes, John we have actually. The main problem, really, is that we've (1)＿＿＿＿＿ all the raw materials we need. Someone in the purchasing department didn't order enough, and now we don't have any more. Also, our supplier doesn't have any available now. This will probably (2)＿＿＿＿＿ the project ＿＿＿＿＿ a bit. I'm recommending that we (3)＿＿＿＿＿ the scheduled completion date for six months.

John: OK, well, that's rather serious isn't it? Is there any way you can (4)＿＿＿＿＿ the shortage?

Mary: Well, no, not really. Without the raw materials, we can't go ahead with the manufacturing. Everything else is ready.

John: I see. Well, don't worry, we'll (5)＿＿＿＿＿ and see if we can find any other suppliers with enough of the raw materials we need. I'm sure we can

(6)_____ something _____. In the meantime, I guess we'll just have to (7)_____ the delay. OK, let's (8)_____ that _____ now and go on to the next item on the agenda, which is the company pension fund.

答案 🔊

小心動詞時態，當你專心檢查意思、介系詞和受詞位置的時候很容易忘記這一點。

(1) used up   (2) put/back   (3) put off   (4) work around   (5) ask around
(6) work/out (7) put up with (8) put/aside

處理工作的 5 個片語動詞

TASK 7.11

請研讀下面的必備語庫。

商用英文必備語庫 7.6 處理工作的片語動詞   MP3 56

work on sth. 處理某項工作	▶	I'm working on a new design for the client.
work towards sth. 努力達成某目標	▶	We're working towards being the market leader within five years.
put forward sth. 提出某想法或議題	▶	He put forward a very interesting proposal for reducing our labor costs.
put effort into sth. 努力做某事	▶	I know you've put a lot of effort into the project. That's why it was successful.
put together sth. 組成團隊；寫報告	▶	We're putting together a new sales team. I'm putting together a report on our recycling program.

Word List   • pension [ˈpɛnʃən] n. 退休金

TASK 7.12

請利用上述片語動詞，完成下面的電子郵件。

Dear Oliver,

Congratulations on your success with the ABC account! We are all very happy with your performance. I know that you (1)_____ a lot of effort _____ the pitch, and we are all impressed. I would like you to (2)_____ the Lika project now. Please read the attached report and then spend some time thinking about how you want to approach this. Once you're ready, I would like you to (3)_____ your proposal to the board on the 1ˢᵗ of next month. Also, can you (4)_____ your own team for this? Choose whoever you think would be best for the job. We'd like to (5)_____ completing this project by the end of the year.

Please don't hesitate to ask me if you have any questions or if you need any more support.

George

答案

(1) put/into   (2) work on   (3) put forward   (4) put together   (5) work towards

常　見　錯　誤　>　>　**use**	
錯　誤	正　確
I am used to speak English at work.	I am used to speaking English at work.
I used speaking English at work.	I used to speak English at work.
・Be used to sth./Ving 意指「現在習慣了某事」；used to V 意指「過去習於⋯⋯」，但現在已沒有這個習慣了。 ・請勿將 be used to 以及 used to 的意思和用法搞混了。	

商業慣用語

　　現在則來學一些含 pay、keep 和 put 的 word partnerships，這些 word partner-ships 屬於慣用語，較不容易記得，得多花點心思。

TASK 7.13

請研讀下面的必備語庫以及例句。

商用英文必備語庫 7.7 含 keep 的慣用語 MP3 57

| keep | · your cards close to your chest
· an eye out for sth.
· your eyes peeled
· your hands clean
· sb. guessing
· a low profile
· up with the times
· sb. on their toes | 將商業計劃保密
密切注意某事
密切注意某事
不接受賄賂或捲入貪污
讓某人猜測
避免引人注意
跟上潮流；注意時事
不讓別人知道你下一步要做什麼 |

 1. A good CEO always keeps his cards close to his chest, and keeps his rivals guessing about his business strategy. That keeps them on their toes!

2. I always keep an eye out for new ideas.

3. When I go to China, I keep my eyes peeled for new business opportunities.

4. Honest people always keeps their hands clean, no matter what is offered to them.

5. We must keep up with the times and produce products which are attractive to young people.

6. I always try to keep a low profile in my company so that my boss doesn't ask me to do more work.

商用英文必備語庫 7.8 含 put 的慣用語 MP3 58

| put | · all your eggs in one basket
· out feelers | 孤注一擲
隨口提議來測試他人的反應 |

put	· your feet up	坐下來，放輕鬆
	· your finger on sth.	掌握某件事情的重點
	· your foot down	運用個人特權阻止某事
	· sb.'s heads together	共同策劃
	· your money where your mouth is	言行一致（通常指付錢）
	· your neck on the line	以個人做擔保
	· sth. in motion	開始運作；處理
	· two and two together	發現兩件獨立事件的關連

1. A good investment strategy is to avoid putting all your eggs in one basket. You should invest in lots of different markets to reduce your risk.

2. I am putting out feelers for a new job. I want to move on.

3. I have to sit down and put my feet up for a bit. I'm exhausted!

4. I just can't seem to put my finger on the problem.

5. My boss put his foot down. No more expense claims over $100.

6. Let's put our heads together and see if we can come up with some better advertising copy.

7. He always puts his money where his mouth is and supports good causes by donating generously.

8. I'm not going to put my neck on the line for you. Sorry.

9. Let's see if we can put this idea in motion.

10. When I saw them having coffee together for the third time, I put two and two together.

商用英文必備語庫 **7.9** 含 pay 的慣用語 ⌒MP3 59

pay	· sb.'s dues	善盡職責
	· your (own) way	自力更生，不依賴他人
	· through the nose	付太多錢買某物
	· top dollar	花了一大筆錢
	· the price	付出代價
	· for itself	某物賺進的錢已經打平成本了
	· sb. back	報復某人

1. I've worked in this department for eight years. I've paid my dues and I really think I deserve a promotion.

2. When I was in college I always paid my own way. I never asked my parents for money.

3. I paid through the nose for my new car. I even paid top dollar for a custom paint job!

4. We didn't do enough research and now we' re paying the price. No one is buying the product.

5. The new machinery we invested in is already paying for itself.

6. I got fired because of her. I'll pay her back, though! You just watch!

✎ 語庫小叮嚀

◆ 請記得我在第四單元中強調的，學習和使用慣用語時，務必確定每一個字都正確無誤。慣用語的任何一個字改變了，就會失去意義，變成沒有意義的怪片語。

◆ 此外，也請記住我在第四單元中的叮嚀，慣用語中只有一個詞可以改變，那就是動詞，動詞的時態和形式請務必正確。

TASK 7.14

請利用你在本節中學到的慣用語來改正下列句子。

1. I always keep my card close to my chest.

_____

2. I can't put my thumb on it.

_____

3. I put one and one together and realized what the problem was.

_____

4. I'm not going to put my neck in the line for you.

_____

5. It was really cheap. I paid bottom dollar for it.

_____

6. It will take some time for the new equipment to pay on itself.

_____

7. Keep your eye peeled for any opportunities over there.

_____

8. My boss always keeps us on our toe. We never know what he is going to do or say next.

_____

9. My mother finds it hard to keep up to the times.

_____

10. Sit down and relax. You look tired. Put your foot up here.

_____

11. The CEO put his feet down and stopped all business trips.

_____

12. We are now paying a price for our earlier lack of care.

_____

答案 🎧
請看下面提供的答案。

1. I always keep my cards close to my chest.

2. I can't put my finger on it.

3. I put two and two together and realized what the problem was.

4. I'm not going to put my neck on the line for you.

5. It was not cheap. I paid top dollar for it.

6. It will take some time for the new equipment to pay for itself.

7. Keep your eyes peeled for any opportunities over there.

8. My boss always keeps us on our toes. We never know what he is going to do or say next.

9. My mother finds it hard to keep up with the times.

10. Sit down and relax. You look tired. Put your feet up.

11. The CEO put his foot down and stopped all business trips.

12. We are now paying the price for our earlier lack of care.

TASK 7.15

請研讀以下 set-phrases 及其意思。

商用英文必備語庫 7.10 慣用語 set-phrases

 MP3 60

· Let me put my cards on the table.	讓我告訴你我最終的決定。
· Put a lid on it!	閉嘴！
· Put a sock in it!	閉嘴！
· I wouldn't put it past him!	那種討人厭的事他就是做得出來！
· Pay up!	給錢！
· There'll be hell to pay.	我們有大麻煩囉。
· If you pay peanuts, you get monkeys.	微薪養蠢才。
· Keep this under your hat!	請勿洩漏此秘密給其他人知道。
· Keep your shirt on!	不要生氣，放輕鬆！
· Keep your pecker up!	打起精神！

TASK 7.16

MP3 61

請閱讀下列對話，並利用語庫 7.10 中學到的慣用語填入空白處，接著聽 MP3 檢查答案。

Conversation 1

A: I'd better get back to the office. Otherwise, there'll be hell to pay.

B: What? You think your boss might fire you for being late back from lunch?

A: He might. (1)＿＿＿＿＿＿＿＿＿＿＿＿＿＿＿＿！

B: Geez. What kind of a boss is he?

A: Well, (2)＿＿＿＿＿＿＿＿＿＿＿＿＿＿, but he's connected to gangsters, so I don't want to make him angry. It's very depressing. I really want to leave but I can't. I don't know what to do.

B: Hey, come on. (3)＿＿＿＿＿＿＿＿＿＿＿＿＿. It can't be that bad. It's just a job!

Conversation 2

A: This is a robbery! (4)＿＿＿＿＿＿＿＿＿＿＿＿＿！

B: (5)＿＿＿＿＿＿＿＿＿＿＿＿！ I'll pay you next week! I get my annual

bonus then, plus some money from my in-laws and some insurance policies are maturing.

A: (6) _____! Pay me now!

B: Well, I'd love to, but my debit card was eaten by the ATM, my credit card is over the limit, and I've only got change for the bus fare home. Will you take a check?

A: Oh, (7) _____!

Conversation 3

A: (8) _____ here. I can offer you NT$35,000 per month. And that's my final offer.

B: Is that a part time job?

A: No, full time. But I'll let you have the weekends off!

B: Well, (9) _____. What can I say?

A: Do you accept?

B: Of course not. Not at that price. Do I look like a monkey?

答案 🔊

如果有聽不懂的地方，可以參閱下方的解答。

(1) I wouldn't put it past him

(2) keep this under your shirt

(3) Keep your pecker up

(4) Pay up

(5) Keep your shirt on

(6) Put a sock in it

(7) put a lid on it

(8) Let me put my cards on the table

(9) if you pay peanuts, you get monkeys

　　好，本詞彙單元的學習到此結束。在繼續往下學習之前，請回到本單元前面的學習清單，確認所有的學習目標都確實掌握了。

　　在第二篇的前面，我曾請你為本篇的 25 個動詞造句，然後勾出覺得難寫的句子，現在來看一看到本篇末你學到了多少。

學習評量

第二篇 結尾 Task 1

請再次研讀下面的動詞，並運用你在本篇中學到的字串，為每個動詞造一個句子。

learn	offer	discuss	continue	request
regret	interest	work	say	become
provide	understand	keep	put	confirm
use	hear	believe	include	suggest
write	ask	attach	pay	follow

第二篇 結尾 Task 2

請比較你在本篇中為開頭 Task 1 與結尾 Task 1 所造的句子，並思考以下問題：

- 你學到了什麼？
- 比起開頭 Task 1，你寫結尾 Task 1 時感覺輕鬆了多少？
- 你覺得在運用哪幾個動詞時還有問題？為什麼？
- 你進步了多少？

PART 3

Biz
Verbs

導讀

在此我們要學的是第三組 25 個動詞，如下。在開始學習之前，請先做與前面兩篇中同樣的兩個 Tasks，等本篇學習結束時便可看出自己進步了多少。

第三篇 開頭 Task 1

請看下列語庫中的動詞，並為每個動詞造一個句子。

第三組25個動詞

· arrange	· return	· inform	· talk	· allow
· tell	· go	· hold	· decide	· apologize
· contact	· mention	· agree	· join	· read
· hesitate	· set	· serve	· bring	· prepare
· consider	· enjoy	· complete	· require	· leave

第三篇 開頭 Task 2

請勾出覺得使用上有困難的動詞，以及難造的句子。

Unit 8 寫作

引言與學習目標

在本單元中我們的學習重點是在寫作中運用這 25 個動詞，包括將 set-phrases 運用在電子郵件中以溝通工作上的業務或維持和收件者的關係，以及用 chunks 增加用語的準確度。

本單元結束時，各位應達成的學習目標如下：

❑ 學到許多用於客戶關係管理的 set-phrases。
❑ 用新學的 set-phrases 做練習。
❑ 學到許多動詞 chunks。
❑ 學到許多雙受詞的動詞 chunks。
❑ 在寫作時有能力更準確、更有自信地運用新學到的動詞。
❑ 知道一些常見的寫作錯誤並知道該如何避免。

Set-Phrases

在本節中，我們將學習更多可用於電子郵件開頭和結尾的 set-phrases，功能包括有提供服務與邀請、提點、表達歉意以及敬請對方不吝給予意見等。

表達願提供更好服務的 Set-Phrases

良好的服務是客戶關係管理的重要環節，良好服務的要點是讓他人感受到你為提供優良服務所付出的努力。經常邀請客戶參加公司舉辦的活動，甚至參加你生活中的私人活動，如派對、家庭聚會等，都是與客戶建立和維持良好關係的方法。那麼，現在我就教你一些適當的用語。

TASK 8.1

請將這些 set-phrases 分門別類，填入下表中。

1. Can you join me for n.p.?
2. Do be assured of our desire to serve you well at all times.
3. Do join us!
4. I hope we can serve you better.
5. I hope you can join me (for n.p.).
6. I hope you will be able to join me (for n.p.).
7. I hope you will join me (for n.p.).
8. I hope you'll let us serve you for many years to come.
9. I invite you to join n.p.
10. It has been our pleasure to serve you.

11. It is always our pleasure to serve you.

12. Please join me (for n.p.).

13. Please join us (on n.p.).

14. Thank you for the opportunity to serve you.

15. We appreciate having the opportunity to serve you.

16. We are always available to serve you.

17. We hope this change will serve your needs better.

18. We look forward to continuing to serve you from our new location.

19. We look forward to continuing to serve you.

20. We look forward to the opportunity to serve you again.

21. We shall endeavor to serve you even better in the coming year.

22. We will try our best to serve you in any way possible.

23. We've been pleased to serve you this past year.

24. Why not join us?

25. You're invited to join me (for n.p.).

Serving	Inviting

答案 🎧

請利用下面的必備語庫檢查答案，「提供服務」一欄裡特別加註了各類字串的使用時機，請仔細研讀。

商用英文必備語庫 **8.1** 提供服務與邀請的 set-phrases　　　　MP3 62

Serving （提供服務）
當客戶對你的服務表示滿意時：
· Do be assured of our desire to serve you well at all times.
· It is always our pleasure to serve you.

Word List　· endeavor [ɪnˋdɛvə] v. 努力……

· We are always available to serve you.

· Thank you for the opportunity to serve you.

· We appreciate having the opportunity to serve you.

· It has been our pleasure to serve you.

欲表達希望未來能繼續和對方保持生意往來時：

· I hope you'll let us serve you for many years to come.

· We will try our best to serve you in any way possible.

· We look forward to continuing to serve you.

· We look forward to the opportunity to serve you again.

欲在年底時向客戶表達謝意，感謝他們一年來的惠顧時：

· We shall endeavor to serve you even better in the coming year.

· We've been pleased to serve you this past year.

告知客戶，公司即使有了變化，也不會影響對客戶的服務時：

· We hope this change will serve your needs better.

· We look forward to continuing to serve you from our new location.

告知客戶，問題已解決並不會再發生時：

· I hope we can serve you better.

Inviting（邀請）	
· Can you join me for n.p.?	· I invite you to join n.p.
· Do join us!	· Please join me (for n.p.).
· I hope you can join me (for n.p.).	· Please join us (on n.p.)
· I hope you will be able to join me (for n.p.).	· Why not join us?
· I hope you will join me (for n.p.).	· You're invited to join me (for n.p.).

✎　語庫小叮嚀

◆ 請注意，提供服務的 set-phrases 中，最好都是用 we 和 our。這是因為你是以公司代表的身分在寫信，此外，若使用可以代表公司全體的 we 或 our，聽起來更是誠意十足。

◆ 你應該也發現到，邀請的 set-phrases 中可以用 I 和 me，也可以用 we 和 us。這裡的考量在於你是以個人還是公司的名義邀請，同時也得考量你和客戶的關係，如果彼此熟悉，並已有長久的生意關係，可選擇使用 I 和 me 等較為親近的語氣。

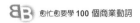
TASK 8.2

請利用語庫 8.1 來改正下面句子中的錯誤，見範例。

1. We'll be ready to serve without delay.

   We'll be ready to serve you without delay.

2. I hope you can join for lunch.

3. It is always our pleasure to service you.

4. Please join us on the anniversary party.

5. We'll be ready serve you without delay.

6. Please join me for we will have lunch.

答案 🔊

請見下列所提供的參考答案，相信這個 Task 並不難，它的目的主要在測試你是否都注意到了 set-phrases 中的小細節。

2. I hope you can join us for lunch.
3. It is always our pleasure to serve you.
4. Please join us for the anniversary party.
5. We'll be ready to serve you without delay.
6. Please join me for lunch.

　　好，現在繼續往下研讀，學習如何在電子郵件中使用提點字串。電子郵件其實就像一種對話方式，所謂提點，就是在對話裡提到之前在電子郵件、會議或電話中談論過的事情。在接下來的章節，我們將學習如何向對方提點之前談過的事情。

用於提點的 **Word Partnerships**

請研讀下面的必備語庫和例句，然後練習自己造句。

商用英文必備語庫 8.2　含 mention 的 word partnerships　(MP3 63)

· I · You · As I · As you · … the n.p. · … be · … as	**mentioned**	· that + n. clause · the n.p. to sb. · the sth. in sth. · to sb. how adj. · something about sth. · in my report · before	· above · during n.p. · earlier · in paragraph X · in item X · on page X · in our email of X · in your email
· … the below- · … the above-		· n.p.	

 1. As I mentioned before, we need to take action immediately.

2. Please see the above-mentioned table for more information on this.

3. I mentioned the problem in my report.

4. You mentioned that you would be willing to help.

5. As you mentioned during our meeting, we look forward to receiving your report.

6. You mentioned to me how interested you were in joining our team.

7. He didn't mention your request to me.

8. Leslie mentioned something about how slow your computer was. Is there anything I can do?

9. The figures mentioned on page 10 of the report are not accurate.

Word List　· table [ˋtebl] n. 表格

193

✎ 語庫小叮嚀

◆ 請注意，由於每次提點的事項都是已經發生了的事情，因此在使用 mention 時，應該用簡單過去式來表示，否定語氣即是 did not mention。

◆ 請注意，使用 As I/you mentioned ... 時，後面必須先加逗號，然後再接另一個子句。

◆ 在 ... mentioned something about sth. 中，第一個 something 指的是所提到的一些具體要點，而不是可以替換的受詞如 sth.。你可以用這個 set-phrase 表示需要更多的具體資訊。

請改正下列句子中的錯誤。請小心，因為有些句子有多個錯誤。

1. As I mentioned it before, we need to take action immediately.
   As I mentioned before, we need to take action immediately.

2. As I mentioned about it before, we need to move quickly on this one.

3. I mentioned about we want to diversify.

4. I mentioned Morris how pleased we were with your work.

5. As I mentioned during the interview we cannot offer you a position soon.

6. Please see the below-mention diagram.

7. As you mention something about your plans, I am interested in knowing more.

8. The proposal mentioned Item 12 has been cancelled.

9. As mentioned their email, they cancelled the project.

Word List　• diversify [daɪˋvɝsə‚faɪ] v. 多樣化；多角化經營

答案

請參考下面提供的答案。如不懂為何你寫的句子有誤，可回頭仔細看語庫 8.2，仔細研讀裡面的小細節。

2. As I mentioned before, we need to move quickly on this one.
3. I mentioned that we want to diversify.
4. I mentioned to Morris how pleased we were with your work.
5. As I mentioned during the interview, we cannot offer you a position soon.
6. Please see the below-mentioned diagram.
7. As you mentioned something about your plans, I am interested in knowing more.
8. The proposal mentioned in Item 12 has been cancelled.
9. As mentioned in their email, they cancelled the project.

常 見 錯 誤 > > **mention**	
錯 誤	正 確
You mentioned about the project.	You mentioned the project.
· 千萬別說 mention about，這是中式英文！	

接著我們來學一些以致歉、希望他人不吝給予意見為目的的 set-phrases。

表達歉意的 Set-Phrases

我們先從含 apologize 的開頭和結尾 set-phrases 開始。

TASK 8.5

請研讀下面的必備語庫以及語庫小叮嚀。

商用英文必備語庫 8.3　表達歉意的 set-phrases　　　MP3 64

· Apologies for the error.

· Apologies for the delay.

· I apologize for any inconvenience.

· I apologize for the inconvenience.

· I apologize for this unfortunate error.

· I apologize for this regrettable error.

· We apologize for any inconvenience.

· We apologize to you for any inconvenience we may have caused.

· Please accept our apologies for any inconvenience we may have caused you.

· We apologize for any inconvenience this may cause you.

· Apologies for the delay in getting back to you, but …

· Apologies for the delay in Ving …

✎　語庫小叮嚀

◆ 最後兩個 set-phrases 在有事無法早點回信時，可於電子郵件的開頭使用。

◆ 其他所有的 set-phrases 則較適合用於電子郵件的結尾。寫電子郵件處理問題或為公司所造成的錯誤致歉時，這些 set-phrases 便非常好用。

◆ We apologize to you for any inconvenience we may have caused.
如果在過去曾為對方帶來不便，想向對方道歉時可以用這一句。

◆ We apologize for any inconvenience this may cause you.
如果預知將來會為對方帶來不便，想預先提醒對方並先致歉，可以使用這一句。

常　見　錯　誤　>　> **apologize**	
錯　誤	正　確
I apologize for our making this mistake.	I apologize for our mistake.
	I apologize for making this mistake.

· 千萬不要用 apologize for our Ving，除非裡面的 Ving 是動名詞當名詞用，否則動詞前面無需再加一個所有格。請用 apologize for n.p. 或 apologize for Ving。

· 美式拼法是 apologize，英式拼法是 apologise，兩者都對。

　　目前為止，你在本書中學過的 set-phrases 大部分都是放在句首，或構成完整的句子。現在我們要學習的 set-phrases 則通常是放在句尾，同時也可電子郵件的結尾。

敬請不吝給予意見的 Set-Phrases

TASK 8.6

請研讀下面的必備語庫與例句。

商用英文必備語庫 8.4　敬請不吝給予意見的 set-phrases（1）　MP3 65

- ..., please don't hesitate to ask me.
- ..., please don't hesitate to call me.
- ..., please don't hesitate to call me on/at X.
- ..., please don't hesitate to call on me.
- ..., please don't hesitate to contact me.
- ..., please don't hesitate to do so.
- ..., please don't hesitate to get in touch.
- ..., please don't hesitate to get in touch with me.
- ..., please don't hesitate to give me a call.
- ..., please don't hesitate to inform me.
- ..., please don't hesitate to let me know.
- ..., please don't hesitate to telephone me.
- ..., please don't hesitate to write to me.

EX
1. If you have any questions about this, please do not hesitate to ask me.
2. If you have any concerns about this, please don't hesitate to let me know.
3. If you need help with this, please do not hesitate to call me on/at 2005-6789.
4. If you have any problems with this, please don't hesitate to get in touch.
5. If you want to call me about this, please don't hesitate to do so.

🖎　語庫小叮嚀

- ◆ Call me on/at X 是說對方「可透過某電話號碼找到我」的意思，X 代表的是電話號碼，美式用 at；英式用 on。Call on me 則是「請對方來拜訪我」的意思。
- ◆ 當然，如果希望使用較正式的語氣，可以用 do not 取代 don't。
- ◆ 通常這些 set-phrases 是放在 if 句的後半部。請再閱讀一次上述例句，以更加了解該如何使用。

TASK 8.7

請研讀下面的必備語庫與例句。

商用英文必備語庫 8.5　敬請不吝給予意見的 set-phrases（2）　MP3 66

> · Please (feel free to) contact me on/at X.
>
> · Please (feel free to) contact me at any time.
>
> · Please (feel free to) contact me at your convenience.
>
> · Please contact me ASAP.
>
> · Please (feel free to) contact me about n.p. ...
>
> · Please (feel free to) contact me again.
>
> · Please (feel free to) contact me directly.
>
> · Please (feel free to) contact me personally.
>
> · Please (feel free to) contact me immediately.
>
> · Please (feel free to) contact me if I can be of further assistance.
>
> · Please (feel free to) contact me if you have any further questions.

TASK 8.8

請改正下列句子的錯誤，見範例。

1. Please contact to me if you need to.
   Please contact me if you need to.

2. If you need help please do not hesitate to get in touch with me.

3. Please feel free contact me at any time if you're not clear about it.

4. Please contact with me if I can be of further assistance.

5. Please contact me about we need to deal with the situation.

6. If the client is not happy with this, please do not hesitate inform me.

7. If you encounter any problems, please don't hesitate to getting in touch with me.

8. If you need to take a few days leave, do not hesitate to you should do so.

答案 🎧

請參考下列提供的答案。如果不了解為什麼有些句子會有錯，可回頭再仔細閱讀一次必備語庫，並注意其中的小細節。

2. If you need help, please do not hesitate to get in touch with me.
3. Please feel free to contact me at any time if you're not clear about it.
4. Please contact me if I can be of further assistance.
5. Please contact me about the situation.
6. If the client is not happy with this, please do not hesitate to inform me.
7. If you encounter any problems, please don't hesitate to get in touch with me.
8. If you need to take a few days leave, do not hesitate to do so.

　　好，現在我們來利用你在本節的五大語庫中所學到的字串做一道 Task，以加深你對這些字串的印象，然後再繼續往下一節學習。

TASK 8.9

請用你在本節中學到的 set-phrases 完成以下電子郵件。注意，有些空格的正確答案不只一個，盡量把你所知道的答案都寫出來，這是測驗你實力的大好機會。

Dear Lulu,

Thanks for your email. Yes, I did get your previous email, and I forwarded your inquiry to the relevant department a few days ago. (1)_____ before, they will contact you soon about this issue. (2)_____.

Dear Nathan,

Please be aware that all our systems are currently down for 24 hours for maintenance. This means that your delivery will be delayed. (3)_____.

Dear John,

I had a very good meeting with the client yesterday. (4)_____ to their managing director. He said he was interested in knowing more about it. (5)_____ . I want to get back to him while he is still interested.

Dear Mr. Tsai,

Thank you for your email and for your kind words. I'm very glad that you found our service useful. (6)_____ .

Dear Joyce,

I had a meeting with the senior analyst of XYS Bank last night. (7)_____ a change in your company's credit rating. If you would like to know more about this, (8)_____ .

Dear Mike,

(9)_____ responding to you, but I have been away. I am a bit confused, as your question about the project schedule was covered in my report. Perhaps you didn't get the last page. (10)_____ , we think it will take about three months. (11)_____ .

Dear Ms. Wu,

As you may know, we have moved our company headquarters to Kaohsiung to take advantage of lower transport costs as we expand our business. We will be having a party to celebrate the move and ten successful years of doing business. (12)_____ .

答案 🔊

請看下面提供的答案。記住，下列雖然提供了多種可能的答案，但在正式寫電子郵件時，可依據你和收件者的關係和電子郵件的內容來調整你的語氣。

1	As I mentioned			please don't hesitate to call me
2	Please (feel free to) contact me at any time.		8	please don't hesitate to call me on/at x
	Please (feel free to) contact me if I can be of further assistance.			please don't hesitate to contact me
	Please (feel free to) contact me if you have any further questions.			please don't hesitate to get in touch
3	We apologize for any inconvenience this may cause you.			please don't hesitate to get in touch with me
4	I mentioned your idea			please don't hesitate to give me a call
	I mentioned your proposal			please don't hesitate to inform me
5	Please contact me immediately.			please don't hesitate to let me know
	Please contact me ASAP.		9	Apologies for the delay in
	Please contact me about this.		10	As I mentioned in Item 12
6	It is always our pleasure to serve you.			As I mentioned on page 12
	We are always available to serve you.		11	Please (feel free to) contact me if I can be of further assistance.
	We appreciate having the opportunity to serve you.			Please (feel free to) contact me if you have any further questions.
	It has been our pleasure to serve you.		12	I hope you can join us.
7	He mentioned something about			I hope you will be able to join us.
				I hope you will join us.

常 見 錯 誤 ＞ ＞ contact

錯 誤	正 確
Please contact with me.	Please contact me./ Please get in contact with me.

· Contact 是動詞的時候，後面無須再接介系詞 with，或者你可以使用 contact 的名詞 chunk: get in contact with。

動詞 Chunks

　　在本節中，我們要學的一些字串模式和前面兩個寫作單元的一樣，但也會學習一些新的用語。請仔細研讀下面的表格，然後再做 Task，以確定掌握了新的字串模式。

TASK 8.10

請將下列動詞 chunks 分門別類，填入下表中，見範例。

1. allow sb. to V
2. arrange n.p.
4. be prepared to V
5. be required to V
6. complete n.p.
7. agree to V
8. consider n.p.
9. consider that + n. clause
10. contact n.p.

11. decide wh-to V
12. decide that + n. clause
13. decide to V
14. enjoy n.p.
15. enjoy Ving
16. inform sb. that + n. clause
17. prepare to V
18. read n.p.

19. allow n.p.
20. require n.p.
21. require sb. to V
22. require that + n. clause
23. tell sb. wh-clause
24. tell sb. wh-to V
25. tell sb. that + n. clause
26. agree that + n. clause

V + n.p	be Ved to V	V sb. that
complete n.p.	be allowed to V	inform sb. that + n. clause

V sb. wh-	V to V	V Ving
tell sb. wh-clause	prepare to V	enjoy Ving

V sb. to V	V that + n. clause	V (sb.) wh-to V
require sb. to V	decide that + n. clause	tell sb. wh-to V

答案 🎧

請利用下面的必備語庫檢查答案。

商用英文必備語庫 8.6　動詞 chunks　🎧MP3 67

V + n.p		be Ved to V	V sb. that
· arrange n.p.　· complete n.p. · consider n.p.　· allow n.p. · enjoy n.p.　· read n.p. · require n.p.　· contact n.p.		· be allowed to V · be required to V · be prepared to V	· inform sb. that + n. clause · tell sb. that + n. clause
V sb. wh-clause	**V to V**		**V Ving**
· tell sb. wh-clause	· prepare to V · agree to V · decide to V		· enjoy Ving
V sb. to V	**V that + n. clause**		**V (sb.) wh-to V**
· require sb. to V · allow sb. to V	· agree that + n. clause · decide that + n. clause · require that + n. clause · consider that + n. clause		· decide wh-to V · tell sb. wh-to V

✒　語庫小叮嚀

◆ 請注意，有的模式乍看之下可能不易理解。例如：be Ved to V，裡面的 Ved 指的是動詞的過去分詞。

◆ 另外，V (sb.) wh-to V 裡的 wh-to V 指的是以 who、what、when、where 或 why 為首的子句。如：I couldn't decide who to invite to the reception.、I can't decide where to hold the New Year's party.。

◆ 此外，也請注意，有的動詞的 chunks 可能不只一個。例如 prepare to V 和 be prepared to V；或 enjoy n.p. 和 enjoy Ving。有的動詞也會搭配介系詞 chunks 使用，這在第十單元中會有更詳細的說明。

　　好，現在來看一些範例，學習如何在電子郵件中運用這些動詞 chunks。

TASK 8.11

請閱讀這些電子郵件，找出必備語庫 8.6 中 的動詞 chunks 並畫底線。注意這些動詞 chunks 的用法。

Dear Lucy,

Just a quick note to let you know what happened on Friday. I arranged the venue as you asked me to, and then returned to the office at around 4:00. However, as I was not wearing my badge I was not allowed to reenter the building. My mobile was dead and I could not contact anyone. I couldn't decide what to do. I begged the security guard at the door to let me in, but he did not allow me to do so. So I went home.

Dear Amy,

I really must complain about your email, which I think was most unfair. You required us—against my advice—to redesign the finance spreadsheet at a very bad time. I only have eight people in my department, as you know, and we simply cannot deal with two complex jobs at the same time. The company was required to file all income tax returns before the end of the month, and we had to give this priority. I told you that my department was not prepared to process such a huge backlog of work. I cannot now take the blame for this decision of yours, especially when I consider that I told you why it wasn't a good idea a few weeks ago. We must now prepare to face huge delays, and possibly a fine for late payment of taxes.

Dear Mike,

Thanks for a great presentation yesterday. I think the clients all really enjoyed it, and I certainly enjoyed hearing about our successes. One of them informed

Word List	
	• venue [ˈvɛnju] n. 集合地
	• badge [bædʒ] n. 徽章；證章
	• dead [dɛd] adj.（電話）中斷的；不通的
	• spreadsheet [ˈsprɛdˌʃit] n. 試算表
	• backlog [ˈbækˌlɔg] n. 積壓

me afterwards that I was lucky to have such a talented presenter in my company. However, when I told him how much I was paying you, he changed his mind! (Just kidding!) After hearing these comments, Lucy and I decided that you should deliver the shareholders' report on Monday. Please contact me as soon as you can.

Dear Edward,

Further to our meeting last week, I read the consultant's report with great interest. As he mentioned, we originally considered a strategic alliance with Global Star, Inc., but they were not prepared to meet our terms. We then decided to give up the idea. The consultant's other recommendations are very interesting. I'd like to arrange another meeting with you and the management team to discuss them in more detail.

Dear Lucy,

Before Macey went on vacation last week, did she complete the report as she agreed to?

If so, where is it? I can't find it! I'm surprised that you allowed her to go on vacation without finishing this really important piece of work. I thought we agreed that she should finish it before she could go. Holiday regulations require that staff need approval from a supervisor before they leave for a vacation. Please let me know if you have it.

答案

請參閱下列答案。

Dear Lucy,

Just a quick note to let you know what happened on Friday. I <u>arranged the</u>

Word List	▪ deliver [dɪˋlɪvə] v. 發表；講述
	▪ shareholder [ˋʃɛrˌholdə] n. 股東

venue as you asked me to, and then returned to the office at around 4:00. However, as I was not wearing my badge I <u>was not allowed to reenter</u> the building. My mobile was dead and I could not <u>contact anyone</u>. I couldn't <u>decide what to do</u>. I begged the security guard at the door to let me in, but he did not <u>allow me to do</u> so. So I went home.

Dear Amy,

I really must complain about your email, which I think was most unfair. You <u>required us</u>——against my advice——<u>to redesign</u> the finance spreadsheet at a very bad time. I only have eight people in my department, as you know, and we simply cannot deal with two complex jobs at the same time. The company <u>was required to file</u> all income tax returns before the end of the month, and we had to give this priority. I <u>told you that</u> my department was not <u>prepared to process</u> such a huge backlog of work. I cannot now take the blame for this decision of yours, especially when I <u>consider that</u> I <u>told you why</u> it wasn't a good idea a few weeks ago. We must now <u>prepare to face</u> huge delays, and possibly a fine for late payment of taxes.

Dear Mike,

Thanks for a great presentation yesterday. I think the clients all really <u>enjoyed it</u>, and I certainly <u>enjoyed hearing</u> about our successes. One of them <u>informed me</u> afterwards <u>that</u> I was lucky to have such a talented presenter in my company. However, when I <u>told him how</u> much I was paying you, he changed his mind! (Just kidding!) After hearing these comments, Lucy and I <u>decided that</u> you should deliver the shareholders' report on Monday. Please <u>contact me</u> as soon as you can.

Dear Edward,

Further to our meeting last week, I <u>read the consultant's report</u> with great interest. As he mentioned, we originally <u>considered a strategic alliance</u> with Global Star, Inc., but they <u>were not prepared to</u> meet our terms. We then decided to give up the idea. The consultant's other recommendations are very interesting. I'd like to arrange another meeting with you and the management team to discuss them in more detail.

Dear Lucy,

Before Macey went on vacation last week, did she complete the report as she agreed to?

If so, where is it? I can't find it! I'm surprised that you allowed her to go on vacation without finishing this really important piece of work. I thought we agreed that she should finish it before she could go. Holiday regulations require that staff need approval from a supervisor before they leave for a vacation. Please let me know if you have it.

雙受詞動詞 Chunks

在本節中我們要學的是雙受詞動詞。記住,這些動詞 chunks 有的可以調換受詞位置,有的不行。請做下面的 Task,看是否還記得在前面寫作單元中學到的雙受詞動詞 chunks。

請將這些動詞 chunks 分門別類,寫在下面的表格中。

1. agree with sb. (about/on sth.)
2. inform sb. (about/of sth.)
3. prepare sth. (for n.p.)
4. return sth. (to sb.)
5. tell sb. sth.

6. talk about sth. with sb.
7. talk to sb. (about sth.)
8. talk to sb. about sth.
9. tell sb. (about sth.)
10. tell sth. to sb.

Non-Invertible	Invertible

答案

請看下面的必備語庫,並仔細閱讀語庫小叮嚀。

商用英文必備語庫 8.7　雙受詞動詞 chunks　　　　　MP3 68

Non-Invertible（不可倒置）	Invertible（可倒置）
· return sth. (to sb.) · prepare sth. (for n.p.) · inform sb. (about/of sth.) · talk to sb. (about sth.) · tell sb. (about sth.) · agree with sb. (about/on sth.)	· tell sb. sth. · tell sth. to sb. · talk about sth. with sb. · talk to sb. about sth.

語庫小叮嚀

◆ 注意，talk 既是可倒置也是不可倒置動詞，表示第二個受詞 sth. 不需要寫出來，但如果想寫出來則需用 about。倘若想調換 sth. 與 sb. 的位置，則 sb. 前須加介系詞 with。

現在來練習使用這些雙受詞動詞，我們就先從不可倒置的動詞 chunks 著手吧。

TASK 8.13

請利用下面提供的片語完成電子郵件。

· about the confidentiality of client records

· about the seriousness of keeping things confidential

· about the seriousness of this breach of trust.

· for us

· of a conversation she had with you last week

· to me

Dear Lulu,

When you joined the company last month, I talked to you _____. I told you then _____. My contact at Jonson & Ronson has just informed me _____. It seems you told her some confidential information regarding their main competitor, G&P. Apparently, you told G&P's current strategy to J&R. I have talked about this case with Malcolm, and he agrees with me _____.

I'm afraid we have no choice but to give you an official warning and to take you off J&R until this matter is resolved. I would be grateful if you could prepare a letter of explanation _____ by the end of this week. Could you please also return all your J&R files _____ before you leave the office at the end of today?

Thanks.

| Word List | ▪ confidential [ˌkɑnfəˋdɛnʃəl] adj. 機密的 |
| | ▪ breach [britʃ] n. 違反；破壞 |

答案

請閱讀下面完整的電子郵件,粗體字為空格內應填入的答案,請比較兩個版本,你注意到兩者間的區別了嗎?

Dear Lulu,

When you joined the company last month, I talked to you **about the confidentiality of client records**. I told you then **about the seriousness of keeping things confidential**. My contact at Jonson & Ronson has just informed me **of a conversation she had with you last week**. It seems you told her some confidential information regarding their main competitor, G&P. Apparently, you told G&P's current strategy to J&R. I have talked about this case with Malcolm, and he agrees with me **about the seriousness of this breach of trust**.

I'm afraid we have no choice but to give you an official warning and to take you off J&R until this matter is resolved. I would be grateful if you could prepare a letter of explanation **for us** by the end of this week. Could you please also return all your J&R files **to me** before you leave the office at the end of today?

Thanks.

　　希望你能看出,第二封電子郵件中的重要資訊比較多,有了這些資訊,郵件內容才會比較清楚易懂。

TASK 8.14

請調換下列句子中受詞的位置。

1. I talked to you about the confidentiality of client records.

_____

2. You told her some confidential information.

_____

3. I talked about this case with Malcolm.

_____

答案🔊

1. I talked about confidentiality of client records with you.
2. You told some confidential information to her.
3. I talked to Malcolm about this case.

　　好，本單元的學習到此結束。在繼續進行下一單元之前，別忘了回到本單元的前面，確定所有的學習目標都確實掌握了。

Unit 9　口說

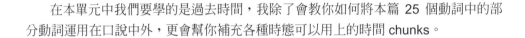
引言與學習目標

　　在本單元中我們要學的是過去時間，我除了會教你如何將本篇 25 個動詞中的部分動詞運用在口說中外，更會幫你補充各種時態可以用上的時間 chunks。

　　本單元結束時，各位應達成的學習目標如下：

- ❏ 對簡單過去式的用法有更清楚的了解。
- ❏ 知道簡單過去式和現在完成式之間的差別。
- ❏ 知道本書 100 個動詞中所有不規則動詞的三態。
- ❏ 知道哪些時間 chunks 該用簡單過去式。
- ❏ 有能力在口說和寫作中用簡單過去式，談論自己過去的職務和經驗。
- ❏ 有能力使用本篇 25 個動詞中的重點動詞來陳述事項。
- ❏ 聽得出動詞加 -ed 後的三種發音，並能夠正確發音。
- ❏ 知道一些常見的口說錯誤並知道該如何避免。
- ❏ 做過一些口說、聽力和發音練習。

時態：過去時間

　　一般而言，若想表達過去的時間（所有的過去時間都算是已結束的時間），可以用簡單過去式。由於商業英文與日常生活的對話裡較少使用過去進行式（was/were Ving）與過去完成式（had p.p.）。因此，本單元的學習重點將偏重在簡單過去式。

　　不過，過去簡單式還是有兩個問題必須注意。第一個問題是，有<u>些</u>動詞的簡單過去式是規則的（動詞後面直接加 -ed），有些是不規則的，要記憶所有不規則動詞的動詞三態並非易事。第二個問題則是，有時很難判斷何時該用簡單過去式，何時該用現在完成式。好在第二個問題不如想像中的困難，因為一旦掌握已結束和未結束時間之間的差別，這兩種時態的差別便顯而易見了。現在我們就先從不規則動詞的動詞三態學起。

TASK 9.1

請完成下面不規則動詞三態的表格。

become	*became*	*become*	leave		
begin			let		
bring			make		
come			meet		
do			pay		
feel			put		
find			read		
get			say		
give			see		
go			send		
have			set		
hear			take		

hold			tell		
keep			think		
know			understand		
learn			write		

答案

請利用下面的必備語庫檢查答案。

商用英文必備語庫 9.1　不規則動詞三態

MP3 69

become	became	become	**leave**	left	left
begin	began	begun	**let**	let	let
bring	brought	brought	**make**	made	made
come	came	come	**meet**	met	met
do	did	done	**pay**	paid	paid
feel	felt	felt	**put**	put	put
find	found	found	**read**	read	read
get	got	got/gotten	**say**	said	said
give	gave	given	**see**	saw	seen
go	went	gone	**send**	sent	sent
have	had	had	**set**	set	set
hear	heard	heard	**take**	took	taken
hold	held	held	**tell**	told	told
keep	kept	kept	**think**	thought	thought
know	knew	known	**understand**	understood	understood
learn	learned/learnt	learned/learnt	**write**	wrote	written

✎　語庫小叮嚀

◆ 這個表格幫你整理出了本書 100 個動詞中所有的不規則動詞，請務必花點心思在這個表格上。

◆ 請注意，learn 可以按一般規則寫成 learned，也可以寫成 learnt，兩者都對，任你選用，但請記住，在同一份文件中務必前後一致。

◆ 請注意，read 的三態拼法都一樣，但過去式和過去分詞要唸成 [rɛd]。

◆ Get 在英式用法裡，較常使用的過去分詞為 got；美式用法則兩者皆可。有獲得或得到的意思時，會用 gotten，如：The movie has gotten some good reviews. 而 got 則用來表示擁有或持有某物，如：I've got a car.。

　　本單元結束前，我們會做一些發音功課，練習其他以 -ed 結尾的動詞。現在我們先繼續往下看，研究我稍早提到的其他問題，也就是何時該用簡單過去式，何時該用現在完成式。

　　如同我們之前學到的，現在完成式是現在時間的一種，這時態是表示現在、尚未結束的時間，有些人會以為是用以表示過去發生的事情，例如：I have been to America.、I have read that book 50 times at least.、I have seen that movie already.。這些句子之所以表示現在時間，是因為動作雖然已經完成，時間範圍卻尚未結束。反之，若動作已經完成，時間範圍也已結束，那麼就可以使用簡單過去式。

　　為鞏固你對這個概念的理解程度，請做下面的閱讀 Task。

TASK 9.2

請閱讀這封電子郵件並完成下面的表格。Jacky 這封電子郵件大約是在何時完成的？

Dear Mavis,

Regarding the report you sent me a few days ago, I have sent it on to Jean. I have also arranged a meeting with the team to go through the report in detail. I have also set up the big meeting room for tomorrow afternoon and have repaired the projector— it was broken last week— so it should be working fine now.

By the way, did you see June this morning? She came in to the office to say

hi. It was really nice to see her. She looked really big and she said the baby is kicking a lot. So exciting!

Anyway, let me know if you have any concerns about the meeting.

Jacky

Finished Time Chunks	Unfinished Time Chunks
you sent me	*I have sent it on*

答案

請利用下面的表格來對照答案。

Finished Time Chunks （已結束的時間 chunks）		Unfinished Time Chunks （未結束的時間 chunks）
· you sent me	· it was really nice	· I have sent it on
· it was broken	· she looked	· I have also arranged
· did you see	· she said	· I have also set up
· June came in		· have repaired

請注意，使用簡單過去式的動詞全是指已結束的時間，如：a few days ago、last week、this morning。

Jacky 這封電子郵件的完成時間大約是在下午。June 是在早上來訪，已經是過去的事情，因此使用的是簡單過去式。Jacky 為會議做的所有安排均用現在完成式，有時間尚未結束的意思，那是因為他還沒下班。如果他已經下班，這封電子郵件是在家中寫的，那麼所有的動詞都可以改用簡單過去式。

請再重新閱讀一次電子郵件並思考我上述的解釋。

接著我們要來學一些可與簡單過去式搭配使用的時間 chunks。

TASK 9.3

請將這些時間 chunks 分門別類，填入下表中。

1. afterwards	7. formerly	13. next	19. this quarter
2. ago	8. immediately	14. once	20. this week
3. at one time	9. in 2005	15. originally	21. this year
4. during that time	10. in March	16. so far	22. year-to-date
5. during this time	11. last quarter	17. subsequently	23. yesterday
6. eventually	12. last year	18. then	

Finished Time Chunks	Unfinished Time Chunks

答案

請利用下面的必備語庫來核對答案。

商用英文必備語庫 **9.2**　時間 chunks

Finished Time Chunks （已結束的時間 chunks）		Unfinished Time Chunks （未結束的時間 chunks）
· afterwards	· in March	· during this time
· ago	· last quarter	· so far
· at one time	· last year	· this quarter
· during that time	· next	· this week
· eventually	· once	· this year
· formerly	· originally	· year-to-date
· immediately	· subsequently	
· in 2005	· then	
	· yesterday	

Word List　▪ subsequently ['sʌbsɪ‚kwɛntlɪ] adv. 其後；隨後

語庫小叮嚀

◆ 請注意，這些只是大略的分法，裡面有些時間 chunks 仍可與其他時態連用。

◆ Year-to-date 永遠是指從今年一月一日至今的時間。

TASK 9.4

請利用語庫 9.2 來改寫下列句子。見範例。

1. I have received your report yesterday.
   I received your report yesterday.

2. So far this morning I sent three emails.

3. During that time I had been to many places.

4. In 1999 I have been worked in Toronto.

5. I write a lot of emails this morning. I think I'll stop and have some lunch.

6. I have given your details to Anne last week.

7. John has talked to Miyuki about my case last night.

8. Did you see John recently?

9. I decide to quit my job last week.

答案 🔘

請參考我在下面提供的答案。

2. So far this morning I have sent three emails.

3. During that time I went to many places.

4 In 1999 I worked in Toronto.

5. I have written a lot of emails this morning. I think I'll stop and have some lunch

6. I gave your details to Anne last week.

7. John talked to Miyuki about my case last night.

8. Have you seen John recently?

9. I decided to quit my job last week.

現在來鞏固目前所學到的新知，然後再繼續學習下一節。

TASK 9.5

MP3 71

請聽 MP3，Willy 和 Alison 下班後在酒吧中聊天。Willy 做過哪些工作？他最喜歡的工作是什麼？Alison 和 Willy 現在從事什麼工作？

答案

Willy 做過服務生、計程車司機、醫院服務員、酒商和會計師，他最喜歡當會計師。現在 Willy 和 Alison 都是會計師。

請先繼續做下面的 Task，我們待會會利用這段對話來做練習，屆時你將可看到完整的對話內容。

TASK 9.6

請再聽一次 MP3，這次請利用必備語庫 9.2，將所有 Willy 用到的時間 chunks 勾出來。Willy 用的是什麼時態？

答案

由於 Willy 談論的多半為自己過去的工作經驗，因此使用的時態大多為簡單過去式。

TASK 9.7

MP3 71

現在請依據你對時態的理解，將下頁動詞改成合適的時態後，填入空格中。有些動詞可多次使用。接著請再聽一次聽力 Task 9.5 中的對話來核對答案。

· be	· go	· know	· study
· come	· get	· learn	· teach
· develop	· have	· need	· travel
· do	· hear	· recruit	· want
		· start	· work

Alison: So, what (1)_____ you do before you (2)_____ to work here?

Willy : Oh, I've (3)_____ lots of different things.

Alison: Really? Like what?

Willy : Well, I (4)_____ out as a waiter. That was when I (5)_____ in college ten years ago. It was my first part-time job. But I (6)_____ about three or four jobs when I was in college to support my studies. I once even (7)_____ as a taxi driver. Then when I quit college. I (8)_____ all kinds of things. I worked in a hospital as an x-ray technician for a while. Originally I (9)_____ to be an accountant, right? So during that time I (10)_____ for my license. But eventually I (11)_____ tired of working at the hospital, so I then got a job in a wine shop.

Alison: A wine shop! Wow. Did you learn a lot about wine?

Willy : Yes, I (12)_____ how to drink it and stay standing! No, I'm kidding. It was interesting. My boss formerly was a wine producer, so he (13)_____ everything about wine and (14)_____ me a lot. Afterwards I really (15)_____ a taste for it.

Alison: That's great. So then what did you do?

Willy : Well, when I got my license I immediately (16)_____ abroad and (17)_____ around for a while.

Alison: Really? You didn't start work then?

Willy : No, I (18)_____ a break after all my studies and jobs. I went to Canada for a while, and next I went to England, which is a really terrible place.

Alison: Yeah, so I've (19)_____ .

Willy : Well, in 2003 I (20)_____ back here and got a job with IDM. Then, in March, your boss (21)_____ me to come over and over work for you guys, so I subsequently (22)_____ here.

Alison: That's quite a career. What did you enjoy the most?

Willy : Oh, I love being an accountant the most.

Alison: Oh, I agree with you.

答案🔊

如果覺得聽力很難，可以參閱下方的解答。

(1)	did	(2)	came	(3)	done	(4)	started	(5)	was
(6)	had	(7)	worked	(8)	did	(9)	wanted	(10)	studied
(11)	got	(12)	learned	(13)	knew	(14)	taught	(15)	developed
(16)	went	(17)	traveled	(18)	needed	(19)	heard	(20)	came
(21)	recruited	(22)	came						

常 見 錯 誤 ＞ ＞ **agree**	
錯　誤	正　確
I agree you. I agree with you to that point.	I agree. / I agree with you. I agree with you on that point.
‧ Agree with sb. (on sth.) 是一個常用的動詞 chunk，意為同意某人（在某事上）的看法，小心不要用錯介系詞了！	

◤ 陳述事項的 Set-Phrases ◢

TASK 9.8

MP3 72

請聽 MP3 中的對話。David 正在向 Judy 敘述他和 Michael 的開會內容。David 和 Michael 在會議中談了些什麼事情？

答案🔊

他們討論了將 Judy 派到中國管理一個三年計劃的可能性。

如果沒有聽懂所有細節，請再聽一次，並參閱下頁完整的對話內容。

David: Michael mentioned to me that head office is looking for someone to go to China to start a new project there.

Judy : Oh. Did he tell you who he had in mind?

David: Well, he mentioned your name.

Judy : Oh. Did he?

David: Yes. He told me that he was looking for someone really efficient and trustworthy.

Judy : Oh. Did he say that about me? Wow, I didn't know he cared about me that much. Did you tell him about the mistake I made with the Ipcress Project?

David: Yes, I mentioned it, but he informed me that the management does not hold you responsible for the mistake.

Judy : Oh. OK. Did he mention to you how long the new project in China would last?

David: Yes. He mentioned three years.

Judy : Oh. Three years is a long time.

David: Yes. I also mentioned to him about your family, and he informed me of the various benefits they have over there for family members, you know, housing, schooling, and so on.

Judy : Oh. That's good. Did he mention to you how much my salary would be?

David: Well, I mentioned to him how much you are earning at the moment, and I also mentioned to him that in my opinion you are currently underpaid.

Judy : Oh. That was nice of you.

David: But I didn't inform him about your problem.

Judy : Oh. So what else did you talk about?

David: We talked about golf after that.

Judy : Oh.

現在來學一些 David 向 Judy 陳述會議內容時用到的 set-phrases。

TASK 9.9

請研讀下列的必備語庫。

商用英文必備語庫 9.3　陳述事項的 set-phrases　　(MP3 73)

· I mentioned to him that + n. clause	· (S)He told me about n.p.
· (S)He informed me that + n. clause	· (S)He told me wh-clause
· (S)He mentioned n.p.	· I mentioned to him about n.p.
· (S)He told me that + n. clause	· (S)He informed me of n.p.
· (S)He informed me wh-clause	· I mentioned n.p.
· (S)He mentioned to me about n.p.	· We talked about n.p.
· (S)He informed me about n.p.	· I mentioned to him wh-clause
· (S)He mentioned to me wh-clause	· (S)He mentioned to me that + n. clause

✎　語庫小叮嚀

◆ 這些 set-phrases 較適合用在想比較正式地陳述事情時。如是非正式的記述或八卦，只要說 (s)he said 就好。

◆ 請注意，所有的動詞都是簡單過去式，這是因為所陳述的事情通常是發生在過去的時間範圍中。

TASK 9.10　　(MP3 74)

請聽 MP3 中的句子，然後利用已學過的 set-phrases 將每一個句子重新陳述一次。做練習時別忘了要把答案錄下來，以便檢查發音或句構是否有誤。

答案　　(MP3 75)

請聽 MP3 裡提供的參考答案。當然，你的答案不同也沒關係，因為可以利用的 set-phrases 本來就有很多個。

發音

在本節裡，我們要學的是規則動詞加 -ed 後的發音。寫作時，所有的規則動詞都會以 -ed 結尾。但是在口說時，-ed 的發音有三種，我現在要教你的便是口說中動詞加 -ed 後的發音。

TASK 9.11

MP3 76

請看下列表格並聽 MP3，你能否聽出這三組動詞間的差別？

1	2	3
asked	agreed	attended
attached	allowed	completed

答案

希望你聽得出來，第一組動詞中的 -ed 是發 [t] 音。[t] 的發音較重，跟動詞的尾音相當接近。請再聽一次，確定聽得出來差別。

希望你聽得出來，第二組動詞中的 -ed 是發 [d] 音。[d] 的發音很輕，並緊接在動詞尾音的後面。同樣地，請再聽一次，確定已聽出其中的差別了。

第三組動詞中，動詞結尾加上 -ed 後，會多出一個音節，變成 [ld] 的音，既然動詞的發音加長了，動詞的音律也改變了。

能夠清楚地發出 -ed 的音很重要，因為如果對方聽不出來，便不知道你所陳述的是過去的事情。

既然你聽得出來 -ed 三種不同的發音了，現在就來學習發音規則。這個規則是以動詞的尾音爲依據。

1. 無聲發無聲：-ed 接在無聲子音 [f]、[s]、[k]、[p]、[ʃ]、[tʃ]、[θ] 後面時，-ed 發無聲 [t] 音。

2. 有聲發有聲：-ed 接在有聲子音 [v]、[z]、[g]、[b]、[dʒ]、[ð]、[l]、[r]、[m]、
   [n]、[ŋ] 後面時， -ed 發有聲 [d] 的音。

3. 接在 [t] 或 [d] 後面：要多加一個音節， -ed 就要發 [ɪd] 的音。

TASK 9.12

MP3 76

請再聽一次 MP3 中這三組動詞的發音，同時回想我剛剛告訴你的規則。你聽出發音
規則了嗎？如果覺得有把握了，請做下面的 Task。

TASK 9.13

下列規則動詞均出自本書的 100 大動詞，請按照 -ed 的發音方式將其分門別類，填入
下表裡。

1. agreed	15. contacted	29. informed	43. requested
2. allowed	16. continued	30. interested	44. required
3. apologized	17. decided	31. involved	45. returned
4. arranged	18. discussed	32. joined	46. reviewed
5. arrived	19. enjoyed	33. mentioned	47. scheduled
6. asked	20. ensured	34. noted	48. served
7. attached	21. expected	35. offered	49. suggested
8. attended	22. followed	36. planned	50. talked
9. based	23. handled	37. prepared	51. tried
10. believed	24. hesitated	38. proposed	52. used
11. caused	25. implemented	39. provided	53. visited
12. completed	26. improved	40. recommended	54. worked
13. confirmed	27. included	41. regretted	
14. considered	28. increased	42. remembered	

[t]	[d]	[ɪd]

227

答案

請利用下列的必備語庫來核對答案。

商用英文必備語庫 9.4 規則動詞加 -ed 後的發音　　MP3 77

[t]	[d]		[ɪd]
· asked	· agreed	· mentioned	· asked
· attached	· allowed	· offered	· attended
· based	· apologized	· planned	· completed
· discussed	· arranged	· prepared	· contacted
· increased	· arrived	· proposed	· decided
· talked	· believed	· remembered	· expected
· worked	· caused	· required	· hesitated
	· confirmed	· returned	· implemented
	· considered	· reviewed	· included
	· continued	· scheduled	· interested
	· enjoyed	· served	· noted
	· ensured	· tried	· provided
	· followed	· used	· recommended
	· handled		· regretted
	· improved		· requested
	· informed		· suggested
	· involved		· visited
	· joined		

✎　語庫小叮嚀

◆ 這些動詞的拼法也有陷阱，不得大意。請仔細看必備語庫中的動詞，有些字須重複字尾後，才能加 -ed；有的動詞如以 e 結尾，便只需加 d；如果是以 y 結尾的動詞，則必須先將最後的母音改為 i，才能加 -ed。

TASK 9.14

請用必備語庫中的不規則動詞練習造句，談論已結束的事情。記得錄下你的句子。你的動詞結尾是否發音清楚？發音是否需要再清晰一點？

常 見 錯 誤 > > **before** 和 **ago**	
錯 誤	正 確
I went to the UK 20 years before.	I went to the UK 20 years ago.

· Before 可用來區別兩個事件的先後順序，如：I went there 20 years before the start of the war.；ago 則較常加在表示時間的名詞片語後使用。

好，本單元的學習到此結束。在繼續往下學習之前，別忘了回到本單元前面的學習目標，確定所有的項目都確實掌握了。

Unit 10 詞彙

引言與學習目標

如同其他篇的詞彙單元，本單元中我們要再來學一些常見又實用的詞彙，搭配本篇 25 個動詞中的部分動詞。我們將從 word partnerships 著手，然後學習片語動詞，最後再學一些慣用語。本單元結束時，各位應達成的學習目標如下：

本單元結束時，各位應達成的學習目標如下：

❏ 學到很多使用頻率高的 word partnerships，可用於商業英文的口說和寫作。

❏ 學到很多片語動詞，可用於商業英文的口說和寫作。

❏ 學到一些很有用的商業慣用語。

❏ 練習如何使用這些新的詞彙。

❏ 知道一些常見錯誤並知道該如何避免。

Word Partnerships

　　本節裡要學的 word partnerships 主要以 bring、leave、hold、set 和 serve 為主，我們現在就先從 bring 和 leave 學起吧。

請研讀下面的必備語庫與例句。

商用英文必備語庫 10.1　含 bring 的 word partnerships

 MP3 78

bring (sth.)	· to sb.'s attention · to sb.'s notice · to V · with you · costs down	· out a new product · a balance forward · out of the red · into the black · up to date

 EX

1. I spent all morning bringing our client records up to date.

2. I brought this problem to your attention three months ago.

3. We've managed to bring the company out of the red by bringing costs down.

4. The new CEO brought the company into the black within three months of taking over.

商用英文必備語庫 10.2　含 leave 的 word partnerships

 MP3 79

leave	· the company · the rest to sb. · us with little profit · word that + n. clause · instructions (for n.p.) · instructions (for wh-)	· us with a small margin · me no choice but to V · a message (for sb.) · sth. out of the calculations · me with no other alternative but to V

EX

1. Joan went on vacation and left instructions for the project. She also left word that it must be finished on time.

2. OK, I think that's it. You can go home and leave the rest to me. Thanks for your help.

3. The increased oil prices have left us with a smaller margin. We need to increase sales.

4. Your behavior leaves me no choice but to fire you.

　　我們等一下再用這些 word partnerships 多做一些練習，現在先學含動詞 hold 的 word partnerships。這些 word partnerships 可根據涵義粗略的分成三大組：有的意指「事件」，如：We held the reception at the Grand Hotel.；有的意指「延遲」，如：A mechanical failure in the factory held up production.；有的意指「擁有」，如：Our company holds the patent for this drug.。除了這三大組之外，還有「其他」涵義的 word partnerships。

TASK 10.2

請研讀以下含 hold 的 word partnerships，將其分門別類後填入下表中，見範例。

hold	· the position that + n. clause · the position (of n.p.) · an insurance policy · a competition · a conference · a dinner · a meeting · a party · a reception · an annual convention · an exhibition · consignments	· detailed discussions with · sb. in the highest regard · sth. for safe keeping · sth. in confidence · stock · the copyright for · the line · the patent for · the price · the shipment · up production · your reservation

Word List

- patent [ˋpætn̩t] n. 專利權
- insurance policy 保單
- consignment [kənˋsaɪmənt] n. 託付物；委託貨物
- stock [stɑk] n. 股票；存貨

Event	Delay	Possess	Other
hold a meeting	*hold consignments*	*hold an insurance policy*	*hold the price*

答案 🔊

請利用下面的必備語庫來核對答案。

商用英文必備語庫 10.3　含 hold 的 word partnerships

Event（事件）	Possess（擁有）
·hold a meeting ·hold a competition ·hold a conference ·hold a dinner ·hold a party ·hold a reception ·hold an annual convention ·hold an exhibition ·hold detailed discussions with	·hold the position (of n.p.) ·hold the position that + n. clause ·hold an insurance policy ·hold stock ·hold the copyright for ·hold the patent for ·hold sth. for safe keeping
Delay（延遲）	**Other（其他）**
·hold up production ·hold the shipment	·hold sb. in the highest regard ·hold sth. in confidence ·hold the line ·hold consignments ·hold your reservation ·hold the price

TASK 10.3

請將下面詞組連結成完整句，有些詞組有多個可能的答案，見範例。

A	
Can you please bring	• a message and I'll get back to you.
I asked her to bring	• costs down considerably.
Hi. I'm away at the moment. Please leave	• to your notice, but I think it's important.
	• the file with you to the meeting?
I hope that these cuts will bring	• the website up to date. It's no
I'm sorry to bring this matter	longer accurate.

B	
Last month's figures were left	• out of the calculations.
Our poor performance last year left us with	• forward to this month's.
	• little profit to fund the expansion.
Tracy? I'm sorry, she left	• the company last week.
The boss is away at the moment, but he left	• word that I should help you.
We are holding	• your consignment until your
We bring the last month's balance	payment is received.

Word List	• aggressively [əˋgrɛsɪvlɪ] adv. 積極地
	• considerably [kənˋsɪdərəblɪ] adv. 相當地；非常地

C We currently hold ◆

We held ◆

We are currently holding ◆

We will be happy to hold ◆

You leave me ◆

We brought out ◆

◆ a dinner for the boss's retirement last week.

◆ a huge stock of products in our warehouse.

◆ a new product at the end of last quarter.

◆ with no other alternative but to cancel the project.

◆ your reservation until you can confirm.

◆ the copyright for this song

答案 🔊

請參閱下面的建議答案。

A Can you please bring

I asked her to bring

Hi. I'm away at the moment. Please leave

I hope that these cuts will bring

I'm sorry to bring this matter

◆ the file with you to the meeting?

◆ the website up to date. It's no longer accurate.

◆ a message and I'll get back to you.

◆ costs down considerably.

◆ to your notice, but I think it's important.

B Last month's figures were left

Our poor performance last year left us with

Tracy? I'm sorry, she left

The boss is away at the moment, but he left

We are holding

We bring the last month's balance

◆ out of the calculations.

◆ little profit to fund the expansion.

◆ the company last week.

◆ word that I should help you.

◆ your consignment until your payment is received.

◆ forward to this month's.

Word List ▪ warehouse [ˋwɛr͵haʊs] n. 倉庫；儲藏室

C We currently hold	◆ the copyright for this song.
We held	◆ a dinner for the boss's retirement last week.
We are currently holding	◆ a huge stock of products in our warehouse.
We will be happy to hold	◆ your reservation until you can confirm.
You leave me	◆ with no other alternative but to cancel the project.
We brought out	◆ a new product at the end of last quarter.

　　我們接著要學的是含 set 以及 set up 的 word partnerships，前者通常有「設定」或「設立」之意；後者通常有「安排」或「創立」的意思。

請研讀下面的必備語庫及例句。

商用英文必備語庫 10.4 含 set 的 word partnerships　　　MP3 81

| **set** | · a time (for n.p.)
· aside a time (for n.p.)
· aside a budget (for n.p.)
· aside funds (for n.p.)
· a date (for n.p.)
· a new standard (for n.p.)
· new records (for n.p.)
· a time limit on
· an example
· the alarm
· targets
· the standard (for n.p.) | · high standards (for n.p.)
· quotas (for n.p.)
· limits (on n.p.)
· priorities (for n.p.)
· prices
· sb. to thinking
· sb. to wondering
· objectives (for n.p.)
· goals (for n.p.)
· a policy
· things right |

Word List　· quota [`kwotə] n. 分配的數量；配額

1. Did you set a date for the next meeting?

2. In the past our products always set the standard for the rest of the industry.

3. Oh, Lord! I think I forgot to set the alarm in the office. I'll have to go back and check.

4. The CEO's job is to set priorities and company policy.

5. It's lucky that we set aside funds for an emergency like this.

商用英文必備語庫 10.5 含 set up 的 word partnerships

set up	· a meeting (for n.p.) · a schedule (for n.p.) · a payment schedule (for n.p.) · a shipping schedule (for n.p.) · a vacation schedule (for n.p.) · an appointment (for n.p.) · a time to meet (to V)	· an account (for n.p.) · an interview (with sb.)(to V) · equipment (for n.p.) · a business · a training program (for n.p.) · a line of credit (for n.p.)

 1. We set up a payment schedule for the new customer.

2. I set up the business in 1975.

3. HR set up a great new training program for the company.

4. I set up my first offshore bank account last week.

TASK 10.5

請用 set 或 set up 填空，完成下面的電子郵件，別忘了要留意時態正確與否。

Dear Lawrence,

Before I leave, I just want to fill you in on what I have done to make it easier for you to cover for me while I am away.

1. I (1)＿＿＿＿＿＿ a meeting for you with the team, so that they can brief you on the project status. You can (2)＿＿＿＿＿＿ a date for the next meeting with them after I get back.

Word List	· offshore [ˏɔfˈʃor] adj. 國外的（享有稅法優惠的） · brief [brif] v. 概述……

2. I (3)_____ targets for the sales team last month. You will need to (4)_____ a schedule and review them periodically.

3. Bonus policy for outstanding sales performance is (5)_____ by the head office, so you just need to (6)_____ aside a time to meet each sales person individually to get their results.

4. I (7)_____ an account for the New Year's Party, and the salespeople usually contribute 1% of their monthly earnings towards this event. I expect you to (8)_____ aside 2% of your own salary to (9)_____ an example to the team.

5. Finally, please remember to (10)_____ the equipment for the CEO's presentation tomorrow, and to (11)_____ the alarm when you leave at night.

Thanks for all your help while I am on my job switch in New York. As you know I will be back in six months. I'm sure I'll find the department in as good a shape as it was when I left it.

Regards and good luck!

A.B. Itch

答案🔈

請利用下表檢查答案，希望你的時態都用對了！

(1) have set up　(2) set　　　(3) set　(4) set up　(5) set

(6) set　　　　(7) have set up　(8) set　(9) set　　(10) set up

(11) set

Word List　• periodically [ˌpɪrɪˋɑdɪklɪ] adv. 定期地；週期性地

TASK 10.6

MP3 83

請閱讀以下 Janice 和老闆開會時的對話，並用 set 或 set up 填空，同樣地，也請特別注意時態是否正確，接著聽 MP3 來核對答案。

Boss: OK, what's next on the agenda?

Janis: Hmm. We need to talk about the Princeton project.

Boss: Oh yes. How's that going?

Janis: Well, the team has been working really hard on it, and they've completed all the objectives you (1)＿＿＿＿＿ for them before the project started. They've (2)＿＿＿＿＿ the payment schedule for it, and the prices (3)＿＿＿＿＿.

Boss: Wow, that was quick. It seems that they've (4)＿＿＿＿＿ new records for project implementation.

Janis: Yes, they've done really well. Because they've done a lot of overtime and put so much effort into it, I'm (5)＿＿＿＿＿ a new vacation schedule for all team members. I think we need to give them some time off.

Boss: Good idea. Actually, I'd like to meet them to thank them myself. Can you (6)＿＿＿＿＿ a time for me to meet them individually?

Janis: Sure.

Boss: OK, anything else?

Janis: Mary Jones.

Boss: Oh yes. Can you (7)＿＿＿＿＿ an appointment for her too? Have you (8)＿＿＿＿＿ the new training program for new employees?

Janis: Yes, it's been done. Actually, that (9)＿＿＿＿＿ me to thinking …

Boss: Yes?

Janis: I think we need to change our training provider?

Boss: Really? You're not happy with the one we're using at the moment?

Janis: Well, it just (10)＿＿＿＿＿ me to wondering whether we might be able to find another one. I think most people are bored with the programs our current provider offers.

Word List
- objective [əb`dʒɛktɪv] n. 目標
- implementation [ˌɪmpləmɛn`teʃən] n. 履行；實行

Boss: OK, well, (11)＿＿＿＿＿ some interviews with some of the others in town, let
　　　 me know what their prices are, and I'll (12)＿＿＿＿＿ aside some extra funds.
Janis: Thanks.
Boss: OK.

答案🎧

建議你先聽 MP3 檢查答案。如果還是有些答案聽不出來，再參考下面的解答。

(1) set　　(2) set up　　(3) have been set　　(4) set　　(5) setting

(6) set up　(7) set up　　(8) set up　　　　　　(9) set　　(10) set

(11) set up (12) set

　　好，現在繼續往下學習本節最後一個動詞，也就是含 serve as 的 word partner-
ships，以 serve as 為主的 word partnerships 可用來顯示事物的關係，「有被用來／被
當作……」的意思，也因此 serve as 句子的前後兩部分通常具有關連，且顯而易見。

TASK 10.7
請研讀下面的必備語庫及例句。

商用英文必備語庫 10.6 含 serve as 的 word partnerships　　　　　🎧MP3 84

serve as	· a model (for n.p.)
	· a reminder (of n.p.) (that + n. clause)
	· a reference (for n.p.)
	· a starting point (for n.p.)
	· an incentive (for n.p.)
	· confirmation (of n.p.)
	· confirmation (that + n. clause)
	· security (for n.p.)
	· a basis (for n.p.)
	· formal notice (that + n. clause)
	· a guide (for n.p.)

Word List　· incentive [ɪnˋsɛntɪv] n. 誘因

1. This memo from the IT department serves as a guide for dealing with all future software problems.

2. This letter serves as formal notice of our decision to terminate our contract.

3. We hope that her dismissal will serve as a warning to other employees.

現在請用下列詞組完成以下句子，見範例。

· Let this mistake	· This letter
· The receipt	· This market study
· These figures	· This memo from the IT department
· These assets	· We hope that the drop in base salary
· This figure simply	· We hope this dynamic sales team

1. *This memo from the IT department* serves as a guide for all future software problems.

2. _____ serves as confirmation of your purchase.

3. _____ serves as a starting point for the new project.

4. _____ serve as the basis for our forecasts for next year.

5. _____ serves as formal notice of my resignation.

6. _____ will serve as an incentive to earn more on commission.

7. _____ serve as security for the loan.

8. _____ will serve as a model for teams in other regions.

9. _____ serve as a reminder that more care needs to be taken.

10. _____ serves as a reference for measuring performance.

 Word List
- terminate [ˈtɜməˌnet] v. 終止；結束
- dismissal [dɪsˈmɪsl] n. 解雇
- commission [kəˈmɪʃən] n. 佣金

答案

請看我在下面提供的建議答案。請記住，句子兩部分之間的關聯必須顯而易見，此外別忘了檢查句子的文法是否正確。

2. The receipt serves as confirmation of your purchase.
3. This market study serves as a starting point for the new project.
4. These figures serve as the basis for our forecasts for next year.
5. This letter serves as formal notice of my resignation.
6. We hope that the drop in base salary will serve as an incentive to earn more on commission.
7. These assets serve as security for the loan.
8. We hope this dynamic sales team will serve as a model for teams in other regions.
9. Let this mistake serve as a reminder that more care needs to be taken.
10. This figure simply serves as a reference for measuring performance.

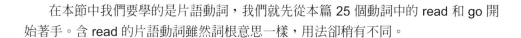

片語動詞

　　在本節中我們要學的是片語動詞，我們就先從本篇 25 個動詞中的 read 和 go 開始著手。含 read 的片語動詞雖然詞根意思一樣，用法卻稍有不同。

含 **read** 的 **2** 個重要片語動詞

TASK 10.9

請研讀下面的必備語庫。

商用英文必備語庫 10.7 含 read 的片語動詞　　　　MP3 85

read sth.	重點在於讀本的形式，如：newspaper, novel, article, report, email。
read about sth.	重點在於讀本的內容，如：macroeconomics, the merger between Compaq and HP, the president's new mistress。
read up on sth.	重點在於閱讀的目的，也就是藉由閱讀來學習新知。

TASK 10.10

請利用下面的片語，完成以下句子，有些空格可填入的答案不只一個。

· all the latest technology

· a new wonder drug

· a book

· the merger between

· the latest developments in our industry

· that article

Word List	▪ macroeconomics [ˌmækroˌikəˋnɑmɪks] n. 總體經濟學
	▪ merger [mɝdʒɚ] n. 合併

245

1. I read up on (1)＿＿＿＿＿＿＿＿＿ last night. Some of these new products are really amazing.
2. I read about (2)＿＿＿＿＿＿＿＿＿ that can cure cancer last night.
3. I was reading (3)＿＿＿＿＿＿＿＿＿ last night when I fell asleep on the sofa.
4. I'm currently reading about (4)＿＿＿＿＿＿＿＿＿ Compaq and HP. It's really interesting.
5. Did you read (5)＿＿＿＿＿＿＿＿＿ on new communication technologies in the Economist?
6. I need to read up on (6)＿＿＿＿＿＿＿＿＿. I'm a bit behind.

答案 🔊

請比較你的答案和下面提供的建議答案。

(1) all the latest technology
    a new wonder drug
    the latest developments in our industry
(2) a new wonder drug
(3) a book
    that article
(4) the merger between
(5) that article
(6) the latest developments in our industry
    all the latest technology
    a new wonder drug

現在我們來研讀含 go 的片語動詞，go 在一般和商業英文中是相當常見的動詞，以下為你在工作上常會用到的片語動詞。

含 go 的 16 個片語動詞

商用英文必備語庫 **10.8** 含 go 的片語動詞

go after sth. 追趕上	▶ We always go after government contracts because they're so lucrative.
go ahead (with sth.) 開始進行……	▶ Please go ahead with the project.
go along (with sth.) 同意……	▶ I can go along with that. It's a good idea.
go back (to sth.) 回到……	▶ I wish we could go back to the old days when it was a small company.
sth. go by 某事溜走	▶ We mustn't let this opportunity go by.
sth. go down 某事減少	▶ Revenues are going down. We need to increase sales.
go for sth. 選擇某事物；以……為目標	▶ I think we should go for the red one. It suits our company image better.
go into details 更詳盡地描述	▶ Without going into details, we had to fire her for misconduct.
go on (with sth.) 繼續做某事	▶ Let's go on with the meeting even though he is not here.
sb. go out 某人出去玩	▶ Are you going out tonight?
go over sth. 檢查某物是否正確	▶ We need to go over those figures one more time. They still don't look right to me.
go through sth. 仔細地檢視某物	▶ We need to go through the report together. There are lots of good ideas in it.
go through with sth. 完成某事	▶ Are we still going to go through with the project?
go with sth. 選擇某物	▶ I'm going to go with the steak. What would you like?

Word List　▪ lucrative [ˋlukrətɪv] adj. 可獲利的；賺錢的

go with sb. 陪伴某人	▶	Would you like me to go with you to the hospital?
sth. go up 某事增加、升高	▶	Transportation costs have gone up considerably.

TASK 10.11

請用上述含 go 的片語動詞，重新改寫這封電子郵件，見範例。

going into

Without <del>descri</del>bing it in too much detail, I think we should choose the propos-al presented on Thursday by Julianne. Once we have checked her figures, I think you'll agree that her proposal is better. We should aim for short-term cash injection. We need to look aggressively for new business. We have let too many months pass without getting new customers. While I agree with Mike's idea of conducting thorough research before we start entering new markets, I think we need to start to implement the project as soon as possible ——once we have examined Julianne's data, of course. I'm just worried that this slow patch will continue for too long. I do not want to return to the early days of the business when money was tight. Margins have been decreasing, while costs have been increasing. I do feel that we should never have com-pleted the restructuring last year.

答案 🎧

請核對你的答案，改寫過的地方以粗體字表示。

Without **going into** too much detail, I think we should **go with** the proposal presented on Thursday by Julianne. Once we have **gone over** her figures, I think you'll agree that her proposal is better. We should **go for** short-term cash injection. We need to **go after** new business. We have let too many

---

Word List　• slow patch 生意較清淡的期間

months **go by** without getting new customers. While I **go along with** Mike's idea of conducting thorough research before we start entering new markets, I think we need to **go ahead with** the project as soon as possible——once we have **gone through** Julianne's data, of course. I'm just worried that this slow patch will **go on** for too long. I do not want to **go back to** the early days of the business when money was tight. Margins have been **going down**, while costs have been **going up**. I do feel that we should never have **gone through with** the restructuring last year.

　　確定上述所學的都已理解後，我們接著就來學習本單元中其他不同涵義的片語動詞。

◤ 安排工作事項的 7 個片語動詞 ◢

TASK 10.12
請研讀下面的必備語庫。

 **商用英文必備語庫 10.9**　安排工作事項的片語動詞　　　　　　　　(MP3 87)

bring sth. up 提及一個新話題，通常是壞消息	▶	I'm sorry to bring this up, but our main customer has just cancelled a major order.
bring sth. about 促成某事發生	▶	If we want to bring this expansion about, someone is going to have to manage it.
prepare for sth. 準備某事	▶	I'm preparing for my certificate exam.
arrange for sb. to V 安排某人做某事	▶	Can you arrange for the new intern to come and see me?

Word List　▪ certificate [sə'tɪfəkɪt] n. 資格證明；執照

249

leave sth. for sb. to V 把某事留給某人做	▶	I'll leave this for you to do. I'm going home.
leave sth. with sb. 把某事留給某人	▶	Leave it with me. I'll do it.
leave sth. to sb. 讓某人獨力做某事	▶	It's not fair to leave it all to me. I have so much work to do already.

TASK 10.13

MP3 88

請利用語庫 10.9 中的片語動詞，完成下面的對話。然後聽 MP3 檢查答案

A: I'm sorry to (1)_____ this _____, but I told you earlier about this problem, and you did nothing about it.

B: Well, hang on. You can't say that I (2)_____ this _____ because I didn't act on what you told me.

A: No, I'm not saying that. What I'm saying is you didn't (3)_____ someone to investigate the problem, and now we're not prepared for it.

B: Well, we can't always be prepared for everything. We don't always know what's going to happen in the future.

A: No, I agree, but you usually (4)_____ these kinds of problems _____ me to deal with, and I don't think it's fair. This time I'm not going to help you. I'm going to (5)_____ this _____ you to solve.

B: OK. (6)_____ it _____ me then.

A: Yes, I will. Grrrr!

答案 🔾

請記住，有時動詞和介系詞會因受詞而分開。

別忘了片語動詞是有時態分別的，也可能出現在否定句中！

如果覺得聽力很難，請參考下面所提供的解答。

(1) bring/up   (2) brought/about   (3) arrange for

(4) leave/to   (5) leave/for   (6) leave/to

出差相關的 5 個片語動詞

TASK 10.14

請研讀下面的必備語庫。

商用英文必備語庫 10.10　出差相關的片語動詞　(MP3 89)

bring sth. along 帶著某物隨行	I brought the report along when I came over on Friday. Didn't you get it?
leave for + n.p. 前往某地	I leave for Amsterdam at 7:00 tonight.
leave + n.p. for + n.p. 離開某地前往他處	Then, I leave Amsterdam for Rome the following Monday.
bring sth. back 帶回某物	I forgot to bring some chocolate back for my wife.
return to + n.p. 回到原出發地	I return to Amsterdam on the Friday after that.

TASK 10.15

(MP3 90)

請利用語庫 10.10 完成下列對話，接著聽 MP3 檢查答案。

A: Where did you go?

B: Well, I (1)_____ Taipei _____ Rome on Sunday last week, right, and flew direct with no stopover, so when I got to Rome I was kind of exhausted.

A: That's a long flight.

B: Yeah. Well, I had a couple of hours in Rome, and then I (2)_____ Amsterdam. That's a short flight. When I arrived in Amsterdam, I thought I was all ready for the presentation, but then I realized I'd forgotten to (3)_____ the presentation materials _____ with me.

Word List　• stopover [ˈstɑpˌovə] n. 中途停留

251

A: Oh God. Really?

B: Yes. So I improvised.

A: Wow, how did it go?

B: Well, I got the new contract, so I think it went OK.

A: Well done. That's great.

B: I (4)＿＿＿＿＿ Taipei on Saturday and when I got home I realized I didn't

(5)＿＿＿＿＿ the contract ＿＿＿＿＿ with me.

A: Ai yo!

答案

如果覺得聽力很難，請參考下列解答。

(1) left/for　　(2) left for　　(3) bring/along　　(4) returned to　　(5) bring/back

改變計劃的 **2** 個片語動詞

TASK 10.16

請研讀下面的必備語庫。

商用英文必備語庫 10.11　　改變計劃的片語動詞　　　🎧MP3 91

bring sth. forward 將某事提前	▶ Let's bring the launch date forward to the end of this month.
sth. be set back 延後某事	▶ I'm afraid the launch date has been set back until the end of next month.

Word List　　• improvise [ˈɪmprəˌvaɪz] v.（演奏、演說等）即席而作

TASK 10.17

請利用上述片語動詞，完成下面電子郵件，記得注意動詞時態。

Dear Willy,

Just to let you know some good news. We have (1)＿＿＿＿＿＿＿＿ the completion date for the Princeton project, as everything is almost finished. Most of the preparations for the launch are now in place and we should be able to start next month. However, the Harvard project is not going so well, and will probably have to be (2)＿＿＿＿＿＿＿＿ until next year. I'll keep you informed about the situation.

Any questions, call me.

Alvin

答案🎧

(1) brought forward   (2) set back

商業慣用語

現在我們來學含 bring、leave、hold 和 go 的一些慣用語。

TASK 10.18

請研讀下面的必備語庫和例句。

商用英文必備語庫 10.12 含 leave 和 bring 的慣用語   MP3 92

leave	· sb. in the lurch	將某人棄之不顧
	· me cold	引發不了興趣，無法被打動
	· a lot to be desired	沒有達到期望
	· well enough alone	不管某事
bring	· out the best in sb.	激發出某人最好的才能
	· sth. to bear on	施壓來影響某個情況
	· sb. to book	警告或懲罰某人（英式慣用語）
	· sth. into line with	讓某事符合……的標準

 1. I used to have my own business, but then my business partner took all our profits and left me in the lurch.

2. The boss's speeches, which are supposed to inspire us to work harder, always leave me cold.

3. The new ads leave a lot to be desired. Whoever designed them was definitely overpaid.

4. Someday we'll have to redesign the system, but for now let's just leave well enough alone.

5. High pressure and an approaching deadline always bring out the best in me.

6. The negotiations only started to go well when he brought his influence with the government to bear on the discussion.

7. If she doesn't improve her work habits, I think we'll have to bring her to book.

8. We need to bring our operating procedures into line with international standards.

商用英文必備語庫 10.13 含 hold 的慣用語　(MP3 93)

hold	· things together · the fort · the purse strings · true for sth. · your ground · all the cards	在困境中堅持下去 代理或代為照料某職務 掌管財務 可應用在某種情況的論證 堅持不退讓 佔盡優勢

EX 1. Our main customer has cancelled an order and the boss is away on vacation. I'm trying to hold things together until he gets back.

2. He left me holding the fort and went on vacation with his wife.

3. Unfortunately, he holds the purse strings, so I can't pay anyone until he gets back.

4. His theory of business holds true in any market: always focus on the next sale.

5. I'm not going to let them win this negotiation. I'm going to hold my ground until I get what I want.

6. Unfortunately, our competitors already held all the cards. It was difficult to steal market share from them.

商用英文必備語庫 10.14 含 go 的慣用語　(MP3 94)

go	· Dutch · nuts · hand in hand with sth. · beyond a joke · back a long way · in one ear and out the other · pear shaped · from strength to strength · to sb.'s head	各付各的餐飲費 非常生氣；抓狂 與某事的關係密切 狀況越來越嚴重 彼此已認識很久 左耳進右耳出 出差錯或未按照計劃進行（英式慣用語） 越來越強大或越來越成功（英式慣用語） 因成功而變得驕傲自大

1. Thanks for inviting me, but I insist on going Dutch.

2. My boss went nuts when he found out I lost another client.

3. High taxes go hand in hand with high profits, I'm afraid.

4. The situation has gone beyond a joke now. We need to fix it.

5. The CEO and I go back a long way. We were classmates in kindergarten, if you can believe it!

6. He never remembers people's names. They go in one ear and out the other!

7. Our plans for expansion have all gone pear shaped since the market for our products started shrinking.

8. The company went from strength to strength in its first 20 years of existence.

9. I'm trying not to let the amazing success of my new company go to my head.

我們現在就利用這些慣用語來做一個 Task。

TASK 10.19

改正下面句子中的錯誤。

1. Figures just go into one ear and out from the other. I can never remember them.

_____

2. Her work leaves a lot of things to be desired.

_____

3. His wife holds the purse string.

_____

4. I'm trying to hold some things together, but it's difficult.

_____

5. Just when things were getting hard, she left me in a lurch.

_____

6. We need to bring her the book if we want her work to improve.

_____

7. While I go away on business, please hold the place for me.

_____

8. Her performance has gone beyond the joke. Fire her immediately.

_____

9. High demand usually goes hand in hand together with high prices.

_____

10. I tried to hold my grounds in the negotiations, but I think I gave away too much.

_____

Word List ▪ shrink [ʃrɪnk] v. 縮小；減少

答案

請參考下面提供的答案。

1. Figures just go in one ear and out the other. I can never remember them.
2. Her work leaves a lot to be desired.
3. His wife holds the purse strings.
4. I'm trying to hold things together, but it's difficult.
5. Just when things were getting hard, she left me in the lurch.
6. We need to bring her to book if we want her work to improve.
7. While I go away on business, please hold the fort for me.
8. Her performance has gone beyond a joke. Fire her immediately.
9. High demand usually goes hand in hand with high prices.
10. I tried to hold my ground in the negotiations, but I think I gave away too much.

　　既然你已經學會了這些慣用語 word partnerships，接著我們就來學一些慣用語 set-phrases。

TASK 10.20

請研讀這些 set-phrases 及其涵義。

商用英文必備語庫 10.15　慣用語 set-phrases　　MP3 95

· Hold on a moment!	等一下！
· Hold it!	等一下！
· Hold your horses!	稍安勿躁！
· Don't hold your breath!	事情多半不可能發生！
· I must love you and leave you.	跟你在一起的時光很快樂，但現在我得走了。（英式慣用語）
· I'm the one who brings home the bacon.	我家就靠我一份薪水。
· I'll bring him down a peg or two.	我要挫挫某人的銳氣。
· Go to the devil!	走開，別煩我！（無禮）
· Go to hell!	走開，別煩我！（無禮）
· There but for the grace of God (go I).	若不是上帝的恩寵，倒楣的就是我了。
· It's all go.	我忙死了。

TASK 10.21

請閱讀這些簡短對話，利用必備語庫 10.15 在空格裡填入適當的慣用語，接著聽 MP3 來核對答案。

Conversation 1

A: Now hold on a moment. (1)_____, so I figure I shouldn't have to do any housework.

B: Well, pal, I'm the one who cooks the bacon! So you should wash the dishes.

A: (2)_____! You shouldn't use so many dishes when you're cooking. I mean this is ridiculous! Look how many there are!

B: Look, I cook, you wash, OK? That's the deal we made. Take it or leave it.

A: (3)_____ —— that's not fair!

B: I do all the housework around here, I clean for you, cook for you, and now you want me to hold horses!

A: (4)_____.

B: Sometimes I think living with you is like living with the devil!

A: (5)_____.

B: I am in hell!

Conversation 2

A: Well, that was fun.

B: Yes, wasn't it. We should do it again some time.

A: Yes, let's. Well, (6)_____. Got an early meeting tomorrow morning at six. New client. Wants us to do some PR for him. Says he's loosing market share. I'm telling you, (7)_____ at our place these days.

B: Six? Wow. (8)_____. So who's your new client?

A: He said his name was Jesus. Some Spanish guy.

B: Oh.

Conversation 3

A: I had a fight with my new boss yesterday.

B: Oh yeah? What happened?

A: Well, I told him he didn't know the business as well as I do. I've been with the company for ten years and he just joined. I'm ten years older than him too, and I simply know more about the business.

B: Right.

A: But because he just graduated with top marks from one of the best business schools in the country, he thinks he knows everything.

B: Oh.

A: But don't worry. (9)_____.

B: So how are you going to do that?

A: I'll wait until he makes a big mistake and then let everybody know he messed up.

B: Do you think he will make a mistake if he's got top marks at business school?

A: Sure. Everybody makes mistakes sometime or other, right?

B: Well, (10)_____.

答案 🎧

請先用聽的增進聽力，順便檢查答案。如有問題，再參考下列解答。

(1) I'm the one who brings home the bacon

(2) Hold it

(3) Hold your horses

(4) Go to the devil

(5) Go to hell

(6) I must love you and leave you

(7) it's all go

(8) There but for the grace of God

(9) I'll bring him down a peg or two

(10) don't hold your breath

常 見 錯 誤 > > **fun** 和 **funny**	
錯　誤	正　確
I always have a funny time on the weekend.	I always have a fun time on the weekend.

· 請記住，fun 是「好玩」的意思；funny 是「好笑」的意思，請不要將兩個字混淆了。這兩者看起來很像，意思卻截然不同。

好，本單元的學習到此結束。在繼續下一單元之前，請回到學習清單，確定所有的學習目標都確實掌握了。

在本篇的前面，我曾請你為本篇的 25 個動詞造句，然後勾出覺得難寫的句子。現在來看一看到現在你學到了多少。

學習評量

第三篇 結尾 Task 1

請再次研讀下面的動詞，並運用你在本篇中學到的字串，為每個動詞造一個句子。

arrange	return	inform	talk	allow
tell	go	hold	decide	apologize
contact	mention	agree	join	read
hesitate	set	serve	bring	prepare
consider	enjoy	complete	require	leave

第三篇 結尾 Task 2

請比較你在本篇中為開頭 Task 1 與結尾 Task 1 所造的句子，並思考以下問題：

- ▸ 你學到了什麼？
- ▸ 比起開頭 Task 1，你寫結尾 Task 1 時感覺輕鬆了多少？
- ▸ 你覺得在運用哪幾個動詞時還有問題？為什麼？
- ▸ 你進步了多少？

PART 4

Biz Verbs

導讀

　　本書即將接近尾聲，我們將要學習最後一組動詞。同樣地，請針對這 25 個動詞再做一遍例行的 Task，如此一來，等本篇結束時，你就可以比較學習前跟學習後的成效，並知道自己進步了多少。

第四篇 開頭 Task 1
現在請研讀下面的動詞，並為每個動詞造一個句子。

第四組 25 個動詞

· expect	· cause	· recommend	· do
· review	· base	· increase	· plan
· implement	· schedule	· show	· note
· begin	· be	· propose	· involveen
· visit	· have	· try	· sure

第四篇 開頭 Task 2
請勾出使用上有困難的動詞，以及難造的句子。

Uuit 11 寫作

引言與學習目標

在最後這個寫作單元中，我們的學習重點在於運用含這 25 個動詞的 set-phrases，在電子郵件中告知收件者注意重要資訊並預先建立你和客戶間的良好關係。我們也將學這些動詞的動詞 chunks，以加強你用語的準確度。

本單元結束時，各位應達成的學習目標如下：

- ☐ 學到許多用於 CRM 的 set-phrases。
- ☐ 用新學到的 set-phrases 做練習。
- ☐ 學到很多動詞 chunks。
- ☐ 學到很多雙受詞的動詞 chunks。
- ☐ 已練習過如何使用這些新的字串。
- ☐ 在寫作時能夠更準確、更有自信的運用這些動詞。
- ☐ 知道寫作中常見的錯誤並知道該如何避免。

Set-Phrases

在接下來的幾個章節裡，我們要再學一些新的 set-phrases，讓你用於電子郵件或報告中，以告知收件者或讀者注意重要資訊、處理智慧財產權的相關問題或是與消費者或客戶建立良好關係。

◀ 告知收件者注意重要資訊的 Set-Phrases ▶

告知收件者重要資訊，是客戶關係管理中的一個重要環節。在下面的幾個 Task 中，我們將學習運用動詞 note 及其變化形式，以提醒收件者特別注意某些資訊。

TASK 11.1

請閱讀下面針對 note、notice 以及 notify 三個動詞所做的說明，並研讀例句。

note 注意；留意
◆ 這個動詞用在 Please ... 或 Please take ... 之後，表示請對方注意相關訊息；若用在 We ... 之後，則表示我方已注意到對方傳達過來的重要訊息。 ◆ Note 也可當作名詞使用，如：This is just a short note to V ...，有告知某事之意。
· Please note that we shall be arriving on the 15th. · This is just a short note to let you know that I will be arriving on Monday. · We note that you will supply references if necessary. · We note that you will be arriving on Monday.

notice 注意到；認知；發覺

◆ 這個動詞可用來告知收件者之前有某個行為造成了錯誤或反常現象，但現在注意到了。

· Upon inspection, we noticed an error in the inventory.

· On checking it, I noticed some discrepancies between the two versions.

· On looking at your report, I notice that you omitted to mention the Jolson case.

· On closer inspection, we noticed that the specs were not quite accurate.

notify 通知

◆ Notify 的語氣較跋扈、直接，適用於下最後通牒時。

◆ 這個動詞若用在 This is to ... 之後，表示告知某人某事；若用在 Please ... 之後則表示要求對方告知某事。

· This is to notify you of our decision.

· This is to notify you that we have changed our address.

· Please notify me when you return from your vacation.

· Please notify us as soon as possible.

TASK 11.2

請將下列 set-phrases 分門別類，填入下表中。

1. Kindly note that + n. clause
2. Please note that + n. clause
3. Please note the following:
4. Please note, ...
5. Please notify n.p. ...
6. Please notify us as to wh-clause
7. Please notify us if + clause ...
8. We note your complaint.
9. I notice that + n. clause

10. Please notify us of n.p. ...
11. Please take note that + n. clause
12. This is to notify you of n.p. ...
13. This is to notify you that + n. clause
14. We note that + n. clause
15. You'll note from n.p. that + n. clause ...
16. Please notify sb. that + n. clause
17. I notice that + n. clause

Word List
- discrepancy [dɪˋskrɛpənsɪ] n. 不一致；矛盾
- omit [oˋmɪt] v. 遺漏；忘記

Notifying	Requesting Notification	Reporting

答案 🔊

請利用必備語庫檢查答案，並閱讀語庫小叮嚀。

商用英文必備語庫 11.1　含 note、notify 和 notice 的 set-phrases　🎵MP3 97

Notifying （告知）	Requesting Notification （請求告知）	Reporting （傳達）
· Please note that + n. clause · Please note the following: · Please note, · Kindly note that + n. clause · Please take note that + n. clause · You'll note from n.p. that + n. clause · This is to notify you that + n. clause · This is to notify you of n.p.	· Please notify us of n.p. · Please notify us as to wh— clause · Please notify us if + n. clause · Please notify n.p. · Please notify sb. that + n. clause	· We note that + n. clause · I notice that + n. clause · I notice from n.p. that + n. clause · We note your complaint.

🖋 語庫小叮嚀

◆ 請注意，note that + n. clause 若是「告知」的意思，後面的子句通常都是用未來式，因為你要知會的通常是未來的事；如是「傳達」的意思，則後面的子句通常都是用過去或現在式，因為你要傳達的通常是已經發生或正在發生的事。

◆ 請注意，I notice that + n. clause 和 I notice from n.p. that + n. clause 中的 notice 比較常用過去式。

請閱讀下面的電子郵件，找出語庫 11.1 中的 set-phrases 並畫底線。注意這些 set-phrases 的用法。

Dear May,

Please notify me as to when you plan to complete the final stage of the project. I need to coordinate the launch with other projects I am in charge of. Also, please note that I will be on leave from the 28th to the 6th of next month.

Thanks and regards,

Dear All,

Kindly note that we will be holding a fire drill next Friday at 10 a.m. Please make sure you have studied the procedures and know what to do. Could the department heads also please ensure the fire extinguishers are in good working order? Please notify me before the end of today if you find any that are not working.

Thanks.

Dear Judy,

Thanks for your report, which I received last Friday. Upon checking through some of the data, I noticed that there seems to be some information missing on page 6. I hope the missing data will be on the way soon! I also noticed that you did not cc Michael. Please cc him in the future.

Word List	• drill [drɪl] n. 訓練；演習
	• cc (= carbon copy) v. 寄副本

答案🔊

現在來練習運用這些 chunks。

Dear May,

Please notify me as to when you plan to complete the final stage of the project. I need to coordinate the launch with other projects I am in charge of. Also, please note that I will be on leave from the 28th to the 6th of next month.

Thanks and regards,

Dear All,

Kindly note that we will be holding a fire drill next Friday at 10 a.m. Please make sure you have studied the procedures and know what to do. Could the department heads also please ensure the fire extinguishers are in good working order? Please notify me before the end of today if you find any that are not working.

Thanks.

Dear Judy,

Thanks for your report, which I received last Friday. Upon checking through some of the data, I noticed that there seems to be some information missing on page 6. I hope the missing data will be on the way soon! I also noticed that you did not cc Michael. Please cc him in the future.

TASK 11.4

請改正下面句子中的錯誤，見範例。

1. Please notify me as when you plan to come.

   Please notify me as to when you plan to come.

2. Please notice that I will be on leave then.

   _____

3. Kindly notify that we will be closed tomorrow.

_____

4. Please notice me before the end of today.

_____

5. I notify that there is information missing.

_____

6. I also note that you did not cc Tom.

_____

7. I notify that you have been absent.

_____

8. This is to notice you that we're fully booked.

_____

9. Please notice us if you intend to cancel your reservation.

_____

答案

請看下列參考答案。

2. Please note that I will be on leave then.
3. Kindly note that we will be closed tomorrow.
4. Please notify me before the end of today.
5. I notice that there is information missing.
6. I also notice that you did not cc Tom.
7. I notice that you have been absent.
8. This is to notify you that we're fully booked.
9. Please notify us if you intend to cancel your reservation.

處理智慧財產權問題的 Set-Phrases

　　在本節裡，我們要來學一些可用於處理智慧財產權問題的 set-phrases。智慧財產權問題是客戶關係管理中一個複雜的環節，若發現顧客未經同意擅用你們公司的

商標或產品圖片，你們原本良好的關係便會破裂。因此，我們現在就來學些要授權給對方以及發現權利被侵犯時可用上的 set-phrases。

TASK 11.5

請將下列 set-phrases 分門別類，填入下表。

1. I have no alternative but to V …
2. You have our consent to V …
3. I have no choice but to V …
4. You have our permission to V …
5. I have no option but to V …
6. You have the right to V …

Taking Negative Action	Giving Permission

答案🅞

請利用下列的必備語庫來檢查答案。

商用英文必備語庫 11.2　處理智慧財產權問題的 set-phrases　　🔊MP3 98

Taking Negative Action （採取反制行動）	Giving Permission （授權）
· I have no alternative but to V … · I have no choice but to V … · I have no option but to V …	· You have our consent to V … · You have our permission to V … · You have the right to V …

✎　語庫小叮嚀

◆ 採取反制行動中的 set-phrases 不僅可用於處理智慧財產權問題，也可用於其他狀況中，例如消費者逾期付款、供應商未按時出貨或違約等狀況。如果想要稍微施加壓力，告知對方將有可能採取法律行動，這些 set-phrases 便非常有用。

Word List　· consent [kən`sɛnt] n. 同意；贊成

273

常　見　錯　誤　> 　> 　**lack**	
錯　誤	正　確
I lack of money.	I lack money.
I have lack of money.	I have a lack of money.

·Lack 可以當動詞也可當名詞用，請小心。
·當動詞時，請用 lack sth.；當名詞時，請用 have a lack of sth.。

建立良好顧客關係的 Set-Phrases

含 have 的 set-phrases 除了可用來建立良好的顧客關係外，也可用來表達支持。如想預先和新的客戶建立良好的關係，或者在知道客戶遭逢一些困難，想表達關心之意時，下列 set-phrases 都非常好用。

TASK 11.6

請將這些含 have 的 set-phrases 分門別類，填入下表中。

1. I hope we may have the pleasure of Ving/n.p.
2. You have my very best wishes for n.p. …
3. I hope we shall have the pleasure of Ving/n.p. …
4. You have my heartiest congratulations.
5. I hope to have the pleasure of Ving/n.p. …
6. You have my sincere appreciation for n.p. …
7. I hope to have a chance to V …
8. You have my sincere gratitude.
9. I hope to have an opportunity to V …
10. I hope we shall have the privilege of Ving/n.p.
11. I hope to have the privilege of Ving/n.p.
12. You have our deepest sympathy.
13. I hope to have time to V …
14. I hope we shall have time to V …
15. You have the full support of n.p. …
16. I hope to have time for n.p. …
17. I hope we shall have time for n.p. …
18. You have our full support for n.p. …

Word List	• gratitude [ˋgrætə͵tud] n. 感謝
	• privilege [ˋprɪvlɪdʒ] n. 專屬某部分人的權利

Building for the Future	Showing Support

答案

請利用下列必備語庫檢查答案。

商用英文必備語庫 11.3　建立良好顧客關係與表達支持的 set-phrases　MP3 99

Building for the Future (建立未來的良好關係)	Showing Support (表達支持)
· I hope we may have the pleasure of Ving/n.p. · I hope we shall have the pleasure of Ving/n.p. · I hope to have the pleasure of Ving/n.p. · I hope to have a chance to V · I hope to have an opportunity to V · I hope we shall have the privilege of Ving/n.p. · I hope to have the privilege of Ving/n.p. · I hope to have time to V · I hope we shall have time to V · I hope to have time for n.p. · I hope we shall have time for n.p.	· You have my heartiest congrat- ulations. · You have my sincere apprecia- tion for n.p. · You have my sincere gratitude. · You have my very best wishes for n.p. · You have our deepest sympathy. · You have the full support of n.p. · You have our full support for n.p.

現在來練習運用這些 set-phrases。

TASK 11.7

請改正下面句子中的錯誤，見範例。有些句子的錯誤不只一個。

1. You have my heartier congratulations.

   You have my heartiest congratulations.

2. You have our permission for reproducing the color photograph in your catalog.

_____

3. I hope have a chance to impress you with our services.

_____

4. I hope to have time for talking to all of your clients.

_____

5. I have no choice to suspend delivery until we receive payment.

_____

6. I hope to have privilege for meeting your office furniture needs in the future.

_____

7. You have full support of everyone here.

_____

8. I have no option but calling my lawyers to deal with this issue.

_____

9. I have not alternative but ask you to return the payment before the end of the month.

_____

10. I hope we shall have a pleasure of meeting again soon.

_____

答案 🔊

請比較你改過的句子和下面的參考答案。

2. You have our permission to reproduce the color photograph in your catalog.

3. I hope to have a chance to impress you with our services.

4. I hope to have time to talk to all of your clients.

5. I have no choice but to suspend delivery until we receive payment.

6. I hope to have the privilege of meeting your office furniture needs in the future.

7. You have the full support of everyone here.

8. I have no option but to call my lawyers to deal with this issue.

9. I have no alternative but to ask you to return the payment before the end of the month.

10. I hope we shall have the pleasure of meeting again soon.

TASK 11.8

請利用語庫 11.2 與 11.3 在空格中填入適當的 set-phrases，有些 set-phrases 可多次使用。

Dear Lucas,

I hear from Macey that you are having difficulties collecting payment from ABC Inc. She has given me a full briefing on the situation. It seems (1)_____ begin legal actions to recover the money. Do please go ahead.

Dear Juli,

My wife and I have recently become members of the Palm Lakes Golf Resort in Chiayi. We (2)_____ enjoying your company there sometime next month. Please let me know if you have a free weekend coming up.

Dear George,

Regarding invoice number 123xyz, your payment is now three months late. I'm afraid (3)_____ refer this case to our legal department for legal action.

Dear Marco,

I know that the current business climate in China is very difficult, and (4)_____ all your efforts to keep the venture going under difficult circumstances.

Dear Mary,

As you may know we have lost a lot of business recently, and there is little prospect of any new business coming in for the foreseeable future. For this reason, I'm afraid (5)_____ lay off 20% of the workforce, and unfortunately your position is one of those that will be eliminated.

Dear John,

Apologies for the delay in replying to your query. I have checked with my lawyer, and apparently (6)_____ sue your former employer for gross misconduct. Please contact me if you would like to go ahead.

Dear Mr. Chen,

I am delighted to hear from Mark that the joint venture project between our two companies has been completed successfully. (7)_____ working with you on other projects in the future.

答案

1	· we have no alternative but to · we have no choice but to · we have no option but to
2	· hope we may have the pleasure of · hope we shall have the pleasure of · hope to have the pleasure of
3	· we have no alternative but to · we have no choice but to · we have no option but to
4	· you have my sincere appreciation for · you have our full support for
5	· we have no alternative but to · we have no choice but to · we have no option but to
6	· You have the right to
7	· I hope we may have the pleasure of · I hope we shall have the pleasure of · I hope to have the pleasure of · I hope we shall have the privilege of · I hope to have the privilege of

　　請注意哪些空格可填入多個答案；哪些空格又只能填入一個答案。請留意標點符號、set-phrases 的結尾和意思，以確切了解原因。

動詞 Chunks

接著，我們要進入的是動詞 chunks 的章節，本節的主要目的在於讓你了解並運用本篇 25 個動詞的使用模式。請仔細研讀下面表格中的動詞 chunks 後做 Task，以確實了解模式。

TASK 11.9

請將這些動詞 chunks 分門別類，寫在下面的表格中，見範例。

1. begin n.p.
2. begin to V
3. begin Ving
4. cause n.p.
5. cause sth. to V
6. ensure n.p.
7. ensure that + n. clause
8. expect n.p.
9. expect to V
10. expect n.p. to V
11. expect that + n. clause
12. handle n.p.
13. improve n.p.
14. increase n.p.
15. involve n.p.
16. involve Ving
17. plan n.p.
18. plan to V
19. propose n.p.
20. propose that + n. clause
21. propose to V
22. propose Ving
23. recommend n.p.
24. recommend that + n. clause
25. recommend Ving
26. remember that + n. clause
27. remember to V
28. remember wh-to V
29. remember wh-clause
30. show sb. that + n. clause
31. show wh-to V
32. show n.p.
33. show sb. n.p.
34. show sb. wh-to V
35. show sb. wh-clause
36. show that + n. clause
37. show wh-clause
38. try n.p.
39. try to V
40. try Ving
41. visit n.p.
42. remember n.p.

V + Ving	V that + n. clause	V + wh-to V
recommend Ving	*expect that + n. clause*	*show sb. wh-to V*

V to V	V + n.p.	V + wh-clause
expect n.p. to V	*remember n.p.*	*show wh-clause*

答案 🎧

請利用下列的必備語庫檢查答案。

商用英文必備語庫 11.4 動詞 chunks MP3 100

V + Ving	V that + n. clause		V + wh- to V
· recommend Ving	· recommend that + n. clause	· show sb. that + n. clause	· show wh-to V
· begin Ving	· propose that + n. clause	· show that + n. clause	· show sb. wh-to V
· propose Ving	· ensure that + n. clause	· expect that + n. clause	· remember wh-to V
· involve Ving	· remember that + n. clause		
· try Ving			

V to V	V + n.p.		V + wh-clause
· expect n.p. to V	· remember n.p.	· propose n.p.	· show wh-clause
· expect to V	· expect n.p.	· try n.p.	· show sb. wh-clause
· begin to V	· begin n.p.	· plan n.p.	· remember wh-clause
· propose to V	· visit n.p.	· involve n.p.	
· try to V	· cause n.p.	· ensure n.p.	
· plan to V	· recommend n.p.	· improve n.p.	
· remember to V	· increase n.p.	· handle n.p.	
· cause sth. to V	· show n.p.	· show sb. n.p.	

✎ 語庫小叮嚀

◆ Show 有兩個涵義，端視動詞 chunk 是否含 sb. 而定。若含 sb.，show 會帶有個人的涵義，表示給某人看某物，如：Show me your resume、Show me your kid's picture.。若不含 sb.，則有非個人的涵義，如：The diagram shows how the electrical circuit works.、These figures show that our market share is increasing.。

Word List · circuit [ˋsɝkɪt] n. 電路；線路圖

◆ 此外，如同前面的單元一樣，有些動詞可有多種模式。例如 recommend that + n. clause 和 recommend Ving；或 ensure that + n. clause 和 ensure n.p.。

現在來看一些範例，學習在電子郵件中運用這些動詞 chunks 的方法。

TASK 11.10

請閱讀下面的電子郵件，找出必備語庫 11.4 中的動詞 chunks 並畫底線。注意這些動詞 chunks 的用法。

Dear Joyce,

Just a few words of explanation about the attached projections. They are based on the results for the three years previous to 2006, and show results region by region using figures which are on file. You will see that, according to the projections, we will only begin to see a satisfactory return after the end of next year. If we want to present a more optimistic analysis, I propose not mentioning the regional results. Of course I don't think this will make much difference, since we will still need to show how we have arrived at our projections.

Dear Joe,

While I am in Beijing, I am expecting a call from Wallis Productions. Please take it for me, and let them know that I have already begun the storyboard, and will begin working on the dialogue when I get back. I don't want my trip to Beijing to cause them a delay.

Word List	• projection [prəˋdʒɛkʃən] n. 預測
	• storyboard [ˋstorɪˏbord] n. 電影拍攝程序的記事板

Dear Connie,

Further to our conversation on the phone, I would like to recommend that we go ahead with the presentation for several reasons. If we can show the board that the department is still able to be of use to the company, then I think we can ensure further funding. It is in our best interest to try to produce an excellent pitch. For this reason I propose that we meet on Thursday to rehearse the pitch and brainstorm any questions the board might have for us.

Dear Lulu,

Please note that Mr. Coginwheel is visiting the plant on Friday. I expect that he will want to see the new loading bay, so please ensure that it is tidy, and that everything is in good order. Also, please remember to ask all of the machinists to wear goggles during his visit. He will expect to see people wearing them. He is looking forward to his visit, and I know with you showing him around, he will be in good hands.

Dear Jonathan,

Please note that I will be arriving at CKS airport on the 29th. I would like to begin my tour by seeing the factories in the North. I would particularly like you to show me the assembly lines and packaging centers. I also plan to see the factories in the South, as I remember that they were underperforming a few months ago. I would like you to show me how you have managed to increase production so quickly there, and how you ensure that production is always on schedule. I then propose to spend some time talking to the machine operators to see if we can get any ideas from them for improvements.

Word List

- pitch [pɪtʃ] n. 宣傳；推銷
- rehearse [rɪˋhɝs] v. 排演；排練
- brainstorm [ˋbren͵stɔrm] v. 腦力激盪
- goggles [ˋgɑglz] n. 護目鏡
- assembly line 裝配線

答案 🔈

看到有些動詞會搭配介系詞 chunks，你可能會覺得不解。別擔心，我會在第十三單元中更詳細的教你如何運用這些動詞的介系詞 chunks 和片語動詞。

Dear Joyce,

Just a few words of explanation about the attached projections. They are based on the results for the three years previous to 2006, and <u>show results</u> region by region using figures which are on file. You will see that, according to the projections, we will only <u>begin to see</u> a satisfactory return after the end of next year. If we want to present a more optimistic analysis, I <u>propose not mentioning</u> the regional results. Of course I don't think this will make much difference, since we will still need to <u>show how</u> we have arrived at our projections.

Dear Joe,

While I am in Beijing, I am <u>expecting a call</u> from Wallis Productions. Please take it for me, and let them know that I have already <u>begun the storyboard</u>, and will <u>begin working on</u> the dialogue when I get back. I don't want my trip to Beijing to cause them a delay.

Dear Connie,

Further to our conversation on the phone, I would like to <u>recommend that</u> we go ahead with the presentation for several reasons. If we can <u>show the board that</u> the department is still able to be of use to the company, then I think we can <u>ensure further funding</u>. It is in our best interest to try to produce an excellent pitch. For this reason I <u>propose that</u> we meet on Thursday to rehearse the pitch and brainstorm any questions the board might have for us.

Dear Lulu,

Please note that Mr. Coginwheel is visiting the plant on Friday. I <u>expect that</u> he will want to see the new loading bay, so please <u>ensure that</u> it is tidy, and

that everything is in good order. Also, please <u>remember to ask</u> all of the machinists to wear goggles during his visit. He will <u>expect to see</u> people wearing them. He is looking forward to his visit, and I know with you showing him around, he will be in good hands.

Dear Jonathan,

Please note that I will be arriving at CKS airport on the 29ᵗʰ. I would like to <u>begin my tour</u> by seeing the factories in the North. I would particularly like you to <u>show me the assembly lines and packaging centers</u>. I also <u>plan to see</u> the factories in the South, as I <u>remember that</u> they were underperforming a few months ago. I would like you to <u>show me how</u> you have managed to increase production so quickly there, and <u>how</u> you ensure that production is always on schedule. I then <u>propose to spend</u> some time talking to the machine operators to see if we can get any ideas from them for improvements.

常 見 錯 誤 > > recommend

錯 誤	正 確
I recommend you to apply for the job.	I recommend you apply for the job.
I recommend that you can apply. I recommend that you should apply. I recommend that you must apply.	I recommend that you apply for the job.

· 千萬不要在 recommend 後面的子句用 can、should 或 must。記住，recommend 後面所接的子句只要用簡單現在式即可。

雙受詞動詞 Chunks

　　在本節中我們要學的是雙受詞動詞。學習至今你應該對雙受詞動詞的用法都非常熟悉，也知道該如何使用了，那現在我們就直接進入正題吧。

TASK 11.11

請將這些動詞 chunks 分門別類，填入下表中。

1. cause sb. sth.
2. show sb. sth.

3. cause sth. for sb.
4. show sth. to sb.

Non-Invertible	Invertible

答案

請利用下列的必備語庫檢查答案，並閱讀其下的語庫小叮嚀。

商用英文必備語庫 **11.5**　雙受詞動詞 chunks

Non-Invertible （不可倒置）	Invertible （可倒置）
	· cause sb. sth.　　· show sb. sth. · cause sth. for sb.　· show sth. to sb.

　　語庫小叮嚀

◆ 看出來了嗎？這兩個動詞都屬於可倒置的雙受詞動詞，也就是你可以隨意調換兩個受詞的位置。這裡需特別注意的是，受詞調換後，要記得加上正確的介系詞。

　　現在我們來做一些練習，讓你更了解這些雙受詞動詞的用法。

TASK 11.12

請閱讀下列句子，練習調換句中兩個受詞的位置。

1. You could try taking it to the sales department and showing it to them.

   You could try taking it to the sales department and showing them the problem.

2. Did you know he would cause us all this trouble?

   _____

3. Do you remember last week I showed you my new software program?

   _____

4. I would like you to show me the assembly lines and packaging centers.

   _____

5. I don't want my trip to Beijing to cause them a delay.

   _____

答案 🔊

請比較你的句子與下面提供的答案。

2. Did you know he would cause all this trouble for us?

3. Do you remember last week I showed my new software program to you?

4. I would like you to show the assembly lines and packaging centers to me.

5. I don't want my trip to Beijing to cause a delay for them.

　　好了，你終於學完最後一個寫作單元。請回到本單元前面的學習目標，確定每一項都懂了。

Unit 12 口說

引言與學習目標

　　在本單元中我們要學的是未來時間，英文中的未來時間對很多人來說可能是一大罩門，使用時也常犯錯。例如，很多人會說：I will have a meeting tomorrow. 或者是 Tomorrow I will go to Hong Kong. 這都不是最精確的用法！稍後會詳加說明。

　　在本單元中我將為你簡介一些實用和實際的方法，以了解英文中的未來時間，此外，更會教你一些可用來表示未來涵義的各類 chunks 和 set-phrases。在接下來的章節裡，我希望你嘗試拋開從前老師教過的未來式用法，重新學習！

　　本單元結束時，各位應達成的學習目標如下：

- ❑ 對談論未來事情的不同用法有清楚的了解。
- ❑ 對 will 和 be going to 的不同有清楚的了解。
- ❑ 有能力使用 25 個動詞中的部分動詞，談論個人的或生意上的計劃。
- ❑ 知道一些常見的口說錯誤並知道該如何避免。
- ❑ 做過一些口說、聽力和發音練習。

時態：未來時間

　　我先為你簡介未來時間的意思，表達未來事情的時候，你有兩點必須先考慮。首先需考慮你要表達的是 personal 還是 impersonal 的未來事件。所謂 personal 的未來事件是指個人的未來計劃、夢想、期望、打算和安排等，以及其他和自己有關的未來人事物；而 impersonal 的未來事件，則是指和你個人較無關連的未來事件，例如經濟前景、所從事的行業前景、政治前景、環境的未來和天氣等，這是你在表達未來事情時的第一個考量。第二個考量是你想表達的事情是 certain 還是 uncertain。我們接著來看一些範例，加深你對這些概念的印象。

TASK 12.1

請閱讀以下電子郵件，判斷內容的整體意思和情況是屬於 personal 還是 impersonal，以及是 certain 還是 uncertain，見範例。

1

Dear Mary,

Please note that I'll be arriving on Tuesday at 3:00. I'm going straight to the hotel as I'll probably be very jet-lagged. Please meet me there tomorrow morning at 10:00 in the lobby. I'll see you then.

▶▶ *personal certain*

2

Dear Oliver,

Thanks for your questions. As I mentioned in my report, the economy will stay much the same next year. Growth will stay steady across the region. Other companies in the industry will all face the same problems, so I think the market situation is going to be more or less the same. I hope this helps.

▶▶ _____

Word List　• jet-lagged [ˌdʒɛt`lægd] adj. 有時差現象的

3

Dear June,

I'm thinking of canceling my holiday this month since we're so busy. I may go to Bali at the end of the year, or I might wait until Chinese New Year and then go to Europe. Sorry to keep you waiting like this, but I'll get back to you with a firm plan as soon as I can.

▶▶ _____

4

Dear George,

Regarding our plans for next year, we hope to increase market share by 0.03% by the middle of the year, and we would like to improve our brand awareness at the same time. We intend to launch several new exciting products and we would like to increase the sales volume of our more popular brands. We are having a meeting with the team on Monday to discuss these plans in more detail. I'll give you a ring later to brief you.

▶▶ _____

5

Dear Frank,

I'm not sure about your forecast for the future. In my view, I think the economy will shrink next year due to the outflow of capital from overseas investors. The government may not be able to stop this trend. Exports could fall as foreign companies order from factories in China instead of Taiwan. Anyway, I guess we'll see.

▶▶ _____

Word List · outflow [ˋaʊt.flo] n. 流出

答案🎧

請看以下答案並閱讀說明文字。

1	personal certain	發信者將此行的安排告知瑪莉,這些安排是個人事情,並且對發信者來說是確定而且不會變動的。電子郵件中只有一個是不確定的未來,你看得出來是哪一個嗎?
2	impersonal certain	發信者在表達自己對他和奧利佛所從事的行業中經濟前景的看法,他的語氣非常肯定,因此是 impersonal certain!
3	personal uncertain	休假是屬於個人的事情,但由於發信者還未決定度假地點及日期,因此是 personal uncertain 的未來事件。
4	personal certain	這封電子郵件談的是個人明年在公事上的計劃,這些事情都已確定,因此是 personal certain。
5	impersonal uncertain	信件內容談的是未來一年的經濟局勢,包括政府方面的作為以及出口方面會受到的影響,但由於發信者不確定自己的預測是否正確,因此是屬於 impersonal uncertain。

好,希望以上說明對你有幫助。現在我們來進一步學習 personal 未來。

你可能從上面的電子郵件內容中已經發現,personal certain 未來大致上可分為兩種:(1) 描述未來的計劃/打算;(2) 描述未來的安排。

計劃/打算和安排的差別在於:計劃/打算表示你即將做某事,但可能尚未著手安排;而安排指的是你已經著手安排的一些預定事宜。舉一個例子,如果我說:I plan to go to Hong Kong. 是表示我已經決定要去香港,但時間、行程等可能都還沒安排。這是確定的未來,因為我已經做好計劃或打算,只是還沒實際行動而已。

Tomorrow I'm going to Hong Kong.,這便是一種安排。因為要去香港前,你必須先訂好旅館、機票,也要先辦好簽證。這些所有安排都需要你先打電話和某人談,或者寫電子郵件給對方。從另一個角度看安排,即:你已經預先處理好一些前置事項,請他人為你安排好某事。

一旦了解這兩個概念,應用時應該就不難了,因為接下來你只要知道該用哪些 chunks 來表達這兩種不同的意思即可,現在我們就來學這些 chunks 吧。

描述個人未來的 Chunks

TASK 12.2

請將下列 chunks 分門別類，填入下表中。

1. ... be Ving
2. Can you make n.p.?
3. Can you manage n.p.?
4. I can make n.p.
5. I can manage n.p.
6. I can't make n.p.
7. I can't manage n.p.
8. It is our intention to V
9. I hope to V
10. I intend to V
11. I may V
12. I might V
13. I need to V
14. I want to V
15. I'm thinking of Ving
16. It is our hope that we can V
17. I would like to V
18. I'll be Ving
19. I won't be Ving
20. I'll probably V
21. I'll probably be Ving
22. I probably won't V
23. I probably won't be Ving
24. I'm going to V
25. I'm not going to V

Personal Certain		Personal Uncertain
Plans and Intentions	**Arrangements**	

答案 🔊

請利用下面的必備語庫來核對答案。

商用英文必備語庫 **12.1** 個人未來用語 (1)　　MP3 102

Personal Certain		Personal Uncertain
Plans and Intentions（計劃與打算）	**Arrangements**（安排）	
· I'm going to V	· ... be Ving	· I may V
· I'm not going to V	· Can you make n.p.?	· I might V
· It is our intention to V	· Can you manage n.p.?	· I'm thinking of Ving
· I hope to V	· I can make n.p.	· I'll probably V
· I intend to V	· I can manage n.p.	· I'll probably be Ving
· I need to V	· I can't make n.p.	· I probably won't V
· I want to V	· I can't manage n.p.	· I probably won't be Ving
· It is our hope that we can V	· I'll be Ving	
· I would like to V	· I won't be Ving	

語庫小叮嚀

◆ 所有含 make 和 manage 的 set-phrases 都可用來建議、接受或拒絕見面時間和地點。請閱讀以下例句：

　A: Can you make 2:00 on Thursday?

　B: I can make 2:00. 或 I can't manage 2:00. How about 3:00?

◆ I may V 的語氣比 I might V 來得強烈一點。I'll probably V 比 might 和 may 的確定程度高，但仍沒有百分之百確定。

◆ 你可能把 I hope to V 當作不確定用語，但因為你已經決定要做某事，所以其實這是確定用語。

◆ 請注意，I want to V 和 I would like to V 經常用於表示未來的計劃和打算。

◆ Be going to V 這個 chunk 與動詞 go 搭配使用時，其中一個 go 可以省略，如：I'm going to go home. 就變成了 I'm going home.；I'm going to go to Hong Kong. 就變成了 I'm going to Hong Kong.。

MP3 102

請用 MP3 練習必備語庫 12.1 中 chunks 的發音。

MP3 103

Joyce 和 David 正在討論週末的計劃，聽完 MP3 中的對話後請列出他們兩人在下列時間的計劃或安排為何。

	Joyce	David
星期五晚上		
星期六早上		
星期六下午		
星期六晚上		
星期天早上		
星期天下午		
星期天晚上		

答案 🎧

	Joyce	David
星期五晚上	和男友吃晚餐	✕
星期六早上	去烏來	打籃球
星期六下午	烏來	✕
星期六晚上	烏來	參加派對
星期天早上	烏來	✕
星期天下午	回台北	✕
星期天晚上	看 DVD	看電影

　　如果第一次沒有完全聽懂，別擔心，請先繼續完成下面的 Task，再閱讀對話內容。

TASK 12.5

MP3 103

請再聽一次對話，並利用語庫 12.1，將所有你聽到的 chunks 勾出來，並思考其意思。

答案 🎧

現在請參考下列完整的對話內容，檢查上面兩個 Task 的答案。

David: Gee, thank God it's Friday!

Joyce: Yeah, you can say that again. What a week! Only a few more hours and then we can celebrate the weekend!

David: So, doing anything nice for the weekend?

Joyce: Oh, yes. I'm going to Wulai on Saturday.

David: Oh, great. Alone or with friends?

Joyce: Well, I'm going with my boyfriend. He's got a motorcycle so we'll be driving up there together. Then we want to stay in a hot spring hotel for the night.

David: Oh, wow? Which one?

Joyce: Don't know yet. We're just going to see which one we like. We both need to get out of the city. So we're coming back late Sunday afternoon.

David: Sounds great. What about Sunday night?

Joyce: Oh, I'll probably be rather tired, so I'll probably just stay home. I might get a DVD or something. Have an early night. But hey, what are your plans for the weekend.

David: Well, I'm going to play basketball on Saturday morning.

Joyce: Oh, right. Is this like a regular thing you do?

David: Yeah. We play every Saturday morning, and then we're going to have a hotpot lunch together. Saturday night I'm going to a party in Gong Guan. Some friends of mine moved into a new apartment so they're having a housewarming party. Should be fun.

Joyce: Sounds good. What about Sunday?

David: Oh, I'll probably have a hangover, so I probably won't be doing much Sunday morning. I'll probably sleep in and spend the day relaxing. I might go to the movies with my roommate in the evening. We usually go to the movies on Sunday night, but if we go I'm not sure what we'd see. We're thinking of going to see the new Ang Lee movie.

Joyce: Oh yes, it's good.

David: So what are you doing later tonight? Want to have a drink together?

Joyce: I'd love to, but I can't make it. I'm meeting my boyfriend for a late dinner.

David: Oh, OK. I'll go by myself then.

我們接著就來進一步探討應該如何運用含 will V 的 set-phrases。

◢◣ 含 Will 的各類不同功能的 Set-Phrases ▶

Will V 的用法常見於各種含 I 或 you 的 set-phrases 中，以表達不同的意思或功能，例如：1. 提議（I'll help you with the figures.）、2. 請求（Will you help me with the figures?）、3. 做承諾（I'll call you back.）、4. 做決定（I'll go by myself.）、5. 威脅（I'll hit you if say that again!）、6. 警告（You'll hurt yourself! Be careful!）、7. 道再見（I'll see you later.）。

Word List	• housewarming party 喬遷派對
	• hangover [ˈhæŋˌovə] n. 宿醉
	• sleep in 早上起得晚

TASK 12.6

請將這些含 will 的 set-phrases 分門別類，填入下表中。

1. I'll be back on Thursday.
2. I'll be free at …
3. I'll be in touch.
4. I'll be late.
5. I'll be really angry.
6. I'll do it as soon as I can.
7. I'll do it later.
8. I'll drop you a line.
9. I'll get it.
10. I'll give you a call.
11. I'll have a cappuccino.
12. I'll have fried chicken.
13. I'll hit you!
14. I'll kill you!
15. I'll put the kettle on.
16. I'll see what I can do.
17. I'll see you then/later/tomorrow.
18. I'll send it tomorrow.
19. I'll talk to him for you, if you like.
20. I'll tell everyone you said that.
21. I'll V, if you like.
22. It'll be all right.
23. She'll be back tomorrow.
24. There'll be lots of people there.
25. We'll see.
26. Will you ask her for me?
27. Will you do it?
28. Will you have time to V?
29. Will you help me with this?
30. You'll be late.
31. You'll hurt yourself.
32. You'll make a mistake.
33. You'll regret it.

Making Offers	Making Requests
Making Promises	**Making Spontaneous Decisions**
Making Threats	**Making Warnings**
Saying Goodbye	**Other**

答案

請比較你的答案和下面必備語庫中的答案。

商用英文必備語庫 12.2　含 will V 的各類不同功能的 set-phrases　MP3 104

Making Offers（提議）	Making Requests（請求）
· I'll get it. · I'll talk to him for you, if you like. · I'll V, if you like. · I'll put the kettle on.	· Will you do it? · Will you help me with this? · Will you have time to V? · Will you ask her for me?
Making Promises（做承諾）	**Making Spontaneous Decisions**（做決定）
· I'll send it tomorrow. · I'll do it as soon as I can. · It'll be all right. · I'll see what I can do.	· We'll see. · I'll do it later. · I'll have a cappuccino. · I'll have fried chicken.
Making Threats（威脅）	**Making Warnings**（警告）
· I'll tell everyone you said that. · I'll hit you! · I'll kill you! · I'll be really angry.	· You'll regret it. · You'll be late. · You'll hurt yourself. · You'll make a mistake.
Saying Goodbye（道再見）	**Other**（其他）
· I'll give you a call. · I'll drop you a line. · I'll be in touch. · I'll see you then/later/tomorrow.	· I'll be free at … · There'll be lots of people there. · I'll be back on Thursday. · She'll be back tomorrow. · I'll be late.

✎　語庫小叮嚀

◆ 在使用這些 set-phrases 時，務必先對背景或狀況有清楚的了解，才能把這些 set-phrases

用對。例如：I'll be in touch. 可能是在做承諾，也可能是道再見。I'll get it. 也可能是表示承諾或者提議，端視使用的情況而定。

◆ I'll drop you a line. 是「我會寫信給你」的意思。I'll put the kettle on. 是「我會煮水泡茶」的意思。

TASK 12.7

請再次閱讀 Task 12.1 中的五封電子郵件，找出含 will V 的 set-phrases，並思考其功能和意思。

TASK 12.8

MP3 105

請聽光碟中的句子，並從必備語庫 12.2 中選出一個含 will 的 set-phrases 來回答。記得把你的答案錄下來以便評量。

答案 🎧

MP3 106

請聽 MP3 中我提供的建議答案。

　　既然我們已經學會 personal 未來的用語，現在來學 impersonal 未來用語吧。要表示 impersonal 的確定未來事件，有兩種 chunks ── will V 和 be going to V，兩者表達的意思一樣，但 be going to V 可強調你有證據說明你對未來的看法是確定的，而 will V 則僅僅是在陳述某件 impersonal 的確定未來而已。

◢ 描述非個人未來的 Chunks ◣

TASK 12.9

請研讀下面的必備語庫。

 **12.3** 非個人未來用語

MP3 107

<table>
<tr><th colspan="3">Impersonal Futures</th></tr>
<tr><th>Certain</th><th colspan="2">Uncertain</th></tr>
<tr><td>· … will V
· … be going to V</td><td>· I think it'll V
· I think n.p. will V
· n.p. will probably V</td><td>· n.p. might V
· n.p. may V</td></tr>
</table>

語庫小叮嚀

◆ 請注意，impersonal 與 personal 的不確定未來用語的用法非常類似，兩者主要的不同在於所使用的主詞，impersonal 的不確定未來用語通常是用物當主詞，如 it 或 n. p.，而 personal 的則均以人當主詞，請比較語庫 12.1 和 12.3 中這兩種用語的用法，以確定我說的你都了解了。

TASK 12.10

MP3 108

請聽 Mark 跟投資顧問 Jennifer 的對話，並回答以下問題：

1. Jennifer 覺得在中國投資的遠景如何？
2. 她建議把錢投資在哪裡？為什麼？

答案

1. Jennifer 對在中國投資的遠景不樂觀。她認為當愈來愈多的公司開始在那裡投資後，人力和原料成本都會高漲。
2. 她認為在越南投資比較好，因為人力成本在一、二十年內仍低，她預期經濟成長後，越南政府會開始鬆綁法規，以利外商投資。
3. 如果還是覺得聽力很難，請閱讀下列完整的對話內容。

Mark　　: So what do you think is going to happen?

Jennifer: Well, as more companies start investing in China, I think the cost of materials will also rise. Also the cost of labor is going to rise eventually. It always does in developing markets. The trick is to get in before the costs get too high, make a lot of money, and then get out.

Mark　　: I see. So what do you suggest?

Jennifer: Put your money in Vietnam, because the cost of labor is not going to rise there for at least one or two decades. Margins are still going to be high.

Mark　　: But what about the political stability?

Jennifer: Well, the government will probably ease restrictions on capital inflow

---

Word List　• restriction [rɪ`strɪkʃən] n. 限制；管制

and outflow as the economy starts to grow. They might even liberalize some of the investment and property laws. That's going to make it easier for foreign companies to buy land and build factories.

Mark　: Hm, interesting.

TASK 12.11

MP3 108

請再聽一次對話，並利用必備語庫 12.3，將所有聽到的 set-phrases 勾出來，注意這些 set-phrases 的用法。

TASK 12.12

你對投資在中國或是越南的看法又是如何呢？請運用剛剛學到的 impersonal 未來用語，給 Mark 一些建議。記得將你的答案錄下來，以便檢查用語是否正確。

答案

我在此就不提供答案了，相信做了這些練習，你已經很會使用這些 set-phases 來表達看法了。

常 見 錯 誤 ＞ ＞ **later** 和 **after**	
錯　誤	正　確
I'll be back two weeks later.	I'll be back in two weeks.
After two years there will be more competition.	In two years there will be more competition.
‧ Later 與 after 多半用來表示過去的時間，意為「過了……之後」，若要表示未來的時間，可以用 in，意為「再過……之後」或者「在某段期間內」。	

Word List ‧ liberalize [ˈlɪbərəlˌaɪz] v. 放寬；放鬆

描述 Personal 未來的 Set-Phrases

TASK 12.13

請聽兩段對話。哪一個是討論個人計劃，哪一個是討論商業計劃？

答案

第一段對話是關於商業計劃。第二段對話是關於個人計劃。

　　如果聽不出來也沒關係，請先繼續往下研讀，我們稍後還會利用這兩段對話做一次練習，屆時將會在答案中附上完整的對話內容。現在來深入學習這些用語。

TASK 12.14

請將下列 set-phrases 分門別類，填入下表中。

1. Doing anything exciting over the weekend?
2. Doing anything exciting tomorrow?
3. Doing anything fun over the weekend?
4. Doing anything fun tomorrow?
5. I expect that I'll V
6. I expect to V
7. I plan to V
8. I propose to V
9. I'm expecting to V
10. I'm planning to V
11. I'm proposing to V
12. I'm scheduling a meeting.
13. My plan is to V
14. We need to schedule a meeting.
15. What are you doing over the weekend?
16. What are you doing tomorrow?
17. What are your plans for the weekend?
18. What are your plans for tomorrow?
19. What do you plan to do about it?
20. What do you propose to do about it?

Asking About Personal Plans	Asking About Business Plans
Describing Personal Plans	**Describing Business Plans**

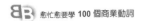

答案🎧

請利用下面的必備語庫來比較答案，並閱讀語庫小叮嚀。

商用英文必備語庫 **12.4**　個人未來用語 (2)　　MP3 110

Asking About Personal Plans （詢問個人計劃）		Asking About Business Plans （詢問商業計劃）
· Doing anything exciting over the weekend? · Doing anything exciting tomorrow? · Doing anything fun over the weekend? · Doing anything fun tomorrow?	· What are you doing over the weekend? · What are you doing tomorrow? · What are your plans for the weekend? · What are your plans for tomorrow?	· What do you plan to do about it? · What do you propose to do about it?

Describing Personal Plans （描述個人計劃）	Describing Business Plans （描述商業計劃）
· I expect that I'll V · I expect to V · I plan to V · I'm expecting to V · I'm planning to V · My plan is to V	· I propose to V · I'm proposing to V · I'm scheduling a meeting. · We need to schedule a meeting.

✎　語庫小叮嚀

◆ 請務必留意哪些動詞可用於商業計劃，哪些可用於個人計劃，哪些則兩者皆適用，並注意這些 set-phrases 中動詞的時態。

◆ 請注意，這些 set-phrases 中，plan 有時候是當名詞用。

TASK 12.15

MP3 109

請再聽一次 MP3 中的兩段對話，並利用必備語庫 12.4，勾出所有你聽到的 set-phrases。

答案

請參閱下列完整的對話內容來檢查答案。

Conversation 1

A: So what do you propose to do about it?

B: I'm proposing to put the project on hold until we can fix the problem. I think we need to schedule a meeting with the client and the whole team so that we can discuss it in more detail. Friday afternoon at 4:00?

A: OK. That works for me.

B: Good.

Conversation 2

A: Doing anything exciting tomorrow?

B: Oh, not really. I expect that I'll go shopping in the afternoon. I'm planning to buy some new clothes.

A: Oh, that's great.

B: What about you? What are you doing tomorrow?

A: Well, I plan to visit some friends in the evening to have dinner together.

B: Nice.

常 見 錯 誤 > > this 和 last	
錯　誤	正　確
I'll be back on this Monday. I went to Hong Kong in last January.	I'll be back this Monday. I went to Hong Kong last January.
·This 和 last 前無需再搭配介系詞使用。	

發音

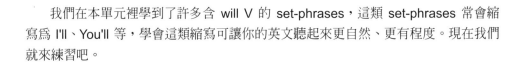

我們在本單元裡學到了許多含 will V 的 set-phrases，這類 set-phrases 常會縮寫為 I'll、You'll 等，學會這類縮寫可讓你的英文聽起來更自然、更有程度。現在我們就來練習吧。

TASK 12.16

 MP3 104

請聽 MP3，練習必備語庫 12.2 裡 will 與主詞縮寫後的發音。

答案

你可能會覺得 I'll 和 You'll 很難發音。說 I'll 時，舌頭應該觸碰上齒正後方的隆起部，輕聲發音。請用鏡子練習。如果說 I'll 時嘴唇會動，嘴形就不正確，因為你應該只有動到舌頭，臉上看不出動作。

請繼續練習，直到發音變得自然為止。

好了，本單元的學習到此結束。請回到本單元前面的學習目標，確定所有內容全部都學會了。

Unit 13 詞彙

引言與學習目標

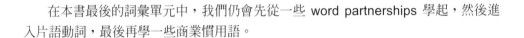

　　在本書最後的詞彙單元中，我們仍會先從一些 word partnerships 學起，然後進入片語動詞，最後再學一些商業慣用語。

　　本單元結束時，各位應達成的學習目標如下：

❑ 學到很多使用頻率高的 word partnerships，可用於商業英文的口說和寫作。
❑ 學到很多片語動詞，可用於商業英文的口說和寫作。
❑ 學到一些很有用的商業慣用語。
❑ 用新學到的詞彙做練習。
❑ 知道一些常見錯誤並知道該如何避免。

Word Partnerships

　　我將在下面介紹你一些常見的 word partnerships，讓你可以搭配 have、implement、schedule、review 以及 do 這五個動詞使用。我們這就從 have 開始學起吧。Have 是商業英文中的動詞，可組成多個 word partnerships，並按涵義分成好幾個種類。第一種為有時間工作或休息的意思，如：If you have a few minutes, I'd like to ask you something.。第二種帶有飲食的意思，如：Do you want to have lunch?。第三種帶有計劃或安排的意思。如：Do you have a reservation?。第四種有和某人交談或討論的意思，如：Can we have a meeting tomorrow?。有時 have 也可以搭配 no，表示沒有⋯⋯的意思，如：I have no intention of resigning.。另一種則表示個人的特質與經驗，如：I have no authority to make a decision about this.。最後，還有很多含 have 的 word partnerships 是無法根據涵義歸類的。

TASK 13.1

請將以下的 word partnerships 分門別類，寫在下面的表格中，見範例。

have	· (no) plans (for n.p.) · a basic understanding of sth. · a bite · a booking · a break · a chance to V · a chat with sb. (about sth.) · a clear idea of sth. · a coffee · a couple of minutes · a day off	· a deal (on n.p.) · a degree in sth. · a discussion with sb. (about sth.) · a flair for sth. · a good sense of humor · a good time · a holiday · a lack of sth. · a lot to offer · a meal

Word List
- booking ['bʊkɪŋ] n. 預約；預訂
- flair [flɛr] n. 才能；天賦

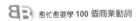
have	· a meeting (with sb.) (about sth.)	· no hesitation in Ving
	· a problem (with sth.)	· no idea (wh-clause)
	· a reason to V	· no intention of Ving
	· a record of sth.	· no objection to Ving/n.p.
	· a reservation	· no way of Ving
	· a rest	· nothing to do with me
	· a talk with sb. (about sth.)	· sth. in stock
	· a taste	· some refreshments
	· a vacation	· some time off
	· a way of Ving	· the authority to V
	· a word with sb. (about sth.)	· the decency to V
	· an arrangement (with sb. to V)	· the good sense to V
	· an impact (on sth.)	· the opportunity of Ving
	· breakfast	· the opportunity to V
	· dinner	· the right to V
	· no option but to V	· time for n.p.
	· experience	· time to V
	· lunch	· trouble Ving

Have Time for Work or Relaxation	Have Food or Drink
have time to V *have some time off*	*have a bite*
Have Plans or Arrangements	**Have a Conversation**
have a reservation	*have a word with sb. (about sth.)*
Have Nothing	**Have Personal Qualities or Experience**
have no hesitation in Ving	*have a degree in sth.*

Word List · decency [ˈdisn̩sɪ] n. 寬容

Have Other Things
have no hesitation in Ving

答案

請比較你的答案和下面必備語庫中的答案，並研讀語庫小叮嚀。

商用英文必備語庫 13.1 含 have 的 word partnerships　　MP3 111

Have Time for Work or Relaxation （有時間工作或放鬆）	Have Food or Drink （飲食）
· have time to V · have time for n.p. · have some time off · have a good time · have a day off · have a break · have a rest · have a vacation · have a holiday · have a couple of minutes	· have lunch · have breakfast · have dinner · have a coffee · have a meal · have a bite · have some refreshments · have a taste
Have Plans or Arrangements （做計劃或安排）	**Have a Conversation** （交談、談論）
· have a reservation · have a booking · have an arrangement (with sb. to V) · have a deal (on n.p.) · have (no) plans (for n.p.)	· have a word with sb. (about sth.) · have a talk with sb. (about sth.) · have a chat with sb. (about sth.) · have a discussion with sb. (about sth.) · have a meeting (with sb.) (about sth.)

Have Nothing （沒有⋯⋯）	**Have Personal Qualities or Experience** （個人特質或經驗）
· have no idea (wh-clause) · have no hesitation in Ving · have no intention of Ving · have no option but to V · have nothing to do with me · have no way of Ving · have no objection to Ving/n.p.	· have experience · have a basic understanding of sth. · have a degree in sth. · have a flair for sth. · have a lot to offer · have the authority to V · have a good sense of humor · have the decency to V · have the good sense to V
Have Other Things （其他類）	
· have a lack of sth. · have an impact (on sth.) · have a problem (with sth.) · have a reason to V · have a chance to V · have a clear idea of sth. · have a way of Ving	· have a record of sth. · have the opportunity to V · have the opportunity of Ving · have the right to V · have sth. in stock · have trouble Ving

✎ 語庫小叮嚀

◆ 在英式英文中，holiday 和 vacation 同義。在英國，國定假日稱作 bank holiday。若需要請假一天則稱作 have a day off，美式用法為 take a day off。

◆ Have a word with sb. 通常是指「與某人很快地談一下某件重要事情」的意思。

TASK 13.2

請將下面詞組組合成完整的句子，見範例。

A Can I have a chat	·	· a bite?
Do you want to go out and have	·	· a couple of minutes?
Have you got	·	· to apologize for his mistake.
He could at least have the decency	·	· for sales. He can sell anything.
He has a flair	·	· with you about my promotion prospects?

B He had the good sense	◆	◆ understanding of investment principles.
I have a record	◆	◆ to tell you.
I have a clear	◆	◆ of your phone calls right here.
I have no idea	◆	◆ to keep his mouth shut when he was asked about his former boss.
I don't have the authority	◆	◆ what you're talking about.

C I have no intention of	◆	◆ an impact on sales volume.
I'm having trouble	◆	◆ doing this extra work unless I'm paid overtime.
I've got a degree	◆	◆ a deal on the price. You want to change it?
I thought we had	◆	◆ understanding her English.
I think our price increase will have	◆	◆ in music. But now I never use it.

D We have lots of these items	◆	◆ nothing to do with me.
Your problem has	◆	◆ a taste?
You have the right	◆	◆ in stock. How many do you want?
I've got an arrangement	◆	◆ to seek legal advice.
That chocolate mousse looks really good. Can I have	◆	◆ with the parking lot attendant to wash my car every week.

答案 🔎

請利用下列表格來核對答案。

A Can I have a chat	◆ with you about my promotion prospects?
Do you want to go out and have	◆ a bite?
Have you got	◆ a couple of minutes?
He could at least have the decency	◆ to applogize for his mistake.
He has a flair	◆ for sales. He can sell anything.

B He had the good sense	✦ to keep his mouth shut when he was asked about his former boss.
I have a record	✦ of your phone calls right here.
I have a clear	✦ understanding of investment principles.
I have no idea	✦ what you're talking about.
I don't have the authority	✦ to tell you.

C I have no intention of	✦ doing this extra work unless I'm paid overtime.
I'm having trouble	✦ understanding her English.
I've got a degree	✦ in music. But now I never use it.
I thought we had	✦ a deal on the price. You want to change it?
I think our price increase will have	✦ an impact on sales volume.

D We have lots of these items	✦ in stock. How many do you want?
Your problem has	✦ nothingg to do with me
You have the right	✦ to seek legal advice.
I've got an arrangement	✦ with the parking lot attendant to wash my car every week.
That chocolate mousse looks really good. Can I have	✦ a taste?

現在來學一些含 implement、schedule 和 review 的 word partnerships。

TASK 13.3

請研讀下面的必備語庫以及例句。

商用英文必備語庫 **13.2**　含 implement 的 word partnerships　　ᴹᴾ³ 112

implement	· a plan · a program · a system · an alternative · a policy	· a change · a strategy · an idea · a suggestion · a project

1. We need to implement these changes as soon as possible.

2. We are willing to help you implement any of the alternatives.

3. I hope we can implement your ideas as soon as possible.

4. Let's implement the new system immediately.

✎ 語庫小叮嚀

◆ 注意，上列語庫右欄中的名詞均可以使用複數。

商用英文必備語庫 13.3　含 schedule 的 word partnerships

schedule	· (a) lunch · a meeting · a project · an appointment · a delivery · a conference · a program	· a visit · a date · a time · an interview · an event · a demonstration

 1. I would like to schedule an appointment with you to discuss the project.

2. We need to schedule a demonstration of the product for next Tuesday.

3. Can you schedule a lunch with John for me please?

4. Let's schedule a time to discuss your ideas.

商用英文必備語庫 13.4　含 review 的 word partnerships

review	· some of the details of the · the details of the · the attached · the following · the above · the below	· situation · results · application · arrangements · contract · list	· proposal · financials · notes · agreement · information · report

Word List	• conference [ˋkɑnfərəns] n. 會議 • demonstration [ˌdɛmənˋstreʃən] n. 實地示範；示範教學 • financials [faɪˋnænʃəlz] n. 財務數字；財務狀況

	· the · our **review** · my · these · this	· guidelines · outline · material · plan	· documents · issues · salary · resume

 1. Have you reviewed the details of the arrangements yet?

2. I'm reviewing the guidelines at the moment.

3. Please review the plan before the meeting.

4. I'd like you to review my salary, if you don't mind.

✎ 語庫小叮嚀

◆ Review sb's salary 意指依某人的年度表現，重新考核其薪水。

現在就來練習運用以上所學到的 word partnerships。

TASK 13.4

請閱讀下列第一封電子郵件，找出含 have、review、schedule 以及 implement 的 word partnerships 並畫上底線。然後在第二封電子郵件中用 have、review、schedule 或 implement 填空。

To All Department Managers:

Please be informed that I intend to have a meeting on Friday afternoon to review the current situation. I hope to have a chat with several of you beforehand to get your ideas on what strategy we should implement.

During the next week, I will be scheduling an appointment with each department head to review the details of the arrangements for severance packages. I hope it will not be necessary to lay off staff, but we are going to need to implement

Word List	· guideline ['gaɪd, laɪn] n. 指導方針 · beforehand [bɪ'for, hænd] adv. 事先；預先 · severance package 資遣方案

changes to the salary structure. In the meantime, please review the attached guidelines for severance procedures.

Dear Mandy,

I have studied your proposal and would like to make the following comments.

It will be difficult to (1)_____ many of your ideas as they now stand. You need to (2)_____ the financials as I think some of the figures may be wrong. Also, if we (3)_____ your suggestions for restructuring, we will have to (4)_____ salaries company-wide next year, something I am not prepared to do. However, I do like your idea of (5)_____ a system of safety checks and emergency measures.

I would like to (6)_____ a visit to the plant for next Thursday, to see for myself the situation you describe. I hope we can (7)_____ lunch together and talk about these issues. In the meantime, I will (8)_____ a word with Michael to see what he thinks about your proposal.

答案 🎧

To All Department Managers:

Please be informed that I intend to <u>have a meeting</u> on Friday afternoon to <u>review the current situation</u>. I hope to <u>have a chat</u> with several of you beforehand to get your ideas on what strategy we should implement.

During the next week, I will be <u>scheduling an appointment</u> with each department head to <u>review the details of the arrangements</u> for severance packages. I hope it will not be necessary to lay off staff, but we are going to need to <u>implement changes</u> to the salary structure. In the meantime, please <u>review the attached guidelines</u> for severance procedures.

(1) implement　　(2) review　　(3) implement　　(4) review
(5) implementing　(6) schedule　(7) have/schedule　(8) have

　　我們接下來要學習的動詞是 do，在英文中這個動詞的使用頻率非常高，許多 word partnerships 都會用到，而且有許多意思。在此我們的學習重點會是商業英文中常見的 word partnerships。在接下來的 Task 裡，請特別注意這些 word partnerships 的形式，並依據這些格式將其分門別類。先參考範例。

TASK 13.5

請將下面的 word partnerships 分門別類，寫在下面的表格中，見範例。

do	· a good job of Ving/n.p.　　　· sb. the courtesy of Ving · something about n.p.　　　· everything we can to V · all we can to V　　　· sb's utmost to V · some sightseeing　　　· everything in our power to V · the calculations　　　· sb. the favor of Ving · everything possible to V　　　· some tests on n.p. · some maintenance　　　· sb's best to V · sth. for sb.　　　· some shopping · some self-evaluation　　　· business (with sb.) · some research (into sth.)　　　· sb. a favor

Do sb. a Favor	*do sb. the favor of Ving*
Do Everything We Can to V	*do everything possible to V*
Do Some Research (into sth.)	*do some sightseeing*
Do Business (with sb.)	*do the calculations*

Word List
- courtesy [ˈkɝtəsɪ] n. 禮遇；好意
- utmost [ˈʌtˌmost] n. 最大限度；最大能力

答案

利用下列必備語庫來核對答案，並研讀例句。

商用英文必備語庫 **13.5**　含 do 的 word partnerships　　MP3 115

Do sb. a Favor	· do sth. for sb. · do sb. a favor · do sb. the favor of Ving	· do sb. the courtesy of Ving
Do Everything We Can to V	· do all we can to V · do everything possible to V · do everything we can to V	· do sb.'s utmost to V · do sb.'s best to V · do everything in our power to V · do a good job of Ving/n.p.
Do Some Research (into sth.)	· do something about n.p. · do some sightseeing · do some maintenance · do some self-evaluation	· do some tests on n.p. · do some shopping · do some research (into sth.)
Do Business (with sb.)	· do the calculations · do business (with sb.)	

EX　1. We are planning to do some tests on the product next week.

2. We will do everything we can to make sure you receive the goods on time.

3. We still need to do some more research into this before we do the cost calculations.

4. How could she decide to close the department without first doing the calculations?

TASK 13.6

請利用語庫 13.5 中含 do 的 word partnerships 填空，完成下面的電子郵件，有些空格的答案不只一個。

Hi Mary,

Can you please do (1)＿＿＿＿＿＿＿＿＿ ? I need some help with the figures

for the report. They don't seem to be working out correctly. I've done (2)_____ at least 15 times, but the numbers still don't work out. Can you please do (3)_____ on them to see if they are correct?

By the way, do you want to do (4)_____ this weekend? There is a sale at Louis Vuitton.

Dear Mr. Johnson,

Please do (5)_____ replying to my letter. I have now written to you three times asking for payment, but so far you have not replied. I have done (6)_____ to provide you with good service, and I believe I did (7)_____ it. Now it is time to pay. I have done (8)_____ to be patient with you. I hope that you can do the same. If I don't receive payment by the end of the month, I shall have no alternative but to do (9)_____. I have already contacted my lawyer.

Notice

Our website is down today as we are doing (10)_____ on it. We will do (11)_____ have it up and working again by the end of the week. Unfortunately, our customer service staff is also not available today and our telephone operators are also occupied, as they are doing (12)_____ average answering times. We are doing (13)_____ minimize the disruption to our service. If you would like us to do (14)_____, please try again tomorrow. It's a pleasure doing (15)_____ you.

Dear Mr. Chen,

I have been doing (16)_____ companies in the UK for a long time. As you know I did (17)_____ there last month during my business trip. I believe there are several exciting opportunities for our company there. I wonder if you could do (18)_____ sparing me ten minutes of your time so that I can put forward my idea to you. I will do (19)_____ keep it short so that you are not unnecessarily inconvenienced.

Word List ▪ disruption [dɪsˋrʌpʃən] n. 中斷

答案

以下是我的建議答案。

(1) me a favor

(2) the calculations

(3) some tests

(4) some shopping

(5) me the courtesy of

(6) my utmost/my best

(7) a good job of

(8) my utmost/my best

(9) something about it

(10) some maintenance

(11) everything we can to/all we can to

(12) research into

(13) everything we can to/all we can to

(14) something for you

(15) business with

(16) some research into/some study on

(17) some sightseeing

(18) me the favor of

(19) my best to

我們接著要學的是 attend 的用法，這個動詞常見於參加正式的會議或儀式時。

 TASK 13.7

請研讀下面的必備語庫以及例句。

商用英文必備語庫 13.6 含 attend 的 word partnerships　　MP3 116

attend	· the meeting · the conference · the reception	· the convention · the opening · the upcoming event	· the annual dinner · the funeral · the wedding

EX　1. Seven people from my company will be attending the conference.

　　2. Would you like to attend the convention in Seattle next month?

　　3. I'm not going to attend the annual dinner this year. It was so boring last year.

✎　語庫小叮嚀

◆ Attend 在英文中的使用頻率不高，除非是極為正式的情況；若為非正式情況，可用 go to。

Word List　· reception [rɪˋsɛpʃən] n. 歡迎會；招待會
　　　　　　· opening [ˋopənɪŋ] n. 開場；開幕

片語動詞

　　在本節中我們要學的是含 be 的片語動詞。英文中含 be 的片語動詞相當普遍，我將在下面告訴你一些商業英文中最常見、最有用的含 be 的片語動詞。

◀ 含 be 的 20 個片語動詞 ▶

TASK 13.8

請研讀下面的必備語庫。

商用英文必備語庫 13.7　含 be 的片語動詞　　　MP3 117

be at odds with sb. (over sth.) 與某人在某事上意見相左	We are always at odds with each other over strategy. We never have the same ideas about it.
be in a better position to V 有更好的地位來……	If we wait a few months, we will be in a better position to enter the market.
be on hand to V 有空做某事	Tomorrow is the product launch. Could I ask you to be on hand to help out?
be in charge of sth. 負責某事	Could you please be in charge of this project?
be of help (to sb.) 幫助某人	You have been of immense help to us.
be in good hands 確信有人會顧及你的利益	I always feel that I am in good hands when I take my business there.

Word List　• immense [ɪˋmɛns] adj. 龐大的

be on file 建檔留存的	▶ Your details are here on file somewhere. Let me see if I can find them.
be in good order 井然有序的	▶ Your monthly report is in good order.
be away (from sb.'s desk) 不在位子上	▶ I'm sorry, I am away from my desk at the moment. Please leave a message.
be in good working order 運作良好的	▶ The copier is now in good working order. Use it carefully so that it doesn't break again.
be in need of sth. 需要某事物	▶ The product is in need of a new image.
be on schedule 如期運作的	▶ The project is on schedule. We will be able to finish as planned.
be in order 正確的	▶ Your application is not in order, so I'm afraid we can't give you the loan.
be in our best interest to V 做……對我們是最有利的	▶ It's in our best interest to offer excellent service. It will help our reputation.
be of use to sb. 幫上某人的忙	▶ I hope we may be of use to you. Please call us if you need some help.
be on the way 在途中	▶ Your documents are on the way. They should arrive this afternoon.
be in place 就定位	▶ Everything is in place for the launch. We can go ahead.
be on sale 打折的	▶ These goods are on sale, but those are not.
be in perfect condition 處於最佳狀況	▶ The goods were in perfect condition when they left our warehouse.
be in sth. 任職於某行業	▶ I'm in pharmaceuticals, and my wife is in medicine, so we are a good team.

Word List
- reputation [ˌrɛpjəˈteʃən] n. 聲望；信譽
- pharmaceuticals [ˌfɑrməˈsutɪk|z] n. 製藥業

 語庫小叮嚀

◆ Be of help to sb. 和 help sb. 同義。
◆ Be in need of sth. 和 need sth. 同義。

TASK 13.9

請改正下面句子中的錯誤。見範例。

1. Your report is at odd with my experience talking with customers in the field.
   Your report is at odds with my experience talking with customers in the field.

2. My new company car is in perfect conditions.
   _____

3. The monitor was for sale, so I got a good deal.
   _____

4. I was away from my desk tomorrow.
   _____

5. This product are not of much use for us.
   _____

6. It is on our best interest to working overtime.
   _____

7. Everything is in good working orders and on place.
   _____

8. Don't worry about the new manager. You'll be in a good hand.
   _____

9. Production are always at schedule.
   _____

10. We are in need to more funds.
    _____

11. Our staff will be in hand with help.
    _____

12. Please let me know if I can be any more help for you.
    _____

13. I hope everything else are at order.

_____

14. We will be on better position entering the market.

_____

15. No, I'm in charge other projects.

_____

答案

請比較你的答案和我在下面提供的句子。

2. My new company car is in perfect condition.

3. The monitor was on sale.

4. I will be away from my desk tomorrow.

5. This product is not of much use to us.

6. It is in our best interest to work overtime.

7. Everything is in good working order and in place.

8. Don't worry about the new manager. You'll be in good hands.

9. Production is always on schedule.

10. We are in need of more funds.

11. Our staff will be on hand to help.

12. Please let me know if I can be of any more help to you.

13. I hope everything else is in order.

14. We will be in a better position to enter the market.

15. No, I'm in charge of other projects.

現在來看一些表示不同意義的片語動詞。

處理人際關係的 4 個片語動詞

TASK 13.10

請研讀下面的必備語庫。

商用英文必備語庫 13.8 用於處理人際關係的片語動詞 MP3 118

have it out with sb. (about sth.) 將某事攤開來講	▶ She really messed up my project. I'm going to have it out with her.
recommend sb. to sb. 向某人推薦某人	▶ You recommended her to me. I'm sorry to disappoint you, but I don't think she's very good.
have (got) sth. on sb. 知道某人的秘密，用來要脅對方	▶ I've got a lot on you. If you fire me, I'll go to the authorities.
have (got) sth. against sb. 因某種原因而不喜歡某人	▶ I've got nothing against him. I just don't like him.

　　語庫小叮嚀

◆ 請注意，你可以使用 got 搭配 have (got) sth. on sb. 和 have (got) sth. against sb.。但在 have it out with sb. (about sth.) 這個片語動詞裡，不可以搭配 got。

◆ Have 和 have got 同義，你可以在非正式的對話中用 have got，或者使用縮寫。

◆ 請記住，片語動詞中的動詞和介系詞有時會因為受詞而分開。請再看一次必備語庫中的例句，確定理解了。

TASK 13.11

MP3 119

請在下列空格中填入適當的片語動詞以完成對話，然後聽 MP3 來檢查答案。請特別注意動詞的時態。

A: Hi. What's up? You look stressed.

B: Oh, I just had a huge argument with Mike.

A: Really? What about? You guys really don't get along, do you?

B: No, we don't. I've (1)_____ him personally, actually. It's just that he's always criticizing my work.

A: Oh, I hate that.

B: I wish you hadn't (2)_____ me. I would never have chosen him for the team. He's not a good worker at all.

A: I'm sorry. I really didn't know he would be like this. What's he done now?

B: Well, he said something which really upset the client. And now the client is complaining to me about him. I tried to (3)_____ Mike, but he denies he did anything wrong.

A: So, what are you going to do?

B: Well, I had another chat with the client, and he told me some things that Mike said about us which he really shouldn't have said. So now that I've (4)_____ him, I'm going to the department head to see if I can get Mike fired.

A: Oh. Wow.

答案 🔾

如果覺得聽力很難，請參閱下方的答案。

(1) got nothing against　　(2) recommended him to

(3) have it out with　　(4) got something on

出差常用的 4 個片語動詞

TASK 13.12

請研讀下面的必備語庫。

商用英文必備語庫 **13.9**　出差常用的片語動詞　　(MP3 120)

arrive at 抵達轉機處	▶ My flight arrives at LAX at 7:45. Then, I've got a one-hour layover before my connection to San Diego.
arrive in 抵達最後目的地	▶ I should arrive in San Diego some time around 9:30.
have sb. round 邀請某人來家裡玩	▶ I'd love to have you round for coffee next weekend.
be based in 辦公室地點位於……	▶ I'm normally based in Shanghai, but my work takes me all over Asia.

TASK 13.13

請利用語庫 13.9 的片語動詞填空，完成下面的對話，然後聽 MP3 檢查答案。　(MP3 121)

A: Can I sit here?

B: Sure. Go ahead.

A: So. Where are you heading?

B: Hm? Me? Oh, I'm on my way to London for a meeting.

A: I see. Where are you from?

B: I'm from Taiwan.

A: Taiwan? Bangkok right?

B: No, actually, that's Thailand.

A: Oh, excuse me. I often get those two mixed up. You guys all look the same anyway. So, London, eh? Well, I'm from Chicago, but actually I'm (1)＿＿＿＿＿ New York. I'm going to London, too. Maybe we can arrange to sit next to each other on the flight? That will be fun.

B: Will it?

Word List	• layover [ˋleˏovɚ] n. 中途停留
	• connection [kəˋnɛkʃən] n. 接駁班機

A: What time do we (2)_____ Heathrow?

B: I'm not sure.

A: I need to (3)_____ London in time for this trade fair I'm attending. I'm staying in my friend's apartment in downtown London. Say, I'd love to (4)_____ for a drink while you're in town.

B: Thanks, but I'm going to be quite busy and I never drink.

答案

如果覺得聽力很難，請參閱下方的解答。

(1) based in　　(2) arrive at　　(3) arrive in　　(4) have you round

表示進行新計劃的 8 個片語動詞

TASK 13.14

請研讀下面的必備語庫。

商用英文必備語庫 13.10　表示進行新計劃的片語動詞　　

begin by Ving 從……開始	▶	Let's begin by looking at the requirements for the project.
involve sb. in sth. 讓某人涉入某事	▶	I don't want to involve too many people in the project.
have to do with sth. 與某事有關	▶	The meeting has nothing to do with sales. It's about Internet marketing or something.
could do with sth. 需要某事	▶	We could do with some more time, to be perfectly honest.
do without sth./sb. 即使沒有……仍繼續下去	▶	Kevin isn't here yet? We'll just have to do without him.

be based on sth. 根據某事物	▶	The idea is based on a similar product I saw at the trade fair last year.
do away with sth. 除去／廢除……	▶	I want to do away with the need for a system check.
base sth. on sth. 根據……來做某事	▶	Can we base it on the model we made last year?

TASK 13.15

MP3 123

請利用上述的片語動詞完成下面的對話，最後聽 MP3 來檢查答案。

Tony ： OK, I'd like to (1)_____ giving you all some background information on the new product. The idea is (2)_____ our main competitor's latest product. We need to come up with a similar product to prevent them from stealing too much market share.

Karen: Isn't that copying?

Tony ： Well, not really.

Karen: Oh. It sounds to me like it's copying. Look, do you have to (3)_____ this? I don't really want to be involved in this new project if we're just basing our products on other peoples' ideas. Can't we be more creative?

Tony ： Well, Karen, if you don't want to be involved, I'm sure we can just (4)_____ you.

Karen: Great.

Tony ： Well, as I was saying, we need to have a similar product on the market. This has (5)_____ maintaining market share.

Mary ： Excuse me, Tony? I agree with Karen. I don't want to be involved either.

Tony ： What? Ah, man. I (6)_____ some support here, you know! I'm only trying to do my job! The boss told me to do this. You think I'm happy about it?

Karen: Let's just (7)_____ the boss?

All ： Great idea!

答案 🎧

同樣地，如果還是有一些難字聽不出來，請參閱下方的解答。

(1) begin by　　(2) based on　　(3) involve me in　　(4) do without

(5) to do with　(6) could do with　(7) do away with

商業慣用語

TASK 13.16

請研讀下面的必備語庫以及例句。

商用英文必備語庫 13.11　含 have 的慣用語　　MP3 124

have	· a lot to answer for	有得解釋了
	· your back against the wall	身陷困境
	· a crack at sth.	嘗試某事
	· an eye for sth.	擅長留意一些特別的事項
	· a/sb.'s finger in every pie	任何小事都插手
	· friends in high places	人脈很好，認識許多有權的人
	· a good mind to	強烈地想要……
	· it on good authority	由可靠消息面獲知某事
	· your hands full	工作滿檔
	· it in for sb.	傷害或批評某人
	· a head start	有某項讓你在競爭中勝出的長處
	· sth. in mind	心中有……計劃或打算
	· a nose for sth.	有天賦認出或找出某事
	· second thoughts (about sth.)	對某事存有疑慮
	· a word with sb. (about sth.)	想和某人討論某個重要議題

 1. Because of him, the company went bankrupt, we lost our jobs, and the bank manager committed suicide. He really has a lot to answer for.

2. We really have our backs against the wall. Unless the market situation improves, we'll have to close the company.

3. This new game I downloaded is pretty fun. Do you want to have a crack at it?

4. She has a very good eye for detail. That's why she's the quality control manager.

5. The company would run a lot better if the boss's wife didn't have a finger in every pie.

6. He's got lots of friends in high places. That's why we get so many government contracts.

7. I've a good mind to report him to the police.

8. I have it on good authority that we are going to buy out our competitor.

Word List　· buy out 收購（企業或公司）的股權

9. Sorry, I can't take on any more jobs right now. I've got my hands full with the Princeton project.

10. I think he's got it in for me. He's always telling lies about me to the boss.

11. They have a head start on us. We need to work really hard to catch up.

12. So what do you have in mind for the new strategy?

13. She's got a nose for the market. She made a lot last year on her investments.

14. I'm having second thoughts about our strategy. I think we're doing something wrong.

15. Can I have a word with you about my salary, please?

商用英文必備語庫 13.12　含 do 的慣用語 MP3 125

do	· a half-assed job · the honors · the rounds · the trick	半途而廢 舉杯為……祝賀 與許多人交談 運作良好

EX

1. He never does a half-assed job. That's why he's always so successful.

2. A: John, would you do the honors please?

   B: Yes, of course. Welcome everybody! We're here today to celebrate Mark's retirement. Let's raise our glasses to him.

3. I've been doing the rounds to personally tell our customers about our new prices.

4. The copier is broken again? Kick it. That should do the trick.

商用英文必備語庫 13.13　含 show 的慣用語 MP3 126

show	· sb. the ropes · sb. the door · what you are made of	向某人解釋新工作 請某人離開 展現你真正的潛力

EX

1. Let me show you the ropes. It's not hard.

2. If you don't stop shouting, I'll call security and ask them to show you the door.

3. I think this difficult project will give me chance to show what I'm made of.

Word List　· retirement [rɪ'taɪrmənt] n. 退休

TASK 13.17

請改正下列句子中的錯誤。

1. Can I have some words with you please?

2. If you have any questions, I'd be happy to show you a rope.

3. I don't have any eyes for details. That's why I'm not good at quality control.

4. I have a plan in my mind.

5. I think she has it on to you.

6. I'm going to show her a door if she gives me any trouble.

7. I'm having second doubts about this.

8. I've got my hand full of work.

9. She has many things to answer to. Because of her, I lost my job.

答案

1. Can I have a word with you please?
2. If you have any questions, I'd be happy to show you the ropes.
3. I don't have an eye for details. That's why I'm not good at quality control.
4. I have a plan in mind.
5. I think she has it in for you.
6. I'm going to show her the door if she gives me any trouble.
7. I'm having second thoughts about this.
8. I've got my hands full.
9. She has a lot to answer for. Because of her, I lost my job.

最後，現在來看有哪些慣用語 set-phrases 可以用在口說中。記住，請小心使用這些 set-phrases。

TASK 13.18

請研讀下列語庫，並利用 MP3 來輔助練習發音。

商用英文必備語庫 13.14　慣用語 set-phrases　　MP3 127

· That will do!	夠了！
· That will do for now.	那目前就先這樣。
· Do me a favor!	閉嘴！不要再說了！（用來回答荒謬的問題）
· Do you want to make something of it?	你想被打嗎？（有威脅、挑釁之意）
· I've got a bone to pick with you.	我需要跟你談一下，你做了某件事情讓我很反感。
· I don't have a clue.	我毫無頭緒。
· I've had it up to here (with sth.)!	我再也受不了……了！
· You have to hand it to her!	不得不佩服她！
· (The) Walls have ears.	隔牆有耳。
· Can I have a moment?	我可以和你談一下嗎？
· Get a move on!	快點行動！
· Let's get this show on the road!	開始吧！
· The show must go on.	儘管遭受到很大的挫折，仍必須堅持下去。

TASK 13.19　　MP3 128

請閱讀下頁的對話，並在空格裡填入適當的慣用語。接著聽 MP3 檢查答案。

Conversation 1

Jon ：Did you hear? The boss was arrested.

Mary: Really? Wow!

Jon : What are we going to do with the Princeton project?

Mary: (1)_____.

Jon : Well, (2)_____.

Mary: I guess you're right. We just carry on as normal, right?

Jon : Well, not normal, or we might get arrested too!

Mary: I see what you mean.

Jon : OK, (3)_____. Jackie you take over sales, Joe you take over finance, June you take over personnel, and Jake you take over strategy. (4)_____ for now. Come on everybody! (5)_____!

Mary: And what are you going to do Jon?

Jon : Me? I'm taking the day off!

Conversation 2

Mike : (6)_____?

Tina : Sure. What's up?

Mike : Well, we need to talk quietly. (7)_____.

Tina : Oh.

Mike : It's about Maria. (8)_____ with her. She's made another mistake with the budget and now we don't have any money left to complete the project. What's worse is that she's been telling the client we can't finish the project ahead of schedule. She told me yesterday she was going to apply for a promotion once the project is finished! She has no idea how bad she is at her job.

Tina : Gee.(9)_____, really. She's got such confidence in herself.

Maria: Hi Guys.

Mike : Hi Maria!

Conversation 3

A: (10)_____!

B: What? What did I do?

A: You used my coffee mug!

B: Oh, gee. I'm sorry? Did someone die?

A: You think it's not serious? You think you can just use what isn't yours? You think you can just come in here and use anything you want? You think you're so fantastic?

B: (11)_____!

A: Do you want to (12)_____?

B: Hey, (13)_____ OK!

A: Sure. How can I help?

答案 🔊

請先用聽的來增進聽力，順便檢查答案。如果還是覺得有困難，請參閱下方的答案。

(1) I don't have a clue

(2) the show must go on

(3) let's get the show on the road

(4) That will do

(5) Get a move on

(6) Can I have a moment

(7) Walls have ears

(8) I've had it up to here

(9) You have to hand it to her

(10) I've got a bone to pick with you

(11) That will do

(12) make something of it

(13) do me a favor

好，本詞彙單元的學習到此結束。請回到本單元的前面，確定所有的學習目標都確實掌握了。

在本篇的一開始，我曾請你為本篇的 25 個動詞造句，然後勾出覺得難造的句子，現在來看一看到本篇末你學到了多少。

學習評量

第四篇 結尾 Task 1

請看下面的動詞，並運用在本篇中學到的字串，為每個動詞造一個句子。

expect	cause	recommend	do	remember
review	base	increase	plan	improve
implement	schedule	show	note	attend
begin	be	propose	involve	handle
visit	have	try	ensure	arrive

第四篇 結尾 Task 2

請比較你在本篇中為開頭 Task 1 與結尾 Task 1 所造的句子，並思考以下問題：

- 你學到了什麼？
- 比起開頭 Task 1，你寫結尾 Task 1 時感覺輕鬆了多少？
- 你覺得在運用哪幾個動詞時還有問題？為什麼？
- 你進步了多少？

附錄

附錄一：100 個動詞

第一組 25 個動詞   p.52

· thank	· let	· give	· find	· accept
· know	· hope	· take	· help	· meet
· like	· appreciate	· call	· need	· want
· make	· send	· receive	· wish	· think
· look	· see	· get	· feel	· come

第二組 25 個動詞   p.114

· learn	· offer	· discuss	· continue	· request
· regret	· interest	· work	· say	· become
· provide	· understand	· keep	· put	· confirm
· use	· hear	· believe	· include	· suggest
· write	· ask	· attach	· pay	· follow

第三組 25 個動詞   p.186

· arrange	· return	· inform	· talk	· allow
· tell	· go	· hold	· decide	· apologize
· contact	· mention	· agree	· join	· read
· hesitate	· set	· serve	· bring	· prepare
· consider	· enjoy	· complete	· require	· leave

第四組 25 個動詞   p.264

· expect	· cause	· recommend	· do
· review	· base	· increase	· plan
· implement	· schedule	· show	· note
· begin	· be	· propose	· involveen
· visit	· have	· try	· sure

附錄二：商用英文必備語庫

商用英文必備語庫 1.1　　　　　　　　　　　　　　　　　　　　　p.45

未搭配介系詞的動詞 （動詞 chunks）		搭配介系詞的動詞 （phrasal verbs）
· arrange n.p. · ask sb. to V · begin to V · believe that ＋ n. clause · continue to V · continue Ving · decide that + n. clause · enjoy Ving · feel that ＋ n. clause · find n.p. · help sb. to V · involve Ving	· offer sb. sth. · prepare to V · recommend that ＋ n. clause · remember n.p. · require sb. to V · send sb. sth. · tell sb. sth. · try Ving · understand n.p. · use sth. to V	· want to V · discuss sth. with sb. · do away with n.p. · do sth. for sb. · get sth. from sb. · go into sth. · go to n.p. · inform sb. about sth. · keep after sb. · keep on at n.p. · look at sth. · look into n.p.

商用英文必備語庫 1.2　動詞 chunks　　　　　　　　　　　　　　p.46

V + n.p.	V that + n. clause	V to V	V + Ving	V sb./sth. to V
· find n.p. · understand n.p. · arrange n.p. · remember n.p.	· feel that + n. clause · believe that + n. clause · decide that + n. clause · recommend that + n. clause	· want to V · continue to V · prepare to V · begin to V	· continue Ving · enjoy Ving · involve Ving · try Ving	· help sb. to V · ask sb. to V · require sb. to V · use sth. to V

商用英文必備語庫 2.1 包含 thank 的開頭與結尾的 set-phrases　　　　p.56

Opening（開頭）	Closing（結尾）
· Thank you for your email about n.p./Ving … · Thank you for your email. · Thank you for sending n.p. … · Thank you for sending me n.p. … · Thanks for your reply. · Thank you for your message. · Thank you for your message about n.p./Ving …	· Thank you very much for your help. · Thanks and sorry for any misunderstanding. · Many thanks for your understanding on this. · Thank you very much. · Thanks in advance. · Thank you in advance for your time. · Thanks in advance for your help. · Many thanks. · Thanks for your help. · Thank you again for choosing n.p. … · Thank you for purchasing n.p. …

商用英文必備語庫 2.2　包含 hope 的開頭與結尾 set-phrases　　　　p.59

Opening（開頭）	Closing（結尾）
· I hope you had a nice weekend. · I hope you had a good trip. · I hope your meeting was successful. · I hope you are feeling better now. · I hope this email finds you well. · I hope you are well.	· I hope this is clear. · I hope we can move this along quickly. · I hope this is OK. · I hope to hear from you soon. · I hope this helps. · I hope this is the beginning of a long and prosperous relationship. · We hope to be hearing from you soon. · I hope to see you there. · I hope you have a good trip. · I hope you understand our position on this.

商用英文必備語庫 2.3　　包含 wish 的 set-phrases　　　　　　　p.60

> · We wish you all a Happy New Year.
> · I wish you great success in your new job.
> · I wish you all the best.
> · We wish everyone there a pleasant holiday.
> · We wish you a Merry Christmas and a Happy New Year.
> · We wish you every success.
> · We wish you good luck.
> · We wish you the best of luck.
> · We wish you success in n.p. ...

商用英文必備語庫 2.4　　感謝、請求和婉拒幫忙的 set-phrases　　　　p.62

Requesting Help （請求幫忙）	Thanking sb. for Their Help （感謝某人）
· I would appreciate your attention to this matter.	· I appreciate all that you have done.
· I would appreciate a prompt reply.	· I appreciate you taking the time to help me with this.
· I would appreciate a response.	· We appreciate having you as a customer.
· I would appreciate any assistance you can give.	· We appreciate it.
· I would appreciate your help with this.	· We appreciate your business.
· We would appreciate it greatly if you could V …	· We appreciate your efforts.
· We would appreciate it if you would V …	· We appreciate your help.
· We would appreciate prompt action.	· We appreciate your interest in our company/products/services.
· We would appreciate prompt payment.	· We appreciate your support.
· We would very much appreciate it if you could help us.	· We very much appreciate your help with this.
· Your help with this would be much appreciated.	

Refusing a Request for Help （婉拒幫忙某人）
· I appreciate your concerns, but I'm afraid I am not able to help you.
· We hope you can appreciate our position.

商用英文必備語庫 2.5　動詞 chunks　　　　　p.66

V + n.p.			V that + n. clause		
· accept n.p.	· like n.p.	· see n.p.	· accept that + n. clause	· find that + n. clause	· think that + n. clause
· find n.p.	· meet n.p.	· want n.p.	· feel that + n. clause	· know that + n. clause	
· know n.p.	· need n.p.				

V to V	V sb. to V	V sb. V	Other
· 'd like to V	· 'd like sb. to V	· help sb. V	· feel adj.
· need to V	· help sb. to V	· let sb. V	· know wh –clause
· want to V	· need sb. to V	· make sb. V	
	· want sb. to V		

商用英文必備語庫 2.6　不可倒置的雙受詞動詞 chunks　　　p.71

· get sth. from sb.	· take sth. from sb.
· call sb. about sth.	· take sth. to sb.
· receive sth. from sb.	

商用英文必備語庫 2.7　可倒置的雙受詞動詞 chunks　　　p.72

· give sb. sth.	· send sb. sth.
· give sth. to sb.	· send sth. to sb.

商用英文必備語庫 3.1　表達看法的 set-phrases　　　　p.82

Giving Opinions（給予意見）	Asking for Opinions（請教意見）	Agreeing（表達同意）	Disagreeing（表達不同意）
· Do you know what I mean? · I think + n. clause · I feel that + n. clause · I find that + n. clause · I really like n.p./Ving … · I don't really like n.p./Ving …	· What do you think? · How do you feel about that? · Do you find that + n. clause?	· I know exactly what you mean. · I feel the same.	· I don't know what you mean. · I don't think so.

商用英文必備語庫 3.2　表達願望或要求的 set-phrases　　p.84

· I wish I could V …	· I wish it would V …
· I really want to V …	· I wish it was Ving/n.p. …
· I wish I had n.p. …	· I really need n.p. …
· I wish I didn't have to V …	· I wish it wasn't Ving n.p. …
· I really need to V …	· I really want n.p. …

商用英文必備語庫 4.1　含 make 的 word partnerships　　p.93

make	· a change · a choice · a comment · a comparison · a contribution to · a copy · a deal · a decision · a difference to · a discovery	· a mistake with · a note about · a phone call · a point of · a presentation on · a profit · a request · a reservation for · a suggestion about · a trip	· an application for · an appointment · an effort to · an impact on · an impression on · an offer · arrangements · inquiries about · money · payment · progress

商用英文必備語庫 4.2　含 get 的 word partnerships　　p.94

get	· a chance to V · a feel for n.p. · a good price for n.p. · a great deal on n.p. · acquainted with n.p. · an/some insight into n.p. · an understanding of n.p.	· approval for sth. (from sb.) · involved (in sth.) · lucky · ready for n.p. · sth. done · started · together

商用英文必備語庫 4.3　含 take 的 word partnerships　　　p.94

take	· some time to V · a taxi · a rest · a chance on n.p. · a course in n.p. · a day off · a long time to V · a look at n.p. · a message to sb. · a picture of n.p. · advantage of	· an active role in n.p. · an interest in n.p. · care of n.p. · control of n.p. · sb. to court for n.p./Ving · effect · legal action against sb. · note of n.p. · part in n.p. · responsibility for n.p./Ving

商用英文必備語庫 4.4　處理訊息的片語動詞　　　p.98

know about sth./sb. 知道很多特定的或專門的資訊	▶	He knows a lot about the bond market. Ask him.
know of sth./sb. 知道某事，但不是很了解	▶	I know of him, but I don't think I know much about his ideas.
let on 洩密	▶	I never let on what I know.
let sb. into sth. (英式) let sb. in on (美式) 告訴某人一個秘密	▶	You never let me into what's going on. You never let me in on what's going out.
look for sth. 尋找某物	▶	We are always looking for opportunities to do business.
look sth. over 快速瀏覽某物	▶	Please look your reports over one last time before you hand them in.
look through sth. 快速瀏覽某物	▶	I usually look through important memos over the weekend when I have more time.
look sth. up 查詢資訊	▶	Can you look her number up for me please?

make sth. up 捏造或編造某事	▶	I usually just make the figures up if I don't have the correct ones.
make of sth. 解讀某事（用於否定句或疑問句）	▶	What do you make of their report? I don't know what to make of it.
send sth. back 因有瑕疵而退還某物	▶	If it's not correct, send it back and ask for another one.
send sth. off 當完成某物時寄給某人	▶	When the report is ready, you can send it off to the client.
send sth. on 將收到的東西轉給別人閱讀	▶	If you find anything interesting, please send it on to the other people on the team.
send sth. out 將某物同時寄給很多人	▶	We send a company newsletter out to all our customers every month.
think of sth. 對某事有何看法 （用於否定句或疑問句）	▶	What do you think of my suggestion? Actually I don't think much of it.

商用英文必備語庫 4.5　處理問題的片語動詞　　　　　　　　　p.101

call for sth. 需要某物	▶	The situation calls for an immediate response.
come down to sth. 回歸到最簡單的因素	▶	It all comes down to the fact that we don't have the resources for this project.
come up against sth. 遇到麻煩或問題	▶	We frequently come up against problems of this kind.
let up 變得較和緩	▶	Business usually lets up over the Chinese New Year period.
look into sth. 調查某事	▶	We need to find someone to look into this and find out what the problem is.
make sth. up 彌補某事	▶	If we work overtime we can make up the delay.

商用英文必備語庫 4.6　處理人際關係的片語動詞　　　　　　　p.102

get after sb. 要求某人盡快將某事完成	▶ Can you get after them? We need the designs quickly.
get on with sb. (英式)	▶ I really get on with my supervisor. She's so nice!
get along with sb. (美式) 與某人相處愉快	▶ I really get along with my supervisor. She's so nice!
let sb. down 讓某人失望	▶ He always lets me down when I ask him to help me.
see sth. through 完成某事	▶ He finds it difficult to see projects through.
take sb. off sth. 使某人退出某專案或任務	▶ We should take him off the project. He doesn't have enough time to help us anyway.

商用英文必備語庫 4.7　處理工作的片語動詞　　　　　　　p.103

get around to doing sth. 抽時間做某事	▶ I haven't gotten around to sorting out my inbox yet.
get down to sth. 講到重點	▶ Let's get down to what our customers really want: low prices.
get on with sth. 繼續進行某項工作	▶ I must get on with this. It's already late.
get through sth. 完成某項工作	▶ I can't get through all the work I have.
see about sth. 安排完成某事	▶ Let me see about getting you a new computer. Yours is too slow.
see to sth. 照料某事	▶ Can you see to it that everything is shipped out by tomorrow?
take sth. on 接下更多工作	▶ We always take more work on at this time of year.

商用英文必備語庫 4.8　　連繫用的片語動詞　　　　　　　　　　p.105

call sb. back 回電給某人	▶	He never calls me back.
get back to sb. 稍後再聯絡某人	▶	You need to get back to me quickly on this.
get through to sb. 聯絡上某人	▶	I always find it hard to get through to him. He never answers his phone.

商用英文必備語庫 4.9　　含 take 的慣用語　　　　　　　　　　p.106

	a bit of getting used to	不習慣某事
	a dim view of sth.	不贊同某事
	the long view (of sth.)	以長遠的角度來看待某事
take	a firm stand against sth./on sth.	不同意某事並預防該事發生
	charge of sth.	掌管某事
	place	發生

商用英文必備語庫 4.10　　含 make 的慣用語　　　　　　　　　p.106

	the best of sth.	用正面的態度來看待某事
	a quick buck	輕鬆賺到錢，但有時手段不正當
	ends meet	努力讓收支平衡
make	a go of sth.	努力讓某事成功
	a killing	快速地賺到很多錢
	do	將就著用

商用英文必備語庫 4.11 含 get 的慣用語　　　　p.107

get	to the bottom of sth.	找出錯誤或問題發生的原因
	sth. off the ground	一開始做某事就很成功
	the hang of sth.	慢慢地知道要如何做某事
	the picture	了解
	fired	因做錯事而被炒魷魚

商用英文必備語庫 4.12 慣用語 set-phrases　　　　p.109

· Take it or leave it.	要不要隨你。
· Take it from me.	相信我。
· Take it easy!	放輕鬆！
· Don't make me laugh!	你的話很可笑！
· Make up your mind!	快一點做決定！
· Make it snappy!	快一點！
· Get your act together.	請有條理和有效率一點！
· Get cracking!	快開始進行！
· Don't get me wrong.	不要誤會我的意思。

商用英文必備語庫 5.1 說明來信目的的 set-phrases　　　　p.117

I am writing	· in response to n.p. · in regard to n.p.	· in connection with n.p. · on behalf of n.p.
I am writing to	· ask about n.p. · confirm n.p. · confirm that + n. clause · cancel n.p. · request n.p. · clear up n.p. · enquire about n.p.	· inform you of n.p. · inform you that + n. clause · let you know that + n. clause · let you know about n.p. · tell you that + n. clause · thank you for n.p./Ving

商用英文必備語庫 5.2　向對方確認或要求確認的 set-phrases　　p.119

Making Confirmation（確認）	Requesting Confirmation（要求確認）
· Just a short note to confirm that + n. clause · This is to confirm that + n. clause · This is to confirm that I will be attending n.p. · I can confirm that + n. clause · I am pleased to confirm that + n. clause · We wish to confirm that + n. clause · We wish to confirm the following: …	· We hereby confirm that + n. clause · Please confirm our n.p. · Please confirm if + n. clause · Please confirm whether + n. clause · Please confirm that + n. clause · Please confirm receipt of n.p. · Please give me a call to confirm that + n. clause · Would you please confirm that + n. clause

商用英文必備語庫 5.3　處理壞消息的 set-phrases　　　　　　　p.122

Giving Bad News （發布壞消息）		Responding to Bad News （回應壞消息）
· We regret to announce that + n. clause · We regret to inform you that + n. clause · We regret we cannot V · I regret to report that + n. clause	· We regret having to V · We regret that + n. clause · We regret that we have to V · We regret to say that + n. clause · We regret to tell you that + n. clause · We regret to advise you that + n. clause	· I'm sorry to learn about n.p. · We're sorry to learn of n.p. · We are sorry to learn from sb. about/of sth. · I am very sorry to learn that + n. clause

商用英文必備語庫 5.4　告知有附件的 set-phrases　　　　　　　p.124

Attaching Information （附加附件）	· n.p. is attached. · I am attaching n.p. for your consideration. · I am attaching n.p. for your interest. · I have attached n.p. · I'm attaching n.p. for your interest. · Please find the attached n.p.	· Please find the attached. · Please find the n.p. attached. · Please refer to the attached n.p. · Please see the attached n.p. · Please see the attached. · Please see the attachment. · Please see the n.p. attached. · The n.p. is attached for your consideration.
Inserting Information （插入附件）	· ... as follows: ... · ... the following: ...	· ... the following n.p. · The following is n.p.

商用英文必備語庫 5.5　動詞 chunks   p.129

V + n.p.	V that + n. clause	V to V	V n.p./sb. to V	V + Ving
· provide n.p. · understand n.p. · keep n.p. · request n.p. · hear n.p. · follow n.p. · believe n.p. · attend n.p.	· understand that + n. clause · suggest that + n. clause · say that + n. clause · request that + n. clause · hear that + n. clause · believe that + n. clause	· offer to V · continue to V	· use n.p. to V · ask sb. to V	· continue Ving · suggest Ving · keep Ving

商用英文必備語庫 5.6　雙受詞動詞 chunks   p.133

Non-Invertible（不可倒置）	Invertible（可倒置）
· ask sb. (about wh-clause) · ask sb. (about n.p.) · attach sth. (to sth.) · discuss sth. (with sb.) · include sth. (in sth.) · say sth. (to sb.)	· offer sb. sth. · offer sth. to sb. · pay sb. (sth.) · pay sth. (to sb.) · provide sb. with sth. · provide sth. to sb.

商用英文必備語庫 6.1　現在時間 chunks   p.145

Present Perfect（現在完成式）		
· so far · yet · now · just	· for · already · since · recently	· lately · never · ever · for ages

Present Perfect Continuous（現在完成進行式）		
· lately · these days · since	· for ages · nowadays · still · recently	· just · for · currently · these days
Present Continuous（現在進行式）		
· at present · nowadays · now	· at the moment · these days · still	· currently · presently

商用英文必備語庫 6.2　慰問的 set-phrases p.151

Asking for Sympathy （尋求慰問）	Showing Sympathy （表達慰問）
· I can't understand it! · Do you understand what I mean? · What I don't understand is wh-clause · … you understand … · Can you believe it?	· I'm sorry to hear that. · I hear you! · I can understand how you feel. · I can understand that. · I find that hard to believe. · I can believe it. · I don't believe it. · I can't believe it. · I can't believe my ears!

商用英文必備語庫 6.3　描述改變的 word partnerships p.152

become	· available (to sb.) · aware of n.p. · aware that + n. clause · clear (to sb.) that + n. clause · dependent (on n.p.) · dissatisfied (with n.p.) · eligible (for n.p.) · familiar (with n.p.) · more + adj. · necessary to V	可用的；可取得的 知道某事 知道某事 某事對（某人而言）是清楚的 依靠某事物的 對……不滿的 對……有資格的 對……熟悉的 更…… 必需的

商用英文必備語庫 7.1 含 keep 的 word partnerships p.162

Communicate Information (傳達訊息)	Store Information (保留訊息)
· keep sb. informed of/about sth.	· keep sth. on file
· keep sb. posted as to sth.	· keep the books
· keep sb. posted as to wh-clause	· keep a record of n.p.
· keep sb. up to date on n.p.	· keep track of n.p.
· keep sb. up to date as to wh-clause	· keep sb. in mind for sth.
· keep sb. updated on n.p/wh-clause	· keep in mind that + n. clause
· keep sb. advised of n.p.	· keep a promise
· keep sb. abreast of n.p.	· keep it in mind
· keep in touch	
· keep in contact	
· keep sb. in the loop (on n.p.)	

商用英文必備語庫 7.2 含 pay 的 word partnerships p.166

Business Costs (企業成本)		Payment Method (付款方式)
· pay a high price (for sth.)	· pay bribes	· pay by check
· pay a realistic price (for sth.)	· pay capital gains tax	· pay by credit card
· pay a total of	· pay income tax	· pay in cash
· pay a visit (to sb.)	· pay interest (on n.p.)	· pay in full
· pay compensation (for sth.)	· pay operating costs	· pay in installments
· pay good money for sth.	· pay overhead (on sth.)	· pay by direct debit
· pay a bill (of #) (for sth.)	· pay rent	· pay by electronic transfer
· pay a fee (of #) (for sth.)	· pay sales tax	
· pay a fine (of #) (for sth.)	· pay wages	
· pay a penalty	· pay taxes	
· pay a premium	· pay off a debt	
· pay back the amount owed (to sb.)	· pay off a loan	
	· pay off a mortgage	

商用英文必備語庫 7.3　含 put 的 word partnerships　　　　　　p.168

Record（做記録）	Abstract Meaning（抽象意義）
· put sth. on file · put sb. on a mailing list/waiting list	· put sb. in the picture · put sth. into perspective · put the matter right
Negative Meaning（負面意義）	**Begin Functioning（開始運作）**
· put a stop to sth. · put a strain on resources/capacity/ 　cashflow · put sb. in a(n) difficult/embarrassing/ 　awkward position · put pressure on sb.	· put sth. into service · put sth. into effect · put sth. onto the market · put sth. to work · put sth. to use
Relationships（人際關係）	**Prioritize（表明優先考量）**
· put oneself out for sb. · put sb. in charge of n.p. · put sb. in touch with n.p.	· put sth. first · put sth. to good use · put sth. to one side

商用英文必備語庫 7.4　處理採購和銷售的片語動詞　　　　　　p.172

work sth. out 計算成本或價錢	I'm working my budget out for next year.
work out to sth. 總計	Your final bill works out to $1,570.
interest sb. in sth. 想推薦某物給某人，希望他人能購買	Can I interest you in our new product?
be interested in sth. 對某事有興趣	We're interested in forming an alliance with your company.
put sth. at (#) 猜測或粗略計算價錢	I put the final cost at $150,000. What have you got?
put in an order 下訂單	If you put in your order before the end of the month, we'll give you a discount.

商用英文必備語庫 7.5　　處理問題的片語動詞　　　　　　　　　　p.173

work around sth. 儘管出現問題阻礙了你， 你仍想辦法處理	▶	We haven't got the resources we need? Well, we'll just have to work around it.
use up sth. 耗光某物	▶	We need to get some more paper for the copier. Somebody just used up the last box.
ask around 四處詢問	▶	Let's try to find a cheaper supplier. Let me ask around.
put up with sth. 容忍某事	▶	We'll just have to put up with his rudeness since he's such an important client.
put sth. aside 暫時擱置某事	▶	Let's put this aside for now and talk about it after the meeting.
put sth.back 拖延某事	▶	This mechanical failure is going to put the project back about two months.
put sth.off 延後某事	▶	Let's put off this project until we can find a buyer for it.

商用英文必備語庫 7.6　　處理工作的片語動詞　　　　　　　　　　p.175

work on sth. 處理某項工作	▶	I'm working on a new design for the client.
work towards sth. 努力達成某目標	▶	We're working towards being the market leader within five years.
put forward sth. 提出某想法或議題	▶	He put forward a very interesting proposal for reducing our labor costs.
put effort into sth. 努力做某事	▶	I know you've put a lot of effort into the project. That's why it was successful.
put together sth. 組成團隊；寫報告	▶	We're putting together a new sales team. I'm putting together a report on our recycling program.

商用英文必備語庫 **7.7**　　含 keep 的慣用語　　　　　　　　　　　p.177

keep	· your cards close to your chest · an eye out for sth. · your eyes peeled · your hands clean · sb. guessing · a low profile · up with the times · sb. on their toes	將商業計劃保密 密切注意某事 密切注意某事 不接受賄賂或捲入貪污 讓某人猜測 避免引人注意 跟上潮流；注意時事 不讓別人知道你下一步要做什麼

商用英文必備語庫 **7.8**　　含 put 的慣用語　　　　　　　　　　　p.177

put	· all your eggs in one basket · out feelers · your feet up · your finger on sth. · your foot down · sb.'s heads together · your money where your mouth is · your neck on the line · sth. in motion · two and two together	孤注一擲 隨口提議來測試他人的反應 坐下來，放輕鬆 掌握某件事情的重點 運用個人特權阻止某事 共同策劃 言行一致（通常指付錢） 以個人做擔保 開始運作；處理 發現兩件獨立事件的關連

商用英文必備語庫 **7.9**　　含 pay 的慣用語　　　　　　　　　　　p.178

pay	· sb.'s dues · your (own) way · through the nose · top dollar · the price · for itself · sb. back	善盡職責 自力更生，不依賴他人 付太多錢買某物 花了一大筆錢 付出代價 某物賺進的錢已經打平成本了 報復某人

商用英文必備語庫 **7.10**　慣用語 set-phrases　　　　　　　　p.181

· Let me put my cards on the table.	讓我告訴你我最終的決定。
· Put a lid on it!	閉嘴！
· Put a sock in it!	閉嘴！
· I wouldn't put it past him!	那種討人厭的事他就是做得出來！
· Pay up!	給錢！
· There'll be hell to pay.	我們有大麻煩囉。
· If you pay peanuts, you get monkeys.	微薪養蠢才。
· Keep this under your hat!	請勿洩漏此秘密給其他人知道。
· Keep your shirt on!	不要生氣，放輕鬆！
· Keep your pecker up!	打起精神！

商用英文必備語庫 **8.1**　提供服務與邀請的 set-phrases　　　　　p.190

Serving（提供服務）
當客戶對你的服務表示滿意時：
· Do be assured of our desire to serve you well at all times.
· It is always our pleasure to serve you.
· We are always available to serve you.
· Thank you for the opportunity to serve you.
· We appreciate having the opportunity to serve you.
· It has been our pleasure to serve you.
欲表達希望未來能繼續和對方保持生意往來時：
· I hope you'll let us serve you for many years to come.
· We will try our best to serve you in any way possible.
· We look forward to continuing to serve you.
· We look forward to the opportunity to serve you again.
欲在年底時向客戶表達謝意，感謝他們一年來的惠顧時：
· We shall endeavor to serve you even better in the coming year.
· We've been pleased to serve you this past year.

告知客戶，公司即使有了變化，也不會影響對客戶的服務時：

· We hope this change will serve your needs better.

· We look forward to continuing to serve you from our new location.

告知客戶，問題已解決並不會再發生時：

· I hope we can serve you better.

Inviting（邀請）	
· Can you join me for n.p.?	· I invite you to join n.p.
· Do join us!	· Please join me (for n.p.).
· I hope you can join me (for n.p.).	· Please join us (on n.p.)
· I hope you will be able to join me (for n.p.).	· Why not join us?
· I hope you will join me (for n.p.).	· You're invited to join me (for n.p.).

商用英文必備語庫 **8.2**　含 mention 的 word partnerships　　　　　p.193

· I · You · As I · As you · ... the n.p. · ... be · ... as	**mentioned**	· that + n. clause · the n.p. to sb. · the sth. in sth. · to sb. how adj. · something about sth. · in my report · before	· above · during n.p. · earlier · in paragraph X · in item X · on page X · in our email of X · in your email
· ... the below- · ... the above-		· n.p.	

商用英文必備語庫 8.3　表達歉意的 set-phrases　　　　p.195

- · Apologies for the error.
- · Apologies for the delay.
- · I apologize for any inconvenience.
- · I apologize for the inconvenience.
- · I apologize for this unfortunate error.
- · I apologize for this regrettable error.
- · We apologize for any inconvenience.
- · We apologize to you for any inconvenience we may have caused.
- · Please accept our apologies for any inconvenience we may have caused you.
- · We apologize for any inconvenience this may cause you.
- · Apologies for the delay in getting back to you, but …
- · Apologies for the delay in Ving …

商用英文必備語庫 8.4　敬請不吝給予意見的 set-phrases（1）　　　　p.197

- · …, please don't hesitate to ask me.
- · …, please don't hesitate to call me.
- · …, please don't hesitate to call me on/at X.
- · …, please don't hesitate to call on me.
- · …, please don't hesitate to contact me.
- · …, please don't hesitate to do so.
- · …, please don't hesitate to get in touch.
- · …, please don't hesitate to get in touch with me.
- · …, please don't hesitate to give me a call.
- · …, please don't hesitate to inform me.
- · …, please don't hesitate to let me know.
- · …, please don't hesitate to telephone me.
- · …, please don't hesitate to write to me.

商用英文必備語庫 8.5 敬請不吝給予意見的 set-phrases（2） p.197

- Please (feel free to) contact me on/at X.
- Please (feel free to) contact me at any time.
- Please (feel free to) contact me at your convenience.
- Please contact me ASAP.
- Please (feel free to) contact me about n.p. ...
- Please (feel free to) contact me again.
- Please (feel free to) contact me directly.
- Please (feel free to) contact me personally.
- Please (feel free to) contact me immediately.
- Please (feel free to) contact me if I can be of further assistance.
- Please (feel free to) contact me if you have any further questions.

商用英文必備語庫 8.6 動詞 chunks p.203

V + n.p		be Ved to V	V sb. that
· arrange n.p. · consider n.p. · enjoy n.p. · require n.p.	· complete n.p. · allow n.p. · read n.p. · contact n.p.	· be allowed to V · be required to V · be prepared to V	· inform sb. that + n. clause · tell sb. that + n. clause

V sb. wh-clause	V to V	V Ving
· tell sb. wh-clause	· prepare to V · agree to V · decide to V	· enjoy Ving

V sb. to V	V that + n. clause	V (sb.) wh-to V
· require sb. to V · allow sb. to V	· agree that + n. clause · decide that + n. clause · require that + n. clause · consider that + n. clause	· decide wh-to V · tell sb. wh-to V

商用英文必備語庫 8.7　雙受詞動詞 chunks　　　　　　　　　p.208

Non-Invertible（不可倒置）	Invertible（可倒置）
· return sth. (to sb.) · prepare sth. (for n.p.) · inform sb. (about/of sth.) · talk to sb. (about sth.) · tell sb. (about sth.) · agree with sb. (about/on sth.)	· tell sb. sth. · tell sth. to sb. · talk about sth. with sb. · talk to sb. about sth.

商用英文必備語庫 9.1　不規則動詞三態　　　　　　　　　p.216

become	became	become	leave	left	left
begin	began	begun	let	let	let
bring	brought	brought	make	made	made
come	came	come	meet	met	met
do	did	done	pay	paid	paid
feel	felt	felt	put	put	put
find	found	found	read	read	read
get	got	got/gotten	say	said	said
give	gave	given	see	saw	seen
go	went	gone	send	sent	sent
have	had	had	set	set	set
hear	heard	heard	take	took	taken
hold	held	held	tell	told	told
keep	kept	kept	think	thought	thought
know	knew	known	understand	understood	understood
learn	learned/ learnt	learned/ learnt	write	wrote	written

商用英文必備語庫 **9.2**　時間 chunks　　　　　　　　　　　　p.219

Finished Time Chunks （已結束的時間 **chunks**）		**Unfinished Time Chunks** （未結束的時間 **chunks**）
· afterwards	· in March	· during this time
· ago	· last quarter	· so far
· at one time	· last year	· this quarter
· during that time	· next	· this week
· eventually	· once	· this year
· formerly	· originally	· year-to-date
· immediately	· subsequently	
· in 2005	· then	
	· yesterday	

商用英文必備語庫 **9.3**　陳述事項的 set-phrases　　　　　　p.225

· I mentioned to him that + n. clause	· (S)He told me about n.p.
· (S)He informed me that + n. clause	· (S)He told me wh-clause
· (S)He mentioned n.p.	· I mentioned to him about n.p.
· (S)He told me that + n. clause	· (S)He informed me of n.p.
· (S)He informed me wh-clause	· I mentioned n.p.
· (S)He mentioned to me about n.p.	· We talked about n.p.
· (S)He informed me about n.p.	· I mentioned to him wh-clause
· (S)He mentioned to me wh-clause	· (S)He mentioned to me that + n. clause

商用英文必備語庫 9.4　規則動詞加 -ed 後的發音　　　　　　　　　　p.228

[t]	[d]		[ɪd]
· asked · attached · based · discussed · increased · talked · worked	· agreed · allowed · apologized · arranged · arrived · believed · caused · confirmed · considered · continued · enjoyed · ensured · followed · handled · improved · informed · involved · joined	· mentioned · offered · planned · prepared · proposed · remembered · required · returned · reviewed · scheduled · served · tried · used	· asked · attended · completed · contacted · decided · expected · hesitated · implemented · included · interested · noted · provided · recommended · regretted · requested · suggested · visited

商用英文必備語庫 10.1　含 bring 的 word partnerships　　　　　　p.233

bring (sth.)	· to sb.'s attention　· out a new product · to sb.'s notice　　· a balance forward · to V　　　　　　　· out of the red · with you　　　　　· into the black · costs down　　　　· up to date

商用英文必備語庫 10.2　含 leave 的 word partnerships　　　　　　p.233

leave	· the company　　　　　　· us with a small margin · the rest to sb.　　　　　· me no choice but to V · us with little profit　　　· a message (for sb.) · word that + n. clause　　· sth. out of the calculations · instructions (for n.p.)　　· me with no other alternative · instructions (for wh-)　　　 but to V

商用英文必備語庫 **10.3** 含 hold 的 word partnerships p.235

Event（事件）	**Possess**（擁有）
· hold a meeting · hold a competition · hold a conference · hold a dinner · hold a party · hold a reception · hold an annual convention · hold an exhibition · hold detailed discussions with	· hold the position (of n.p.) · hold the position that + n. clause · hold an insurance policy · hold stock · hold the copyright for · hold the patent for · hold sth. for safe keeping
Delay（延遲）	**Other**（其他）
· hold up production · hold the shipment	· hold sb. in the highest regard · hold sth. in confidence · hold the line · hold consignments · hold your reservation · hold the price

商用英文必備語庫 **10.4** 含 set 的 word partnerships p.238

set	· a time (for n.p.) · aside a time (for n.p.) · aside a budget (for n.p.) · aside funds (for n.p.) · a date (for n.p.) · a new standard (for n.p.) · new records (for n.p.) · a time limit on · an example · the alarm · targets · the standard (for n.p.)	· high standards (for n.p.) · quotas (for n.p.) · limits (on n.p.) · priorities (for n.p.) · prices · sb. to thinking · sb. to wondering · objectives (for n.p.) · goals (for n.p.) · a policy · things right

商用英文必備語庫 10.5 含 set up 的 word partnerships   p.239

set up	· a meeting (for n.p.) · a schedule (for n.p.) · a payment schedule (for n.p.) · a shipping schedule (for n.p.) · a vacation schedule (for n.p.) · an appointment (for n.p.) · a time to meet (to V)	· an account (for n.p.) · an interview (with sb.)(to V) · equipment (for n.p.) · a business · a training program (for n.p.) · a line of credit (for n.p.)

商用英文必備語庫 10.6 含 serve as 的 word partnerships   p.242

serve as	· a model (for n.p.) · a reminder (of n.p.) (that + n. clause) · a reference (for n.p.) · a starting point (for n.p.) · an incentive (for n.p.) · confirmation (of n.p.) · confirmation (that + n. clause) · security (for n.p.) · a basis (for n.p.) · formal notice (that + n. clause) · a guide (for n.p.)

商用英文必備語庫 10.7 含 read 的片語動詞   p.245

read sth.	重點在於讀本的形式，如：newspaper, novel, article, report, email。
read about sth.	重點在於讀本的內容，如：macroeconomics, the merger between Compaq and HP, the president's new mistress。
read up on sth.	重點在於閱讀的目的，也就是藉由閱讀來學習新知。

商用英文必備語庫 **10.8** 含 go 的片語動詞　　　　　　　　　　p.246

go after sth. 追趕上	▶ We always go after government contracts because they're so lucrative.
go ahead (with sth.) 開始進行……	▶ Please go ahead with the project.
go along (with sth.) 同意……	▶ I can go along with that. It's a good idea.
go back (to sth.) 回到……	▶ I wish we could go back to the old days when it was a small company.
sth. go by 某事溜走	▶ We mustn't let this opportunity go by.
sth. go down 某事減少	▶ Revenues are going down. We need to increase sales.
go for sth. 選擇某事物；以……為目標	▶ I think we should go for the red one. It suits our company image better.
go into details 更詳盡地描述	▶ Without going into details, we had to fire her for misconduct.
go on (with sth.) 繼續做某事	▶ Let's go on with the meeting even though he is not here.
sb. go out 某人出去玩	▶ Are you going out tonight?
go over sth. 檢查某物是否正確	▶ We need to go over those figures one more time. They still don't look right to me.
go through sth. 仔細地檢視某物	▶ We need to go through the report together. There are lots of good ideas in it.
go through with sth. 完成某事	▶ Are we still going to go through with the project?
go with sth. 選擇某物	▶ I'm going to go with the steak. What would you like?

go with sb. 陪伴某人	▶	Would you like me to go with you to the hospital?
sth. go up 某事增加、升高	▶	Transportation costs have gone up considerably.

商用英文必備語庫 10.9 安排工作事項的片語動詞　　　　　　　p.249

bring sth. up 提及一個新話題，通常是壞消息	▶	I'm sorry to bring this up, but our main customer has just cancelled a major order.
bring sth. about 促成某事發生	▶	If we want to bring this expansion about, someone is going to have to manage it.
prepare for sth. 準備某事	▶	I'm preparing for my certificate exam.
arrange for sb. to V 安排某人做某事	▶	Can you arrange for the new intern to come and see me?
leave sth. for sb. to V 把某事留給某人做	▶	I'll leave this for you to do. I'm going home.
leave sth. with sb. 把某事留給某人	▶	Leave it with me. I'll do it.
leave sth. to sb. 讓某人獨力做某事	▶	It's not fair to leave it all to me. I have so much work to do already.

商用英文必備語庫 10.10 出差相關的片語動詞　　　　　　　p.251

bring sth. along 帶著某物隨行	▶	I brought the report along when I came over on Friday. Didn't you get it?
leave for + n.p. 前往某地	▶	I leave for Amsterdam at 7:00 tonight.

leave + n.p. for + n.p. 離開某地前往他處	▶	Then, I leave Amsterdam for Rome the following Monday.
bring sth. back 帶回某物	▶	I forgot to bring some chocolate back for my wife.
return to + n.p. 回到原出發地	▶	I return to Amsterdam on the Friday after that.

商用英文必備語庫 10.11　改變計劃的片語動詞　　　　　　　　p.252

| bring sth. forward
將某事提前 | ▶ | Let's bring the launch date forward to the end of this month. |
| sth. be set back
延後某事 | ▶ | I'm afraid the launch date has been set back until the end of next month. |

商用英文必備語庫 10.12　含 leave 和 bring 的慣用語　　　　　p.254

| **leave** | · sb. in the lurch
· me cold
· a lot to be desired
· well enough alone | 將某人棄之不顧
引發不了興趣，無法被打動
沒有達到期望
不管某事 |
| **bring** | · out the best in sb.
· sth. to bear on
· sb. to book
· sth. into line with | 激發出某人最好的才能
施壓來影響某個情況
警告或懲罰某人（英式慣用語）
讓某事符合……的標準 |

商用英文必備語庫 10.13　含 hold 的慣用語　　　　　　　　　p.255

| **hold** | · things together
· the fort
· the purse strings
· true for sth.
· your ground
· all the cards | 在困境中堅持下去
代理或代為照料某職務
掌管財務
可應用在某種情況的論證
堅持不退讓
佔盡優勢 |

商用英文必備語庫 10.14　含 go 的慣用語　　　　　　　　　　　p.255

go	· Dutch	各付各的餐飲費
	· nuts	非常生氣；抓狂
	· hand in hand with sth.	與某事的關係密切
	· beyond a joke	狀況越來越嚴重
	· back a long way	彼此已認識很久
	· in one ear and out the other	左耳進右耳出
	· pear shaped	出差錯或未按照計劃進行（英式慣用語）
	· from strength to strength	越來越強大或越來越成功（英式慣用語）
	· to sb.'s head	因成功而變得驕傲自大

商用英文必備語庫 10.15　慣用語 set-phrases　　　　　　　　　p.257

· Hold on a moment!	等一下！
· Hold it!	等一下！
· Hold your horses!	稍安勿躁！
· Don't hold your breath!	事情多半不可能發生！
· I must love you and leave you.	跟你在一起的時光很快樂，但現在我得走了。（英式慣用語）
· I'm the one who brings home the bacon.	我家就靠我一份薪水。
· I'll bring him down a peg or two.	我要挫挫某人的銳氣。
· Go to the devil!	走開，別煩我！（無禮）
· Go to hell!	走開，別煩我！（無禮）
· There but for the grace of God (go I).	若不是上帝的恩寵，倒楣的就是我了。
· It's all go.	我忙死了。

商用英文必備語庫 11.1　含 note、notify 和 notice 的 set-phrases　　p.269

Notifying （告知）	**Requesting Notification** （請求告知）	**Reporting** （傳達）
· Please note that + n. clause · Please note the following: · Please note,	· Please notify us of n.p. · Please notify us as to wh-clause	· We note that + n. clause · I notice that + n. clause

· Kindly note that + n. clause · Please take note that + n. clause · You'll note from n.p. that + n. clause · This is to notify you that + n. clause · This is to notify you of n.p.	· Please notify us if + n. clause · Please notify n.p. · Please notify sb. that + n. clause	· I notice from n.p. that + n. clause · We note your complaint.

商用英文必備語庫 11.2 處理智慧財產權問題的 set-phrases　　　p.273

Taking Negative Action （採取反制行動）	Giving Permission （授權）
· I have no alternative but to V … · I have no choice but to V … · I have no option but to V …	· You have our consent to V … · You have our permission to V … · You have the right to V …

商用英文必備語庫 11.3 建立良好顧客關係與表達支持的 set-phrases　　　p.275

Building for the Future (建立未來的良好關係)	Showing Support (表達支持)
· I hope we may have the pleasure of Ving/n.p. · I hope we shall have the pleasure of Ving/n.p. · I hope to have the pleasure of Ving/n.p. · I hope to have a chance to V · I hope to have an opportunity to V · I hope we shall have the privilege of Ving/n.p. · I hope to have the privilege of Ving/n.p. · I hope to have time to V · I hope we shall have time to V · I hope to have time for n.p. · I hope we shall have time for n.p.	· You have my heartiest congratulations. · You have my sincere appreciation for n.p. · You have my sincere gratitude. · You have my very best wishes for n.p. · You have our deepest sympathy. · You have the full support of n.p. · You have our full support for n.p.

商用英文必備語庫 11.4 動詞 chunks　　　　　　　　　　　　　　p.280

V + Ving	V that + n. clause		V + wh- to V
· recommend Ving · begin Ving · propose Ving · involve Ving · try Ving	· recommend that 　+ n. clause · propose that + 　n. clause · ensure that + n. 　clause · remember that 　+ n. clause	· show sb. that + 　n. clause · show that + n. 　clause · expect that + n. 　clause	· show wh-to V · show sb. wh-to V · remember wh-to V
V to V	**V + n.p.**		**V + wh-clause**
· expect n.p. to V · expect to V · begin to V · propose to V · try to V · plan to V · remember to V · cause sth. to V	· remember n.p. · expect n.p. · begin n.p. · visit n.p. · cause n.p. · recommend n.p. · increase n.p. · show n.p.	· propose n.p. · try n.p. · plan n.p. · involve n.p. · ensure n.p. · improve n.p. · handle n.p. · show sb. n.p.	· show wh-clause · show sb. wh-clause · remember wh-clause

商用英文必備語庫 11.5 雙受詞動詞 chunks　　　　　　　　　　　　p.285

Non-Invertible （不可倒置）	Invertible （可倒置）	
	· cause sb. sth. · cause sth. for sb.	· show sb. sth. · show sth. to sb.

p.292

商用英文必備語庫 **12.1** 個人未來用語 (1)

Personal Certain		Personal Uncertain
Plans and Intentions（計劃與打算）	**Arrangements**（安排）	
· I'm going to V	· ... be Ving	· I may V
· I'm not going to V	· Can you make n.p.?	· I might V
· It is our intention to V	· Can you manage n.p.?	· I'm thinking of Ving
· I hope to V	· I can make n.p.	· I'll probably V
· I intend to V	· I can manage n.p.	· I'll probably be Ving
· I need to V	· I can't make n.p.	· I probably won't V
· I want to V	· I can't manage n.p.	· I probably won't be Ving
· It is our hope that we can V	· I'll be Ving	
· I would like to V	· I won't be Ving	

p.297

商用英文必備語庫 **12.2** 含 will V 的各類不同功能的 set-phrases

Making Offers （提議）	**Making Requests** （請求）
· I'll get it.	· Will you do it?
· I'll talk to him for you, if you like.	· Will you help me with this?
· I'll V, if you like.	· Will you have time to V?
· I'll put the kettle on.	· Will you ask her for me?
Making Promises （做承諾）	**Making Spontaneous Decisions** （做決定）
· I'll send it tomorrow.	· We'll see.
· I'll do it as soon as I can.	· I'll do it later.
· It'll be all right.	· I'll have a cappuccino.
· I'll see what I can do.	· I'll have fried chicken.
Making Threats （威脅）	**Making Warnings** （警告）
· I'll tell everyone you said that.	· You'll regret it.
· I'll hit you!	· You'll be late.
· I'll kill you!	· You'll hurt yourself.
· I'll be really angry.	· You'll make a mistake.

Saying Goodbye（道再見）	Other（其他）
· I'll give you a call. · I'll drop you a line. · I'll be in touch. · I'll see you then/later/tomorrow.	· I'll be free at … · There'll be lots of people there. · I'll be back on Thursday. · She'll be back tomorrow. · I'll be late.

商用英文必備語庫 12.3　非個人未來用語 p.298

Impersonal Futures		
Certain	**Uncertain**	
· … will V · … be going to V	· I think it'll V · I think n.p. will V · n.p. will probably V	· n.p. might V · n.p. may V

商用英文必備語庫 12.4　個人未來用語 (2) p.302

Asking About Personal Plans （詢問個人計劃）		Asking About Business Plans （詢問商業計劃）
· Doing anything exciting over the weekend? · Doing anything exciting tomorrow? · Doing anything fun over the weekend? · Doing anything fun tomorrow?	· What are you doing over the weekend? · What are you doing tomorrow? · What are your plans for the weekend? · What are your plans for tomorrow?	· What do you plan to do about it? · What do you propose to do about it?

Describing Personal Plans （描述個人計劃）	Describing Business Plans （描述商業計劃）
· I expect that I'll V · I expect to V · I plan to V · I'm expecting to V · I'm planning to V · My plan is to V	· I propose to V · I'm proposing to V · I'm scheduling a meeting. · We need to schedule a meeting.

商用英文必備語庫 13.1　含 have 的 word partnerships　　　p.309

Have Time for Work or Relaxation （有時間工作或放鬆）	Have Food or Drink （飲食）
· have time to V · have time for n.p. · have some time off · have a good time · have a day off · have a break · have a rest · have a vacation · have a holiday · have a couple of minutes	· have lunch · have breakfast · have dinner · have a coffee · have a meal · have a bite · have some refreshments · have a taste
Have Plans or Arrangements （做計劃或安排）	**Have a Conversation** （交談、談論）
· have a reservation · have a booking · have an arrangement (with sb. to V) · have a deal (on n.p.) · have (no) plans (for n.p.)	· have a word with sb. (about sth.) · have a talk with sb. (about sth.) · have a chat with sb. (about sth.) · have a discussion with sb. (about sth.) · have a meeting (with sb.) (about sth.)

Have Nothing （沒有……）	Have Personal Qualities or Experience （個人特質或經驗）
· have no idea (wh-clause) · have no hesitation in Ving · have no intention of Ving · have no option but to V · have nothing to do with me · have no way of Ving · have no objection to Ving/n.p.	· have experience · have a basic understanding of sth. · have a degree in sth. · have a flair for sth. · have a lot to offer · have the authority to V · have a good sense of humor · have the decency to V · have the good sense to V
Have Other Things （其他類）	
· have a lack of sth. · have an impact (on sth.) · have a problem (with sth.) · have a reason to V · have a chance to V · have a clear idea of sth. · have a way of Ving	· have a record of sth. · have the opportunity to V · have the opportunity of Ving · have the right·to V · have sth. in stock · have trouble Ving

商用英文必備語庫 **13.2** 含 implement 的 word partnerships　　　　p.312

implement	· a plan · a program · a system · an alternative · a policy	· a change · a strategy · an idea · a suggestion · a project

商用英文必備語庫 **13.3** 含 schedule 的 word partnerships　　　　p.313

schedule	· (a) lunch · a meeting · a project · an appointment · a delivery · a conference · a program	· a visit · a date · a time · an interview · an event · a demonstration

商用英文必備語庫 13.4 含 review 的 word partnerships p.313

review	· some of the details of the · the details of the · the attached · the following · the above · the below · the · our · my · these · this	· situation · results · application · arrangements · contract · list · guidelines · outline · material · plan	· proposal · financials · notes · agreement · information · report · documents · issues · salary · resume

商用英文必備語庫 13.5 含 do 的 word partnerships p.317

Do sb. a Favor	· do sth. for sb. · do sb. a favor · do sb. the favor of Ving	· do sb. the courtesy of Ving
Do Everything We Can to V	· do all we can to V · do everything possible to V · do everything we can to V	· do sb.'s utmost to V · do sb.'s best to V · do everything in our power to V · do a good job of Ving/n.p.
Do Some Research (into sth.)	· do something about n.p. · do some sightseeing · do some maintenance · do some self-evaluation	· do some tests on n.p. · do some shopping · do some research (into sth.)
Do Business (with sb.)	· do the calculations · do business (with sb.)	

商用英文必備語庫 **13.6** 含 attend 的 word partnerships   p.319

attend	· the meeting · the conference · the reception	· the convention · the opening · the upcoming event	· the annual dinner · the funeral · the wedding

商用英文必備語庫 **13.7** 含 be 的片語動詞   p.320

be at odds with sb. (over sth.) 與某人在某事上意見相左	We are always at odds with each other over strategy. We never have the same ideas about it.
be in a better position to V 有更好的地位來……	If we wait a few months, we will be in a better position to enter the market.
be on hand to V 有空做某事	Tomorrow is the product launch. Could I ask you to be on hand to help out?
be in charge of sth. 負責某事	Could you please be in charge of this project?
be of help (to sb.) 幫助某人	You have been of immense help to us.
be in good hands 確信有人會顧及你的利益	I always feel that I am in good hands when I take my business there.
be on file 建檔留存的	Your details are here on file somewhere. Let me see if I can find them.
be in good order 井然有序的	Your monthly report is in good order.
be away (from sb.'s desk) 不在位子上	I'm sorry, I am away from my desk at the moment. Please leave a message.
be in good working order 運作良好的	The copier is now in good working order. Use it carefully so that it doesn't break again.
be in need of sth. 需要某事物	The product is in need of a new image.

be on schedule 如期運作的	▶	The project is on schedule. We will be able to finish as planned.
be in order 正確的	▶	Your application is not in order, so I'm afraid we can't give you the loan.
be in our best interest to V 做……對我們是最有利的	▶	It's in our best interest to offer excellent service. It will help our reputation.
be of use to sb. 幫上某人的忙	▶	I hope we may be of use to you. Please call us if you need some help.
be on the way 在途中	▶	Your documents are on the way. They should arrive this afternoon.
be in place 就定位	▶	Everything is in place for the launch. We can go ahead.
be on sale 打折的	▶	These goods are on sale, but those are not.
be in perfect condition 處於最佳狀況	▶	The goods were in perfect condition when they left our warehouse.
be in sth. 任職於某行業	▶	I'm in pharmaceuticals, and my wife is in medicine, so we are a good team.

商用英文必備語庫 **13.8** 用於處理人際關係的片語動詞　　　　　p.324

have it out with sb. (about sth.) 將某事攤開來講	▶	She really messed up my project. I'm going to have it out with her.
recommend sb. to sb. 向某人推薦某人	▶	You recommended her to me. I'm sorry to disappoint you, but I don't think she's very good.
have (got) sth. on sb. 知道某人的秘密，用來要脅對方	▶	I've got a lot on you. If you fire me, I'll go to the authorities.
have (got) sth. against sb. 因某種原因而不喜歡某人	▶	I've got nothing against him. I just don't like him.

商用英文必備語庫 13.9　出差常用的片語動詞　p.326

arrive at 抵達轉機處	My flight arrives at LAX at 7:45. Then, I've got a one-hour layover before my connection to San Diego.
arrive in 抵達最後目的地	I should arrive in San Diego some time around 9:30.
have sb. round 邀請某人來家裡玩	I'd love to have you round for coffee next weekend.
be based in 辦公室地點位於……	I'm normally based in Shanghai, but my work takes me all over Asia.

商用英文必備語庫 13.10　表示進行新計劃的片語動詞　p.327

begin by Ving 從……開始	Let's begin by looking at the requirements for the project.
involve sb. in sth. 讓某人涉入某事	I don't want to involve too many people in the project.
have to do with sth. 與某事有關	The meeting has nothing to do with sales. It's about Internet marketing or something.
could do with sth. 需要某事	We could do with some more time, to be perfectly honest.
do without sth./sb. 即使沒有……仍繼續下去	Kevin isn't here yet? We'll just have to do without him.
be based on sth. 根據某事物	The idea is based on a similar product I saw at the trade fair last year.
do away with sth. 除去／廢除……	I want to do away with the need for a system check.
base sth. on sth. 根據……來做某事	Can we base it on the model we made last year?

商用英文必備語庫 **13.11** 含 have 的慣用語   p.329

have	· a lot to answer for	有得解釋了
	· your back against the wall	身陷困境
	· a crack at sth.	嘗試某事
	· an eye for sth.	擅長留意一些特別的事項
	· a/sb.'s finger in every pie	任何小事都插手
	· friends in high places	人脈很好，認識許多有權的人
	· a good mind to	強烈地想要……
	· it on good authority	由可靠消息面獲知某事
	· your hands full	工作滿檔
	· it in for sb.	傷害或批評某人
	· a head start	有某項讓你在競爭中勝出的長處
	· sth. in mind	心中有……計劃或打算
	· a nose for sth.	有天賦認出或找出某事
	· second thoughts (about sth.)	對某事存有疑慮
	· a word with sb. (about sth.)	想和某人討論某個重要議題

商用英文必備語庫 **13.12** 含 do 的慣用語   p.330

do	· a half-assed job	半途而廢
	· the honors	舉杯為……祝賀
	· the rounds	與許多人交談
	· the trick	運作良好

商用英文必備語庫 **13.13** 含 show 的慣用語   p.330

show	· sb. the ropes	向某人解釋新工作
	· sb. the door	請某人離開
	· what you are made of	展現你真正的潛力

商用英文必備語庫 13.14　慣用語 set-phrases　　　　　　　　　p.332

· That will do!	夠了！
· That will do for now.	那目前就先這樣。
· Do me a favor!	閉嘴！不要再說了！（用來回答荒謬的問題）
· Do you want to make something of it?	你想被打嗎？（有威脅、挑釁之意）
· I've got a bone to pick with you.	我需要跟你談一下，你做了某件事情讓我很反感。
· I don't have a clue.	我毫無頭緒。
· I've had it up to here (with sth.)!	我再也受不了……了！
· You have to hand it to her!	不得不佩服她！
· (The) Walls have ears.	隔牆有耳。
· Can I have a moment?	我可以和你談一下嗎？
· Get a move on!	快點行動！
· Let's get this show on the road!	開始吧！
· The show must go on.	儘管遭受到很大的挫折，仍必須堅持下去。

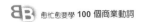

附錄三：學習目標記錄表

利用這張表來設立你的學習目標和記錄你的學習狀況，以找出改進之道。

第一欄：寫下你接下來一週預定學習或使用的字串。
第二欄：寫下你在當週實際使用該字串的次數。
第三欄：寫下你使用該字串時遇到的困難或該注意的事項。

預計使用的字串	使用次數	附註

國家圖書館出版品預行編目資料

愈忙愈要學 100 個商業動詞 ＝ Biz English for Busy
People: 100 Business Verbs / Quentin Brand作；
金振寧譯. －－初版. －－臺北市：貝塔，2006
〔民95〕
　　面：　　公分

　　ISBN　957-729-595-9（平裝附光碟片）

　1. 商業英文－動詞

805.165　　　　　　　　　　　　95009719

愈忙愈要學 100 個商業動詞
Biz English for Busy People: 100 Business Verbs

作　　者 / Quentin Brand
譯　　者 / 金振寧
執行編輯 / 廖姿菱

出　　版 / 貝塔出版有限公司
地　　址 / 100台北市館前路12號11樓
電　　話 / (02)2314-2525
傳　　真 / (02)2312-3535
郵　　撥 / 19493777貝塔出版有限公司
客服專線 / (02)2314-3535
客服信箱 / btservice@betamedia.com.tw

總 經 銷 / 時報文化出版企業股份有限公司
地　　址 / 桃園縣龜山鄉萬壽路二段 351 號
電　　話 / (02) 2306-6842

出版日期 / 2006年6月初版一刷
定　　價 / 380元
ISBN：957-729-595-9

Biz English for Busy People－100 Business Verbs
Copyright 2006 by Quentin Brand
Published by Beta Multimedia Publishing

喚醒你的英文語感！

對折後釘好，直接寄回即可！

廣　告　回　信
北區郵政管理局登記證
北 台 字 第 1 4 2 5 6 號
免　貼　郵　票

100 台北市中正區館前路12號11樓

貝塔語言出版 收
Beta Multimedia Publishing

寄件者住址 ☐☐☐

讀者服務專線（02）2314-3535　　讀者服務傳真（02）2312-3535
客戶服務信箱 btservice@betamedia.com.tw

www.betamedia.com.tw

謝謝您購買本書！！

貝塔語言擁有最優良之英文學習書籍，為提供您最佳的英語學習資訊，您可填妥此表後寄回（免貼郵票）將可不定期收到本公司最新發行書訊及活動訊息！

姓名：＿＿＿＿＿＿＿＿＿＿＿　性別：□男 □女　生日：＿＿＿年＿＿＿月＿＿＿日

電話：(公)＿＿＿＿＿＿＿＿＿(宅)＿＿＿＿＿＿＿＿＿(手機)＿＿＿＿＿＿＿＿

電子信箱：＿＿＿＿＿＿＿＿＿＿＿＿＿＿＿＿＿＿＿＿＿＿＿

學歷：□高中職含以下　□專科　□大學　□研究所含以上

職業：□金融　□服務　□傳播　□製造　□資訊　□軍公教　□出版
　　　　□自由　□教育　□學生　□其他

職級：□企業負責人 □高階主管　□中階主管　□職員　□專業人士

1. 您購買的書籍是？＿＿＿＿＿＿＿＿＿＿＿＿＿＿＿＿

2. 您從何處得知本產品？(可複選)

　　　□書店 □網路 □書展 □校園活動 □廣告信函 □他人推薦 □新聞報導 □其他

3. 您覺得本產品價格：

　　　□偏高 □合理 □偏低

4. 請問目前您每週花了多少時間學英語？

　　　□ 不到十分鐘 □ 十分鐘以上，但不到半小時 □ 半小時以上，但不到一小時

　　　□ 一小時以上，但不到兩小時 □ 兩個小時以上 □ 不一定

5. 通常在選擇語言學習書時，哪些因素是您會考慮的？

　　　□ 封面 □ 內容、實用性 □ 品牌 □ 媒體、朋友推薦 □ 價格□ 其他＿＿＿＿

6. 市面上您最需要的語言書種類為？

　　　□ 聽力 □ 閱讀 □ 文法 □ 口說 □ 寫作 □ 其他＿＿＿＿＿

7. 通常您會透過何種方式選購語言學習書籍？

　　　□ 書店門市 □ 網路書店 □ 郵購 □ 直接找出版社 □ 學校或公司團購

　　　□ 其他＿＿＿＿＿＿

8. 給我們的建議：＿＿＿＿＿＿＿＿＿＿＿＿＿＿＿＿＿＿＿＿＿＿

＿＿＿＿＿＿＿＿＿＿＿＿＿＿＿＿＿＿＿＿＿＿＿＿＿＿＿＿＿

喚醒你的英文語感！

Get a Feel for English !

喚醒你的英文語感！

Get a Feel for English !